afterglow

sidetracked part 3

s.k. kelley

Adapted Edition: August 2024

Library of Congress Control Number: 2022900352
ISBN: 978-1-955240-10-9
(digital ebook): 978-1-955240-16-1
Published by Bleeding Heart Books
skkelleyauthor.square.site

~ ∞ ~

*for every teacher who encouraged
my creativity over the years*

I couldn't have done it without you

~ ∞ ~

Books by S.K. Kelley

Sidetracked
(Part 1)

Borderline
(Part 2)

Afterglow
(Part 3)

<u>COMING SOON</u>

Resignation
(Part 4)

Follow S.K. Kelley on Bluesky or Twitter @skkelleywrites
or visit skkelleyauthor.square.site for updates!

Sidetracked is a four-part new adult
contemporary fantasy psychological drama series
with slice of life, romance, and thriller elements

**A CONTENT WARNING IS AVAILABLE
IN THE BACK OF THE BOOK
ON PAGE 579**

one

Centennial Memorial Hospital looms outside, the clean white marble and dark glass filling me with more dread than looking up at Reid Manor's dilapidated exterior ever did. I stare through the tinted passenger window several seconds too long before thanking Taylor for the ride.

"Yeah. Good luck with your little problem." He says *good luck*, but his voice is low and somber and suggests he feels no sympathy for me.

"Thanks," I mutter.

He smiles, but it doesn't reach his pale eyes. "See ya around."

God, I hope not.

With a sigh, I pop the door open and step out onto the sidewalk. I watch from the curb as Taylor drives out of the parking lot. I stand there as the black car turns onto the main street, and I don't move even after it leaves my sight, heading north toward Riverview General.

I feel awkward standing around doing nothing, and my legs are starting to get tired, so, finally, I turn back to face the hospital. The ride here was bad enough, but all the courage in the world couldn't prepare me for this moment, and I find myself hesitating outside the front doors. Another step forward, and they'll slide open.

But I can't move.

I don't know how long my phone's been shut off, but James must have called at least once. I bet he was terrified, wondering where I went and what happened to me. Even if he guessed it had something to do with Ice, all he'd have to go on was Jesse's word that I said I was only stepping out for a minute.

I *told* Jesse to have James call if he woke up before I got back. He must have called. And I never answered. I couldn't. Because I was unconscious in a hospital bed clear across town.

How am I supposed to face him?

He'll know something's wrong the moment he sees me.

Yesterday, I swore I'd tell James the truth from now on, but how am I supposed to walk into his recovery room and admit that I met with Ice?

What if he hates me for it?

What if he won't *forgive me?*

The hospital doors slide open, bursting my quiet panic bubble. An older woman with violet eyes walks through. She studies me for a second before stepping aside. Forcing back my nerves, I dip my head to be polite and pass through the door.

It slides shut behind me.

The hospital air is cold and dry compared to the summer heat. My weak, bruised left arm aches as I hold it. I waffle in the sparsely populated lobby, desperately wishing I could turn around and leave, but I eventually suck it up and make my way to the reception counter.

"Is James Reid still in room...R-138?"

The receptionist clicks around on his computer for a moment before lazily glancing up. I don't recognize him, but he must know who I am because the fact that I'm human doesn't seem to give him pause.

"R-138," he confirms. "I believe he's waiting for you. I heard there was something of a fuss yesterday."

Great. I force a smile. "Thanks."

I step away from the counter, take a moment to remember which direction James' room is in, and leave the lobby.

Centennial Memorial is not empty—far from it—but I feel so alone. I walk through the halls on shaky legs. I ease the plastic Riverview General bracelet over my right hand and drop it in the next trash can I pass. I cycle through a million things I could say to explain where I've been, but I know I won't use them. No more excuses. My inaction nearly got him killed. I can't lie about what's been going on with Ice anymore.

James deserves the truth.

I take a deep breath and, without knocking, push open the door of room R-138. Three heads turn to look at me, and I freeze under their collective gaze as the room falls silent.

James is awake, sitting up in bed. His face is so blank, it's impossible to tell whether he's relieved or worried or surprised or upset or angry to see me. He just *stares*. The bruise at his temple is now a deep purple—a proper black eye.

Matthew was smiling when he first glanced over, but his eyes widen as he recognizes me. I'm sure he knew I was missing.

The third face belongs to a younger girl with large amber eyes and short, curly hair dyed firetruck red. She doesn't seem nearly as surprised, and she watches me with childlike inquisitiveness.

The door swings shut with a loud click, breaking the silence and trapping me inside the small room with them.

James lurches forward in the raised hospital bed, looking like he desperately wants to stand, while Matthew does stand, seeming to sense his friend's urgency.

"Jayde—" James' scratchy voice rises agonizingly. He's already on the verge of tears. "Where were you?"

A pit in my stomach.

The same three words in a different voice.

James' question doesn't hold a trace of Ice's cold accusation —he just sounds afraid and upset and tired—but it leaves me at a loss for words.

Matthew relaxes, having watched me for a moment, and turns back to James. "See, man; I told you she was fine. You don't gotta be paranoid all the time."

James nods, but his frown grows more pronounced and acutely concerned as he stares me down. He must sense something off. *But what?* My nerves? The bruising on my arm? The hot pink bandage on the other? How pale I am? The new outfit?

What does he see, looking at me now?

I glance at the floor. At my feet. The clean leather boots.

"Maybe we should go," the girl says, voice lilting questioningly. When I look up, she's watching James instead of me. "I'm sure they wanna be alone now that Jayde is back?"

Matthew glances at her, at James, and then at me again before agreeing. He grabs a backpack from the floor while the girl stands from her chair and smooths the front of her oversized hoodie.

"Thanks," James says blankly.

Matthew pats him on the shoulder. They talk for a moment, but I'm distracted by the girl. She's watching me again. Her expression is level, mild. She tips her head, then looks to James as Matthew leaves his bedside and walks toward the door.

I step aside, offering Matthew a weak smile. He returns the smile without hesitation and steps out of the room, holding the door open.

"C'mon, Cass," he says.

The girl waves him off, smiling, and whispers something to James. His eyes narrow, but she laughs at his reaction. Then, after patting his arm, she turns away.

Our eyes meet as she approaches the door. Her smile is bright and warm, but her gaze is strangely penetrating.

"Everything will be alright," she says. "James loves you."

I can't bring myself to respond.

She looks past me, still smiling, and steps through the door to join Matthew. The door clicks shut as they leave.

Now, all I hear is the ticking clock and my own breathing.

Well, this is it.

I'm back.

James is awake, and we're alone. But I don't know what to say. I kept so much to myself the past couple weeks. Dangerous secrets and silly white lies.

Where should I even start?

two

After a moment spent staring at each other in silence, James asks if I want to sit. I absolutely do, so I take the chair beside the bed. It's more comfortable than standing, but I still can't look him in the eye. With my hands balled in my lap and my head hung low, I must look terribly guilty.

I am guilty, but I...

A finger brushes the hot pink bandage over my elbow. The bruise on my forearm—the purplish imprint of a hand wrapped around it. There's no real pain, but it's like a shockwave passes through me at his touch. A rush of some terrible emotion. His fingers are warm, but I still feel cold, and my hands close around the hem of my new cotton shorts.

"What happened?" he asks softly.

"Long story." My voice feels so far away. I don't know why, but I laugh, and the words come a bit faster. "The bruise is from the other day, when Ice caught me by the arm. He pinned it behind my back, you know? But, um... Ha... You'll be so mad. I mean, I kinda hate myself right now, so... It's hard to explain."

"Just tell me. I won't hate you."

I ignore the heat in my cheeks and force myself to look up.

The blank surprise on his face is gone, his expression more concerned than anything else. He must know I have nothing good to say, but he doesn't seem particularly upset, and it frustrates me.

"You should be mad."

He laughs weakly, wincing as he glances at the ceiling. "Oh, I *am* mad. But I don't think I could ever hate you."

You sure?

"But I…" Trailing off, I look down again.

Starting from the beginning makes the most sense, but *when* did it really begin? *What should I say?*

James rests a hand on my shoulder—a gesture that should be reassuring but instead leaves a pit in my stomach. "I know this has something to do with Ice. I know that. I'm not stupid, but… Please. I need to know."

I panic, hearing his name again.

"James, I— I tried to ignore him. I really did." My voice trembles, but each word is another weight lifted off me. "I ignored the texts. I blocked his number. But he got a new one. He threatened Rose, so I… I agreed to meet."

"You met with him? When?"

The smallest trace of pain—

"He found out about us. Like, that we're together—or dating, I mean." A breath from crying, the words pour from my chest like hot blood through my fingers. "He said you promised to leave in July. But you didn't, and he was pissed that I asked you to stay. He said I'd regret it. Then *that* happened. He stabbed you, and I… I really thought it was over."

"You—I…"

I stare at my hands without blinking as tears fill my eyes. Maybe it's from reliving the memories I've been trying to ignore. Maybe it's just guilt. Either way, I can still picture the blood.

James coughs. "Okay, yeah, sure. But that was a few days ago, right? What happened yesterday? Jesse said you told him you'd be right back, but that was a few hours before I woke up. You never showed, and you never answered your phone."

"I know. I'm sorry." I stare at the pink scar on my palm. "I wasn't expecting to be gone this long."

"Where'd you go?"

"I…stepped out to call Ice. He asked to meet with me again, in the morning. For a *chat*. I didn't want to leave the hospital, but he nearly killed you. I couldn't just sit here and do nothing. I guess I thought I could bargain with him or something…"

"Bargain with—?"

He sighs. I glance up to find his jaw set and one hand held over his eyes. So far, I can't tell whether this is going better or worse than I imagined.

"And you agreed to meet?" he asks, eyes still closed as his hand falls from his face. "What happened?"

"Well… He picked me up—"

James' eyes snap open, blazing. "He did *what*?"

I flinch, hands at chest level. My involuntary reaction seems to alarm him, and he quiets before glancing away with a whispered apology. I sigh and drop my hands to my lap, but I feel bad for being so on edge.

"We went to his house." I pause. James doesn't interrupt, but his face is tense, eyes focused on nothing in particular. "I mentioned what happened—how you morphed, and how the doctors here explained it."

"You talked about me?" he asks, gaze flicking to my face. "Why?"

"I don't know. Because he asked, I guess."

His eyes harden, and he looks away again. I knew this would hurt him. I wish I could end the story there. I wish all we did was go out to Westbrooke and talk.

But I won't lie, so I have no choice but to continue.

When I finally get around to Ice's *idea*, James' interest swings back to concern. I admit to returning the knife, though I leave out my attempt at stabbing him with it, and he looks at me like he thinks I'm an idiot. Maybe he's not wrong, but I only make matters worse by stammering something more directly related to Ice's theory as to how I *might* be able to activate the River Sapphire before I can stop myself.

At first, his eyes narrow thoughtfully. Then he glances at the medical wrap on my arm again. And a fire ignites in his eyes as he catches on.

"You let him do *what*?" he cries. "While I was comatose in the fucking hospital? You seriously went and let him—? *Why*, Jayde? What were you thinking?"

Dr. Corel's words echo in my mind.

You aren't suicidal, are you?

"What choice did I have?" My voice breaks, wavering as I struggle to finish what I started. "Weren't you listening? Last time I ignored him, he tried to kill you."

He doesn't respond, but I can't bear the horrible understanding clear on his face. My hands ball into fists as I press them to my eyes. My left arm aches, and my cheeks are damp from crying, but I feel lighter. Maybe telling the truth is helping. At least a little.

"I thought if I went along with it—if I just gave Ice what he wanted for once—things might get better. It's my fault you're in this mess, you know? I begged you to stay. I asked you to trust me. But I still hid the text messages from you. I thought I was going to die yesterday. I really did. But I got the key to my house back. Ice promised he wouldn't make another copy, and I didn't die. And he...returned my stupid boots, so..."

"Jayde..."

"I'm sorry." Tears well in my eyes again, spilling over, but I feel strange. Conflicted. Scared. Relieved. "I should've told you sooner—that he was texting me or that we met before. Maybe none of this had to happen. Maybe everything would've been fine..."

"No, Jayde— That's not what I..."

The bedsheets rustle, but I don't move my hands from my face even as James drags the metal chair closer and pulls me into an awkward hug. He says it's not my fault—what happened to him or anything Ice did. He didn't realize how I felt. How much pressure I was under. He shouldn't have made the deal with Ice in the first place. It was a mistake. He regrets it.

I listen, but all I can do is cry. Even if I could think of something I wanted to say, I wouldn't be able to say it.

He continues murmuring and rubbing my back while I don't move at all. My arm goes numb, but I manage to stop sobbing, and breathing comes easier. Though, I'm suddenly exhausted.

Some time passes, quieter than before. Then James tenses, his hand freezing on my back.

"Wait," he says. "Ice's fucked plan— It worked?"

I nod against his shoulder. He sits back, pulling away from me. I immediately miss his warmth in the cold room, but I straighten myself up too. He stares at me. His face is blurry through my tears, but his eyes are wide.

"You...morphed?"

I sniffle and nod again, drying my face with the back of my hand. "If I hadn't, I would've bled to death right there. It was that bad."

He stares into the void for a moment—processing everything I've said, I guess—then shakes his head. He meets my gaze with a fiery darkness I wish I didn't have to see.

"If he touches you again, I will kill him."

My breath catches, but I can't bring myself, the hypocrite who tried to stab Ice with his own knife, to argue. So I look away. I hug my arms to my chest, ignoring the pins and needles, and the room falls quiet again.

Tick, tick, tick...

Eventually, James sighs. "Hey, I..."

He's about to apologize, but I—

"Why'd you do it?" I ask under my breath. My nails dig into my arms, but I keep my eyes low, on my knees. "Why make a deal with Ice in the first place? Why agree to leave? Was it really just because you thought it'd keep me safe?"

Tick, tick...

"Yeah," he says. "And I..."

He sighs again. I finally look up, but he glances away with his hands balled in his lap. His expression is guarded, leaking sadness.

"I tried to go through with it too, y'know? I did." He sighs *again*. "But every time I brought it up, you'd just look at me and say you didn't want to be alone. At first, it was kind of annoying. I couldn't understand why you wanted to stick around, but then— I stopped caring. I didn't want to send you off somewhere else. I didn't want to leave. I liked being with you and hanging around your house and pretending that everything was gonna be okay. And you told me to stay, so…"

He flashes a miserable smile, glancing up with watery eyes. "It's messed up, right? How I never said anything even though I figured blowing him off would come back to bite me in the ass? I guess I thought it was worth it—those few weeks with you, I mean. I dunno. Anyway, I knew this was coming longer than you did, and I never said a thing either."

"But I *knew*, and I—" My mouth is dry again, and I drop my hands to my lap. "I talked to Ice. Responded to his texts. I hid in the bathroom to answer phone calls. He told me to make you leave *or else*, but I still—"

"Nah," he says tiredly. "I mean, yeah; obviously, I wish you hadn't done it, but what I did was way worse. You just wanted me to be happy. You didn't want me to worry. But I… To be honest, I didn't care what Ice might do to me…or how much it might hurt you." His jaw sets, but it's hard to tell if he's upset or embarrassed. "I just…clung to every tiny scrap of affection you gave me, knowing it couldn't last forever. I wanted to be with you. I wanted to wake up every morning and see you there. And you told me you loved me. But then I... I couldn't even bring myself to fight him—to give myself a real chance. I just... I'm sorry. For not telling you. Or for giving up so easily. I'm sorry that my dumb choices drove you to do this."

"James..."

He kind of laughs, though he winces and raises a hand to his injured side. "I guess what I mean is: Don't feel bad for me. I had it coming. Seriously. I practically asked for this. But, yet again, it's my fault he hurt you. I'm sorry, Jayde."

"I'm fine," I say, glancing away.

I am fine. And I also did nothing to stop Ice, so... I guess we both messed up.

I let out my breath. "Anyway, who was here visiting with Matt?"

"Oh, uh—" He blinks, looking past me—to the door, I think. "That was Cassidy, his kid sister—or, sibling, I mean. Sorry. Anyway, they're alright. Kinda weird, but I wouldn't mind getting them close to Ice for a second just to figure out what's going through his head. I knew he was fucked up—takes one to know one, I guess—but Jesus Christ..."

Right...

"So, Cassidy is—"

"—a telepath," he says, chewing his thumbnail. "They read minds, yeah. Why didn't I think of that earlier? If only he went to the Fourth of July party... Dammit..."

"James?"

He sighs but finally meets my gaze again. "Sorry. I'm okay.

Sounds like you saved my ass back there, though."

I don't know about that.

"Did you tell them what happened?" I ask.

"Cass heard just about everything, so…" He frowns. "I had to explain the gist of it to Matt too. Before this, he didn't know shit. He, um… He took it better than Rose did, I think, but he already knew that I have problems with Ice, so…"

He stares at his lap like having to open up to his friend was the worst thing in the world.

Ugh.

"You don't have to talk about it if it bothers you."

He sighs, glancing up as he scratches the back of his neck. "How is Rose, anyway? She pissed at me or what?"

Rose.

"I don't know," I admit, chest tight. "I mean, she drove us to the hospital, but she saw you morph. Someone from Human-Immortal Affairs took her away while we were still out in the waiting room. I'm sure she's fine, but I haven't heard from her since. I still haven't turned my phone on yet."

He grimaces. "Shit. I'm sorry. I know you didn't want her to find out…"

"It's fine." I brush my hair out of my face and force a smile. "Like you said, it was only a matter of time. Anyway, I'm sure I'll find a million texts from her too."

"Ah, man—" He averts his eyes, ears turning red. "Yeah, I hope you don't think I'm a desperate idiot when you listen to those voicemails."

It's silly, but I feel a bit better seeing him get embarrassed.

"It can't be worse than what's been running through my head all morning," I say with a smile that falters after a second. "Meeting with Ice was…pretty dumb. I wasn't sure how you'd react."

"Yeah…" The tired, nervous pain crosses his face again, and he worries his scarred hand in his lap. The knuckles on his other hand are bruised. "You have to swear you won't scare me like that again. You can't trust Ice, you know? You can't believe a word he says. And, *please*, tell me if he talks to you again."

I nod, and I mean it. "I will. But you have to promise me the same. And don't let whatever he's said get to you. If you're worried, talk to me."

A hint of tension in his jaw, amber eyes focused on his hands in his lap. Then he lets out a breath and looks up.

"I'll try," he says mildly.

"Then it's a deal."

three

We're alone for a couple hours, then a nurse comes by with a lunch menu for James. He looks it over before asking if he can eat in the cafeteria instead, since he's not hooked up to any machines.

The nurse says it's fine and leaves after checking his vitals.

"Are you hungry?" he asks.

I nod. I haven't eaten since breakfast—though, I barely had an appetite then. Now that I know I haven't ruined everything just yet, I'm starving.

"A nurse gave me a few cafeteria vouchers yesterday," I say, digging them out of the tote bag I left on the bench in the window-sill—thankfully, everything's still here. "But are you sure you're okay to get up?"

"It won't kill me to walk, if that's what you mean."

I'm not even sure what I meant, but I watch without interjecting as he stands from the tall hospital bed. He's wearing a cotton gown, sweatpants, and fuzzy nonslip hospital socks, and he seems to be seriously favoring his left side. It doesn't look comfortable.

"You sure you're okay?" I ask again, meeting him near the

bed.

"I'm fine."

"What meds do they have you on—do you know?"

"Percocet." He winces as he glances at his chest. "It does the job swell if I don't move, but my ribs are pretty rough. I guess I cracked a couple."

I hold out a hand. He hesitates before taking it, but his hand is as warm as I remember. Just yesterday, I worried I'd never be able to hold his hand again. Because I thought he might die. *And then I thought I would.*

Moisture pricks my eyes, but I turn to face the door and wipe my face to curb the tears before they have a chance to fall.

"Ready to go?" I ask.

"Yeah." His grip on my hand tightens. "Let's go."

James knows where the cafeteria is, so I follow his lead. We arrive in under ten minutes, both slightly winded from the trek across the hospital. The cafeteria isn't crowded—only a few tables are taken—so we opt to sit at the nearest table and rest for a moment. I watch through a large window looking out on a courtyard. The rose bushes are blooming. Pink and red and yellow, some flowers impressively large. An elderly man and female nurse are sitting at a bench in a strip of sunlight.

"So, ah..." James' knuckles tap against the tabletop. "You said Rose drove us to the hospital? I imagine she saw...everything, huh?"

"Um..."

Her shrill scream as blood slicked my hands and dripped from my elbows to my thighs. The crack of James' head hitting linoleum. A ginger cat's faint, labored breathing. An uncomfortably familiar voice on the phone. Bone-white knuckles gripping the steering wheel in the fading light.

But all I say is, "Yeah."

"God," he breathes. "If I knew, I—"

"It's not your fault." I take a deep breath before looking back to James. He's upset, surely imagining whatever he thinks must have happened after his memory cut out, but I try not to mirror it. "Have you heard from Human-Immortal Affairs at all?"

He shakes his head, but his expression mellows slightly. "No. I saw RSP, though—Riverview Special Police, the immortal cops. I think I mentioned them before? Anyway, two guys stopped by a couple hours after I woke up. Jesse was still there, but I asked him to leave when they came in. They, uh— Well, they already knew what happened."

"With Ice?"

"With everything," he says in frustration. "Sounds like Human-Immortal Affairs kept them in the loop this whole time."

"I believe it," I mutter. "What did they want?"

"Nothing." He glances out the window, eyes narrowed. "They know exactly what Ice did, but their hands are tied because you're involved. Because he's your sponsor. 'Cause of that, everything he's done falls under Human-Immortal Affairs jurisdiction. RSP is cooperating with them—they're *looking into it* or some shit— but that's about all they had to say."

When I don't respond, he kind of laughs. "The one cop told me to try deescalation next time. Can you believe it? RSP is useless as always."

Deescalation? Ugh.

He sighs, and the spark of dark humor fades as he looks to me again. "Anyway, thanks for calling Jesse. If you hadn't, he probably wouldn't know I'd been hurt at all. Unless Matt decided to tell him. 'Cause I doubt I could've brought myself to."

"I had to call someone," I say. "I wish I knew the immortal emergency number, though." When he tips his head, it's my turn to be frustrated. "You were bleeding out in my kitchen. If I'd known the number, I could've gotten help sooner instead of calling Jesse to ask where to go."

His mouth closes, his eyes still wide. "Oh, sorry. It's 119."

Really? Just 911 reversed?

"Why didn't you just ask me?"

"Just *ask* you?" I hide my face in my hands, but I can't stop laughing. "James. I asked you a *million* times, but you were so out of it. You yanked the knife out, and—"

"I did *what?*"

Wet, hot blood splashing my chest, soaking into my shirt. The knife clattering on the floor. The blank, blank look in his eyes. And the blood. Oh god, the blood—

I shake it off and take another deep breath. "Never mind. It all worked out in the end. You're fine, and I'm fine, and I'm sure Rose is fine wherever she is, so..."

"Yeah..."

He looks intensely concerned, but I appreciate him dropping it for now. I'm not quite ready to face everything that happened the other day in my own mind, let alone talking about it *with* James.

"What'd you say to Jesse, anyway?" I ask. "He was there when you first woke up, right? All I said is that you were in a fight…"

He nods, massaging his left hand, eyes glued to the table. "A fight. Yeah. That's all I said too. It was a stupid fight. The other guy pulled a knife, and I was lucky you were around. That's about it. He… Jesse doesn't need to know about Ice right now."

I bite my cheek.

I was hoping he told Jesse the truth—especially considering how much he nagged me to tell Rose about my scars. But I get it. It's easier said than done, and he doesn't want to risk dragging his brother into our mess.

Still annoying, though.

"Come on," James says, forcing a smile. "Let's eat. You said you're starving, right?"

I agree, and we make our way to the front of the cafeteria.

The guy behind the counter looks like he can't be much older than I am, but Centennial Memorial Hospital's cafeteria is practically a restaurant. There's a digital menu board with professional photos and everything.

It's kind of weird, but I hand over my paper meal voucher and get a turkey sandwich with a side of chopped fruit. James orders a hot dog and fries. We get a fountain drink to share, then return to the table. He drops his tray, the plastic clattering loudly against the tabletop, as he takes a seat. I sit across from him more carefully.

"You talked to Ice," he says.

"Yeah. I said that already."

He stares at his food. His hands are in his lap under the table, and his expression is complicated—like he isn't sure whether to be upset or angry.

"You talked about me."

I frown. "A little, I guess."

"Did it bother him at all—stabbing me, I mean?"

"I—"

When I first met with him yesterday, he was acting normal and unaffected. Like it was nothing. Like the past month of unrelenting conflict hadn't happened at all. Like he truly feels he did nothing wrong.

"No," I say finally, rubbing the bruise on my forearm. "I don't think it did. But, like I said, he didn't force me to meet up with him or go along with his crazy plan. Sure, maybe I had no real choice. I don't know. But it felt like I did. And he was…actually kind of nice to me—in a totally messed up way."

"He hurt you, Jayde."

"I—" *Why is this so difficult?* "I know. I know that. Obviously. I could've died yesterday. I almost did. But I let him do it, and he didn't let me die, so…"

"You still think he doesn't want to hurt you."

I never wanted to hurt you.

Isn't that what he said?

I'd hate to kill you.

Isn't that what he said?

"I don't know what he wants," I admit lamely. "He wasn't upset to hear that you survived, and he seemed relieved when I woke up. He was nice to me. Told me what happened while I was out. Bought me new clothes to replace the ones I trashed and returned my boots and the key, but—"

He thinks someone has to die.

"You can't trust a word he says, Jayde." James' voice is low and dark. "Nothing. I'm serious. He's so full of shit. Always has been."

"I…"

I stuff a chunk of honeydew in my mouth to avoid having to speak. Because, as much as I'd hate to contradict James or defend Ice in any way, I don't know if I agree completely.

How am I supposed to know when Ice is being genuine or not? What's a front and what isn't? What's the truth and what's a lie? After yesterday—*after this morning*—I have no idea.

But I can't bring myself to admit that to James.

"Just don't meet with him like that again," he says quietly. "Never. Please. I can't stand the idea of him hurting you, but I can't even *try* to protect you if I'm not there."

I sigh. "I already said I won't, and it's not like I want to talk to him or anything. Yesterday sucked. But I'm a fully-fledged human immortal now, with a feline form and everything… So, there's that at least."

A heavy silence settles over the table, so I take a bite of my sandwich as though it eases the tension at all.

"I can morph too," he mumbles.

"Oh? You've tried it since you woke up?"

He stares at his untouched tray, frowning deeply. "Just once. When the doctor said I arrived in feline form, I didn't believe him. He told me to give it a try. It's like…flipping a switch. Instinctive.

After how many times I tried as a kid, it's not fair how easy it was. It's not fair it took almost dying like that. You know?"

"But it's nice that you can now, isn't it?"

"I guess." His eyes flick up, the emotion behind them unfathomable. "How's it work for you?"

Now that we're not talking about Ice, I feel better, and the hunger sets in again. I take another bite of my sandwich, actually tasting it this time. It hardly tastes like cafeteria food, more like the type of thing you'd find at a nice diner.

"I have to wear the River Sapphire," I say. "I mean, I haven't tried yet, but I was told I can't wear the necklace at all without morphing."

The table falls quiet again. I eat a piece of cantaloupe. James picks at his fries. Peeking at him from the corner of my eye, he looks less upset than before, but I feel like I need to say something. To kill the silence or reassure him somehow.

"I'll show you later," I offer. "I wanna know what I look like as a cat, anyway. The River Sapphire didn't activate until after I lost consciousness, so…"

"Yeah, it's cool. Glad it worked out for you."

My breath catches, and I stammer an apology, but he forces a smile that manages to soften his features.

"Nah, it's fine," he says. "I'm just glad you're okay."

four

I step through the door and find James sitting in bed with a meal tray in his lap. He looks up and flashes a smile, halfhearted but more genuine than the one he offered before I left.

"Your phone went off," he says.

"A call?" I ask, walking faster on my way across the room. When I finally gathered the nerve to turn my phone on, it turned out to be dead rather than just powered off, so I have no idea what to expect.

"Just a text, I think. When it first came on."

I unplug my phone, sit on the vinyl bench in the windowsill, and check my notifications. There are dozens of missed calls, unread texts, and FaceSpace messages from James. I was expecting that, but at the top of the list—

That could have gone worse, don't you think?

Oh.

It takes a moment to even register his name above the message. *Ice Monroe, 14 hours ago.* I was hoping to find a text from Rose, but…

"What's up?" James asks, still picking at his food.

"One second."

There's an image too. I unlock my phone to pull it up, but I'm not sure what to think. The photo looks like it was taken in Ice's backyard at night. The lighting is bad, but I recognize the wrought-iron fire pit and can just make out the corner of a wooden planter in the background.

It looks like...*burning clothes*.

"It's a text from Ice," I say. I glance up to find James staring at me, but I shake my head. "It's stupid. I wouldn't worry about it."

He's not convinced.

With a sigh, I move to stand by the bed. He sets his food tray aside, takes the phone when I offer it to him, and squints at the image on the screen. The yellow flames leave the photo washed out and overexposed, so it's probably impossible to understand without context.

"Seems like he burned the clothes he wore yesterday before I morphed."

James looks up from my phone's screen with sharp eyes. *"That could have gone worse*? Are you fucking kidding me?"

My bare knees squishing against wet carpet. I think Ice was wearing jeans, and we both ended up on the floor. *I think.* His clothes must have been soaked.

"To be fair, it really could have," I say. "I lost a lot of blood."

I take my phone back and try to play it off as the stupid text I said it was, but I can't shake the nagging concern.

Why burn the clothes? Even then, why tell me? It's dramatic and petty, which isn't off-brand for Ice, I guess, but... This doesn't feel the same as the obnoxious, ultimately meaningless, or vaguely threatening texts he sent before. And he's never sent a picture. But I don't know what it means—assuming it means anything.

"Block him," James mutters.

"I can't," I say, careful to keep my voice level. "This happened *because* I blocked his number last time. There's no way I'm risking it again. I'd rather put up with this, and one text is nothing compared to what I dealt with before, anyway."

"Well—" His expression darkens as he looks away, but he quickly looks back. "Just be careful. Okay?"

"Of course." I offer a smile. "I already promised to tell you if I hear from him, and I won't respond to anything he says unless it's an emergency. Try not to worry. I learned my lesson."

"Right," he agrees, though his smile is weaker than mine.

* * * * *

I'm trying to sleep.

I really am trying, but my body aches, and an uncomfortable tingling fills my left arm. I'm cold even wearing scrubs as pajamas, and the hospital tote bag with clothes stuffed inside makes for an awful pillow. I should've asked the nurse for a real one before she left. And this vinyl bench pad sucks. It's worse than the floor mattress at Reid Manor. And the clock is *so* loud and annoying.

I wanna go home. I miss my bed. I miss my pajamas. I miss...

A rustling behind me quiets my thoughts. The sound of James

shifting in bed, disturbing the crinkly sheets. *What time is it?* He should be asleep by now.

"Jayde," he whispers. "Hey. You awake?"

I hesitate, but I don't expect I'll fall asleep any time soon, so... "Yeah."

I roll over, groaning as the tingling in my arm worsens. My back and hips protest too, but I manage to drag myself up and sit. The room isn't so dark that I can't see James sat up in bed, watching me with a nervous frown.

"Are you okay?" he asks.

"Just sore," I mumble. "How about you? Everything alright?"

He smiles—surely, he can relate to being sore—but his expression falters, then he scratches his shoulder and glances at his lap. "I can't sleep. I keep thinking... Imagining...things. Last night, without you, I couldn't fall asleep either."

I bite the inside of my cheek, eyes darting to the hot pink bandage I haven't had the nerve to take off. The bruise above it. The dark imprint of fingers. I wish I had a coat I could wear to cover it up. Might help with the cold too.

But the mess I got myself into yesterday is nothing compared to what happened to James. I have no right to feel so sorry for myself.

I look up. "Can I help?"

"Can you...come here, maybe?"

I take a deep breath, half because I'm nervous and half because I don't trust my legs. But I leave the bench and cross the room. It's only a few feet, but it feels like a mile. I stand in front of James and stare at the edge of the bed to avoid his gaze. My hands ball into fists as a mess of emotions well in my throat.

What *did* he imagine while I was gone? What went through his mind as morning became afternoon and the sun eventually set? Did he think that Ice kidnapped me? Did he think I was hurt? Did he think I abandoned him—that I wasn't coming back?

"I didn't want to be out so long," I say, my wavering voice hardly a whisper. "I didn't want to worry you. When I left, I wasn't expecting…"

He sighs. "You're here now. You're here, and you're okay, and that's… Like I said, that's all I care about."

"James, I…"

I don't know what to say, but he doesn't seem to mind. Slowly, his hands move from his lap to my face, and I glance up. Tears well in his eyes as he smiles in a way that only seems to highlight his pain. But he looks relieved too.

"I love you," he says. "I was worried, but I don't care what happened with Ice. At all. It doesn't matter."

"I—"

I hardly deserve his sympathy considering what I did. Hiding my contact with Ice nearly got him killed. I almost wanted him to hate me for it. Just for a day. Just for a minute. A second. I wanted him to scold me for being thoughtless and selfish and stupid. He shouldn't be so nice to me. I *hurt* him.

But I don't say anything.

Instead, I raise a hand to touch the bruise at his temple. The discolored skin is puffy and warm. His eyes close as he leans into my touch, and I want to kiss him, but my fingers creep down, from his cheek to his jaw to his collarbone.

The soft fabric of the hospital gown.

I freeze and drop my hand, which returns to being a fist at my side as my gaze flicks down. The gauze taped over the long central incision on his chest pokes out from the gown's neckline. His wounds are severe, and so recent...

"How do you feel?" I ask, the words awkward and stilted. "I'm sorry. I think I forgot to ask earlier."

His hands leave my cheeks, and he laughs, wincing as he seems to do every time he laughs now. He scoots over in the small bed. I sit on the edge, watching him with a wariness I know I can't keep off my face.

"Oh, I am fucked up," he says, his honesty surprising me. "But they have me on a whole cocktail of drugs. Painkillers, antibiotics. I mean, you saw it. And I feel way better now that you're here. It's not so bad. I feel like I can relax a little."

I let out my breath. "Good. I'm glad."

He flashes another smile. The warmth of it brightens his eyes, and, for a second, I believe it—that he is fine, and he doesn't hate me, and we're going to be okay.

"I'm not sure I can fall asleep just yet, though," he says, scratching his jaw. "So... Ah... Maybe you can stay here with me? For a little bit. We could—I dunno—cuddle? Maybe?"

It's so stupid, it makes me laugh. "Is that okay? I don't wanna hurt you."

"You won't hurt me. It's fine."

Still, I hesitate before pulling my legs up onto the bed. We can both fit, but there's not much extra space, and it's not the most comfortable. For some reason, I feel unreasonably nervous despite the fact we've been sleeping in the same bed for weeks now.

He brushes a few stray hairs behind my ear, and his expression softens. "I'm glad you're here. And safe. And with me."

"You said that already," I mumble.

"And I mean it."

Something in his voice sets off my tear ducts, and I hide my face in my hands. "I really thought you might die."

Arms wrap around me, drawing me closer. He's warm, and the sensation of being hugged is familiar and comforting, but he smells like the hospital. Like antiseptic ointment and freshly laundered linens. My chest feels so tight I can barely breathe.

"When you pulled the knife out... When you passed out... And seeing you here, still asleep after so long... Hours. It was morning. I didn't know what to do. I felt like it was all my fault. I just wanted to help—to fix things. I wasn't...thinking about anything else. I'm sorry."

The last few days don't even feel real. How is it possible that James nearly died? That Ice nearly killed him? That Ice nearly killed me? That I let him do it?

How is it possible?

"I'm okay," James says. "You're okay."

Yes. That's right.

I am okay.

I have to be okay.

five

The door handle engages with a click, and I look up as James steps out of the small adjoined bathroom. I drop my phone to the bench and jump up to meet him.

He looks good, wearing normal clothes instead of a hospital gown, and seems to be in a decent mood, so I can only assume the shower wasn't too painful despite being his first real one since his surgery. He flashes a smile that's still a bit too tired. I feel better today too—physically, anyway—but I don't imagine either of us slept great while sharing the hospital bed, even if I have a feeling he would've slept worse without me there.

"How do you feel?" I ask, just to be sure.

"Clean," he says.

I laugh. Unfortunately, I know that feeling all too well. How many times has it been now? How many showers have I taken after being drenched in blood?

Too many.

Way too many.

I clear my throat. "You're not in too much pain, though, right?"

"I'm sore as hell, but I'll be fine."

He walks past me to sit on the edge of the bed. I follow, but I don't sit. I just stand in front of him and run my fingers through his hair. Damp, soft. The dark bruise near his eye. His cheek. The line of his jaw, a bit scruffy.

He leans into my hand, eyes closing, looking serene for the first time. And, the same as last night, I really want to kiss him. More than anything.

But I can't.

I'm too scared.

James wouldn't reject me. I *know* he wouldn't. Maybe he even wants me to kiss him. But I… I feel like I don't deserve it yet. I'm still too mad at myself for messing up. Or for not doing more. And for leaving him alone—even if it was only for a day.

I sigh, dropping my hand to his knee, and his eyes open.

"You okay?" he asks.

"Yeah, I just—"

"Oh." He touches his bruised eye and averts his gaze, flashing a nervous smile. "Yeah, I guess he got me pretty good, huh? I suck at fighting in general, but Ice is a real pain in the ass, so… Sorry if it's gross."

"Gross?" I laugh again, caught off guard and oddly relieved. "That's not what I was thinking at all. It's just a bruise. I mean, you never thought any of mine were gross, right?"

He blinks. "No."

I roll my eyes and sit beside him, pulling my hair over one shoulder. "It's not your fault he hit you, but a bruise like that will heal in no time, right?"

His eyes flick down, and his fingers brush the bruise on my

arm. I stare at the purplish marks between the pink, scarred heart on my wrist and the tiny, stitched wound in the crook of my elbow.

"That'll heal too," I say.

Tick, tick...

James clears his throat. "Hey, uh, so— What do you look like as a cat?"

A flicker of sympathetic concern in sharp blue eyes. A soft, tired frown. An expression I wish I never saw. An expression that made everything so much more complicated.

"A brown tabby," I say, glancing up from my arm. "You wanna see? I haven't had a chance to see it either."

He smiles. "Sure. If that's cool with you."

We watch each other for a quiet moment. I can't tell if he's genuinely interested in my feline form or if he only brought it up to get off the topic of our injuries, but I am curious, so I nod and step away to grab my wallet. The River Sapphire is clean and free of blood. Someone must have cleaned it at Riverview General— but who? Ice? Dr. Corel? Night?

I guess it doesn't matter.

I return to the bed, climb up, and sit cross-legged facing James. He looks interested, not upset or worried, but it's still hard to maintain eye contact. As I stare at the vibrantly blue gemstone in my hand, I realize—

I wore the River Sapphire almost every day since Ice gave it to me, but, now, because it finally works, I can't. Unless I *want* to turn into a cat, I can never wear it again.

"What does it feel like?" I ask. "Morphing, I mean?"

James shrugs. "Doesn't feel like anything, really. One second, you're a person, and then—*poof*—you're a cat. It's instantaneous. There's nothing to feel, I don't think." Then he laughs. "I mean, it's no agonizing werewolf transformation or anything."

I roll my eyes. "Well, I figured that much. It's not like I've never seen anyone do it."

Still... I haven't tried to use the River Sapphire in weeks. I wore it out of habit, but I stopped trying. I stopped caring. Sure, I hoped it wasn't a lost cause, but it might not have bothered me if it never activated. Now, it shouldn't be a problem. Now, all I have to do is put the necklace on.

Why am I so nervous?

I unclasp the thin chain and hold it up to my neck. The instant I fasten the clasp again, I lose my balance. Like my legs gave out beneath me, I fall forward. My face bumps James' knee, but the impact seems less jarring than it should.

He laughs again. "See? It just happens. You alright?"

"Yeah. And I guess the necklace works," I say, still collapsed with my nose in the crisp sheet and my whiskers folded against his leg.

My mouth opened reflexively when I spoke, but the sound didn't come from my throat—the same way voices never seem to when immortals speak in feline form. Experiencing it firsthand is strange, almost as strange as the sensation of my scratchy tongue brushing the roof of my mouth.

I shift, preparing to right myself, but—

Oh. *Oh, no.*

My body feels entirely wrong. I stop moving, allowing myself a moment to process my new, much smaller form and the way my feline body is laid out.

"You stuck?" James asks.

"Um…"

I push myself up with my forelimbs to get my face out of the bedding and assume a rough approximation of a seated position with my rear legs awkwardly tucked beneath me. *I don't know what I was expecting, but…* I'm suddenly quadrupedal, and it feels as though I have an extra set of joints in all four limbs. I'm not sure how it's all meant to work together.

I do my best, though, and I manage to remain upright long enough to balance myself and keep from toppling over again.

Then I look at my hands—or *paws*, I guess. They're small, covered in short, cream-colored fur. Further up my arm—*leg?*— I find that Ice was right. I am a brown tabby, covered in chestnut fur, similar to my human hair color, with darker stripes and speckles.

"Where does all my stuff go?" I ask. "Dr. Corel told me that I have separate forms, which I guess is super rare, but I've never understood what happens to someone's clothes and stuff when they morph. Do you know?"

He thinks for a moment before shaking his head. "It's weird, right? You morph, and everything on you is gone, but it's still there when you turn back. Clothes, backpack, the junk in your pockets. But I don't know how it works. It's just how it is, you know? I doubt most immortals ever think about it."

I glance over my furry shoulder, my head turning more than it ever could in human form, to check out my tail. It's also a striped brown. With some conscious effort, I swish my tail from side to side.

Yeah. This is definitely weird.

"What's that about separate forms, though?" James asks.

"Oh, um… It basically means that my human and feline forms aren't connected." I try to remember exactly what Dr. Corel said, but convincing my tail to curl itself over my paws and stay in place takes a lot of focus. "Like, when I first morphed… I was bleeding out, right? But my feline form wasn't injured. The cut wasn't there at all—not like when you morphed and kept bleeding. That's what saved my life."

"I've never heard of that. I wonder if… Hey, wait. Look at me for a second."

I glance up. His eyes lock onto my face, narrowing in thoughtful confusion. He frowns as he studies me and doesn't say anything for a long while, which makes me nervous.

Then he grabs his phone from the bedside table. After fiddling with it, he turns the screen to show me. The front-facing camera is on, so I'm met with a mirror image of my feline self. A brown tabby with small ears, white whiskers, and light patches on the chest and muzzle.

Right now, that's me. I'm a *cat.*

"Weird."

"Yeah," he agrees. "But check out your eye."

What?

Oh!

My right eye is green—round and feline, but about what I expected it might look like—but my left eye is different. Like an abstract painting, streaks of bright blue cut through the darker, more muted green. The blue is the same color as the clear afternoon sky. The same color as a water immortal's eyes—*as Ice's eyes.*

It's pretty in a vaguely unsettling way.

"Huh…" I fight the urge to raise a hand to touch my face. "I wonder if that's normal for human immortals."

"No clue. You're the only one I've seen like this."

Has he met Taylor?

I assume they at least knew each other in passing if they went to the same school growing up, but I don't want to ask. I do not want to talk about Taylor Corel right now.

My two-toned eye *feels* normal, though—the same as the other one, anyway—so I shrug it off as a random quirk associated with assuming feline form as a human. Maybe it has to do with how the lab-created gemstone interacts with the human body to trigger the transformation. *Or something.*

James puts his phone away.

"I'd show you mine," he says, his smile a bit off, "but it was rough the other day. I felt like I was gonna pass out and could only maintain it for a minute, so…"

My eyes lock on the tip of the pink incision visible above his shirt collar. *And a single dark stitch.*

I feel my ears angle back.

The surgeons had to split his rib cage open, didn't they? To get inside and control the bleeding? They mentioned a damaged artery near his heart…

"It's fine," I say. "I don't want you to hurt yourself."

"Once I heal up, we can work on it together." He's still smiling, but more obvious discomfort creeps into his expression as he glances away. "It felt…pretty unnatural the first time, so I can only imagine how it is for you."

"It's different, for sure."

Careful and awkwardly low to the mattress, I crawl closer and make my way into James' lap. Even without touching his chest, I can hear his heart beating. Hear how his breath is slightly uneven. Smell the generic hospital soap on his skin and the fabric softener on his shirt. But, when I finally look up from my paws, I can't tell what he's thinking.

Then he lifts a hand and pets my head. My ears fold in response to being touched. In this form, his hand doesn't feel nearly as warm, nor does the room feel so cold. But my flesh prickles as the sensation of touch is transferred through the fur to my skin.

And I feel it. When he catches the River Sapphire's chain with his fingers. A cryptic sadness crosses his face as he slips the necklace over my head.

I panic.

The transformation is just as abrupt as before, but my frantic thoughts of how I wanted my body to be positioned must have had some effect, as I return to human form sitting perpendicular in James' lap with my legs hanging over the edge of the bed. I almost fall, but he catches me by planting a hand on my back and pulling me back up.

Our faces are close, only a few inches apart. His eyes are wide. And my breath catches.

Then something—a flash of complicated darkness—flickers through his eyes. As his expression shifts, I relax upon accepting that I'm not about to fall and drop from his lap, off the bed and to the floor.

I force a smile. "Sorry. I'll get the hang of it eventually."

"You're fine..."

He doesn't look directly at me, but he faintly mirrors my smile before holding the River Sapphire out. I feel like I should say something. But I can't think of anything, so I just take the necklace. As I glance up again, there's a knock at the door.

Oh, thank god.

I step back from the bed as a nurse enters the room. I recognize her as the same woman who was working when James was first moved into the recovery room.

She acknowledges me with a smile.

"You took a shower, right?" she asks, stopping beside the bed. When James nods, her smile brightens. "Perfect. It looks like you feel better than yesterday too. Mind if I check your incision real quick?"

"Go for it."

He lifts his shirt from the bottom hem, and I avert my gaze before retreating to the padded bench in the window. I tuck the River Sapphire away, sit down, and unlock my phone.

I'm not really *doing* anything on my phone, but I listen as the nurse asks James several questions. It sounds like he's healing well. *No signs of inflammation. Good.*

He opts to have his incision covered with gauze again, but I don't have the nerve to watch, and I desperately try to zone out the rest of their conversation.

Rose still hasn't answered my texts. Another call went ignored this morning. *The same as yesterday.*

I'm sure she's fine—probably just freaked out or pissed, but… *I don't know.* I hope the Human-Immortal Affairs agents were nice to her. I hope she's safe at her parents' house, hanging out with Kyle and watching TV, not worrying about immortals. I think she was scheduled to work yesterday too… If she took the day off, I hope she didn't get in trouble for it. More than anything, I hope she doesn't feel as helpless and trapped as I have the past couple months.

When the nurse finally leaves, James stands from the bed, and I glance up from my phone. He stretches, though he winces quite obviously before turning to me with a totally normal-looking smile.

"Wanna go for a walk or something?" he asks. "I can't stand sitting around here all day."

I pocket my phone. "Sure."

We head to the cafeteria first, making better time than we did yesterday. We talk about nothing over lunch, and then I point out the courtyard. With some prodding, James agrees to check it out. It's something to do to kill time, I suppose.

The closest way out is off to the far side of the cafeteria, a set of spotless glass doors. It's hot outside, but the fresh air is nice, and the sun feels amazing on my shoulders.

Hospitals are always so cold.

"Why is that?" I ask.

James sighs. "The cold makes you want to leave sooner."

I laugh and wander further out.

The rectangular courtyard is empty. We're alone with the large bronze statue of a pregnant woman. There's an ornate wooden bench with a memorial plaque, a variety of rose bushes, and a small rock garden with a short Japanese maple in the center. The space is cute and comforting, and it's quiet compared to the hospital's busy interior. Peaceful. I really like it out here, but all four walls are lined by large windows, so it leaves me feeling kind of exposed too.

I turn back to James. He's sitting at the bench, watching me. Maybe he's tired from walking around. Maybe he's a bit messed up because of his meds. Or, maybe it's the heat.

"Matt asked if you were okay," he says before glancing through the window looking in on the cafeteria. "After they left yesterday, I mean. He texted to ask about that bruise on your arm."

"What'd you tell him?" I ask, once again wishing I had *something* to cover up with.

He kicks a small rock that somehow ended up on the paved walkway. "I said Ice grabbed you, and that's why we fought."

That is…partially true—*I guess*—but I'm beginning to wonder how abridged the version of events he gave to Matthew were. If the younger sibling knows everything after reading James' mind, why hide what really happened? I know he hates bothering his friends, and I understand not wanting to get anyone else involved, but…

"And you never mentioned Ice to Jesse at all?"

"No," he says under his breath.

I sit beside James, and he glances at me, worrying his hands in his lap. I think I know exactly how he feels, and the guilt leaves a pit in my stomach.

"He asked me about Ice," I say, though I force a smile and look away before I catch his reaction. "We were still stuck in the waiting room, and he asked if this had anything to do with him—because he knew I was with Ice in June or whatever. But I, um…"

Why would Jesse ask if James hurt himself?

"I panicked and said I wasn't there when it happened."

He nods slowly. "Yeah… I suck at talking to him too. I always have, ever since Mom… Ugh." He takes a deep breath and looks up, at the slice of blue sky visible above the courtyard. "Anyway, he's doing so much better than me—moving out and going to university and all. I don't wanna mess that up for him. He shouldn't have to deal with this shit. I'm an adult, and it's my problem, and he's got enough on his plate as it is, you know?"

I want to pat him on the shoulder and say, *It's okay to ask for help when you need it*, but I'd feel like the worst kind of hypocrite if I said something like that.

I lied to Jesse and Matthew too. I lied to Rose until I literally couldn't keep it up any longer. And my own brother doesn't even know that Ice exists—let alone that I've landed myself in the hospital multiple times in the past month. Last time we talked, I told him I was fine.

"That's messed up, isn't it?" James mumbles.

"Maybe a little, but I get why you didn't say anything. This whole situation sucks. And it's honestly kind of embarrassing. But it'll get better, right?"

He stares at me for a moment, eyes wide like he has no idea how to respond. Then, as he looks away again, he nods.

six

"So soon?" I glance between James and Dr. Edwards. "I know immortals heal fast, but it hasn't even been three days since his surgery. He nearly died."

The surgeon blinks, seemingly amused. "The incision is healing as expected, no complications, and his strength has sufficiently returned. Everything checks out, so, unless James would prefer to extend his stay, he's free to leave today."

James stands and stretches his arms over his head.

"I'm ready to get out of here," he says.

His eyes are bright, and his discomfort is less obvious than it has been the past couple days, but I still catch a shift in his expression just before he drops his arms back to his sides. A slight, stifled wince. Maybe that's why the thought of leaving bothers me.

"If you're sure," I agree slowly.

"I am."

He smiles easily, exchanging a look with Dr. Edwards, who dismisses himself soon after. They both seem to know better than I do, and I did walk out of the hospital barely twenty-four hours after almost bleeding to death myself, but James had a punctured lung and a few ribs cracked too. He underwent major surgery.

But I still haven't seen the incision myself. I couldn't bring myself to look over whenever someone came by to check on it or change the wound dressing.

"Are you sure you're okay?" I ask. "Absolutely sure?"

He nods with some confidence, humor evident in his smile. "I'm fine, Jayde. Seriously. I'll show you later, but there's nothing to worry about."

"Okay. I trust you."

"Great. Almost ready to go?"

I frown and glance at my things, strewn about the vinyl bench across the room. James looks ready to walk out the door right now, but—

"Go where?" I ask.

"Ah…" His smile grows fixed, then he drops it and rubs his jaw. "I thought about it after you asked last night, and… Well, I mean, we can't go back to your house or the manor, you know? They're not safe at all. I thought about getting a motel room again, but I don't want you to worry about money either, so… I'm thinking we should stay at my place until things calm down. Uh… Have you heard anything from Rose yet?"

"No. She's still ignoring me, but… *Your* place?"

"My dad's place, anyway."

"But I thought—"

He shushes me, glancing away with a shadowed expression made more intense by the harsh overhead lights and yellowing bruise beside his eye. "Just— Don't. It's not like I wanna go back, but we'll be safe there. Ice knows how I feel about my dad. He'd never think to look for me there—let alone think I'd take *you* there."

I glance at my feet. The leather boots.

What is James' father like? He doesn't talk about him often, and nothing I've heard was particularly good. Even with how little I know, I'm not sure it's a good idea to stay there. I mean, I love my parents, and my relationship with them isn't *that* bad, but I still can't imagine crawling back to either of them.

Then again, it's not like I have any better ideas. *If this is what James thinks is best...*

"Okay," I say.

At this point, I'm just glad we have any sort of plan. I'd rather go home, obviously, but I wasn't looking forward to the gory mess we left behind.

"Give me a minute to grab my stuff."

James nods, and I return to the bench, where I start organizing everything. I don't have much, so it should all fit in the hospital tote bag.

Behind me, James mutters, "I wanna stay with Matt, but he's still living with his parents—and out in Westbrooke too. He barely knows anything, and Cassidy is always there."

A glance over my shoulder suggests he's talking to himself. He's pacing while messing around on his phone, texting or something.

Then he sighs. "Fuck. He's gonna be pissed."

"Matt or your dad?" I ask dryly.

"Both," he says. "But mostly my dad. We haven't talked since I stormed out in May, and I'm in deep shit this time—none of the petty shit he's used to. Doubt he'd even care to know what's happened, though. Or that I can morph or anything. I bet he's still hung up over the stupid TV."

"Sorry I asked."

"Hey, I'm sure you've got your own reasons for not talking about your folks much, right? You deserve to know what you're in for if you're gonna meet him."

"Now I'm really sorry I asked."

He laughs. And then coughs.

I realize I only have the clothes I'm wearing, so I fold the cotton scrubs and stuff them into the bag with everything else. At the very least, they make decent pajamas.

"Anyway," he says, "I had Matt drop my car off this morning, so let's just get outta here before I change my mind about this."

I nod, sling the hospital-branded tote over my shoulder, and follow James out of the room. We stop only to pick up a couple prescriptions from the on-site pharmacy before leaving the hospital through the front entrance. His car is parked in visitor parking, not far from the building.

The car is already unlocked, and he opens the passenger door for me. His hand hesitates before falling away from the handle, and he turns to me with a terse expression.

"Jayde, about Ice—"

"If he wanted to kill me, he would have," I say, unsure where the words are even coming from. "He said enough the other day that I know you're the one in danger now. Not me. If you think your father's house is the safest place for us, I trust you. And I'll stay with you either way, so let's just go."

He averts his eyes and nods. Then we both climb into the car, and we're off—though I'm still not exactly sure where we're going.

I watch the scenery change through the window as we head north. After stopping to eat, we pass through downtown Riverview. Then we turn left, heading toward unfamiliar neighborhoods on the eastern side of town. Compared to Westbrooke's consistently glamorous, manicured lots, these houses are mismatched, existing in various stages of upkeep—or disrepair. The roads are narrow and uneven, and half the lawns are weedy and dry.

I'm not surprised to learn that James' father lives in this part of town. I grew up in a similar neighborhood to the south. *Well, my neighborhood was a little nicer than this, but it's still similar.*

James sighs heavily as he parks his car on the curb in front of a modest two-story house with a very small and very dead front lawn and a beat-up, blue pickup truck in the cracked drive-way. The mailbox is crooked, and the house could use a fresh coat of oatmeal-colored paint, but it matches the general vibe of the rest of the neighborhood.

Unremarkable part of town aside, I doubt being here would bother me so much if James wasn't so obviously upset. It's hard to say whether it's the neighborhood or the house or the prospect of seeing his father again or some combination of factors. I wish I could help in some way, but I honestly don't want to know exactly what has him so stressed. I'm sure the answer would only make me more nervous.

"Should we go in?" I ask after a good five minutes spent sitting in silence in the uncomfortably hot car.

James lifts his head from the steering wheel to offer me a bleak look, but he nods and pops his door open. I follow suit, and, as we make our way up the overgrown stepping stone path to the front door, he looks over the dead grass in mild disgust.

"What's the point of installing sprinklers if you never turn them on?" he mutters.

We stop on the landing as James hesitates. He stares at the door with wide eyes and a taut frown and scratches his arm with his bruised hand. I follow his gaze to the intricately carved wooden plaque hanging on the brown door.

{ The Reid Family }

The cutesy sign does little to ease my nerves. If anything, it's kind of sad to think a loving family might have once lived here. Plus, the space smells strongly of tobacco smoke. There's an old coffee can with a hole cut into the lid beside the door—a makeshift ashtray surrounded by a few stray cigarette butts.

"Should I knock?" James asks, his voice low. "Or can I just walk in? He kicked me out, and we haven't talked in months. I— What am I gonna say? What's *he* gonna say?"

I frown. "I don't know. This was your idea."

He drags his hands down his face and takes a deep breath before reaching for the doorknob.

It's unlocked.

The front door opens into a kitchen. The air is stale and sour and smells about as smoky as the landing, and *god it's a mess*. Old pizza boxes, empty takeout containers, and at least a dozen tall beer cans line the counters. The sink is full of unwashed dishes, and a plastic garbage bag overflowing with more empty cans sits on the grungy linoleum floor beside the trashcan at the end of the counter.

The house's semi-open floorplan leaves only part of the living room visible beyond the kitchen. A TV plays rather loudly just out of sight—it sounds like sports of some kind, but it's hard to tell.

James sighs and crosses into the living room while I, overwhelmed by the mere thought of stepping inside this house I already dislike, carefully close the front door and hang back in the cluttered, dimly lit kitchen.

"Dad," James says, his voice flat like he's desperately trying not to convey any particular emotion.

When he receives no response, he repeats himself louder, and the TV volume drops several clicks. Even from behind, James' stiff posture clearly communicates his frustration and discomfort, and being acknowledged by his father doesn't seem to have helped.

I creep a few steps closer to James, hoping to see further into the living room, but I don't want to completely expose myself just yet, so he still blocks most of my view.

"Jesse? No, wait— *James*?" His father's voice is slurred and a bit rough. "Where the fuck have you been?"

James bristles. "Where have I—? You kicked me out, remember? Memorial Day weekend?" He pauses, waiting for a response, but he doesn't receive one. "God… Why am I not surprised?"

"Smartass."

"How am I—? Ugh. Forget it. If you can't even remember, I guess it doesn't matter."

James shakes his head and glances back—presumably to make sure I haven't bolted considering his fleeting relief as I force a smile I can't maintain. He offers a hand to me, and I take a breath before inching closer to accept it. I end up standing half behind and half beside him, just past where the linoleum gives way to brown carpet.

From here, I can see the rest of the living room. It's also poorly lit and littered by a mess of paper plates and beer cans, more covering a small dining table and falling onto the wooden chairs and floor below. Beyond that, James' father sits on the couch in front of a flat-screen TV set up on a low stand.

He looks like a painfully unpleasant sort of person. Bored and annoyed and holding a beer can in one hand—like a terrible, deadbeat dad in a sitcom from the 2000s. He probably hasn't shaved in weeks. *Or washed his shirt.* But the man has fair skin and messy, rust-colored hair, and I hate to admit I can see the resemblance between him and James.

"A girl?" the man asks in gruff surprise.

"Yep. Jayde, this is my dad, Jonathan. Dad, this is my girlfriend, Jayde. Alright, cool, let's go."

With that rushed introduction out of the way, James starts leading me through the small living room toward a staircase, but his father stammers something absolutely unintelligible, and we stop. James winces, his grip on my hand tightening as he slowly turns back to face the couch.

"A *human* girl?"

James laughs, the sound short. "Yeah, long story. No time to explain—not that you'd remember if I tried."

We start moving again, and he stops us a second time. Jonathan Reid stares at his son for a long, tense moment. Just being here, witnessing this interaction, makes me wish I could sink into the carpet and disappear.

"What's up with your face?" he asks. "Someone hit ya?"

"Wow. Haha. It almost sounds like you care." James' gaze turns icy as his eyes narrow and his shoulders quirk up. "Better question: Why haven't you called once since I left—especially if you forgot you kicked me out? And why wasn't anyone able to reach you while I was *literally dying* in the hospital the other day?"

His father's eyes glaze over as he stares at us, and I can't tell what's going through his mind. Is he speechless after being caught off guard? Did anything James said reach him at all?

"Did you even listen to the voicemails?" James asks. "Jesse and the hospital both left at least one." He waits a moment, but his father *still* doesn't respond. Then he shakes his head. "Whatever. Good to know you're as shitty as ever. C'mon, Jayde."

Why'd we come here, again?

seven

Upstairs, James shuts us inside a bedroom at the end of the hallway. He lets go of my hand, and I glance over. With his back against the door, he breathes heavily, one hand clutching the loose fabric of his t-shirt while the other smooths his hair back.

"Are you okay?"

It feels like the stupidest thing I could've asked, but he nods as he collects himself.

"Yeah. Just— Probably. Ugh." He turns the privacy lock on the doorknob and relaxes slightly. "I am so sorry you had to see that. Being a belligerent asshole runs in the family, apparently."

I frown. "I think I understand why you were staying at Reid Manor."

"My dad isn't why I—" His blank expression shifts slightly. Then he clears his throat, glances past me, and steps away from the door. "Anyway, uh… It sure is weird being back."

James' bedroom is small and squarish. The air, while more breathable, is hotter and stuffier than the air downstairs, where I believe an old window AC unit was doing its best to cool the first floor.

The twin-size bed in the far corner of the room is rather

haphazardly made with vaguely childish bedding, and the only other pieces of furniture are a small wooden dresser acting as an end table with a half-empty water bottle and red spiral notebook on top, a near-empty bookcase, and a plastic wastebasket with no liner. Several cardboard boxes are stacked in one corner of the room, and the small closet—which doesn't have a door despite looking like it should—contains only a broken skateboard, a guitar case covered in quarter machine stickers, and a white box fan. The warm, off-white walls are bare too, save for at least a dozen silver thumbtacks with torn bits of colored paper still clinging to them.

What kind of posters were hanging in here before he took them down?

James grimaces as he pokes around the room, and, as I look again too, something about it feels strangely *off*.

I drop my bag beside the tall, thin bookcase and swipe a finger over an empty shelf, exposing the dust covering it. But the dust is thicker at the front than at the back, so I imagine there were books on it not too long ago.

What is this feeling, though?

I turn to face the room.

James grabs the spiral notebook from the top of the dresser and opens it to the first page. His frown deepens, his expression some combination of anger and sadness, as he reads whatever is written inside.

"I doubt he came in here once while I was gone," he says, closing the notebook.

"Your father?"

He answers not with words, but with a pleading look.

Then he crosses the room again, where he sets the notebook on the very top of the bookcase before opening the nearest cardboard box. The box, resting on top of three others beside the bookcase, has *BOOKS* written on the side in dark permanent marker, and the contents do not disappoint as he holds up a paperback novel.

"Wanna help put these away?" he asks, voice still low.

"Oh. Sure."

We spend several awkwardly quiet minutes filling the bookcase. The books in the box span various genres. High fantasy, crime thriller, mystery, sci-fi, young adult fiction, classic novels, non-fiction, history and science and nature, and the occasional fairy tale anthology or book of poetry. Most have resale stickers on the cover or spine and likely came from secondhand stores or yard sales, but it's a decent collection. I could barely fill one of these shelves with all the books I own.

When we get to the first box labeled *CLOTHES*, he doesn't look inside. But, as he prepares to pick it up, I move to stop him.

"Where do you want it?" I ask. "I'll move it for you."

He averts his eyes, one hand hovering over his sternum, before pointing to the closet. He steps back, and I pick up the box. It isn't *that* heavy—maybe thirty pounds—but I'm certain he shouldn't lift even this much weight yet.

I set the box on the floor in the closet. After moving a second clothing box, I sit on the edge of the small bed. I stare at my clean boots. At the short, brown carpet beneath my feet.

Across the room, James starts putting away shirts using the plastic hangers that were all pushed off to one side of the closet rod. It looks uncomfortable—bending down and standing up and wincing and pressing a hand to his injured side for a second—but I don't mention it. And I don't stop him because I know it sucks feeling like you can't do anything for yourself.

Something about this room, though...

"Why's all your stuff packed up like that, anyway?"

"I guess I thought I'd never come back," he mumbles, "so I just boxed everything up before I took off. Thought it'd be easier to move with it all in boxes—or something like that."

"Oh?"

I listen as he explains how he spent the whole month of June couch-surfing. He was kicked out after he broke a TV. He knocked it over during an argument with his dad. James had been out late—at a party, I guess. He was kinda drunk. Sounds like his dad is almost always drunk. It was an accident, but he was told to leave, so he did. He stopped by to pack his things a few days later and never came back.

He didn't set himself up at Reid Manor until July.

But I don't ask *when* in July, too afraid the answer might be what I expect.

He puts the last article of clothing away and dismantles the cardboard box, tucking it with the other empty boxes in the back of the closet. Then he picks up the box fan—which *should* be light enough for him to safely carry—and turns to face me again.

He flashes the sort of off-putting smile I'd probably offer someone while trying to convince them that I'm fine after I spent an hour crying in secret. Though, his black eye might be clouding my perception.

"It's not so bad with you here," he says. "Still hot as hell, though."

"It is hot in here."

He adjusts his grip on the fan, and his smile falters as he looks around the room again. "Fuck… I got rid of just about everything, didn't I?"

Something about this…doesn't feel right…

"At least we have a fan," I say lamely.

He sighs, unimpressed by my attempt at humor, and crosses the room. The only window is behind me. No screen, so I just push it open and crawl out of the way, leaving James ample space to position the fan. Then I plug the fan in, having to reach behind the bed to find the outlet. When I sit up again, the air blowing in is hot on my face, but any air circulation at all is an improvement.

James sits in the middle of the bed and stares at the ceiling. I move closer and watch him. But I don't say anything. I don't touch him at all, keeping my hands on my knees.

Eventually, he glances down, and his eyes meet mine.

What is it…?

"Back in the hospital—" I stammer. "You said you wanted to show me something?"

He perks up and nods. "What happened the other day was bad. Don't get me wrong; when Ice stabbed me, I thought I was done for. But I'll be okay. It'll heal, so you don't need to worry about me."

"You still shouldn't have pulled the knife out, you know? If I had panicked, you'd probably be dead right now."

"Yeah…" He laughs, a hand pressed to his side. "I know, and I'm sorry. I don't even remember doing that, but— Here.

Just look."

James grabs ahold of the back of his shirt as though he intends to pull it off over his shoulders, but he hesitates and instead pulls the shirt up from the bottom hem to expose his chest. His left side is badly bruised, and his sternum is covered by a long gauze pad, but the small stab wound on the right side of his chest is uncovered, stitched, and scabbed over. No redness or weeping. It's healing well.

I touch it without thinking

His skin is so warm. He has freckles on his chest too.

"See?" he says. "You can take the bandage off if you want. I don't really need it anymore."

"Okay..."

Slowly, I pick at the edge of the medical tape adhering the gauze to his skin. Our eyes meet for an instant, and he smiles. I'm still not sure I want to see it, knowing what the surgery entailed, but I peel the gauze away.

"Oh."

The incision is several inches long, running down the center of his sternum. I expected bruising or staples or *something*, but it's just a perfectly straight line held together by a row of small, dark stitches. It seems less healed than the stab wound, and the skin is still in the process of bonding together in a few places, but I guess it looks good—for what it is, anyway.

Either way, I do not touch it.

"Does it hurt?" I ask, glancing up.

"Well..." He pauses to think, expression neutral, before shaking his head. "I'm still sore from the fight, but, uh... I feel alright considering they sawed my rib cage in half or whatever."

I feel my frown harden. "James…"

He drops the hem of his shirt, takes the spent gauze from me, and leaves the bed. After tossing the gauze into the wastebasket, he sighs, and his shoulders dip ever so slightly. I watch his back for an uncomfortably long moment, but he seems to shake off whatever came over him.

"Nah. What's real cool is that, pretty soon, I'll be able to morph whenever I want." As he plants a hand on his hip, he turns to face me with a smile. "I'll show you once I heal up a bit more, but I guess you can say I'm not defective anymore—if I…ever was."

That reminds me of the missing weight of the River Sapphire, where the pendant used to rest just below my collarbone. It's still in my wallet. *And thinking about it—*

"That makes two of us, huh?"

Another moment of silence.

James frowns, glancing away. It looks like he wants to say something as he stares across the room at nothing. His frown deepens in a way that feels significant, but he soon shakes his head again. With a quiet laugh, he sits on the edge of the bed.

I scoot closer, but the bitterness in his expression—a soft smile with knitted brows—surprises me. Then he takes my left hand in both of his, and my breath catches.

"Thank you," he says, holding my gaze. "Seriously. I bet it sounds stupid to you, but *thank you* for everything you've done for me. Everything you've given up. I'm sorry for causing so much trouble, but I… I'll try not to scare you like that again."

I can't look away. "Does that mean you won't fight anymore?"

"If that's what—" He glances aside, but only for an instant, and kind of laughs as he returns my hand. "Yeah... I mean, I sure as hell won't try something like *that* a second time. I'm no good to you dead, right? But I won't just stand by if Ice tries to start shit either."

"Oh. Well." I scratch my wrist. "I guess that's all I can ask. I hardly have the right to tell you what to do after..."

His eyes flick to my left arm—the tiny scab in the crook of my elbow or the hand-shaped bruise or the scarred heart; I don't know—but he doesn't mention it. He doesn't chastise me for meeting with Ice. He doesn't even tell me it's okay. He says nothing, and I don't speak either.

We're both quiet for a while, glancing around to avoid eye contact and stewing in the hot room while the fan buffets the back of our heads with equally hot air.

Then, out of nowhere, James takes my face in his hands. He stares into my eyes, and I stare back, suddenly more worried than I have been all day. His amber eyes are wide, but I can't get a good read on him—just an...uncomfortable level of focus.

"Please," he says. "You can't leave me alone like that again."

"What? I—"

He shakes his head and pulls me into a tight hug, effectively cutting off whatever I was going to say. Warm breath tickles my ear as I stare at the wall past him. At a scrap of shiny, black paper trapped by a piece of clear tape.

What is he thinking? What should I be thinking? What is even going on right now?

"I don't trust myself," he whispers. "I can't, even now, so…"

My breath catches again, and I carefully reciprocate the hug. His back is warm beneath my hands. He's always so warm. *But*…

"Why was your stuff in boxes?" I ask again. "Is it really just because you were planning to move out?"

He freezes and breaks off the hug. His frown is nervous, his cheeks a bit pale, and I detect a hint of misty dread in his wide eyes. I feel bad asking a second time. I don't even care if he doesn't want to tell me—or if he deflects or lies. But I have to ask. I can't keep thinking about it without saying *something*.

"Why were you really at Reid Manor in July?" My mouth feels dry, but I keep talking. "Couldn't you have stayed with Matthew? He seems like a good guy, and you said you stayed with him for a while in June. He would've helped you, right? Even if he still lives with his parents?"

"Uh…" He blinks a few times, then sighs and glances around.

I look too. Even after putting away a good deal of the things that were packed up and moving the last few boxes to the closet, the room feels empty.

In a way, it reminds me of Ice's bedroom. He doesn't keep much in his room either. It's minimal and neat and clean, but it still feels like a bedroom. It feels like a place someone actually lives in.

This room feels *lonely*, like a tidy guest room, missing the belongings of whoever is going to stay in it next. But James grew up here. A bedroom that someone grew up in shouldn't feel like this.

I don't like this room, and I don't like this house.

"Life sucks," James says, his voice low. "I'm sure you get that, after everything you've dealt with this summer, right? I mean, I don't— Well, it's not like I want to...stop...living. Obviously not. But..." He flashes an uneasy smile that leaves a pit in my stomach. "It sucks, you know?"

He is deflecting.

I feel my frown grow more pronounced. "I guess, but..."

He meets my gaze with no meaningful expression. "Haven't you wished he'd just get it over with?"

Get it over with? Like—

"Ice?" I ask sharply. When I realize exactly what he said, my eyes dart to my lap. "Well... Maybe I have thought that once or twice, but—"

"I know. You never meant it."

"Of course, I never meant it. How could I?"

"How could you?" he echoes with a sigh.

I look over as James falls back onto the bed and stares at the ceiling. He looks deep in thought and sort of lonely, reflecting the emptiness of the room we've trapped ourselves in. It's like a nagging itch in my brain. The room. This conversation. Our entire situation. *But, honestly, what's new?*

"Are you okay?" I ask.

His eyes close. "Mm... I'll try not to scare you like that again. I've freaked you out enough as it is, and I feel bad that you have to deal with my personal shit on top of everything else too now."

That doesn't answer my question.

"You sure you wanna stay here?" I ask, giving up.

He groans and sits up slowly, favoring his side. We watch

each other for a long moment. His expression is still mild but less murky than before.

"It'll be fine. Just boring, and we have to put up with my dad when he's home. He's annoying as hell, but he won't *hurt* us or anything. And, as much as I hate it, we're probably safer here than anywhere else." He looks around for the umpteenth time. "Though, I sorta wish I sold the guitar instead of my electronics. It'd be nice to play video games or watch TV or whatever, right?"

"We can always swing by my house and grab my laptop."

He pales again, but he must realize we can't avoid the cottage forever, even if it's just to pick up a few things.

I only have the obnoxiously expensive outfit that Ice left me with and a set of nurse's scrubs, and he doesn't have his backpack. Considering the state of his bedroom, he might want it back sooner than later. *For now, though...*

"Okay, fine. But where will I sleep?"

He glances at the bed we're sitting on and flashes a sheepish smile. "Not a lot of options, huh?"

"You sure you don't mind being that close to me?"

He shrugs, smile widening. "I got a sleeping bag out in the car. Might hurt a bit, but I can take the floor if you don't wanna share."

I fake a frown to mask my relief, and he laughs. Then he pulls me closer. He kisses my hair. The side of my head. I feel his heart beating through his shirt—a bit fast, same as mine. He's as warm as ever, and I feel myself relax for the first time since we walked into the house.

"No," he murmurs. "I think I can handle it now."

eight

James sits cross-legged in the middle of the bed and covers his eyes with his hands. I roll my eyes, but I pull my shirt off over my head without saying anything. The t-shirt I borrowed is probably a size too big for him and falls over the hem of my cotton shorts, but I don't have a camisole, and it's more comfortable than the flashy blouse or blue scrub top.

"You know," he says, "I haven't had a girl stay the night since eighth grade."

"Am I supposed to be impressed?" I ask with a laugh.

"Nah. She slept on the floor."

I laugh harder, and he accuses me of judging him. Maybe I am judging a little, but I'd never stayed the night alone with a boy before that night at Reid Manor during the rainstorm. *And he slept in a chair clear across the room.*

When I turn to check, he's still covering his eyes.

"Okay," I say, smoothing the shirt. "It's safe to look now."

His hands fall to his lap, and he blinks as he stares at me. "You look good."

"Huh?"

"Oh." His face and ears flush red, and he covers his eyes

again. "Sorry. Blame the oxy if I say anything too stupid, okay? It makes me dumb as hell. Also kinda sleepy."

The medication?

I step closer and comb my fingers through his hair. He lowers his hands, and he looks me over as though seeing me for the first time. Golden eyes wide and glittering, his mouth ever so slightly agape until our eyes meet again.

He flashes a smile and scratches the back of his neck. "Nothing like almost dying to make you feel alive, right?"

"That's not funny."

"It's not?" With a laugh that doesn't make him wince, he pats the empty space on the bed beside him. "Come here a sec."

His expression mellows as I humor him by climbing onto the bed to sit beside him. He turns to face me properly, and we stare at each other for a moment. A long moment. It's getting dark outside. *I wish I had a hair tie.* The best I can do to keep my hair out of my face is pull it all over one shoulder. The air blown in by the fan still doesn't hold a touch of coolness, but I doubt it would help even if it did.

I'm in James' bedroom. I'm in his bed.

"Hey, I, uh—" His eyes flick to my lips, and he swallows hard. "Actually, I'd really like to kiss you right now."

I laugh. "Just do it, you dork."

His expression shifts as his hands leave his lap. He brushes my bangs out of my eyes and holds my face for a moment. Soft. Careful. His attention flicking between my eyes. When I *finally* close the distance, beating him to it, our mouths come together with a hungry desperation I wasn't expecting. His fingers tangle in my hair. I inch closer until I'm in his lap with his face in my hands.

His breath comes faster. Mine does too.

I grasp the fabric of his shirt, pulling him impossibly close, and melt into him. The room is hot, and his body radiates warmth as always, but I don't care. All I feel is *relief*. Relief that I'm okay. Relief that he's okay and still so warm and so *alive*. Then, slowly, his hands slide down. My neck. My shoulders. His hands trace the curves of my body until they come to rest at my hips, and I gasp as an unfamiliar heat floods me head to toe.

No one has ever touched me like this.

I break away to catch my breath, and we both open our eyes. Our faces so close, our noses still touch. With our chests pressed together, can he feel my heart racing? Can he hear every beat? I think I feel his heart—*it's racing too*.

"You okay?" he asks, hushed and breathless.

His eyes are bright, his smile soft and welcoming. He looks less nervous than I expected—less nervous than I feel. His fingers brush a sliver of exposed skin near the crumpled hem of the t-shirt he let me borrow, sending a warm, pleasurable shiver down my spine. And I want *more*.

I want to kiss him again, draw a hand up his arm, and run my fingers through his hair. I want to see how far he'd let me take it. I would give James *everything*.

And, right now, I want to, but...

His black eye is nothing, but I can't ignore the incision beneath his shirt or the cracked ribs that still hurt him when he laughs. Even if he insists he's fine, and the medication dulls the pain, he was seriously injured.

I... *I can't justify this right now.*

"I'm fine." I hug him, burying my face in his neck. He smells like body wash. Normal body wash, not the hospital stuff. And that *stupid* vanilla deodorant. Cool. Clean. A bit sweet. *Ah... Damn it.* "But we should get to sleep, right?"

He lets out a breath and kisses the side of my head. Then his hands move to my back again. The absence of his fingers against bare skin fills me with an aching sense of loss.

But I can wait.

We're together, and we're safe, and we have time.

I can wait.

"Yeah, okay," he agrees softly. "You're right."

He kisses me again with far less intensity, then lies down. I'm left straddling his hips, *which really isn't helping*, but he just stares at the ceiling with his arms folded behind his head. Seems like he's lost in thought all of a sudden.

I was kinda hoping he might put up more of a fight, but I smash those impure thoughts deep *deep* down and won't dare admit to them. I can't even bring myself to ask what he's thinking.

My face still feels like it's on fire, so I glance around to distract myself.

The bed is small, and we're about in the middle of it, but I shift to his good side. Without looking at me, he slips an arm out from behind his head. I mold myself to his side and carefully rest a hand on his chest. I can feel the stitches through his shirt, but... With him holding me like this, I feel safe.

For the first time in weeks, I *am* safe. *We're both safe.*

"I love you," I say.

"Mm... Love you too."

He combs his fingers through my hair, and I watch his profile as he frowns. The expression is soft, not too different from his thoughtfulness, but it reflects just enough unease to worry me.

"Are you okay?" I ask.

"Yeah," he says, and, for once, I actually believe him. "I'm okay. But y'know what, Jayde? I don't give a shit if you're human. I wanna be with you more than anything."

"Aah... Am I even human anymore, though?"

"Oh, right. I keep forgetting." His eyes flick to my face, and he flashes a curious smile. "You can do the whole cat thing now."

"We both can."

His smile falters, and he looks back to the ceiling. "I might've mentioned it already, but, when I first woke up—" He laughs, but bitterness creeps into his expression. "I mean, I freaked the fuck out 'cause you weren't there, but that's not— Uh... Anyway, the surgeon guy said you brought me in as a cat. I didn't believe him, but he said I was probably...misdiagnosed? That I probably wasn't really defective to begin with. I still don't know if I believe that. What does that even mean—*misdiagnosed?* How the hell do you misdiagnose something like that? But... I did it. I morphed on my own, and it was *easy*, so maybe it is true."

James...

"Isn't that good?" I ask.

"Dunno." He laughs again, sounding tired. "It's...weird. I don't know how to feel about it, to be honest. I mean, fuck; I should be happy, right? Or relieved, or whatever, at least. And maybe I was a little—maybe I *am* a little—but I think I'm more… *pissed?* Like, if I was never actually defective my whole life, why couldn't I do it before? What was wrong with me before? Why'd it take almost dying, you know?"

My first impulse is to say I understand, but I stop myself. Even if my experience with the River Sapphire is similar on a surface level, it's not the same at all.

I've known about immortals for two months, but James grew up in that world. He was supposed to turn into a cat and see in the dark and develop some cool special ability as a kid. *Years* ago. But he never did. For years, that expectation must have haunted him. In school. In every relationship and social interaction he endured. It seems like he was treated differently by everyone around him for a long time.

Sure, I was picked on a few times in middle school—who wasn't? But James was bullied for *years*. I don't understand the first thing about what he went through.

"Sorry," he huffs. "I should just shut up and be happy about it, shouldn't I? I mean, I'm not sure being able to morph makes me any less of a freak, but at least I finally have a *chance* to be normal, right?"

"Maybe," I mumble, stuck on the idea of a younger James working alone as the rest of his classmates paired up with friends during group projects.

"Well… I guess I'll never be normal if I stay with you."

My mouth quirks into a smile. "Oh? What's that supposed to mean?"

"You're human." He rolls onto his side to kiss me again. Soft.

I feel the smile on his lips before he pulls away. "It's weird, right? Totally crazy. Maybe liking you just makes me even more of a freak."

"Does that bother you?"

His smile widens, eyes sparkling. "Fuck no. You are perfect. Just like this. And so beautiful. And I—" His breath hitches, and he laughs as his cheeks flush. "Sorry, uh…"

I don't know why I start laughing—*maybe it's a subconscious attempt to relieve the suffocating sexual tension between us*—but it seems to soothe us both. James returns to lying flat on his back. He stares at the ceiling, and I rest my head on his shoulder.

"You don't have to apologize," I say, as though saying it makes me any less frustrated. "I want to be with you too, but… It's late. We really should get some sleep."

"I know."

We're quiet for a moment. A few minutes—several, maybe—with my hand on his chest and his arm holding me close. His eyes eventually close, and I find myself staring across the room at the closet with the few remaining cardboard boxes lined up against the wall.

There's that weird feeling again…

I clear my throat. "Here, I'll, um—" As James' eyes open, and he looks at me, I start over, "I'll go turn the light off."

"Okay."

He hesitates before moving his arm. A strange coolness settles over me the instant his hand leaves my shoulder, but I force myself to follow through. I leave the bed and flip the light switch. The room falls dark—or *darker*, anyway, as a neighboring house's floodlight illuminates the room enough I can still see clearly.

I wanna get back to cuddling. But I can't bring myself to move. I stand beside the door for a few, long seconds. I listen to the buzzing box fan set up in the window behind me, but my eyes are locked on the vertical orientation of the doorknob's privacy lock.

Safe or not, I wish we weren't here.

I wish we weren't stuck at James' unpleasant father's equally unpleasant house. I wish we weren't recovering from grievous injuries. I wish no one got hurt at all.

It's summer. Relaxing might be out of the question at this point, but I want to at least try to take it easy and move on from the bad. Right now, I just wanna be able to fool around with James for more than thirty seconds without being overcome by so much guilt I have to stop myself.

I'm nineteen years old! This isn't fair.

After carefully smoothing my expression, I turn away from the door. James is sat up on the far side of the bed. He watches me, eyes reflecting green in the low light. And he smiles warmly and sleepily as I cross the room to join him.

Surely, one day, we can get what we want.

* * * * *

James is asleep.

The room is still uncomfortably hot.

And I am thirsty.

Careful to avoid disturbing James, I roll onto my other side and reach for my phone on the dresser. I turn it on just to check the time—12:37AM. No important notifications. Nothing from Rose. But it's only at 12% battery. I turn it off again and drop my face to the flat pillow.

Is James' father downstairs? Still out in the living room?

I'm too thirsty to put it off, so I slip out of bed. The privacy lock turns with a soft click, and I crack the door open. The hallway is dark, but I hear the TV. The bathroom is at the other end of the hall—I can use that sink—but I need a cup first.

It's late. Maybe he's asleep.

I creep down the hallway, keeping my footsteps light and reminding myself to breathe. A light still on somewhere down-stairs casts a soft glow up to the turn in the staircase. I make my way down and peek around the corner. The TV blocks my view of the couch, but I hear snoring over whatever late-night infomercial is playing on it.

As I walk past the TV, it's clear that Jonathan Reid is passed out. He's sitting up with a beer can in his hand, but his eyes are shut, head lolled to one side. I quicken my pace into the kitchen, where a yellow light is turned on over the sink.

I have half a mind to swipe a dirty cup off the counter and wash it upstairs, but I resist the urge. Instead, I scan the cabinets above the cluttered counters.

Which has cups in it?

I check the cabinets one at a time. Cooking oil and spices above the stove. Half-empty liquor bottles above the sink. Finally, beside the fridge, I find a cabinet with dishes inside. Seems like the majority of dishes in this house are elsewhere at the moment, but there's a single plastic cup that looks like it's about as old as I am.

Good enough.

I grab the cup and carefully close the cabinet before turning back. The tip of my middle finger bumps an empty beer can on the counter, and I freeze as it knocks over several others. At least five or six cans fall off the counter and clatter on the floor. The noise quiets after a few seconds, but I don't move, the inside of my cheek caught between my teeth.

Because the snoring in the other room stopped too.

Heart racing, I speed out of the kitchen before freezing again when I see that James' father is wide awake and noticed me. *Of course he noticed me.* But I only made it halfway across the living room.

"You— James brought ya, right?" His voice is slurred and drowsy, and he points at me with a wavering hand.

Ugh... I doubt I can avoid this conversation without making things worse for myself *and* James, so I try to play it cool and nod while inching closer to the stairs.

Jonathan Reid watches me with something that might be a scowl. Or drunk confusion. Or maybe that's how he always looks, and it doesn't really mean anything.

"You staying here or something?" he asks.

"Oh, yeah, I guess so," I say. "Is that okay?"

He doesn't answer my question one way or the other, but his expression shifts slightly. He takes a drink from the can in his hand. "You're human?"

I swallow. "Yes?"

"What're ya doin' down here?"

"Um..." I raise the cup, grasping it too tightly in an attempt to keep my hand from trembling. "I was just...looking for a cup. For water. I'm sorry if I woke you up."

He squints at me. "How old are you, girl?"

"Nineteen."

"Huh." For some reason, he has to think about that.

I smother my grimace, forcing a smile instead. "Well, um, I should get back to bed. Thanks for letting me stay."

Without waiting for a response, I head for the staircase at a controlled pace. He doesn't stop me or move from the couch, and I manage to make it back upstairs and shut myself in the bathroom without further incident.

I lock the door, set the cup on the counter, and drag my hands down my face. That was nothing compared to what happened when we first got here, but if this is the kind of thing James has had to deal with his whole life, I don't blame him for running away and staying at Reid Manor instead.

Forget about it.

With a sigh, I fill the cup with water.

I feel better after taking a drink, so I head back to the bedroom. I close the door, turn the privacy lock, and walk to the bed. James doesn't seem to have moved at all since I left. He still has his back to the wall and is breathing softly and slowly.

Good.

If I can help it, he will never wake up alone like that ever again.

nine

~ ∞ ~

A light breeze, gentle and calming, disturbs my loose hair. When I open my eyes to inky darkness, I realize I'm in the dreamscape. It's been awhile. Can't say I missed it, though.

"Jayde."

Night.

I snap out of my frustration and turn, but I don't see her. I call her name, scanning the light-speckled dark around me, and, after a moment, she materializes out of a misty light several feet away. She's wearing sweatpants and an oversized t-shirt, and she looks dead tired. Eyes downcast, hugging her arms.

What a mood.

"I am so sorry," she says, voice wavering. "What Ice did was— And what happened to James…" She shakes her head, hands held over her chest. "I should have known better. Of course, Ice was up to something. I should've recognized that. You should've told me. I asked if you were okay, but— If he already had the knife to your arm, why didn't you say anything?"

My gaze snaps to my feet, and I feel my jaw set.

The only way Night would know that Ice had the knife to my arm when she knocked on the door is if he told her himself. He was honest with her about what happened in that room?

Why does that annoy me so much?

"If I knew, I could have stopped him. You know I would have, right?"

"Of course, I know that," I mumble. "That's why I…"

"Oh."

Her hands fall from her face, and she looks away, cycling through understanding, surprise, and disappointment in quick succession. Then her eyes water, and her lip trembles, and the tiny firefly lights flicker a pale red as they flit around in the dark.

"He was serious, then. You agreed to it."

"Mm-hm." I feel kinda bad, imagining she spent the past few days thinking she could've prevented it. "It's not your fault, and everything worked out. Ice gave me the key he was using to sneak into my house, and I can morph now. And James doesn't hate me for it, so…"

She shakes her head, her expression having shifted the second I mentioned James. "Oh… I had no idea that Ice was planning to hurt him. I swear. I never thought he'd take it this far. When you walked in with him, I didn't know—"

That James was in the hospital?

"I believe you," I say. "And that wasn't your fault either. You warned me to be careful after I met with Ice the first time, and I still didn't tell James that he threatened us. It's no different from what happened at your house."

Her tense posture eases up slightly as she steps closer. She's not crying—she hasn't shed a single tear—but she wipes her eyes. Then she nods and takes a deep breath, and the tiny lights around her slow and regain their usual soft white color.

"How is James?" she asks. "Ice said he…stabbed him, and that he was in the hospital this weekend?"

"He's fine now. Out of the hospital, and he can morph too."

"He can? Oh. I see." The beat of surprise fades, and she smiles softly even as she avoids my gaze. "I hope he finds life a bit easier from now on."

That makes two of us.

"It was bad, though," I admit. "He almost died, and he's super upset that I met with Ice—that I went out to Westbrooke and…left him alone like that. To be honest…I'm kinda worried about him."

She frowns. "Mm… James has a habit of underestimating himself. He's more capable than he thinks. Ice, on the other hand… I've never seen him act like this before. When he came back from the hospital that night, he—"

Night hesitates. Her cheeks take on some color as an unfamiliar and more complicated emotion flickers across her face. Then she hugs her arms close and glances away again.

"He was honest with me," she says, her voice level. "I know he didn't tell me everything. That much is obvious. I'm not surprised he doesn't want to confide in me, but what he did say was more than enough for me to understand the severity of his actions, and I… I'm really so sorry for what he's put you and James through the past few months."

Ice? Honest? How can she tell?

I laugh despite myself. "What do you have to be sorry for? You never wanted me to learn about immortals in the first place, right? You said you tried to stop him—"

"I should have stopped him." She looks at the floor, fire in her eyes, the hem of her shirt balled in her hands. "I should've tried harder. I shouldn't have let him drag you into this mess— our lives, immortals, his…stupid emotional baggage. Any of it. You don't deserve this. I should've known better than to believe he could handle this himself."

As her eyes grow misty, the floating lights flicker between white and red and zip through the air with more energy. The floor trembles. Night doesn't seem to notice, but I glance at my bare feet, worried the solid darkness might give way at any moment.

"He's calmed down a little," she continues briskly, growing more upset by the second, "but this weekend wasn't great. No matter what I say, he refuses to see reason. He knows what he's done and how badly he's hurt everyone, and he knows it was wrong, but he doesn't care. Or, if he does care, he won't admit it. His misery is insufferable, as always. I don't know how to stop him from making these…*choices*. I've never been good at reading him when he's like this. I just don't know what to do anymore."

"What do you mean?" I ask, taken aback by the intensity in her voice. "Why do you always act like he's your responsibility?"

"Ice *is* my responsibility!"

Oh—

She shakes her head, anger and sadness further muddying her expression. The fairy lights flicker again as weightless tears fly from her eyes and drift through the air, sparkling like liquid crystals illuminated by impossible light.

"I know he shouldn't be." She presses her hands to her eyes. "I know it's messed up. I know that. But he clearly doesn't know how to be responsible for himself. Someone has to take care of him, and someone has to apologize to the people he hurts."

Wait... What did Ice tell her after he left the hospital?

I step closer. "If you know why he's doing this, you have to tell me. Ice wants to *kill* James. He almost did. If there's anything I can do—"

She freezes. The sparkling tears fall from the air, opaque and red as blood as they splatter on the black ground. Then she laughs, the sound tired and hollow and echoing throughout the void.

"Do you think Ice knows why he did any of this?" She flashes a miserable, twisted smile. "Of course not! He's so childish and impulsive. He's always been this way. The illusion of control is there, but he sabotages every good thing he's ever had. Squanders every opportunity presented to him. And he doesn't know *why* he does it. He doesn't have the slightest idea. I doubt Ice has ever understood that part of himself, and he's certainly no closer to understanding now. Frankly, I don't think he wants to. I don't think he wants to face it at all. After all, it's *so* much easier to ignore it and pretend that everything's *fine*."

My teeth click as I hold back from interjecting.

Why can't she just tell me what she knows?

The floor shifts again, nearly throwing me off balance. As I steady myself and step back, the tiny lights turn a deep, dangerous red. They cast a warm glow like burning embers and dart around like angry hornets, but Night still doesn't seem to notice.

I hate this. If she knows Ice better than anyone and can't figure him out, what hope is there for me?

Tears roll down her face as her shoulders droop in defeat. "Maybe there's nothing I can do. Maybe he can't stand seeing anyone happy. Maybe hurting others makes him feel better about himself. Or, maybe he wants everyone else to feel the way he does, and he finally found the perfect way to do that. To hurt everyone who ever cared about him…all at the same time."

"Night. Slow down—"

"I'm sorry," she gasps. "I should have—"

She drops to her knees. The dark ground beneath her seems to liquefy, and she slowly sinks into the tarry floor. Still, she doesn't react to her surroundings. It's like she doesn't see it or feel it at all.

Then a violent tremor rocks my dreamscape, so powerful that I can't catch myself. The tiny, floating lights flash a blinding, all-encompassing white. The sharp burst of a thousand shattering light bulbs gives way to silence and pitch darkness.

And I fall right through it.

~ ∞ ~

ten

"James. I need to go home."

He glances around the small room we've trapped ourselves in for two full days, only leaving the relative security of the second floor to scrounge for food or bounce for two hours to eat in the broiling hot car in the parking lot of a nearby fast food restaurant. His strained expression carries a relatable helplessness, but I can't do this anymore.

"I know you don't want to go back," I say. "I get that, and we don't have to *stay* there, but I need clothes. My phone is dead, and I'd love to have my laptop, so we can at least entertain ourselves. Besides, don't you want your bag? It seemed like you kept basically everything you need to live in there."

"Eh… You're not wrong, but—" He scratches his arm before looking to me with a grave frown and furrowed brows. "I bled a lot, right? Aren't you worried about…the mess?"

I shrug. "The mess won't magically go away. It'll only get worse the longer we avoid it. Either way, I'd like to wear my own clothes again."

We exchange a grimace, but he eventually relents. We need to grab something to eat, anyway. I watch from my spot on the carpet as he drags himself off the edge of the bed and looks around the room again.

His reluctance is frustrating, but I'm nervous too. I remember the crime scene I left in the kitchen all too well, and I have no idea what we'll find when we finally go back. *A room full of week-old blood, worse than James' car looked after he drove me to the ER? A pile of pink towels laid over the ruined linoleum?*

I can't imagine that Rose would have cleaned the mess for us. I doubt she even went back unless it was just to pick up a few things before taking off again. But we live there. Our names are on the lease. The complex manager would kill us if she found it in the state we left it in, and police would definitely get involved.

"It'll be fine," I say as we slip out of the house—thankfully undisturbed by Jonathan, who was passed out on the couch.

"You say that now," James mutters.

"Um, I literally jammed my fingers into your chest to keep you from bleeding to death. I'm not afraid of blood at this point."

He hits me with a pleading look before walking around to the driver's side of his car. We've barely talked about what *actually* went down in the kitchen last week, but I shrug unapologetically and wait for him to unlock the passenger door.

Once we're both in the car, we stare at each other for a long moment. Neither of us say anything. I doubt he really wants to talk about it. *I know I don't.* Then he starts the car, and we're on our way.

The drive through town is quiet. Quiet enough that it eats at me, and I find myself sighing.

"I'm sorry," I say.

He glances over. "Huh? Sorry? For what?"

"Giving you such a hard time."

"Pft—" He stifles a laugh and returns his attention to the road. "Yeah, well, I'm sorry for always being such a downer. Seriously. You don't have to apologize. If I had the cash, I'd put us up in a motel right now, but I don't. It's just— Being home again... I never wanted to go back, you know?"

"Maybe if we clean up my house..."

"Maybe," he agrees, though his frown deepens slightly.

I sigh again.

He doesn't think my house is safe, but how is his dad's house any better? James' bedroom is small and stuffy, and leaving it for anything more than a trip to the bathroom at the end of the hall risks running into the house's *other* occupant. The few times I've interacted with Jonathan Reid have told me everything I need to know about the type of person he is.

The rest of the drive is tense and quiet, as my house is our first stop. James parks in Rose's empty space in front of the angular, brown cottage. There's no visible blood around the exterior of the building, so I step out of the car and walk up the concrete path to the front door before I have a chance to overthink it, while James, who is clearly more on edge, hangs a few steps behind.

I peek through the window beside the door. The closed blinds obscure all but a thin vertical strip of the living room. I still don't see any blood, but I can't see into the kitchen from here.

"Let's just go in and get it over with," James says, having joined me on the landing.

I take his hand in mine, offer a reassuring smile, and move

to the front door. The door is locked. *Interesting.* I don't know if Rose has been back at all, but I doubt either of us thought to lock it before we left for Centennial Memorial.

Still, I take a deep breath to steel myself before I unlock the door and push it open. A harsh, chemical scent hangs in the cool air. Bleach or…*something.* The living room furniture looks to have been slightly rearranged, and the small, round dining table and matching chairs are neatly stacked on the carpet near the staircase on the far side of the room. But I still can't see most of the kitchen. I drop James' hand as I rush ahead, heart racing, but I stop abruptly before leaving the carpeted living room.

When?

How?

I swear I still smell the metallic tang. Still see the crimson red pooling on the white floor, slicking my hands and soaking into my clothes. But the kitchen is spotless. No blood. No broken window or sparkling glass littering the floor. The linoleum is pristine. Even the grey scuff marks from our cheap dining set are gone.

James stops beside me, but I can't bring myself to look at him, worried I'd only imagine more blood if I did.

"Do you think—?"

I shake my head. "Someone replaced the linoleum, for sure. It was either Ice or…Human-Immortal Affairs, maybe. I doubt it was Rose—she's not broke, but she doesn't have that kind of money."

"Sure, but *why?*"

Honestly, I can't be bothered to care why. I've all but given up on trying to understand why anyone around me does *anything.*

"At least we don't have to deal with it," I say mildly.

I glance over my shoulder to gauge James' reaction. He nods, but he looks uncomfortable and deep in thought.

What all does he remember?

I force a smile and pat his arm. It doesn't seem to help much, but I'm relieved that he didn't have to see the mess. *And that I didn't have to either.* For days, I was dreading the prospect of cleaning the kitchen myself.

After moving the dining set back to its proper place, we head upstairs. Both the study area and my bedroom look the same as I remember before we left for the farmer's market. Nothing appears out of place, and nothing new seems to have been left behind.

Good.

I drag my empty duffel bag out from underneath the bed and get to packing while James searches the room for whatever of his things weren't already inside his backpack. It doesn't take either of us long, and, once I slide my laptop into its travel case, we're essentially ready to go.

James returns downstairs while I change clothes, out of the outfit Ice left me with and into my own clothing. Then I grab my duffel and turn to leave, but I hesitate as I catch my reflection in the mirror.

Have I always looked this tired?

I step closer, but I ignore the mirror and instead look over the top of my dresser more carefully. A textbook from spring term that I still haven't decided what to do with. A few pieces of unopened junk mail. A cool rock James picked up during our swimming trip out Rock Creek. My jewelry box…

The River Sapphire is in my wallet.

I open the jewelry box and look through the necklaces I own. It'd be nice if I could slip the River Sapphire over my head without having to undo the delicate clasp, but none of the few chains I have are much longer than the one it's already on—a downside of not being a jewelry girl, I guess.

Oh, well. I'll find something else.

I close the jewelry box and step out of the room.

Downstairs, James is standing near the door with his backpack slung over one shoulder. He turns to me, looking even more tired than my reflection did.

And I pause again.

Being here again is surreal, considering the way I left. I didn't expect coming home to feel so *normal*. I thought I'd be more anxious, and I was at first. I thought I'd be walking into a disaster, but it wasn't like that at all. I missed my house. I missed my queen-size bed. I missed the air conditioner—which was left on the whole time we were gone and feels lovely. I missed the familiarity of it all.

"Are you sure we can't stay here?" I ask.

James takes a deep breath and looks at me in a way that feels desperately conflicted. "We can hang out for a couple hours—eat here, I guess—but I don't wanna push our luck."

I don't agree that staying here is pushing our luck any more than staying at his father's house is, albeit for different reasons, but I'll drop it for now. Even a few hours spent in an air-conditioned space sounds like a good deal.

We leave our bags beside the front door. James opens the

blinds and heads for the couch, where he sits and immediately pulls out his phone. I plug my phone in, leaving it to charge on the coffee table, and wander into the kitchen.

The farmer's market produce we bought on Saturday is still in the fridge and still good, save for a small carton of raspberries that molded. I grab a nectarine and make a mental note to bring the rest with us when we leave.

On my way back to the couch, I freeze as I pass by Rose's bedroom. *How is she?* I tried calling before my phone died, but...

I crack the door and peek inside. No clothes on the bed. A couple pillows are missing, along with her favorite quilted blanket. Fewer things seem scattered around her desk and dresser than usual. No laptop either. She must have come back at some point, even if only for a few minutes.

After the place was cleaned, I hope.

I haven't heard from her since those Human-Immortal Affairs agents whisked her away. She's ignored every call and message I've sent. Everyone made it sound like she'd be fine, like they only wanted to learn exactly what happened and have her sign a Secrecy Agreement. They told me I'd probably see her in a couple hours.

But she never came back.

She is home with her parents, right? I almost want to stop by or ask someone just to be sure, but...

I close her bedroom door and return to my phone. It's powered on, so I give calling Rose another shot. It rings once before the call is rejected and an electronic voice sends me to her chipper voicemail. *"This is Rose MacArthur. If it's important, leave a*

*message, and I'll get back to you. If it's not, text me instead.
Thanks!"*

Ouch.

I end the call without leaving a voicemail or sending a text and set my phone on the arm of the couch. If she listened to any of my previous voicemails, she knows that James is fine and we're both safe. There's not much else I can say. And it sucks, but I can't blame her for not wanting to talk to me. If she needs space, she can have it. For as long as she needs. Ice crashed in, but I basically let it happen by keeping quiet, and she knows that. I'll understand even if she never forgives me for hiding the full extent of my problems with him.

I drop to sit beside James.

"You called Rose again?" he asks. "You think she's alright?"

"She hung up on me this time, so I'm sure she's fine."

His mild expression shifts to more overt discomfort. "What happened after I blacked out? I remember looking down and seeing the knife after he stabbed me, and I kinda remember you guys coming out of the bathroom, but you said I pulled the knife out? I don't remember that at all."

I sigh, but I have been actively avoiding the fine details, and it seems like he barely remembers anything after I came out of the washroom.

"You passed out," I say, glancing away. "We thought you were dead for a second. Then you morphed, and I used your phone to call Jesse—it was the first name I recognized. Anyway, he told me to take you to Centennial Memorial, so Rose drove us there. After the doctors took you in, I explained the deal with Ice and everything to her, and we sat in the waiting room until Human-Immortal Affairs came. After that, I was alone until Jesse showed up. I guess he had to drive up from San Francisco?"

Our eyes meet for an instant, but he quickly looks away.

"Yeah," he mumbles. "He goes to school down there."

"He lives there? Renting?"

James laughs, wincing. Then he looks back to me with a more genuine smile. "He splits rent on a house with three or four other guys who go to USF, and they're all immortals, so they make it work." As I nod, trying to do the math in my head, his smile slips. "There's no reason for Jesse to come up for the whole summer, you know—the way our dad is? Right now, I think he's staying with a friend in town."

"He seemed worried about you," I say carefully. "Both him and Matthew were, when we talked."

"Yeah…"

Change the subject—

"Anyway, about Rose; I'd hang up on me too, if I were her." I pause to take a bite of nectarine. "You were totally out of it after you pulled the knife out, but it was awful. Seriously the worst thing I've ever seen. Blood everywhere. I yelled at her for wanting to call 911. I think she had a full-blown panic attack. And then you turned into a cat, and I made her drive us halfway across town without explaining anything."

"And you still don't regret asking me to stay?" he asks, staring at his hands. "What if she never talks to you again?"

"If you left like Ice wanted, you might be dead right now. I can still fix things with Rose, probably, but…"

"No. You're right." After a moment of hesitation, he looks up from his lap. *Grim and resolute.* "It was a stupid deal, and I figured his plan might be to catch me alone and take me out if I went through with it. He never said that, exactly, but— Ah… To be honest, I never wanted to leave."

I know.

He flashes a self-conscious smile and scratches his shoulder. "I guess, what I mean is: I'm glad you talked me into staying."

"Good." I lean on his shoulder. "You need to stop being so hard on yourself all the time."

"I know, and… I'm trying."

eleven

We eat lunch and fill a cloth tote with food to bring back to his house. I leave a note for Rose on the dining table in case she drops by again, and then I return to the front of the house, where James is waiting.

When I finally stop gazing out the window, wishing I didn't have to leave, I notice the spare key on the bookcase beside the door. I moved it inside weeks ago, and it's exactly where I left it. My key is attached to my purse, and the brass copy Ice made is in my wallet's zippered coin pocket with the River Sapphire.

Hm…

I take the spare key off the bookcase and offer it to James. He stares at it for a long moment before tucking his throw blanket and pillow under one arm, accepting the key, and looking up in confusion.

"Do we have to leave?" I ask.

"Jayde…"

"Listen; when I met with Ice, he handed over the key he copied. The one he used to sneak in and hide out until we got back on Saturday. That was part of the deal—that he return the key and swear not to make another. As long as Rose still has her key, all of the keys are accounted for. And you said you'd consider staying here if the cottage wasn't a total wreck, so…"

He frowns, glancing around.

James liked it here. After the first couple days, he seemed more comfortable than he ever was at Reid Manor or the motel.

Why choose his dad's house over this?

But he shakes his head, shifting his weight—though, he pockets the key. "I can't. I'm sorry, but I just can't trust that guy. Even if he swore on his life that he doesn't have another key, I have no reason to believe him. But it's not like we're gonna stay at my dad's the whole summer."

"No? I was starting to think we might be stuck there forever."

"Hell no," he says with a half-hearted smile that makes him wince. "Don't worry, I can set us up in a motel in a couple weeks."

I hate the thought of spending even a couple more weeks at his dad's house, but it's better than nothing, so I agree.

"Where do you get this money, anyway?" I ask. "You've been paying for stuff like it's nothing ever since we met."

His hand falls away from the doorknob, and he squints at me. "Huh? You're telling me you don't know about SIP—that we get paid out checks every month?"

"No. I've literally never heard of that before."

"Did Ice and Night explain *anything* to you?" When I force a smile, he sighs. "Well, now you know. Anyway, uh… I get about eight hundred dollars a month right now. You get more if you work and pay taxes, and you get more the more money you make—for investing, or whatever. Kinda backwards and fucked, if you ask me, but it's…kept me alive since I turned eighteen and actually saw the damn payments myself."

Monthly payments…

"Why don't humans get anything like that?"

He shrugs. "I don't know how it works, but I'm not one to complain about free money. Anyway, we should get outta here before I change my mind."

"I wish you would change your mind," I mutter. He ignores me and unlocks the door, and I grab my duffel bag from the floor. "Well, do you mind if I at least text Ice and ask if he knows who replaced the linoleum?"

He groans, disgust flashing across his face before he looks away and steps outside. "I wish you'd just block him, but I'm not gonna be that guy. I won't stop you as long as you don't make a habit of it."

"It's not like I *want* to talk to him." I hold my phone up, pursing my lips. "I just wanna know who was in my house."

"That…is fair," he relents.

We're in the car, heading north again, before I actually bring myself to open our text conversation. Ice hasn't sent anything since the annoying *that could have gone worse* nonsense, but I suck it up—dreading the possibility of sparking an actual *conversation*—and type something out.

> **Me:** Were you at my house this week? Did you clean it?

I wait a moment, holding my breath as the text is marked as read. He starts typing right away.

Ice: I may have stopped by on Tuesday.

Me: You don't have a key, right?

Ice: I do not have a key to your house, nor did
I need one to get inside. The door was
unlocked when I let the work crew in, and
I instructed them to lock it when they left.
I was only there for a moment.

Ice: Why ask? Did they not lock the door?

Work crew…

Of course, he paid someone else to take care of it.

I read the messages aloud, exactly as written because I am determined to stick to my word and keep James in the loop when it comes to my dealings with Ice. His eyes narrow as he watches the road ahead.

"Bet he only did it to cover his tracks," he says.

"Maybe," I say slowly. "But the complex manager is human, and all of the tenants I've met since moving in are too, so Human-Immortal Affairs might have forced him to clean up his mess to keep anyone from looking through the broken window and finding a literal crime scene inside."

"That's possible," he agrees through another grimace, "but I still wouldn't trust anything Ice says. Especially not over text."

twelve

I watch James' back as he sits on the edge of the bed. He's on his phone—texting, I think. This is the third morning he's woken up before me, but his posture is far more relaxed.

He seems okay now, but, ever since we came here…

I reach out to touch his back. Warmth wicks into my palm through his t-shirt, and he starts slightly, but he grins as he glances over his shoulder to look at me.

"Morning," he says. "Good news; I made plans to get out of the house again for a few hours. Matt wants to play basketball with Jesse and a few other guys, and he said you can tag along."

Oh? This *is* good news.

I sit beside him. "Are you okay to play sports, though?"

He tugs at his shirt collar to peek inside. I don't look too closely, but he frowns before running a thumb down his chest, where the healing surgical incision is hidden beneath his shirt. Then he twists his torso and mimes throwing a ball overhand.

His smothered wince isn't lost on me, but he nods. "Yeah, I'll be fine. Basketball's no contact sport, but I bet they're only playing HORSE, anyway."

"You sure?"

"What? Don't believe me?" he asks, cracking a smile. "I'm just sore. The dumb stuff always takes the longest to heal, and I was hit in the side damn hard—hard enough to crack my ribs, you know?"

I want to believe him, but…

He sighs, rolling his eyes. "I'm serious, Jayde. Look—" He pulls his shirt up from the hem. The incision over his sternum is now a reddish-pink scar, partially scabbed over and missing half of the thin, dark stitches that originally ran along the entire length of it. "I'm healing a bit faster than I'm used to, so…"

This time, I place my hand over the pink line without hesitation. His skin is warmer than the surrounding air, and his heart beats steadily beneath my palm. His left side is still bruised, though the color has faded from purple to a yellowish grey. I suppress the urge to kiss the small, closed stab wound and instead let my hand fall to my lap.

With a sigh, he drops the hem of his shirt. "See? It's not nearly as bad as you think. Besides, Matt knows I was real fucked up. He wouldn't invite me if he didn't think I could handle it."

"Okay. Just promise you won't push yourself too hard."

"Yeah, yeah," he says mildly, looking away to respond to a text that lit up his phone's cracked screen. "I'll sit out if it gets bad."

I feel kinda weird going out to meet more of his friends considering our situation, but I think I can handle it. Getting out of here at all will be good for us both. I fix James' damp, messy hair, and he kisses my cheek.

He must sense my concern because his smile softens. "Don't

worry, babe. I'll be okay."

* * * * *

We stop to eat before heading to the basketball courts behind Riverview Community Center. They're open to the public, but I rarely see anyone use them. Today, there are a few cars in the aged parking lot and several people gathered in the grass around two picnic tables near the edge of the asphalt.

As we park beside a red convertible, I pick out Jesse and Matthew among a few other guys standing around the table nearest to the parking lot. Two others are sitting at the furthest table in the shade of a large maple tree. Neither are facing us, but I recognize Cassidy's wild, fiery hair and assume they're both part of the guys' group too.

James glances at me, surprisingly nervous. Then we leave the car and walk across the lot to meet up with everyone. Matthew flags us down right away, and we stop just before reaching the table. There are five guys total. Jesse, Matthew, Carmen Choi's boyfriend...*Lucas?*—and two I don't recognize.

The one who is clearly the youngest looks up from his phone and gasps. "Dude, James, where the hell have you been, man? It's been so long, I thought Matt was fucking with me when he said you were coming."

"You also didn't believe he had a human girlfriend," Lucas says dryly, "yet here she is."

James laughs, still harboring a hint of nerves. "I'm fine, guys. Just been keeping to myself, taking it easy, you know?"

He's dead set on keeping everyone in the dark, huh? *Why? Who is he trying to protect?* I mean, I wasn't planning to broadcast my problems to a bunch of strangers either, but it bothers me considering my scars are out in the open and at least one of these guys knows I didn't have them a couple months ago.

The young guy, an air immortal with messy blond hair, squints at James. "Taking it easy? Uh-huh... What's up with that black eye, then?"

As I scan the faces of everyone in the group to monitor their reactions, Matthew's pleasant expression falters. His attention flicks to me for an instant, but James doesn't seem to notice. He just smiles at his friends, and, as he scratches the back of his neck, his casual, understated embarrassment is convincing even to me.

"You guys know me. I got in a dumb fight over the weekend. Cracked another rib too."

"Sick! Who'd you fight?"

"Just some guy," he says mildly, glancing aside. "Doesn't really matter, though; I lost."

"Damn."

His friends have no reason to question his story, and neither Matthew nor Jesse say anything to contradict him. They can only see the yellowing bruise on his face and, perhaps, tell that he still favors his left side. They can't see the long incision healing beneath his shirt. They have no idea that he was stabbed and nearly died hardly a week ago. *These people don't know a thing about what Ice has done to us.*

A fresh wave of insecurity hits me, and I'm suddenly missing the knit wristband I threw away. Feels like all I can really do is keep my left wrist out of sight.

"Anyway," James says, "this is Jayde. Y'all probably know who she is already, but we've been together a few weeks now."

He proceeds to introduce the guys. I already know Jesse, Matthew, and Lucas—to James' surprise. Stephen, the blond air immortal, is seventeen. He's the youngest of Matthew's friends, as I assumed. The last guy, a tall, muscular water immortal with short brown hair, is Alex. They're all wearing brand-name athletic clothing, except for Lucas, who wears dark skinny jeans and a band shirt with the sleeves cut off.

They all seem friendly enough, but I don't learn much about anyone past their names because the conversation quickly turns on me again. I answer a few inane personal questions. I'm nineteen years old. I go to Riverview Community College. I've lived here my whole life. And, obviously, I know about immortals.

"Weren't you with Ice Monroe back in June?" Alex asks. He doesn't seem to notice the flash of panic before I manage to suppress it. "I feel like I remember hearing about you. From Matt, maybe—or was it Carmen?"

I fix an apologetic smile on my face and nod, frustrated by how mechanical the motion feels.

"We broke up," I say. "In July."

"I heard they weren't technically dating," Matthew says, which reminds me that James and I both insisted I was *never* dating Ice when we first met. *So much for that.* Still, his willingness to jump to my defense even though he knows James is lying is a relief.

"Carmen was convinced they were dating," Lucas says. "Pretty sure she said Ice told her as much himself."

Hearing that only makes me more frustrated.

Ice said *"something like that"* when Carmen asked if we were a thing. He never outright told anyone we were *dating*, and, when I asked, it was pretty clear that he never viewed our relationship that way.

Matthew laughs. "We're talking about Carmen here, man. She's great, but you can't believe everything she says."

"That's rich coming from you."

The lighthearted banter continues, shifting away from the topic of me and Ice and whether or not we were ever actually dating, and I take some solace in the fact that no one seems to care about my scars—or the bruise on my arm, which has thankfully faded to the point you can no longer tell exactly what caused it. Not even Lucas' attention lingers on my arms for more than a second or two, but I don't let up on hiding the worst offender on my wrist.

"Whatever, James," Alex says, flashing a warm smile. "It's good to see you, man. I was starting to think you up and died on us for real this time. No one heard shit from you until a couple weeks ago."

James' smile grows strained. "Well, I'm not dead, so…"

"Alex, shut up." Matthew laughs easily. "He was just too busy with his new girlfriend to hang out. You were the exact same when you first got with Dawn. Blew me off like ten times. Asshole."

They start bickering, and James lets out a breath as the conversation is once again derailed toward something unrelated. Jesse, who has barely said a word since we arrived, pats his brother on the shoulder.

"You doing alright?" he asks, keeping his voice low. "Matt said you're back at Dad's?"

James grimaces. "Yeah, uh… It's just for a while, though. A few days. Maybe another week. It's just… Jayde's having some problems with her roommate after… Well, you know?"

Jesse glances at me with some level of understanding. He must know it's related to James' *fight*, and James must have mentioned Rose to him at some point—that she drove us to the ER or hasn't been talking to me since or something—but it doesn't sound like James explained the whole story. *Or even half of it.*

Jesse sighs before looking back to James. "You can tell me if you're in trouble. You know I don't mind helping out if there's anything I can do."

James glances away. "I'm not in trouble. Dunno what you've heard since you got in town, but we got everything under control. Don't worry about me. I'm fine."

Under control? Right.

Stephen howls laughing over something Matthew said, distracting us. The guys proceed to talk about something that went down at a house party a couple weeks ago. A stupid, reckless stunt that James missed out on because he was busy ghosting everyone. But he laughs *for real* at Matthew's dramatic recreation, which makes me laugh too.

"WAIT—" A distant but loud female voice rings out over the lively conversation. "No fucking way! They really showed up?"

thirteen

Carmen.

"Jayde, get your ass over here," she calls, waving from where she stands on top of the second picnic table several yards away.

For a second, James looks like he might pass out.

I laugh again. "I should go, so you guys can get on with your game."

He breathes and nods, then kisses my forehead.

"Have fun," I say, flashing a smile.

I wave to the guys and jog to Carmen at the other picnic table. Her fluffy hair is now bleach-blonde, and she's wearing shorts, a cropped t-shirt, and well-worn combat boots. Cassidy sits at the far bench, playing a Nintendo Switch. They drop a pair of over-the-ear headphones to their neck and offer a mild smile.

Carmen jumps down from the table, landing beside me with a grin. "It's been a while, huh? I see you're still with James. How's that going for ya?"

"Fine," I say, anxiety flaring in my chest as I press the inside of my wrist against my thigh.

"Yeah?"

She pauses, seeming to notice *something*, and her expression shifts. Muted surprise. Confusion. Concern. Her brows furrow, and she glances over her shoulder at Cassidy, who immediately averts their gaze, before looking to me again. *Now I really wish I had a flannel.*

"Oh, ah…" She clears her throat and shakes her head, shedding most of the intensity in her expression. "Sorry. Anyway, have you heard anything from Night yet?"

"No. Still nothing."

I meet Cassidy's eyes by mistake. They frown softly but don't contradict me. Somehow, their silence makes me feel even worse. Carmen is one of Night's closest friends. I could easily reassure her, but I don't want to mention the dreamscape.

Carmen sighs. "I have half a mind to drive over there and see how she's doing myself. Would you back me up if I did?"

And go with *you?*

"No," I say a beat too quickly.

She purses her lips, tilting her head side to side. "Oh. I mean, that's fair. Wouldn't want to run into your ex, huh? How messy was the breakup with Ice, anyway?"

"Ah—" My eyes dart to my feet.

As much as I want to give her even an abridged version of the truth, I feel like I shouldn't. James is deliberately hiding it from his friends, and I don't know how well I trust Carmen to keep anything I say to herself. I like her, but—

"Hey, Carmen," Cassidy says brightly. "Did you know that Jayde can turn into a cat now?"

Her eyes grow wide, and she turns on the young teen. I take the second she isn't looking at me to let out my breath, which is for the best because she quickly turns back with a grin.

"For real?" Her violet eyes sparkle. "You finally got that necklace to work, huh? I see you aren't wearing it now."

I nod, trying to mirror her enthusiasm. "I morph if I wear it, so I can't anymore."

"Makes sense. Can you show me?"

I laugh.

The basketball court is up against the community center—a huge, gymnasium-type building—on one side and is mostly out of sight from the nearest road at the top of a berm on the far end of a soccer field, so the area is pretty secluded. There's no real reason I couldn't throw the necklace on for a minute, but I don't have much practice taking feline form yet. I'd probably embarrass myself.

"Sorry, but I don't have it on me," I say, relieved when Cassidy doesn't bat an eye despite knowing that the necklace is in my wallet, which is in the purse I left in James' car...which is almost certainly unlocked.

Carmen puffs out her cheeks. "Okay, fine, but you have to show me next time we hang out. I'm serious. I'll hold you to it."

"No problem."

"I hope I can see too," Cassidy says rather dreamily. "I bet you and James are absolutely adorable as cats."

"Hold up— James can morph too? Since when?"

"Aren't all cats cute?" I ask, ignoring her abject shock. "But, yeah, we can both morph now. It's a long story, though. You'll have to ask him about it."

Carmen glances between me, Cassidy, and the group of guys gathered on the basketball court. I can practically hear the gears turning in her head, but, considering how little she knows, I can't imagine what she might be thinking.

Even so, she flashes another smile. "Hey, are you going to the bonfire this weekend? It's for the Reid twins' birthday—not that James tends to go, but if anyone can convince him, it's you. Anyway, you could both show off your feline forms there. I'm sure everyone'll eat it up."

James' birthday? This weekend?

Cassidy bursts into laughter. "He never told you it's almost his birthday?"

"No," I say blankly.

Well... I have seen his driver's license before, but how was I supposed to memorize everything on it after looking only a couple times? I remember it was in the vertical format. James is only twenty. *Maybe it was an August birthday...*

"Seriously?" Carmen lets out an exaggerated sigh. "Now you *have* to come. Kick his ass if he gives you trouble. But, believe me, you'll have a great time. Matt Barnett always throws killer parties. This one's right on the beach, and it's supposed to be an all-nighter kinda thing."

The beach? James mentioned liking the beach—the sound of the waves or whatever—and it would mean a full night out of his dad's house.

I smile. "I'll talk to him about it. But we have nothing going on, so I'm sure we can make it."

"Sick! Can't wait."

I sit at the picnic table across from Cassidy, who got distracted by the guys on the basketball court. They haven't started playing yet—still busy hanging out and chatting amongst themselves. Then Matthew bounces the ball, and everyone focuses on him instead. After a moment, the others nod in agreement to whatever he said, and he looks in our direction.

"You ladies wanna play?"

Carmen and I both wave him off, and he shrugs, but the fact he asked at all makes me wonder if she usually plays with them. She doesn't seem like the sporty basketball player type. But, then again, neither does Lucas.

The group wanders from the center of the asphalt toward the hoop closest to the parking lot. Matthew passes the ball to James as they walk. He fumbles the catch, but they both laugh. Their voices carry a genuine, comfortable warmth, and I feel better thinking that James might have finally relaxed a little.

"So... James has been staying with you, huh?" Carmen asks, joining me in sitting at the picnic table.

I feel like I already said so, but I nod. "He was staying at my house for a while, but— I mean, I... I got into an argument with my roommate this weekend, so we're at his dad's right now."

"His dad's?" she asks in surprise before glancing aside. "James was all over the place in June—I swear to god I saw him just about everywhere. Then I guess he took off early from Matt's party on the Fourth, and it was like he disappeared off the face of the earth. Until you shared that picture and I saw you guys at Riverside, no one heard from him at all."

Not even Matthew? Carmen learned he was with me before *his best friend*? That bugs me, but I'd rather throw up than address the issue of James ghosting everyone.

"I don't want to be at his dad's," I mutter. I rest my arms on the table, careful to keep my wrist out of sight. "But I'm hoping it'll only be for a few more days."

She smiles. "Yeah? It must be weird spending all your time with immortals now, huh? It was lowkey crazy just talking to you back when Night first introduced us, so I can't even imagine how it's been for you."

"I wouldn't say it's weird, exactly. But, to be honest, I still feel like I don't really understand the difference between humans and immortals—like why everything is the way it is, you know?" My eyes pass over the pink scars on my arms, and I return my hands to my lap. "Anyway, I've had a lot going on lately. I haven't had much time to think about how weird being around immortals is. It's just how it is now, I guess."

Carmen thinks a moment longer, glancing at Cassidy, who seems to be completely ignoring us, before looking down at the table with a mild frown. Her glossy, black nails tap against the painted wood. When she looks to me again, dread settles in my throat, but I desperately try to keep a straight face.

"Level with me for a second," she says. "Does this have anything to do with whatever happened between you and Ice back in July? It's just kinda unexpected that you'd end up with James so fast. I didn't realize you even knew each other."

My head fills with static, but I don't feel my expression change at all.

"We met in June," is all I manage to say.

"Hey, wait a second," Cassidy says sharply, though they flash a bright smile as our eyes meet. "James told you I can read minds, right? I mean, obviously I know he did, but still—"

I nod, and they point toward the group of men on the basket-ball court. Since I last looked, they've formed a single-file line in front of the hoop to throw trick shots at the basket one at a time. I guess James was right about them playing HORSE.

"Okay, so my brother has the coolest ability," they continue, voice dramatically hushed. "Have you seen it?"

"No."

Their smile widens to a mischievous grin. "Watch this—" Turning to face the basketball court, they cup their hands around their mouth. "HEY MATT; come here a sec!"

Matthew, standing in the middle of the line, stops what he was doing, glances over in mild confusion, and then vanishes. *Vanishes.* In the same instant, he reappears near the picnic table with a hand on his hip. It startles me, but Carmen and Cassidy don't react in the slightest.

"Sup?" he asks.

Cassidy laughs. "Nothing. I just wanted you to teleport over so Jayde could see it."

"Whatever, Cass." He rolls his eyes, then turns to me with a smile. "It is pretty sweet, though, right?"

"I'm sure it comes in handy," I say, distracted as my ever-changing perception of reality tries to reconfigure itself.

"Also," Cassidy says before Matthew has a chance to respond, "can I go to the beach party or whatever? Carmen was just talking about it, and I really wanna go."

He grimaces. "Oh, shit. I still gotta talk to James about that. I'll get back to you later; deal?"

Cassidy nods, and Matthew flashes another grin, dipping his head before teleporting back to his place in line. I watch curiously as he turns to James. After a moment of talking, Matthew points at us. He makes the *I'm watching you* gesture at Cassidy, who grins and rubs a fist over their sternum, before he looks to James again and laughs.

"He'll totally let me go," Cassidy says.

Carmen chuckles. "You know the twins are turning twenty-one this year, right? There's gonna be a shit ton of alcohol—more than usual—so I wouldn't get your hopes up. It's a grown-up party, after all."

Oh, great. Alcohol.

"Stephen's not an adult, and he's going," Cassidy protests, glancing between us with wide eyes. "Besides, not everyone will drink it just because it's there."

I take the bait. "I can keep an eye on you if you come."

"Yes!" They beam at me, small hands curled into excited fists. "I knew you'd have my back."

Carmen sighs, and her smile softens as she glances from Cassidy to me. "Lemme guess; you don't drink?"

"Turns out I'm kind of a stupid drunk," I admit.

She laughs. "Fair enough. If it makes you feel any better, Natalie doesn't drink much either. I tease her about it sometimes, but it's really not a big deal."

"How is Natalie?"

"Going through her quarter-life crisis, I think," she says, though her tone remains lighthearted. "She lopped her hair off in the bathroom last week. I mean, I fixed it up for her once she calmed down, but it's shorter than mine now."

"Wow."

When I last saw Natalie, her hair was long—similar in length to mine, falling to her waist at least. Cutting it so short on a whim is a drastic change. I wonder what happened…

A breakup, maybe?

"Past that, she's doing great. Busy with summer classes, modeling gigs, taking commissions—odd jobs like that. She's always busy, but I guess working so much keeps her mind off the annoying things."

Maybe I should've found a summer job.

Carmen rests her elbows on the table and props her chin in her hands. As she stares at nothing in particular, I get the feeling she was more worried about her sister than she's letting on. Then she looks to me again, still not quite smiling.

"Anyway, how have you been? I mean, it seems like you've been through…*something* since I last saw you, but I figure I should ask."

"Um…"

I catch a slight shift in Cassidy's expression, and they pointedly return to watching the guys on the basketball court. *I guess I'm on my own this time.*

"I heard some rumors," Carmen says more seriously. "About you. And Ice and James. Everyone knows those guys don't get along, so it's no surprise people are talking about it since you're mixed up with both, but…" She sighs, glancing aside. "Anyway, I don't know. You don't have to tell me shit if you don't want to. You barely know me. I get it."

What has she heard?

"Yeah, I'd…rather not go into it right now." Ignoring the small pit in my stomach, I force a smile. "But, maybe you can read about it in my future memoir."

She laughs. "Hey, some of the stories I've heard around town are wild. Seriously insane. If the truth is half as interesting, it might make a good read—or a good TV drama if you'd rather go that direction."

"Hm…"

I've never seriously considered writing a book—not even when James mentioned it a while back—but it's not a bad idea. If I changed the names, over-dramatized a few events, and sold it as pure fiction, I might have a successful novel on my hands. It might even be cathartic.

Then again… Publishing a book would definitely break the Secrecy Agreement. I might have to change immortals into vampires. Or werewolves.

Cassidy laughs, and I glance up from the table's chipped green paint.

"Sorry," they say with a hand over their mouth and golden eyes still crinkled by a hidden smile. "It's just that you're super positive. It's kinda nice. I mean, I get anxious just listening to what other people think sometimes."

I sigh, avoiding their gaze as I gather my ponytail and draw it over one shoulder. "Someone has to stay positive, right? James has more trouble with that. I guess he's been through a lot—before this summer too, so…"

"Oh, no," Cassidy says with a hint of surprise as they drop

their hands to the edge of the table. "James is a good guy. For real. Even if he has some problems, he's still a really good guy and Matthew's very best friend. Ah— But he hates when I talk about him, so I won't. Anymore. Sorry."

Carmen laughs. "Aww, Cass. I miss when you were a tiny scrub and randomly told me the innermost thoughts of random strangers without hesitation. It was so cute, and *so* funny, but I get it. You wanna respect privacy, and I respect that. It's a sign that you're growing up."

She doesn't understand at all.

"Too many people have gotten mad at me for spilling their secrets," Cassidy says.

They flash a contrite smile and turn to watch the game of HORSE playing out on the basketball court. I don't think I've seen anyone play HORSE since middle school, but it looks like they're having fun. No one's out yet either—though the trick shots are slowly getting more and more ridiculous.

I mean... Throwing the ball over your shoulder while facing away from the hoop *and* in a squat? *And* making the shot?

"Matt's just showing off at this point," Carmen mutters, smiling as she watches the group play. "We dated for a few months in high school, you know, and he was on the varsity team as a sophomore. I doubt any of these guys are as good as him."

James is up next. He misses the basket but laughs easily as Matthew writes a letter on the back of his hand with a marker.

"These guys are all friends?" I ask.

"Oh, yeah." She glances at me, seemingly curious. "I'm pretty sure they all met through Matt—well, except for Lucas; he met most of them through me—but they get along well enough."

"How much do you know about them?"

Her eyes narrow. "Did James even bother introducing you?"

"He introduced us," I say hastily. "But I only really caught their names. I'm just curious because James said he doesn't have many friends."

"Ugh." She rolls her eyes. "What a drama queen… Of course, we're his friends too. Like I said, they've all asked about James at least once since he basically blinked out of existence on the Fourth. But, sure, I can tell you a bit more about everyone. You already know Lucas, Matt, and Jesse, so…"

Carmen points out Stephen as he takes his shot. The ball goes low, hitting the pole instead of the hoop, and he groans while the others laugh.

"That's Stephen Cook," she says. "He's my cousin, actually —on my mom's side. Anyway, he's a few years younger than us and a huge dork, but these guys are all dorks, so it's whatever. The other guy is Alex…Valdez, I think? I don't know him too well, but he played basketball in high school too. And I think he's in the National Guard now? Definitely military, anyway—I mean, just look at him."

Alex is an athletic guy and significantly beefier than the others, so I can only assume he's into bodybuilding or something similar. I wouldn't be surprised if he is in the military, but I'm not sure I'm willing to take Carmen's word for it.

I thank her, but watching them like this…

James successfully makes his next shot. Stephen gives him a high-five, and Jesse pats him on the back. He grins like he's having a great time and speaks to all five guys with apparent ease. As far as I've seen, no one here has treated him any differently than they treat each other. They were all happy to see him when we showed up. They all look like they're having fun—like a bunch of happy, close friends hanging out.

What is James' problem?

Is it just that he can't let go of the past?

It sucks that other immortals treated him badly when he was younger. I wish it hadn't happened—the same way I wish none of *this* happened—but he needs to accept it and try to move on from it. Things clearly aren't the same as they were back then. Dwelling on it forever will only hurt more.

James deserves happiness. Everyone does.

No one deserves whatever happened to him as a kid or any of what either of us have been through this summer. But it happened anyway. We can't change it. And I know that healing and moving forward won't be easy. I know that, but I know we can do it.

fourteen

As the guys wrap up their third game of HORSE, my mind is stuck on Matthew's tattoo—because it's almost identical to James' tattoo. Both are the bold outline of a twenty-sided die on the back of one leg, just below the knee, but James' has a 20 on the top face while Matthew's has a 1.

James explained that it's a game reference when we first talked about it, but I didn't realize *Matthew* was the friend who thought he'd benefit from the critical success' good luck or that they got *matching tattoos*.

Now, though, it seems they're done playing, so I excuse myself from the table to meet up with James.

The guys have already split into two groups. James, Jesse, and Matthew moved to the dry grass between the basketball court and picnic tables, while the others are still hanging out near the hoop. James scratches his cheek as Jesse praises him for playing a good game—it seems he hasn't played with everyone like this in a long time. He looks kind of embarrassed, but his face lights up as I approach, and he slings an arm over my shoulder without his usual hesitation.

"Did you have fun?" I ask, trying to ignore the warmth in

my cheeks. "I only watched a little, but it looked fun."

"Yeah. It was nice to get out, anyway."

The twins lost all three games—judging by the three sloppily written, complete *HORSE*s on their hands and forearms. Matthew won two games, and I think Alex won the other. But no one seems to mind who won or lost.

"You need to get out more," Matthew says. "You're rusty."

James glares at him, but both laugh as their eyes meet. I smile, feeling far less nervous than I did when we first got here.

"Did Matt talk to you about the bonfire yet?" I ask.

James hesitates as we watch with bated breath. I tip my head to prompt an actual answer, and he sighs—almost a groan.

"Yeah… But I hate parties. And I haven't gone to a bonfire in years—" Understanding flickers across his face, and he grimaces. "Oh. You wanna go, huh?"

"I think it'd be fun," I say, unsurprised by his reaction considering what Carmen and Cassidy said earlier. "I'm not big on parties either, you know, but I haven't actually gone to the beach in a long time. Besides, it's for *your* birthday. Shouldn't you go?"

"You should," Matthew agrees with a fake pout.

James looks between us several times, his expression some combination of exaggerated dismay and uncertainty. I pat his back in an attempt to encourage him to make *some* kind of decision.

He sighs, glancing from me to Matthew for the tenth time. "It's Friday, you said?"

Matthew nods, and he sighs again more heavily.

"I'll think about it."

James glances aside, and Matthew flashes a low thumbs-up

while he isn't paying attention.

"Hey, Jayde," Cassidy calls as they approach separately from Carmen, who went to join the other group. "Did you ask about the party yet?"

When I nod, they grin.

"So, what do you think?" they ask, bouncing on their heels as they turn to Matthew. "Can I go?"

He shrugs. "You should ask Mom, not me."

"Mom thinks you should take me out to do more things," they retort. "She thinks that *all the time*. But Jayde and Carmen said they'd keep an eye on me, so you won't have to watch me the whole time."

"Ask Mom," he says again. "I'm not telling you no, Cass, but it's not a party for little kids. We're gonna have drugs and alcohol and—"

"Ugh. Fine." Cassidy waves their smirking brother off and smiles at me again. "You're coming, right?"

"James said he'll think about it."

They hit him with a sharp look. "You *have* to come. I need to know what your cat forms look like. I bet you're so cute!"

James' attention darts past Cassidy—Carmen and the rest of the guys are heading this way. He prickles, eyes wide as he looks back to us.

"Okay, okay," he says under his breath, hands up. "We'll go. Just—"

"Hold up," Stephen says loudly, breaking away from the others to reach us first. "You can morph now, and you didn't think to mention it?"

I guess they were within earshot.

"It's not a big deal," he protests lamely.

"And your girlfriend too?"

His wide lavender eyes are full of innocent curiosity, but I have no idea what to say. Then Carmen laughs and cuffs him over the side of the head, and he jumps back with a yelp.

"Jayde's a human immortal, dumbass," she says, planting her hands on her hips. "That's sorta what it means, y'know?"

He glares at her, rubbing the spot she hit. "You don't think it's weird?"

"No weirder than you."

Lucas laughs, Stephen turns to face him in humored defiance, and the three get into a lighthearted spat with Alex playing the part of referee. James lets out his breath while Matthew rolls his eyes.

"To be fair," Jesse says mildly, "you never mentioned that she could morph too."

James' expression darkens for an instant. He looks to me, so I force a smile and reach for his hand. As he seems to relax again, I look back to the others.

"Seriously, it's not a big deal," I insist. "Thanks to the necklace, it was only a matter of time for me. James is the real medical miracle here."

"Yeah, I guess it's cool," James says. "But we should probably head out now."

Matthew's pleasant expression shifts slightly—a vague air of concern. "Already? Aren't you staying at your dad's place? We don't mind if you hang out a while longer. Right, guys?"

Everyone agrees, nodding and murmuring or at least shrugging in passive confusion, and I find myself growing frustrated. James obviously had fun playing HORSE with his friends. It's super nice outside right now too. The bedroom was miserable this morning, and it'll only be worse now that it's the hottest part of the day.

Why is he in such a hurry to leave? Is he trying to avoid more questions he doesn't want to answer, or—

James laughs, a mildly derisive sound that cuts through my thoughts. "It's alright, man," he says, his voice just as dry. "It's no worse than before, anyway. Can you guys believe he forgot he kicked me out?"

Everyone falls awkwardly quiet, even Matthew and Carmen, who now seem at a complete loss. Cassidy sort of frowns. It looks like they want to say something as they stare at James, but they glance at their feet instead.

"Yeesh," Matthew mutters.

James shrugs, surprisingly unaffected by everyone's reaction. I squeeze his hand, and he seems to snap out of it.

"Oh, uh—" He sighs before forcing a smile. "Sorry, guys. Thanks for the offer to hang out, but I really should take it easy a while longer."

Right! I totally forgot.

"How'd your ribs hold up?" I ask.

"They held up fine," he says, his expression softening. "I'm kinda sore and missed some easy shots because of it, but it's not like I've never cracked ribs before."

One of Carmen's eyebrows shoot up. "Oh, yeah? You get in fights that often, huh?"

He pauses before laughing, but he doesn't answer her question.

fifteen

Our relief is tangible when we pull up to the house and find his father's blue truck missing from the driveway.

"He's probably out on a job," James says. Jonathan is some kind of on-call contractor, so his schedule is wildly unpredictable. "If we're lucky, he'll be gone most the day."

Stepping inside, the first floor is such a sad mess that it catches me off guard despite having seen it many times. And, even without his father here, it's not a fun place to be for the ten seconds it takes to walk through on our way to the staircase.

"That wasn't so bad," James says, dropping to sit on the edge of his bed. "I expected the guys to push more and ask where I've been or why I'm with you or exactly what happened, but they didn't. It was…kinda normal."

Is that true?

He looks up, my prolonged silence having distracted him from untying his shoes. "You okay? Did Carmen say something?"

Carmen.

"Not really," I say. "She said she heard rumors. About you and me and Ice, I guess. It's just crazy stuff people have made up since no one heard from any of us in so long, I think—even

Night hasn't been talking to anyone—but..."

"Ah—" His focus darts back to his shoelaces. "Can't say I'm surprised. There are always rumors about me going around."

"Oh?" I drop my purse beside the bookcase.

He kicks his shoes off, falls back onto the bed, and stares at the ceiling. "Someone sees me at the mall after I don't go out for a couple weeks, and a rumor goes around like, '*Wow, I guess James* is *still alive.*' I'm used to it, so it's whatever. But I'm sorry you've gotta deal with that shit now too."

I step closer to the bed. James watches the ceiling with a tired frown, but he just spent a couple hours playing basketball in the sun and doesn't appear particularly bothered or upset past that.

I sit beside him, and amber eyes meet mine.

"Did she tell you what they're saying?" he asks.

"I didn't ask."

He glances away again, smothering a grimace with his hand. "Yeah. It's probably better if you don't know."

"Do you know?"

"No. But I know what they were saying back in June, so..."

He's right. I don't want to know.

He hefts himself up and flashes a smile that doesn't quite reach his eyes. "Hey, uh... Thanks for not saying anything to anyone today. It's fine if they know we can morph and all, but I... I can't deal with the rest right now."

"It's okay," I mumble. "I'm not ready to deal with it either. I don't even want to hear the rumors."

Then I remember the River Sapphire in my pocket, and I turn to James. "This is random, but do you have a necklace or cord I could borrow? I need something long enough to slip over my head—for the River Sapphire. Maybe an extra wristband too? I lost the one I stole from Rose."

He thinks for a moment, rubbing his jaw as he looks around the room. "Yeah... I might have something. Hold on a sec."

I wait while he crosses the room to poke around in the closet. He opens a box labeled *MISC.* and digs through it. A cartoon figurine missing an arm and a leg. An empty CD case. Four red permanent markers held together by a rubber band. After a moment, he tosses a grey knit sweatband over, and I manage to catch it with both hands.

It's well-worn and stained by faded marker doodles, but it'll work to hide the heart on my wrist. I drop it over the foot of the bed, onto my unzipped duffel bag.

"This might work," James says slowly.

I look as he lifts a tangled length of dark brown twine from the box. He studies it for a moment before returning to the bed. While he works to untangle the cord, I slide the River Sapphire off its thin, presumably expensive silver chain and toss the chain aside. I'm not sure if it landed in my bag, but I can't be bothered to care as James reveals the newly untangled necklace—a wire-wrapped shark tooth on an unnecessarily long hemp cord.

"That'll work," I say.

He unties the knot in the cord, wiggles the shark tooth off, and passes the cord to me before throwing the pendant across the room. It bounces off the closet's back wall and lands in the open *MISC.* box.

"Still got it," he says with a wry smile and fleeting glance at the three iterations of *HORSE* scrawled on his arm in black marker.

I roll my eyes and thread the River Sapphire onto the new cord. I tie a couple slip knots and adjust the length until I'm sure it can fit over my head but shouldn't trip up my small feline form.

"You gonna try it out, or what?" he asks, leaning back. "It was weird as hell the first time, but you might need the practice since everyone's dying to see you morph this weekend. A human immortal in the flesh."

"Everyone wants to see you morph too," I remind him. "And I haven't seen your feline form yet either."

He laughs nervously. "Yeah, I guess you have a point. We can give it a shot right now if you want."

"You sure you're okay to?"

"Yeah, I'm fine." His smile warms. "I mean, I played HORSE no problem, so I doubt I'll pass out or anything."

"Okay." I hop off the bed and turn to face him, trying to pump myself up. "Want me to go first?"

He nods, and I glance at the deep blue gemstone in my hand. I'm less nervous than last time, and it wasn't so bad then. *Just a bit awkward, so...*

This'll be fine.

I take a deep breath, slip the cord over my head, and promptly lose my balance. I tumble forward, but I don't fall far. My face bumps the rough carpet, irritating my sensitive whiskers as I land on my side.

James laughs. "You good?"

I shift, preparing to right myself, but— *Oh.* Once again, I have no clue what I'm doing or how to move.

"Still works," I say, my face still on the floor.

I struggle to remember how I oriented myself the first time before carefully testing my limbs. After a moment, during which James joins me on the floor—still very much in human form—I manage to stand. Somehow, standing seems easier than sitting.

He hesitates before patting my head, and then *almost* grimaces. "God, it's just as fuckin' weird."

"You're telling me."

I survey the room, strangely unsettled by how large the small bedroom now feels. The low vantage point isn't new—I've spent plenty of time lying on the floor in an attempt to cool down—but I take up less space than I'm used to. The world is so much bigger.

Well, no... I'm just smaller.

I look back to James. "Alright, it's your turn." When he frowns, I laugh. "Don't worry. It can't be any more embarrassing than me falling on my face, right?"

He laughs too. "Okay, fine. Here goes."

After taking a deep breath of his own, he morphs, appearing as a short-haired ginger cat sitting on its hind legs with its front limbs in the air. Though, he drops his paws to the floor without face-planting and assumes a more convincing feline sitting position than I managed last time. He smiles, baring teeth—sharp, feline fangs included—and I laugh even harder.

"See, that wasn't so bad," I say.

He tips his head in an almost cartoonish way. "If you say so."

We practice moving in feline form for several minutes. Walking in circles and straight lines and sitting and stretching.

It's certainly more complicated than moving around in human form. I'm unsteady on my feet, unsure exactly where my center of balance is, and periodically trip or pick up the wrong leg at the wrong time. James seems to have similar luck, but it could be worse. As long as I think carefully about every single movement I make before I make it, I should be fine.

"Watch this," James says.

He's crouched low to the carpet. Then he jumps—an attempt to make it onto the bed, I think. But he falls short. Like something from a funny cat video compilation, his claws stick into the side of the mattress, and he scrabbles the rest of the way up with his fur standing on end.

I laugh so hard I'd probably cry if I were in human form.

He spins to face me, orange fur still fluffed up as he glares at me from atop the bed. Ears flat against his head, tail thrashing side to side.

"Oh, shut up," he stammers. "It's not like you could do any better."

"Wanna bet?"

His eyes narrow, but he steps aside, moving toward the pillows to watch from a safe distance.

I huff and look back to the section of bed in front of me. The top feels so far away, which is both impressive and sad considering the cheap, metal frame is relatively low to the floor. It kinda sucks being the size of a small house cat. Even with practice, I'm not sure the benefits will ever outweigh the cons, and I'm already less confident than I was a second ago.

But I already agreed to jump, so I have to try.

I think back to those cat video compilations. I picture the way a cat looks right before they jump, and I do my best to imitate that posture. Rear legs tucked beneath the body like springs. Bend my forelimbs. Keep my center of gravity low. Imagine how the jump should go in my head. *Angles. Distance. The ideal trajectory.* I took geometry and physics in high school. I should be able to do this.

"What are you waiting for?" James asks, humor tempering the otherwise scathing remark.

I hesitate.

Comparatively, jumping the distance from the floor to the top of the bed would be nearly impossible for a human. But I'm not human right now. I'm a cat, and cats are designed for this sort of thing.

Right now, I am literally made for this.

Ignoring James, I wiggle my hips to loosen up and get a better feel for my new musculature. Then I push off the ground with my back feet. I stretch my forepaws out, reaching for my target, eyes zeroing in on the unmade bedding, and I somehow land on top of the bed instead of smacking into the side of it. But the River Sapphire's long cord tangles in my legs, and I have to awkwardly scramble to free my limbs and reposition myself.

Not perfect, but better than expected.

The sharp sound of clapping assaults my sensitive cat ears, and I look up from my paws to find that James already returned to human form. He smiles warmly, confirming my suspicion that his competitive spirit was exaggerated.

"You did better than me," he says mildly. "Guess I shouldn't be surprised you're a natural."

"A natural? What's that supposed to mean?"

I tip my head so far that my right ear and whiskers brush my shoulder. But he just smiles and shakes his head. Then he reaches for the cord looped around my neck and lifts it away, and I'm back to normal in an instant. Our eyes meet, and my heart quickens as we stare at each other.

I'm not a cat anymore. Now, I'm just a human girl, sitting in the middle of my boyfriend's bed, as confused as I am curious.

He drops the River Sapphire. I watch the pendant land on the bed and fall into a crease in the blanket, but my eyes flick up again as James' thumb brushes my jaw. When he kisses me, I melt with no regard for how hot the room is.

sixteen

I sit in front of the window and watch the quiet neighbor-hood through the dusty, spinning fan blades. The air coming in is even hotter than before, but there's still something mildly refreshing about the sensation of moving air on my face.

Still can't decide which is worse, though: the heat or the boredom.

We dropped by the cottage to pick up my swimsuit and beach towel, but we didn't stay long, and that was hours ago. Since then, we've done nothing but sit in this bedroom. Messing around on our phones or lying on the floor to escape the heat or huddling close to watch an episode of some random docuseries.

I glance over my shoulder.

James is still sitting on the edge of the bed. He's on his phone —reading, probably. He's been going through sci-fi novellas like nobody's business. That's nice for him, but I hate being cooped up in one room so long. Trapping myself in my bedroom while avoiding Rose was bad enough, but at least I had air conditioning.

The heat hardly seems to bother James anymore, though.

"Hey—" I pause, but I decide to ask anyway. "Has your dad always been like this?"

He doesn't react. For a moment, I wonder if he's ignoring me. Or if he heard me at all. Then he sighs and falls back onto the bed. He looks up at me, phone still held in one hand.

"You really wanna know?" he asks.

"I was just wondering."

"Okay, ah…" He sighs but looks more resigned than upset. "It's a long story. But, no, it wasn't always like this. My dad… Well, he used to be a decent guy—like a normal dad, I guess—but Mom's death kinda messed us all up."

"Oh."

Whatever "normal dad" means…

He drops his phone, rolls onto his side, and buries his face against my thigh. His hands are warm. His breath is warmer. And my breath catches as his lips brush my bare skin, but I recover and comb my fingers through his hair.

"When did your mom die?"

"About twelve years ago," he mumbles. "It was a car accident. A couple months after, I was officially diagnosed as defective—metabolic inability to morph, or MIM, or whatever the fuck it's actually called. It felt like my life was falling apart. Our dad tried to keep it together for a while, but he fell apart too, so I… I don't know. I guess I'm not defective after all… Still feel pretty fucking useless, though."

Defective…

"Dr. Corel said it might have been psychosomatic," I say slowly. James' head turns slightly, one eye peeking at me, and I force an apologetic smile. "Before I left the hospital, I mentioned that you morphed, and he said it's possible."

His visible eyebrow—the one with a scar through it—furrows. "You talked about me?"

"He seems to know you."

"Well, yeah." He sits up and tips his head, frowning. "I mean, he's not the one who diagnosed me as defective, but he used to be a, uh…therapist for kids. Working at some center downtown. Anyway, that's why it threw me off to see him in the ER back in July."

He was a therapist?

James grimaces, shielding his mouth as he glances away. "He really thinks it was all in my head, though, huh?"

Well... We've talked about James a few times, and I always got the feeling that Dr. Corel feels sorry for him in some way—which makes sense if he used to be a children's therapist.

"I don't think he meant it as a bad thing," I admit.

He meets my gaze more seriously. "Have you ever had to see a therapist?"

"No. But I'm starting to think I should."

"Ha… Yeah…"

Wait. Dr. Corel gave me his psychiatrist friend's phone number. He said he worked with human immortals before, so maybe I will call once things calm down more. Maybe talking to someone would help.

James flashes a wry smile. "I haven't gone in years—which might be a mistake on my part, but at least I can admit that now. I guess."

Behind his smile, I catch a hint of familiar emptiness. The slightest hint of the tired, angry darkness that filled his eyes in

July. His eyes seem brighter, and he smiles more freely now...
But it hits me. A pit in my stomach. The awareness that nothing
has really changed.

The pain James carries goes so far back, I doubt I'll ever be
able to understand it. Not fully, anyway.

But I don't want to pick at old wounds, so I just hug him,
pulling him close to hide the shift in my expression. I wonder
what goes through his mind as he gasps softly. Wonder how he
really feels about our situation as he holds me tight and presses
his lips to my neck.

I stare out the window.

"We should get out of here," my voice says.

"And do what?"

"Literally anything. I don't care."

"Anything, huh? Mm..." He sighs, breath tickling my ear,
then leans back to offer a weary smile. "There is something I've
been thinking about for a while, but, uh... I doubt you wanna
help me with it."

"Oh?"

He frowns. "Reid Manor."

"*Oh.*"

"Yeah." He glances away. "The blood, and... Anyway, I
need to clear the rest of my shit out of there. And I think it'd be
nice to have the mini-fridge up here."

Reid Manor.

He's right, though.

My time spent there feels like a total blur now, but Ice *shot*
me, and James broke a window without properly patching it.

The building wasn't in great condition to begin with, but his family owns it. Who's to say when someone else might stop by to check it out. I'd hate for anyone to find the pool of blood I left upstairs.

Damn it...

"And you wanna do that now?" I ask.

James' hands slide down my arms and fall to the sliver of bed between us. "The sooner, the better, right? It's not like I *want* to take you back there after what happened... But I don't want to go alone either. It's not... I mean, it's really not a good place for me right now."

"And your dad's house is?"

He laughs, and I frown. Pointedly.

"No, you're right," he says, still smiling. "It's not much better here. Somehow, I think it's *less* hot there."

With a sigh, I glance over my shoulder, at the locked bedroom door. Then back at James, who seems concerned—like he asked me to do something truly awful. And I sigh again.

"I'll go," I say. "I wasn't kidding when I said I'd rather do anything else if it meant not sitting in here all day."

He nods, relief slipping into his expression. "Alright."

seventeen

We stop by a hardware store before making the drive to Reid Manor. Through downtown, to the south. Down the winding gravel road through a sea of trees. The final bend reveals the large house, and we park in the dry, weedy gravel lot out front.

As we exit the car, the dust settles, and James apologizes for dragging me out here for what must be the tenth time. I assure him once again that I don't mind tagging along.

Obviously, this won't be fun, but I'm starting to think I wanted to get out of his father's house more than he did.

I look from James' nervous frown to the dilapidated Victorian manor looming nearby. Dark even in broad daylight, with peeling paint and mossy brick and boarded-up windows, the house is as intimidating as it is depressing.

I wasn't sure I'd ever see this place again.

Hell, last time I was here, I wasn't sure I'd *survive* and have the chance to come back—let alone expect I'd willingly return to clean up the mess I left behind.

"I can't remember if I told you," James says. "But I used to come here all the time as a kid to play or hang out or get away from home for a while or whatever. I'd catch a bus or ride my bike all the way out here. It wasn't in much better condition back then, really, but…"

I pat his back and walk past him, toward the large front doors. "That's why I want to help. I fell out of the ceiling onto a guy holding a gun. It's my blood, so it only seems fair I clean it up."

"Right…"

He stops me as I move to open one of the heavy doors. Our eyes meet, and he looks unreasonably concerned.

"You sure you're okay with this?"

I nod, trying not to laugh. "It's just blood, James. I've seen more than enough. I can't be bothered to care anymore."

"Yeah… Right. Sorry."

I kiss his cheek, swear *again* that I'll be fine, and we finally walk inside. James leaves the bucket full of everything we picked up earlier just beyond the small vestibule, and we head further into the building. The ground floor seems the same as I remember —dusty and cluttered with cobwebs in the corners where the walls meet the ceiling. The only drop of dry blood I find is easily scraped off the bottom step of the main staircase.

I glance back. "Should we start at the top or the bottom?"

James watches with furrowed brows as I pick flakes of blood out from underneath my fingernail.

"Shouldn't you wear gloves?" he asks.

This isn't the first time I've had to clean blood from my nails —not even close. But, if it bothers him that much, maybe we should leave the blood for last.

I grab the thick roll of plastic sheeting from the supply bucket. "Let's take care of the window first—get the hardest thing out of the way."

He looks at me like I'm insane, but I hold his gaze with a smile I refuse to let slip, and he gives up.

We climb the stairs to the second floor, ignoring the sporadic black stains on the hardwood steps, then take the rickety staircase at the back of the house up to the third. I pointedly avoid looking down the hallway as we step out of the small room at the top of the stairwell, but the air is hot and musty and strangely sweet. With James walking ahead, we dip into the bedroom one door down, and I close the door behind us.

"I don't like this," he says.

"Uh-huh…"

I glance to the right. A tiny, blackened hole in the wall a few inches above the decorative wood molding. The ghost of ringing echoes in my head. But I look away, facing James and the large, haphazardly covered window across the room instead.

He patched the empty frame with cardboard right after the encounter with Ice that shattered it. I vaguely remember the glass fragments sparkling in the light as he swept them up, and I tried to stay awake. But the duct tape and thin, aging cardboard won't hold up for long or protect the room from the elements come winter. Even if we can't replace the glass, sandwiching fresh cardboard between layers of plastic and stapling it all to the original window frame should do the trick.

Or so James hopes.

We cover the window with a large panel fashioned from cardboard, tape, and plastic, then take a few minutes to collect the remaining broken glass hiding around the room.

The process is surprisingly quick, and we make our way back downstairs to take a break in the first-floor bedroom we camped out in before. The mini-fridge still contains several drinks, so we take our pick, sit on the mattress, and hang out for a while.

As James finishes his soda, he says he wants to bring the rest of his stuff out to the car. We argue about whether or not he's healed enough to move the fridge himself, but I can barely carry it across the room even after emptying it, so I have no choice but to turn it over to him.

He rolls his eyes and lifts the fridge without much effort. "Told you. Just grab the bags."

I grab the bags. Then I follow James out to the car, wait for him to pop the trunk, and set the bags inside.

"There's more you wanted to bring out, right?" I ask, to which he shrugs in agreement. "I'll head upstairs, then. You can meet me there when you're done."

I figure I can get started on the blood while he brings out whatever else, but he stops me before I even turn back to the house.

"You sure you wanna go up alone?" he asks, a hand still resting on my arm.

I look up from the thin, pale scar half-covered by his hand. His expression is tense. I have a feeling he wasn't able to avoid looking at the blood on the floor when we first went up.

"I'll be fine." I smile for good measure, desperately trying to ignore the faint, buzzing thoughts. *Like the hole in the wall.* "Just meet me when you're done, okay?"

He looks at me like there's something else he wants to say,

but he sighs and shakes his head. Then his hand falls from my arm, and he glances away.

"Okay," he says. "I'll be up in a minute."

He kneels to pick up the mini-fridge, and I walk back into the house. I grab the mop bucket full of cleaning supplies and slowly make my way upstairs. I keep to the main staircase, following the black droplets and splotches and partially formed shoe prints all the way up to the third floor.

When I come out on the landing, I'm...*surprised*. I bled less than I thought I did. My memory of what happened between my hand slipping and waking up in the hospital is mainly limited to a sharp pain in my wrist and seeing bright red blood *everywhere*. It seemed bad at the time, like I might have nearly bled to death, but the pool of cracked, blackened blood beneath the open crawl-space door hardly covers more than a square foot of hardwood.

In a way, it's underwhelming.

Maybe most of the blood soaked into my clothes instead of ending up on the floor? I don't know, but this is nothing compared to what I've seen since.

The way James bled after he pulled the knife out...

That was bad. I thought I'd never wash it all from my skin. Thought the image seared into my eyes would never fade and the scent of blood would haunt me forever. I'm still relieved the mess was gone by the time we went back to the cottage.

I stop in the bathroom to fill the bucket with water and mix the cleaning solution, and I feel fine. I return to the hallway and set the bucket down, and I feel fine. As I kneel beside the bucket at the edge of the crusty bloodstain, the small scab in the crook of my left arm catches my eye, and—

What did the cream carpet in Ice's bedroom look like after I lost consciousness?

Okay, I'm a little queasy now.

I ignore the discomfort, dunk a rag into the bucket, and get to work. The blood turns a rusty reddish brown the moment liquid touches it, and I realize with a pang of electric regret that I should have chipped the dry, caked blood off the floor first. Even worse, the rehydrated blood gives off a mild, sickly odor that doesn't pair well with the lemon-scented floor cleaner.

Damn it...

All I can do now is commit to what I've started.

eighteen

By the time James makes it upstairs, the floor is a disgusting mess. The liquid in the bucket is a ruddy brown, the blood on the floor looks like red-black sludge, and there's a dark stain on the wood that I doubt will ever come out no matter how hard I scrub.

James doesn't care about the mess, though.

He doesn't care that I forgot to put gloves on or have watered-down blood halfway up to my elbows. He doesn't care when I say the floor might be irreversibly stained. I'm not sure if he sees the mess around me at all.

I think he only sees that I'm crying.

I don't feel particularly upset or anything, but fat tears stream down my cheeks all the same. And he makes a sound, like a gasp. Then he drops to the floor beside me and holds my damp face in his hands. He stares into my eyes, his expression unclear through my *stupid* tears. After a quiet moment of me staring back at him, he kisses me softly, and I admit that I have no idea why I'm crying.

"Sorry," I mumble, willing myself to *not* swipe my nasty hands over my eyes. "I'm fine. This just…happens sometimes?"

He wipes the worst of the tears from my face with his thumbs.

"Where are the gloves?" he asks.

"I think…" I look back to the floor and pick up the rag I was using before he distracted me. "I probably left them in the bathroom."

He steps away, returning a moment later with both pairs of obnoxiously colored rubber dishwashing gloves. Kneeling again, he pulls one pair of gloves on, leaving the other pair on the floor between us. I watch from the corner of my vision as he surveys the damage before taking a wet rag from the bucket to join in mopping up the horrible, bloody mess I made in the middle of the hallway.

God, I am so stupid.

"It doesn't bother me," I say lamely. "Seriously. I just—"

"It's alright." He looks up with the fakest smile I've ever seen. "You should take a break, though? Okay?"

Shit… I want to comfort him somehow, but it feels useless. My hands are drenched in bloody water. How could I possibly convince him that I'm fine when I'm like this?

What should I do?

Should I offer to stay? Or take a break like he asked?

I get the feeling he wants a minute alone—and I really need to wash my hands—so I just nod and pick myself up off the floor.

"At least let me refill the bucket and rinse these rags out first."

He nods without looking up.

I hesitate, sure there's *something* more I should say, but I force myself to pick up the bucket and walk away. I step into the bathroom, closing the door and leaving James alone in the hallway.

I set the bucket on the toilet lid. I wash my hands. My arms. I upend the bucket into the stained porcelain bathtub and watch the spent cleaning solution swirl down the rusted drain. I rinse the bucket and rags. Mix a new batch of floor cleaner. Rinse my hands a final time, shut the water off, and turn to leave.

But I stop and stare at myself in the water-spotted mirror until the weight at the end of my arm becomes uncomfortable.

After taking a breath and adjusting my grip on the plastic handle, I bring the bucket and clean rags back out to James. He doesn't seem to have made much progress in the few minutes I was gone.

"You sure you don't want me to stay and help?"

"Give me…five minutes," he says, his voice low.

My hands ball into fists at my sides. *But what can I do?*

"Okay," I agree.

I wring out a rag to take with me, and I leave James behind. I walk down to the second-floor landing and begin the tedious, mind-numbing task of wiping up the blood that was tracked and dripped on the steps between the second and third floors.

I'm sure he heard me coming up, but, once I'm done, I sit on a step just out of sight of the hallway and check my phone.

No messages. Nothing of note on FaceSpace.

So I rejoin James.

He seems better, like he's at least recovered from the shock of walking in on me crying while trying to mop up a puddle of my own blood. And I'm not crying anymore, so he doesn't stop me from pulling gloves on and sitting down to help him. We're even able to talk normally, as I ask about the book he was reading this morning in an attempt to distract us both from the morbid reality of the task at hand.

We rinse and refill the bucket twice more in the process, but we eventually finish clearing the floor of actual blood. Neither of us care about the dark stain left behind on the wood. It's as clean as it will get using generic floor cleaner and cotton rags.

James shuts the crawlspace door and stashes the folding step stool in the bathroom. Once he double-checks that I'm still okay —I am *fine*—we head downstairs, easily wiping up the last bits of dried blood as we go. Then we wash our hands in the first-floor bathroom, scrubbing our skin with diluted floor cleaner because we don't have hand soap, gather everything we brought with us, and shove it all into the backseat of James' car.

I slide into the passenger seat and buckle my seatbelt. We should be ready to go. I certainly am. But, as James sits in the driver's seat with the key in the ignition, he doesn't turn it.

The car doesn't start.

Instead, he rests his hands on the steering wheel and stares up at the old manor house through the windshield. He looks…*sad*.

"What's up?" I ask.

"Coming back here with you was a mistake."

I laugh. "Why? Just because I cried for a second? That was nothing, I swear. I don't regret coming. I would've felt bad if you had to do it yourself, but, honestly, it was nice to get out of your dad's house for a while, even if it was to do this. I know you don't like being cooped up there either."

"Yeah, but—"

"We can always go back to the cottage."

He sighs heavily. "We talked about this… Your place isn't safe, and you know it."

"Is anywhere safe? I'm sick of hiding from Ice, feeling like we're running scared all the time. And I don't like your dad. Staying at his house really seems to mess you up. It's not fair."

"My dad? Not fair?" He covers his eyes with one hand and massages his temples. "Ice tried to *kill* me. He tried to kill me right in front of your best friend—your *human* best friend, who, by the way, now refuses to talk to you. And Ice probably still wants me dead. Shit's even worse than it was before, so we're safest right where we are."

"But—"

He looks up sharply. "Do *not* defend him."

"I wasn't going to," I say through my teeth.

The fire in his eyes softens, and he shakes his head. "Sorry. But I don't want to put you in danger if I can help it. Not again. If keeping you safe means staying with my dad a while longer, I can handle it."

I frown, and bleak exhaustion washes over his features.

"You hate it there," he says. "I know. I hate it too. But what else can I do? I feel like a coward. Like I've already lost. All I can do is sit in my room and hide while the rest of the world is on fire. But it feels like I don't have another option. I'm *stuck.* You know what I mean, right?"

Like we don't have another option…

"Maybe," I say slowly. "But, even if we are stuck right now, and even if it's our own fault, that doesn't mean… I mean, *I* don't think you're a failure."

"No?" He laughs weakly. "All I ever do is fuck things up. For myself. For you. For my family. My friends. I can't do anything right. All I've wanted to do since I saw you waiting for me in the *stupid* police station lobby was protect you. But I can't even do that without trapping you somewhere almost as bad as dealing with Ice. I'm just...not strong enough to actually *do* anything."

I shake my head, painfully aware of how wide my eyes are. "That's not true. You're doing your best."

I reach out to touch his arm, but I stop at the last second. I hesitate and retract my hand as he turns away from me. His shoulders slip, and he holds his head in his hands.

"My best?" His voice breaks. "My best isn't enough. It never was. Never will be. What if something else happens? What if we leave my dad's, and something... Fuck, I don't know. But I can't get hurt like that again, and I just—"

"James!"

My sharp voice startles us both, but it works. He stops rambling and glances at me, wiping his damp eyes with the back of his hand.

"What?" he asks.

"You're doing everything you can," I say, hands balled in my lap to keep them from trembling. "I trust you, but we're just two people in a seriously messed up situation. We can't control everything—that's impossible—but stressing yourself out like this won't change anything either."

He searches my face for a moment. Then his jaw sets, and he frowns more miserably.

"I'm sorry," he mumbles.

I sigh. "Don't apologize. This isn't your fault."

"Sorr—" He laughs breathlessly, averts his gaze, and scratches his shoulder. "I guess… I mean, I don't think you're wrong. I'm probably overthinking the whole thing. I get that. But I still…" He looks to me again, struggling to maintain his soft smile. "I feel like you're not taking this seriously. Ice could kill you. He almost did."

Kill me?

"He could," I say mildly. For some reason, the tension leaves my shoulders, and my hands relax in my lap. But I can't look James in the eye *because I want to be honest.* "Of course, he could. I'm just a weak, pathetic human girl. But Ice doesn't want to kill me. I've told you a million times; he only messed with me to get to *you.* And I think it worked. Because it's starting to sound like you don't care if you're in danger."

When I look up, he offers another smile, but his eyes don't meet mine. He won't even deny it.

"I worry about you," I admit.

He still doesn't respond, so I look at my lap again. The car is quiet. And hot. Even with the windows rolled down, the air is stale and hard to breathe. But I don't feel that hot—as hot as I think it is in here, anyway. *Why don't I feel that hot?*

Eventually, James sighs, and the car sputters to life.

I watch Reid Manor's reflection in the side mirror. As we drive away, I wonder if *this* will be the last time I see it. A tiny reflection of a ruined house that disappears as the road bends.

I look from the mirror, now reflecting only the dusty road behind us, to the trees. Tall evergreens and gnarled oaks. They pass by like green blurs as my eyes lose focus, and, again, I feel like I should say something. Just a little more. Something to reassure James. But I can't think of anything.

So, as usual, I end up thinking about Ice.

My eyes narrow as my mood sours further. I rest my elbow on the door and prop my chin in my hand. But I can't seem to stop thinking about it now.

I haven't heard from him in a while.

Our last exchange was innocent enough, but I know that means nothing to James. The mere *thought* of Ice existing somewhere in Riverview hangs over us like a storm cloud. Dark and dangerous, a looming threat that could let loose a lightning bolt and electrocute us at any moment.

And James feels it worse than I do. He's so desperate to keep me safe that he fully believes he has no choice but to stay somewhere he'll never feel comfortable. In his mind, knowing that Ice can't act even if he figures out where we are is worth hiding out in his hot, cramped, depressing bedroom for god knows how long.

I understand why he feels that way—I can't even pretend I don't. But that doesn't make me hate it any less.

James clears his throat as the car leaves the gravel road behind. The sound rescues me from the depths of my wandering thoughts, but I act like I didn't hear, worried that acknowledging him might make him reconsider saying anything.

"Hey," he says. "Are you mad at me?"

I turn away from the window, shocked because I thought *he* was mad at *me*, and say, "No."

He sighs—in relief, I think. He's still far from anything I'd dare consider relaxed, but it looks like the momentary silence calmed him down a little. Still, even with me watching, he doesn't take his eyes off the road.

"I'll think about what you said." His voice is tired and mild. "I mean it. 'Cause I hate this too. I don't wanna spend the rest of my life bumming at my dad's house or hiding out in cheap motels either, you know? I just— It sucks. I mean, I'm trying, but I don't know what to do. And I don't wanna mess things up worse."

I still can't get over the idea that he thought I was mad.

"It's okay," I say. "We'll have a chance to clear our heads soon. We're still going to that party, right?"

"Shit." But he laughs. "Well, yeah. I'd hate to let Matt down again, so I'd better suck it up and go."

"It'll be good to get away. Plus, it's for your birthday."

His expression softens further. "That too, I guess."

Good.

I smile and lean back in my seat. "Hey. We should stop and eat before we head back."

"Huh? For real?" He laughs again, though the grimace slipping through betrays underlying disgust. "You're seriously hungry after all that?"

"A little," I admit.

It was a lot of work.

nineteen

James seems fine now.

His dad wasn't here when we got back—having gone out on another job, I suppose—so we didn't have to deal with that drama, and we're free to spend the evening hanging around the bedroom as usual. I watch through the box fan's spinning blades as the broad, green leaves on a tree in the neighboring yard shift in a light breeze. James is sprawled out in the middle of the room behind me.

We're just talking, mostly about things we've discussed a little before. Like my admittedly unformed ideal college career path and increasing uncertainty as to what I should do with myself in the future. And his slowly growing interest in fantasy world-building and passing thoughts of actually writing a novel.

"What kind of book would you write?"

"Dunno," he mumbles. "Sword and sorcery, I guess. And I think I'll set it somewhere cold. Like…a high fantasy version of Norway or something."

I laugh and glance over my shoulder. He's still lying on the floor with his throw blanket balled up behind his head, staring at the ceiling like he's bored out of his mind—which is probably true.

"Speaking of the weather," I say. "How can you stand it?"

His eyes flick to me. "What do you mean?"

I flash a smile and tug on my camisole's thin fabric, letting it go to snap back against my skin. "Wearing a shirt. It's been so hot all week. If I were a man, there's no way I'd be wearing a shirt right now. If I didn't think it'd kill you, I'd change into a sports bra and wear only that."

"Oh—" His expression shifts, and he glances away for an instant, but he laughs with a touch of red in his cheeks as he meets my gaze again. "Uh. Yeah. It's hot as fuck, sure, but I'm more comfortable wearing a shirt."

"How modest—like you haven't complained about the heat all week too."

He sighs and looks back at the ceiling. "Maybe the heat affects you more than it affects me, since you're human and all."

"You think so?" I ask, having never considered that we might perceive the heat differently. "Well, either way, I'll melt if I have to deal with it much longer."

"Sorry."

Frustrated with myself, I turn to the window before echoing his apology. "I don't mean anything by it, you know? I guess I'm just tired of sitting around."

"I know," he says, more unbothered than I expected. "Sitting around here doing nothing sucks. It's always sucked, and it's even worse in the summer. This year's no different."

I glance at my hands on the window sill, turning my right over to see the scar on the palm. It's almost completely healed now. Just a pink scar that rarely impacts my ability to use it. I can't remember the last time it really hurt or ached or went numb for a minute.

"We won't be here much longer?" I ask.

"No. I still don't have a real plan, but…" His voice moves as he joins me on the bed, sitting fairly close. "I just want to be with you."

I fix my hair before turning around.

The same as when we left the restaurant, he looks fine. He smiles at me in the sweet, adoring way he does when he's in a good mood. Like the last time we went to Riverside Park. Like when we went swimming with Rose. His expression carries a faint tiredness, but patching the window must have worn him out. *Not to mention watching me cry on the floor surrounded by blood…*

But he took more painkillers about an hour ago, so it could be that. It's probably just that—and the manual labor. Even if his ribs are bothering him a little, I'm sure he's fine.

Right?

"I am with you," I say.

"God, I wish it wasn't so fucking hot in here."

"Yeah?" I think about it for a moment, and it hits me— "What if one of us slept in feline form to counteract the body heat of two adults sharing a twin-size mattress?"

He laughs, averting his eyes. "That is…not what I meant. But it's not a bad idea either."

What did *he mean?*

"You think we should try it?" I ask.

"Hm…" He leans back, eyes trained on the ceiling. "Sure.

I'll take cat duty, so you don't have to deal with the necklace. Why? You getting tired?"

It's still light outside—the sky just beginning to darken, the warm air blown in by the fan a touch cooler than before. I peek at my phone to check the time, and it's almost 9PM.

"No," I say mildly, scrolling down my FaceSpace newsfeed. "The heat makes it hard to get comfortable enough to fall asleep this early."

"That's what I'm saying. I wanna hang out up here with you, but it's at least five degrees cooler on the floor. I keep thinking about falling asleep down there."

"I'm not opposed to it at this point," I mutter.

"Wouldn't it hurt your back?"

"*My* back?" I ask sharply, turning to face him again. "What about you? You just had your rib cage sawed in half and stapled back together or whatever."

He sighs. "I told you a million times; I'm *fine*. I'd say you could punch me to prove it, but, honestly, I don't think you would."

"What? You're on painkillers, right? How would punching you prove anything?"

"I feel pain just fine," he says, nearly doubled over in laughter, a hand held to his left side. "It's not like Percocet nerfs my nerve endings or anything. Ow, ah— See?" He's still laughing. "I just don't think you have the guts to actually punch me."

"Oh, yeah?" I ask, feeling a smile spread across my face.

He grins too, recovering from his laughing fit. "Yeah!"

I look from his face to his chest to the scar on the palm of my hand. I ball the hand into a fist, draw my arm back, and…gently tap my fist against James' sternum. I feel the raised incision against the back of my fingers, just beneath the fabric of his shirt.

A memory.

In the dark. In a musty room.

I hit him once before, haven't I?

It's like…I can't actually *remember* doing it. I don't remember thinking it through at all. But I remember the *smack* of my hand striking his cheek. That sound ringing in my head. And I remember the sharp stinging in my scraped palm.

With a frown, I meet James' eyes again. His smile is soft and mild, and I get the feeling he's waiting for me to say something.

But how is this the same person?

How are we the same people?

"No, you're right," I say with a sigh. "I can't hit you."

Glancing away, he scratches the back of his neck. "Aw, man… I was ready to pretend I was in excruciating pain and everything."

"Hey!"

I punch him harder, on the shoulder, and he laughs. A reassuring, warm sound that makes me laugh too. Then his arms wrap around me, and I squeal as he falls back onto the bed, pulling me down on top of him. I barely catch myself, hands landing flat on the bed. Head empty with stray hairs falling over my eyes, I stare down at James' smiling face.

My heart races.

He's fine, right? I'm fine, right?

Suddenly, I realize what he meant earlier, and I also wish it wasn't nearly so hot in here.

* * * * *

My phone...ringing.

My phone...

Oh. My phone is ringing.

My eyes snap open.

It's dark, but I slip my arm out from underneath the warm ginger cat snuggled up to me and roll over to grab my phone from the bedside table...dresser. *Whatever.* I look at the screen, but I hardly believe the name displayed there.

Ice?

"What is it?" James mumbles behind me.

"Um—"

I don't *want* to answer. I almost feel like I shouldn't. But I know that ignoring Ice is dangerous, so I suck it up, tap the green button, and bring the phone to my ear.

"Hello?" I ask, my voice low and rough from sleep.

I wait a second, but all I hear is a faint electronic static, the buzzing fan in the window, and James shifting in bed behind me.

I clear my throat. "Hello? Anyone there?"

Still no answer.

What the hell... Was the call an accident? Did he pocket dial me? *At two in the morning?* God, that seems ridiculous, but I'd rather believe that than think Ice would intentionally call me in the middle of the night just to not say anything.

"What do you want?" I ask, frustration leaking into my voice. "Well? Is it important? I'm kinda busy, you know?"

Busy avoiding you. And sleeping. Ugh.

I listen with all the patience I can muster, resisting the urge to hang up, but I only hear dead air. A faint, digital hum without the slightest indication of someone breathing or any other meaningful background noise.

James yawns. "It's still dark… Who is it?"

"Oh, it's, um…" *Damn it.* "It's Ice, I think."

"What?" he asks, sounding much more awake now.

After another moment of *nothing*, the soft static cuts out. I pull the phone from my ear to confirm the call ended.

Seriously?

I drop my phone on the dresser and turn to find James sitting cross-legged on the bed in human form. He scratches his arm as he watches me with obvious concern.

"What'd he say?" he asks.

"Nothing. He didn't say anything—not a single word. And he hung up, so…"

"Well, it's…" His frown softens, and he glances off to the side. "I mean, that's fine, right? We're safe here. Even if he knows we're here, he'd never wanna start shit with my dad, so… I guess we should…"

"Just go back to bed?"

He looks back to me with a hint of tired desperation. "Yeah. Exactly. Come here."

As we lie down, he kisses my hair and pulls me closer. And I close my eyes, ready to drift back to sleep, snuggled safely in his arms.

twenty

~ ∞ ~

I open my eyes. I'm flat on the floor, staring into an inky void dotted with tiny lights that drift through the air but cast no light.

I'm asleep.

In the dreamscape.

An uncomfortable coolness seeps into my back, so I sit up and look around. The space is empty as far as I can see, though it's impossible to tell how far that is. There's nothing. No one. I'm alone, a shining beacon in the dark, surrounded by flickering fairy lights that always seem both miles away and just out of reach.

How big is my dreamscape, anyway? I've never found an end to it—not that I've really tried, I guess.

So, having nothing better to do, I pick a direction and start walking. I keep an eye on my surroundings, hoping to catch even the slightest change, but several minutes pass and nothing has yet to stick out.

The atmosphere is oddly neutral. I sense nothing threatening, but nothing too welcoming either. The space simply exists, and

I exist within it, and I have no idea why I'm here or what my subconscious could possibly want to tell me by showing me absolutely nothing.

It's kind of annoying...

As I walk and see nothing new, I eventually wonder if Night is also asleep. But I have no idea how to find anything on purpose, let alone another person, so continuing forward feels like the best course of action. Perhaps, eventually, I'll find *some* meaning in this dream. So, clinging to that small hope, I walk and walk and walk, one silent step after another, for a long time.

After a while, new flickering lights stop appearing ahead of me, and I pass them all, heading alone into pitch darkness.

Somehow, the dreamscape feels even quieter than I'm used to. It's like walking through nothing. The soft sound of my breathing and the unnatural light cast on my body are the only things keeping me grounded and feeling *real*.

Past that, the silence is tangible. It's lonely, but there's nothing outwardly disturbing or upsetting about it. Though, I wish the dream would hurry up and end if this is all it intends to be.

I never feel well-rested after coming here.

But I walk a while longer and *finally* spot something off in the distance. A fuzzy point of color in the dark, like the light at the end of a long tunnel.

I quicken my pace, more curious than nervous. Eventually, the indistinct blur comes into focus and forms the wavering image of concrete buildings against a blue sky. On the far side of an empty parking lot, Night stands with her back to me in a manicured patch of grass beneath a blossoming plum tree. The shade casts a mottled pattern of light and shadow on the school uniform she's wearing.

What is this place? Or…where?

My foot, previously bare but now wearing a leather fashion boot, hits the dark pavement. That contact is the first meaningful sound I've heard in what feels like hours, but a gentle breeze and muted city soundscape follow as I leave the darkness and enter the strange urban scene.

As I cross the parking lot, I spot the ghostly image of a young boy standing in front of Night. It seems they're talking, their voices far too soft to make out—until the boy's attention darts past her. His eyes meet mine for an instant, then he flickers out of reality.

Night starts slightly and glances over her shoulder.

Her expression is inexplicably sad as she turns to face me, but it quickly mellows. I stop on the raised curb encircling the patch of green grass, just beyond the edge of the plum tree's shade.

"Jayde." Her voice is mild and distracted. "You're…here."

"Where is here?"

I look around again, but the building I assume the parking lot belongs to is blurry, shimmering like a mirage in summer and somehow more indistinct than the generic city backdrop around it. It's two stories tall, made of concrete and metal and glass, but I can't pick out any real distinguishing features, and I can't decide if I recognize it or the surrounding area at all.

When I look back to Night, she hugs her loosely crossed arms while staring in the direction of the fuzzy building.

"This is my dreamscape," she says. "I… I'm sorry. It's not

always like this. Most nights, I have more control over it."

"Who were you talking to just now?"

"Oh, he's no one important." I catch a hint of disgust in the line of her mouth before she meets my gaze with a soft smile. "In fact, he's not even real—merely the illusion of an old childhood friend."

A friend?

She partially blocked my view of the boy, so I was only able to discern messy blond hair and wide blue eyes before he vanished, but I won't push for answers. It's her dreamscape, and my arrival clearly caught her off guard.

"Are *you* real?" she asks sharply, taking a step closer.

"Uh—" I glance at my obnoxiously expensive outfit. "Yeah, I think so?"

She massages her temples. "Sorry to ask such a strange question. But I... I haven't been sleeping well. How'd you even find this place?"

"I walked," I say. "I woke up in my dreamscape—the black void with the little lights, you know?—and, after walking for a while, I ended up here. Somehow."

She looks up, eyes wide, then quickly glances aside again with furrowed brows, pursed lips, and her chin in her hand. But she seems more thoughtful and curious than upset or concerned.

At the very least, I don't think she's *mad* to see me.

"Somehow is right," she says slowly. "Current theory suggests all dreamscapes are connected in some way. With my ability, I've learned to travel between them, but I've never...literally walked from one dreamscape to another. To be honest, I've never thought to try."

She looks to me with an unreadable expression, and her hand falls to her side. "I'm not sure how you managed it."

We stare at each other for a moment. *And I—* I sit on the curb, tired of standing after walking for so long. And I look at my hands. A heart-shaped scar on my left wrist. A slice across my palm.

I feel myself frown. "Do you think it might have something to do with the River Sapphire?"

Her expression shifts, but she doesn't speak, and I feel my own expression grow strained. *I want to trust Night. She's in direct contact with Ice. Maybe she knows something. Maybe she can help.*

"I never had dreams like this before Ice gave it to me."

"When was the first?"

I hesitate, surprised by her haste, but answer honestly: *The Fourth of July.*

"The Fourth— Hm…" She crosses the grass to sit beside me on the curb. She looks more like how I remember her. *Gentle and caring.* "I suppose it's possible the two are related. What do you know about the necklace?"

With a nod, I rehash everything I know. I can't remember exactly what the letter from Human-Immortal Affairs said, but I know the gemstones are created in a laboratory, and Ice obtained the River Sapphire so quickly, I can only assume it was made on-site at the office in Seattle. Each one is specially designed for the individual, so they work differently for each user. Mine activates by putting it on and taking it off—but she already knows that.

And it contains my DNA, somehow combined with fragments of immortal DNA—

Night holds up a hand. "Where do you think Human-Immortal Affairs gets the immortal DNA used in the process? Rather, is the source different for each gemstone?"

"I... I've honestly never thought about it."

Eyes narrow with intense focus, she holds a hand over her mouth. "What did Carmen say...? Your gemstone is blue, and, if I recall correctly, Taylor Corel's is violet..."

"It is," I confirm, able to clearly picture the rough, amethyst crystal intricately knotted into a pendant at the end of a dark cord.

"You met him?" she asks with a poorly stifled grimace.

I do not mask my grimace as I nod, and she apologizes on his behalf without me saying a single word as to how he behaved. After meeting him in person, I completely understand why the man has a bad reputation.

"In any case," she says, "it's likely that the gemstone's color corresponds to the donor immortal's DNA."

"So...whose DNA was used for the River Sapphire?"

"And could that DNA have any effect on the human wearing it?"

My eyes feel wide as we watch each other, but I catch what she's hinting at. *And it makes sense.* Night is a psychic water immortal who can travel between dreamscapes. The River Sapphire is blue, and I never had strange dreams before Ice gave it to me.

Why didn't I make that connection sooner?

"You think—"

"Yes. Taking everything you've told me into consideration, I believe Ice offered my DNA when he commissioned your necklace from Human-Immortal Affairs."

I shake my head, my mouth a bit dry. "But... Why?"

"It's hard to say..." She smooths the front of her pleated skirt and glances away. "Perhaps he learned there was a small chance that the unique abilities of the donor immortal could be transferred through the gemstone. I can't imagine he would offer his own DNA if he had any reason to think such a thing were possible."

Maybe, but... "The letter didn't say anything about that—a transfer of powers or anything. Just that it was supposed to let me turn into a cat."

"You're giving Human-Immortal Affairs more credit than they deserve, Jayde." Her eyes narrow dangerously as she once again tries and fails to mask her disgust. "Do you honestly believe they disclose everything they're trying to gain from their little science experiment to the human participants? They claim the Program is designed to support human integration into immortal society— like it's meant to *help* you—yet they stand idly by while—"

She pauses, teeth grit and eyes wide, and glances around as though remembering where she is. Then, with a quick apology, she takes a breath and continues more calmly, "The Human Immortal Program is a controversial study run by a government agency that happily admitted you without your permission. Ice hardly seems to know much about it himself, so I'm sure they're not opposed to hiding key information from the humans involved too."

With her hands balled in her lap, she stares at the grass near her feet. And I have no idea how to feel.

"Jayde, I…" Her voice is little more than a whisper, and her shoulder trembles slightly. "I saw what they did in the hospital. Ice tried to convince them to hold off on their tests until you recovered, but… To those scientists in Seattle, I'm afraid you're essentially a guinea pig."

Right.

I lost a lot of blood—enough that I went into shock and fell unconscious. It was bad, but Ice said that Human-Immortal Affairs swarmed the hospital. He said they forced me to shift between forms and took several blood samples. He seemed pissed about the whole thing. I figured it was just because he hates being told what to do, but…

Night was there too, huh? For how long?

Well… If Ice is as useless as she says, it makes sense. I bet she's the one who picked out this outfit for me after all. *And he just took credit for it.*

I sigh, wishing I were more surprised.

"You seriously think your DNA is in the River Sapphire?"

She nods, seemingly disappointed. "If Ice had to supply both DNA samples himself, I can't think of any other explanation. It would explain your connection to the dreamscape—the one your mind developed in July, and the fact you managed to make your way into mine."

She's probably right.

I want to ask about her dreamscape—like why it's currently taking the form of some random parking lot, for one—but there are more pressing matters at hand. If her theory is correct, and her DNA gave me a taste of her ability through the River Sapphire... *I have concerns.*

"You said you're sort of psychic, right?" I ask, forcing a smile. "You mentioned seeing things in dreams sometimes. Things that ...might happen in the future?"

Wariness creeps into her soft frown. "On occasion, yes... Why? Have you seen anything?"

"Nothing in a while—I mean, nothing *bad* in a while, anyway —but I think I might have before. A couple times. Maybe."

"Oh, no..." She sets an elbow on her knee and props her chin in her hand to watch me, weary and serious. "Do you remember what I told you about my dreams? About how hard it is to predict the future with any degree of certainty?"

When I nod, she nods too.

"I meant that," she says. "Every word. You cannot trust the things you see or hear or feel in your dreamscape. The future isn't set in stone—there are countless possible outcomes in any situation—and the visions are rarely as straightforward as they appear."

Large, green eyes. A sick smile. Blood dripping in ribbons. A sinking feeling, deep in my gut. Faint, nightmarish images I can't seem to place. A shiver tickles my spine, but I can't pin down the source of the emotion.

"I'll keep that in mind," I say, though I'm no closer to under-standing than I was before. "Thanks for the advice, anyway."

She smiles like she feels sorry for me. "Of course. Feel free to tell me if you see anything especially troubling. The dreamscape isn't always…gentle with its messages, but a second opinion might ease your mind."

"Can I text you, or are we only on talking terms here?" I ask, biting my tongue as my tone comes across far more scathing than intended.

"Ah…" Hurt flickers across her face, but her voice remains level. "Ice still doesn't know we're meeting in dreams. I'm sure he suspects we're communicating somehow, but, by only speaking this way, he can't prove we've talked at all since you left."

"Dreams it is, then."

She looks up at the plum tree, her lips thinning. "It's better this way. He doesn't need to know. It would only make things worse."

Worse for who?

I'm frustrated, but she looks upset, and I remember what Carmen said the other day. Night hasn't spoken with anyone since she learned about my injuries. I don't understand her relationship with Ice at all, but isolating herself like that can't be easy, especially not if she's stuck living with him.

Speaking of—

"He called me."

"Who?" she asks sharply. "Ice? When?"

"Tonight," I say. She grows more and more confused as I explain how I woke up to a phone call at *2AM*. "I answered—I didn't want to completely ignore him, you know—but he hung up without saying anything."

She shakes her head, brows knitted. "I don't know why he'd call you. In fact, he hasn't mentioned you in days, and he's seemed alright compared to before. He's eating again, and…" She sighs. "Well, anyway, I was hoping he was trying to get over it."

"Get over it? Last time we talked, he told me someone has to *die* before any of us can get over anything."

She blinks. "He said that to you?"

"Yeah. He did. Right before he left the hospital after I woke up. He said it's gone too far, and there's no other way."

"Oh." She forces another smile, but her eyes remain uncomfortably wide as she turns away. "I can't promise it will help, but I can talk to him if you want."

Yeah. Whatever.

I don't want to be mad at her. None of this is her fault. But what is talking really going to accomplish?

Talking to Ice is hard. He's impossible.

"Sure," I say, unable to keep the dryness from my voice as I stand from the curb. "If you think it'll make any difference, go for it. Talk to him. But I'm gonna head out and try to get more sleep."

She looks up at me, eyes glistening with moisture, but she nods even as her smile slips. "I… I hope James is well."

It wasn't exactly a question, but I don't know how to respond, so I just dip my head and turn to leave. I cross the parking lot, my hands as loose fists at my sides. I take the first silent step into darkness, and Night's urban dreamscape fades away.

Once again, I'm left wandering the void.

~ ∞ ~

twenty-one

"These movies are kinda overrated, aren't they?" I prop my chin in my hands. "I mean, I can barely follow what's happening on screen. Why should I care about any of these characters? Is there even an actual plot?"

James laughs. "You said you've only watched a couple of these movies, right? No wonder you have no idea what's going on."

My groan is cut off by a yawn.

"It's a two-hour-long, flashy action sequence," he continues. "What more do you want from it? At least the special effects and costume design work is cool."

"I guess it is pretty cool."

But I hate feeling like half the jokes go over my head because I haven't watched a superhero movie in years.

Movie aside, the heat is getting to me. We've been hanging out on the floor for the past *three hours*, just watching Netflix. I slept like garbage last night—no thanks to Ice waking me up at 2AM and getting stuck in my dreamscape. If I rest my head on the pillow acting as a buffer between my elbows and the carpet, I'm sure I could take a nap, but I'm not sure it's a good idea.

Even so, I'm considering it.

"What time is it?"

I'm the one who asked, but I reach for my phone to check for myself. The instant my fingers brush my phone's plastic case, it vibrates and dings, alerting me to a new FaceSpace message.

Weird timing.

Curious, I turn the phone over.

> **Messenger**   now
>
> Carmen Choi: Yo! You and James coming to the bonfire or no?

Oh, right! It's Thursday. The party's tomorrow. Things have been so slow around here, I forgot what day it is.

> **Me:** Yeah. We'll be there.
>
> **Carmen:** Sweet!!
>
> **Carmen:** You staying together still? At his dad's?
>
> **Me:** Yeah, we're still at his dad's. There's no AC and we're stuck in the bedroom all day. It sucks.
>
> **Carmen:** Oh?? Don't you have an apartment or smth?
>
> **Me:** I rent at the new cottage cluster near RCC, yeah.
>
> **Carmen:** Why not stay there??

Don't mention Ice. Make something up!

Me: Drama with my roommate. "Cat" stuff, you
know? Pretty sure I can't talk about it over
FS.

Carmen: Ok... (◔_◔)

Me: I'm serious!

Me: She found out (• - •);

Carmen: Oh shit oops lmao

Ugh... She might ask about it later, but I can only hope that morsel of truth is enough tea to tide her over until then.

Me: But we're fine and going to the party, so
don't worry!

Carmen: Awesome! See ya there!

I drop my phone and rub my eyes.

"You good?" James asks.

"Mm-hm. It's just Carmen, checking in to make sure we're going to the bonfire."

"Ah, shit. That's tomorrow, isn't it?"

I meet his mildly disgruntled gaze with a smile. "You're real worked up about this party, huh?"

With a heavy sigh, he taps the space bar to pause the movie. His seriousness surprises me, and I drop my smile, anticipating whatever I've dredged up this time.

"It's not the party," he says. "It's the *people*. Bonfires are cool and all, and Matt knows how to have a good time. I won't deny that. But everyone he invites brings whoever else they want, and there always ends up being someone who hates me. Even if they don't go out of their way to start shit, just knowing they're there, whispering about me behind my back or whatever, makes me wanna bail."

After the past few months, I get that.

But I pat his shoulder. "Well, this year, you won't be the only awkward weirdo there, and I *know* everyone will be talking about me, so… Anyway, if you start feeling like you want to leave, we can just hide out in your car until you feel better. Even if we're stuck there the whole time, at least we'll be together."

He stares with wide eyes for a few seconds, his jaw a bit slack. Then his expression cracks, and he laughs without wincing at all.

"What?" I ask, unsure whether to be relieved or offended.

With another sigh, he shakes his head, still smiling. "I thought you said you didn't wanna see me sleeping in my car."

"Oh!" I sit up sharply. "That's right! I totally forgot Carmen said it's an overnight thing. We're camping on the beach?"

"If you want," he agrees, repositioning to sit cross-legged in front of me. "We don't have to stay the night."

"No, it sounds amazing." I temper my elation and flash a more muted smile. "I haven't gone camping in years, and I've never camped near the ocean before. Does it get cold at night?"

He shrugs, his smile unaffected. "Not too cold. The weather's pretty mild. Gets windier at night, but I'm sure it'll feel great compared to sitting in here all day."

I bet.

"The last time I went to the coast, it was February." I glance at my hands as I feel my expression shift. "Rose wanted to go whale-watching. A friend mentioned it to her, but their plans to check it out together fell through, so I went with her instead."

I laugh, but it almost hurts to think about now. "It was freezing, and it rained the whole day. But we'd gone all the way out there, and she was dead set on seeing at least one whale. We just...sat in her car at an overlook right off the highway and watched the ocean through the windshield."

"Did you see any whales?"

"We saw three—I think."

"I mean... That's cool, right?"

"Yeah." I sigh. "But I think it would've been cooler if we had binoculars. I can't believe we didn't think to pick some up before we left town."

I look up from my lap and force a smile. Talking about Rose is miserable right now, but I am hyped to get out of this house —and Riverview—for a couple days. The fact we're going to the beach is a bonus.

Note to self: message Rose before we leave. Just in case.

After a moment, James scratches his arm and glances away, suddenly looking...*embarrassed?* "A while back, you said something about going to the coast. When you said that, I... I thought about it, but—" He looks up with a hesitant smile. "I guess I never imagined I'd actually get the chance to take you there."

Oh.

When we had that conversation, he was still planning to leave, wasn't he? He was still trying to find some way to follow through on his "deal" with Ice. And I had no idea.

I can't imagine how that must have felt.

My fingers find the hem of my shorts. I glance down, unable to maintain a smile as my cheeks flush with frustrated heat.

"To be honest, I said it without thinking. When I realized what I said, I kinda panicked. But, um… I did want to go with you—specifically *you*, I mean. So I'm glad it worked out this way."

I listen to the fan buzzing in the window. That sound is *always* there. It's never really quiet in this room because of it, but I still feel the soft tension as neither of us speak for a long moment. Then I feel a gentle hand come to rest on the top of my head, and I look up. James watches me with a mild warmth that, for some reason, I feel like I don't deserve.

"Thanks," he says.

Thanks? "For what?"

"For telling me that."

I feel my face flush hot again, and I brush his hand off my head. "You're welcome, I guess. Anyway, we're going to the party tomorrow, and I'm gonna make sure you have fun."

"Oh, yeah?" He laughs, leaning back. "That almost sounds like a threat."

"Maybe it is."

I turn away to unpause the movie.

twenty-two

I spend several minutes towel-drying my hair while debating how to style it. We're going to the coast. It's in my best interest to wear my hair up, right? James said the weather should be reasonably warm, but it'll be windy.

My hair and the wind are *not* friends.

I brush my hair and gather it into the best bun I can manage near the top of my head. It's not so neat that it stops looking fun but still secure enough that it shouldn't come out unless I want it to. The style surely isn't up to Carmen's standards, and my bangs might get in my eyes, but I'll be fine.

I apply mascara and check myself out in the mirror.

The teal straps of my bikini top poke out from my blouse's scoop neckline. *As do a few inches of a certain pink scar.* I didn't even think about it when I first picked my clothes, but this outfit leaves most of my scars visible.

That's fine, right?

Everyone who saw me at the basketball court knows about the scars, even if they don't know *how* I got them, and they all seem cool enough. No one mentioned them or asked about it, except for Carmen in a roundabout way, but I don't know who else will show up or if every new person I meet will be so friendly.

It can't hurt to stuff a flannel in my bag just in case.

And, as much as I dread the idea, I might have to suck it up and ask Carmen about the rumors. I don't *really* want to know what everyone's been saying, but it weighs heavily on my mind.

I glance from my reflection to the grey sweatband on my wrist. I forgot that James gave it to me until I found it while packing last night. It doesn't fit as well as the one I stole from Rose, but it does the job.

Even with the heart hidden, though, I know the rumors will get worse as more people see the other scars. Everyone knows who I am. They know I was with Ice in June. Surely, some even saw us together once—at Riverside or who knows where else. What will they think when they see me in a bikini top with scarring on my shoulder and a pink slice across my side?

Ugh... Stop worrying, Jayde. You look fine.

Everyone at the party will be cool. No one will say anything. Everything will be fine. There's no way we'll actually spend the whole time hiding out in James' car.

I take a deep breath, gather my things, and make a beeline back to the bedroom out of habit.

Oh.

James is still asleep. Sprawled out on his back on the small bed, wearing a loose t-shirt and boxers with only his feet covered by the thin sheet we're using as a blanket. The room is hot already, but he looks more comfortable like that than he usually does when he's awake.

"You should probably get up soon," I say.

"Yeah, yeah…" After opening one eye to look at me, he drags himself up to sit on the edge of the bed, stretches, and rubs the sleep from his eyes. "Hey, thanks for letting me sleep in, though."

"No problem."

I drop my stuff on top of my duffel before joining James at the bed. As I stand in front of him and fix his messy hair, he flashes a sleepy, self-conscious smile.

"You sure we have to go?"

"Don't be like that," I say with a laugh. "It'll be fun."

His expression warms. "Yeah?"

"Yeah. Worst case scenario, we ignore everyone and pretend it's just the two of us."

"Mm… Ignore everyone, huh?" He hugs me, his hands on my back and ear to my chest. "That doesn't sound too bad, you know. Plus, I know the perfect place to hide."

I stare out the window behind the bed. Green leaves. Blue sky. The warmth of James' body does *something* to me.

I compensate by laughing even harder. He releases me, I sit beside him, and he kisses me on the cheek. Then his phone vibrates on the dresser—a bit unexpected, considering it usually doesn't vibrate at all, but the sound saves me from my complicated feelings.

Still, he hesitates before retrieving his phone. The notification was a text from Matthew. He plans on stopping by before we leave town. James jokes that it's probably to make sure we don't bail.

"Should I make breakfast?" I ask. "I think your dad's out of the house again, so it should be fine to hang out downstairs."

He blinks at me. "Oh? I mean, yeah, if he's not here, sure. Do whatever you want."

"Okay."

He stands when I do, but he walks to the closet and starts rearranging the cardboard boxes as though looking for a specific one. He seems fine, so I swipe my wallet and phone off the dresser, tuck both in my back pocket, and head for the door.

"Should I make enough for Matt and Cassidy?" I ask, slinging my bag over my shoulder.

"Uh… Yeah. Sure. Sounds good." He's not visible from where I'm standing, but I hear him clear his throat. "I just…gotta grab a few things, and I'll meet you down there."

"Okay."

I leave James to whatever he's doing and go downstairs. The first floor is a mess, but it's quiet, and a quick glance out the kitchen window confirms the blue pickup truck's absence. So I clear some counter space, moving several cans to the half-filled contractor bag near the front door, and poke around for break-fast possibilities.

Um… There aren't a lot of options, so… French toast, it is.

It's fast and easy. There's a bottle of table syrup in the fridge. And this loaf of cheap white bread is nearing its best-by date, anyway.

James joins me while I'm in the middle of cooking. He's wearing dark board shorts and the vaporwave Arizona t-shirt that Rose gave to him. He apologizes for the huge mess and busies himself with tidying up a little.

Just as we sit to eat at the breakfast bar-style island, which is now *almost* clean, a vehicle pulls into the driveway. It's not James' father—that much is obvious from the engine's clean sound—so we don't bother moving. A moment later, Matthew walks in the front door, engaged in conversation with Cassidy, who follows close behind. Cassidy's soft, gold eyes flick in my direction, shadowed by the dramatically wide brim of their straw sunhat, and their face splits in a grin. They rush past their brother to stand across the counter from me.

"Good morning, Jayde," they say. "Good morning, James."

I return their greeting and acknowledge Matthew's *hello*, but James says nothing. He's not quite looking at anyone, and his fork taps against his paper plate, betraying some emotion.

Cassidy glares at him before smiling again. "Looks like you made extra. Don't mind if I do."

While they scramble to put together a plate, Matthew slides an empty stool closer and joins us on the opposite side of the breakfast bar. He picks up a slice of french toast, rolls the dry bread into a cylinder, and takes a bite.

"Sup, man? Not looking forward to the party I spent weeks planning for you?"

James rolls his eyes but cracks a smile. "This party is hardly for *me*, and you know it, but I... I am looking forward to it, so... Thanks, anyway."

Matthew laughs.

Cassidy slaps their plate on the table next to mine, interrupting their conversation and startling me. As I catch my breath, they apologize with a nervous laugh and sit to my right.

"I've never been to a bonfire party before," they say. "I'm so excited."

Matthew sighs. "You invited yourself, Cass. Just remember: you are not allowed to drink *anything*. Mom would kill me."

Cassidy purses their lips and, having just pocketed their phone after taking a photo of their food, picks at the syrupy mess of drowned french toast on their plate with a plastic fork. Matthew, watching James with a curious silence, downs another rolled slice of bread in three bites.

"So, any big plans next week?" he asks.

"Oh, uh—" James glances at me. I shrug, and he shakes his head before looking back to Matthew. "I haven't thought about it much. We're taking things one day at a time right now, y'know?"

"Fair."

Cassidy gasps. "Hey, can I ride with you guys?"

"Sure," I say.

"Yes! Thanks, Jayde."

Matthew raises a hand to cover his smirk. James hits me with a shocked look but doesn't try to overturn my offer, and I shrug unapologetically. I like Cassidy—they're a breath of fresh air amidst *everything*.

They grin. "I won't be any trouble. Promise."

When we finish eating, I leave the last two slices of french toast on a paper plate in the fridge even though I fully expect to find it still there when we get back. Then James and I grab our bags and meet Matthew and Cassidy outside.

"I'll follow you guys out," Matthew says, motioning for us to continue past him and the cute, red BMW in the driveway.

James agrees—he was probably right about Matthew's ulterior motives—and Cassidy grabs a florescent pink gym bag from the back of their brother's car before joining us on the curb near the Honda. Then we pack everything into the trunk, pile into the hot car, and we're off, driving through the neighborhood with Matthew close behind.

Cassidy, who took the middle seat in the back, leans forward with their hands on the center console. "You don't mind that I'm coming, right?"

"No," James says.

He spoke quickly, but their smile falters, and his posture seems more tense than usual. Both hands on the steering wheel at ten and two. Eyes focused on the road ahead. And I remember—

James' offhand comment about getting them close to Ice just to figure out what he's thinking.

Cassidy said they avoid talking about the private thoughts of others, but I can only imagine that's exactly what James is afraid of. Is he worried they'll mention something he doesn't want me to know? Or is he uncomfortable with the idea of them reading his thoughts in general?

They glance between us, their expression pleasant but curious and attentive. I'm sure they're used to people worrying about their ability by now.

Too many people have gotten mad.

Cassidy averts their eyes and clears their throat. "So, James... Matt said the party's at a private beach. We brought tents. Is there a campground?"

"There's no campground, but there's plenty of space to set

up tents on the sand."

Oh?

"Right on the sand?" Cassidy echoes.

"My family owns the land around the cove. It's fine."

"We didn't bring a tent," I say.

James sort of shrugs. "I have a tarp and a sleeping bag in the trunk. You have your necklace, right?"

"I do."

"Might as well use it."

I promised to show Cassidy and Carmen my feline form. That's fine, and I don't mind, but I wasn't planning to spend much time as a cat. It's like having too many legs and not enough arms and a spine made of cooked spaghetti. I haven't practiced nearly enough to feel comfortable moving around. It's awkward.

"You want to sleep on the beach as cats?" I ask. "Even if the weather is mild, won't we get cold?"

He flashes a hesitant smile. "I guess we'll find out."

And to think I almost didn't pack a blanket.

"It's a cute idea," Cassidy says with a laugh. "I used to sleep outside all the time—just for fun, y'know? Most times, I'd wake up totally covered in dew. But it usually wasn't too cold."

James sighs. "Must be nice to be a kid."

"Your family owns the beach, though?" they ask. "Don't they own an old house in town too?"

"Reid Manor is owned by someone on my dad's side, and the beach is owned by someone on my mom's, but, yeah..." He frowns thoughtfully. "I guess most of my extended family is pretty well-off—or used to be, anyway. I heard they wanted to build a beach resort there back in the eighties. Or something like that, right? But, for whatever reason, development never began. There's still a road leading up to the beach, but the land's all unimproved."

"And you can visit whenever you want?" they ask in awe. "A whole private beach to yourself?"

"Yeah." He laughs, eyes meeting mine for an instant. "I used to dream about building a house out of driftwood up on the cliffs, but I... Honestly, I wouldn't even know who to ask for permission for something like that."

A house on the beach, huh?

Cassidy hums, swaying side to side. "I wanna live on the beach too. Getting away from everyone in town and living alone sounds super dreamy. And quiet."

"And quiet," he agrees.

Cassidy's expression shifts, dimming for half a second. Then, as the lull in conversation grows longer, they move to the window seat behind James. They set their large sunhat aside, pull a phone out of a small tote bag, and don a pair of mirrored sunglasses and colorful over-the-ear headphones. The music they play is so loud, I can hear the muffled, poppy bass over the air blowing in through the rolled-down windows.

And James' shoulders relax slightly.

I look from his profile to the child in the backseat. Cassidy angled themself toward the window with one elbow propped against the door and their chin held in their hand. I think their eyes are closed, but I can't quite tell. Then I look back to James.

"You don't trust them?" I ask under my breath.

"No," he says. "It's not that I don't trust Cassidy. It's just—They can't control what they hear. I haven't spent much time with them in a while, and maybe that was…intentional, but they weren't always great at not commenting on stuff."

I glance through the window. We're out of town now, heading west on the highway. Yellow grass dotted with trees. Fields. Farmland. I don't come out this way very often.

"What are you so worried they'll say?" I ask.

He doesn't answer immediately, so I turn to watch him. There's a hint of tension in his jaw, and I start to wonder if he'll answer at all, but he eventually shakes his head.

"That's not it," he says slowly. "I mean, yeah; I don't want everyone to know the random, messed up shit going on in my head. But, mostly, I feel bad that they can't help hearing it whenever I'm around. Cassidy's just a kid, you know?"

"That's it?"

He rolls his eyes. "What? You wanna know every time I think about my dead mom?"

He's obviously being sarcastic, but I can't help averting my gaze. I pat my thighs just to give my hands something to do.

"You never talk about your mom."

"Trust me; there's a good reason for that. She was a great mom—the best anyone could ask for, really. But, mostly, I remember the accident and everything that went wrong after."

"Sorry," I mumble. "I don't mean to upset you. Or pry."

He laughs, and I glance up to find him smiling. "You're fine, babe. Cassidy's a sweet kid. And I'm sure they know I think that even if I lock up whenever they're around. I don't know how they do it—putting up with everyone else's thoughts all the time, you know? I mean, fuck, I can hardly handle my own some days."

"Yeah, I…"

I hold a hand over the sweatband on my wrist as an image of myself flashes through my mind. Something I must have seen but can't…quite remember. *Another me, sneering as she asks if I want to die.*

"I think I know what you mean."

twenty-three

The terrain changes as we leave the National Forest and again as we near the coast and turn onto Shoreline Highway heading south. The sky is clear and blue, but the air pouring in through the window is cooler now and carries a salty tang.

And I can see the ocean, which feels more welcoming and less desolate than it was in February.

I check on Cassidy—still fast asleep. After a bit of internal back and forth, I reach into the backseat to wake them. They stretch and yawn before dropping their headphones to their neck and pushing their sunglasses up.

"We're almost there?" they ask.

"About twenty minutes, and we will be," James says.

I point out the window. "You can see the ocean out this side."

They gasp and unbuckle their seatbelt to switch seats, but, when they try to roll down the window, it only goes halfway— not for lack of trying. After another moment of struggle, they release the crank handle and fold their arms over their chest.

"You should at least fix the windows. And the AC too."

"Yeah?" James asks dryly. "I'd rather save up for a new car. One with AC and a bluetooth stereo."

"You said it; not me."

I laugh, and Cassidy grins, glancing between the two of us. James seems less anxious than before, which does wonders to improve the mood inside the vehicle even as the highway leaves the ocean view behind.

"So, you can both turn into cats now?" Cassidy asks, sliding into the center seat.

"Seems so," James agrees as I nod.

"Is it hard to morph? —Oh, never mind." They laugh before backtracking. "Does this mean you're not defective anymore?"

"Kinda sounds like I never was. Still no superpowers or anything, though."

Cassidy's eyes flick to meet mine.

They know about my dreamscape, and they know I haven't told James, but they don't mention it. *Probably for the same reason they haven't outwardly reacted to any of James' innermost thoughts either.*

"Superpowers aren't everything," they say. "They're not even always fun. Turning into a cat is the most important part, right?"

"I..." He blinks, though his eyes remain on the road. "I guess you're right. I never thought about it like that."

"I'm not the only immortal who hates their ability either. I'm not the only one it causes a lot of trouble for. And there's nothing we can really do about it, you know?"

"You're right," he says again.

Their smile softens, betraying a flash of sadness. Then they turn to me and start talking about music.

Cassidy knows a lot of bands and artists, but I don't have much to contribute to the conversation since I mainly listen to the same music I listened to when I was in middle school and random pop stations that Apple Music recommends.

The car falls quiet as the discussion ends. James struggles to get the car radio working, but every frequency plays garbled static.

"Whatever," he mutters. "We'll be there in a few minutes."

Cassidy unbuckles their seatbelt and turns to watch Matthew's car out the rear windshield. I can't bring myself to stop them— nor do they seem bothered by the fact that I think they should practice proper car safety.

After another mile or so, we turn off the highway and onto an unpaved road marked only by a metal sign with a few bullet holes punched through it:

PRIVATE ROAD
NO TRESSPASSING
NO PUBLIC BEACH ACCESS

Less than a mile up the dusty road, we reach our destination —a sandy turnout with five vehicles parked in the sand. I feel like I recognize a couple from the community center, but I'm not sure who any of the vehicles belong to.

Ocean waves and seagull cries hang in the air as I step out of the car. The sun is warm on my shoulders, tempered by a cool wind that sprinkles my hair and cheeks with mist. I can't see the water from here, but the marine scent is pleasant and mild. We must still be some distance above the actual beach.

Matthew's red convertible pulls to a stop beside James' car, and he hops out. As he joins us, James turns to him with a frown.

"How many people are here?"

Matthew looks over the parked vehicles. "Jesse, Nick, Stephen, Carmen—with Lucas and Nat, I'm sure—and, uh...the Porter twins, I think. Dunno who else might've tagged along, but pretty sure those are the cars."

"Who all did you invite?"

"A lot?" Matthew shrugs. "More plan to show up later. Mina, Tyler, Alex... But, y'know, *I* didn't invite the Porter girls if that's what you're getting at."

James sighs. They keep talking, but the number of names being thrown around is making my head spin, so I ignore them and walk around the car to open the trunk. Cassidy peeks into the trunk, then shoves their tote bag, oversized sunhat and all, into their pink gym bag before running back to the guys.

"Matthew," they call, pointing at him. "Take our stuff down, so I can race Jayde to the beach."

Uh, oh.

Matthew stops talking mid-sentence and turns to Cassidy with a hand planted on his hip. "Why should I? I already have to take the cooler down—and most the shit in there's for you."

"Then take two trips! It's way easier for you to carry stuff like that, anyway. You don't even have to walk."

He pulls a face but agrees to take our bags down, so I drop mine back into the trunk.

"Don't forget to shut the trunk like you mean it," James says. "I swear to god I'll lose it if I come up here later and the battery's dead again."

"Yeah, yeah."

As Matthew looks over the bags, James turns away and heads up a wide, sandy trail bordered by yellow grass and scraggly brush. When I look to Cassidy again, they flash a guilty smile.

"Sorry. I really wanna see your cat forms. I hear thoughts—not see them." Their eyes dart to the side, a hint of darkness in their otherwise pleasant smile. "Thankfully."

"It's...fine."

But I suddenly have a much better understanding of what James said about their ability earlier.

The warmth returns to their expression, and they turn back to the car to pester Matthew some more. He fends them off with generic, glancing comments that suggest he's not listening to a word they're saying as he removes our bags from the trunk, but Cassidy continues their one-sided conversation undeterred.

I leave them to it and go after James.

The sandy trail leads up to a ridge overlooking the vast ocean, and I pause to take it all in. This beach is *nice*—a large, secluded, crescent-shaped cove surrounded by tall sandstone cliffs. Gentle waves wash up on the sandy beach below, but I spot a rockier area dotted with tidepools at the far end to the south.

I look up, shielding my eyes to block out the early afternoon sun. The cloudless sky is a bright, summery blue. In a few hours, it might be warm enough to swim.

Will I have the nerve?

"This is awesome," Cassidy croons as they come to an abrupt stop beside me. "What a cool beach. It's so *big*!"

Matthew appears up the trail ahead of us, closer to James than where I stopped at the trail's crest. He's carrying a large, red cooler with two backpacks piled on top—mine and James'—and wearing a third that must be his own. He doesn't seem at all burdened by the weight, so I can only assume his mild irritation over "carrying *so* much" is for show.

I continue forward, but I pause again a few feet away from the guys as James' frown grows more severe.

"I was hoping you were wrong about the Porter girls," he says.

Matthew sighs. "Man... Does it matter who is or isn't here? Don't you plan on avoiding us all, anyway?"

James hits him with a dirty look. Matthew laughs, shattering his false air of annoyance, and looks out over the beach. I step closer to see for myself. There are several people split between two groups, gathered near an arrangement of plastic coolers and pop-up day shelters—specks of cheerful color on the expanse of pale sand.

"Okay, okay," Cassidy says eagerly. "How do we get down?"

James points left, where the trail continues at an angle down the cliffside. We're at least fifty or sixty feet above the beach, so I get the impression the trail has more than a few steep switch-backs on the way down.

"Should be a piece of cake as cats."

That's easy for you to say!

Cassidy meets my nervous gaze and flashes a grin and double thumbs-up. "Just trust your feline instincts, Jayde."

Yeah... I'm not convinced I have those.

"I'll leave your bags at the bottom of the trail," Matthew says. "That way, you won't have to talk to anyone right away if you don't wanna."

"Do I have to talk to them at all?" James asks dryly. When Matthew rolls his eyes, he glances the other way. "Ugh. Thanks anyway, man."

Matthew nudges him with his shoulder before vanishing.

I take the last step to James' side and follow his line of sight to find that Matthew reappeared near one of the groups down on the beach. He drops his cooler and receives a warm welcome. Then he points at us, and the five others turn to look. Two of them—namely Jesse and...*Carmen?*—wave at us.

James groans, but I wave back.

"Okay, so we're good to race now, right?" Cassidy asks, voice and eyes bright.

James and I exchange *a look*.

Obviously, we don't think racing is a good idea. We haven't practiced nearly enough for this to be in any way safe—what if one of us trips? And I have no idea what condition the trail is in.

But he shrugs, so I feel obligated to play along.

Cassidy pumps their fist in the air. "Yes! Let's do this."

I take the River Sapphire from my pocket and slip the cord over my head. Fortunately, the transformation catches me less off guard this time. I do not fall on my face, and the lower vantage point—while unexpectedly different—isn't nearly as alarming.

I shake my head, letting the motion flow down my flexible spine to get a better feel for my new body, before looking up at the others.

Cassidy beams down at me, hands pressed to their cheeks. "A little tabby? And one of your eyes is different? That's so cool!"

At least someone thinks so.

Cassidy morphs next. Their feline form is a small, coppery-red shorthair—the fur closer in color to Matthew's ruddy hair than their human form's unnaturally bright red—with a thin frame and a short, kinked tail.

We both turn on James, who looks between us with a soft frown before finally morphing himself.

"Aww, James," Cassidy coos. "You're super cute too."

Whiskers twitching, his ears flatten against his head. "What's that supposed to mean? I look like a normal cat, right?"

Cassidy laughs, prodding his shoulder with one paw. I glance away and take a few slow, cautious steps forward to get a feel for the sandy ground beneath my paws.

"Are we racing or not?" I ask.

"Oh, yes, of course!"

Cassidy bounds to the start of the trail, right before it begins sloping down. Their feline movements appear effortless, and they glance over their shoulder with an air of confidence. But James and I are in no way accustomed to coordinating on four legs, even if only to walk in a straight line.

I have to think carefully about each step, and being so low to the ground is strange and unsettling, with the nearby foliage feeling too large and a bit too close. The pungent ocean scent is so strong I taste it on my prickly tongue, and the breeze shifts my sensitive whiskers and fur. The foreign sensations are distracting and only complicate movement further.

Even so, we manage to join Cassidy at the trailhead without bumping into each other or tripping over our own feet.

"Are we seriously doing this?" he asks wearily—*as though he wasn't the first of us to agree to it.*

"It's probably not safe," I admit.

Cassidy looks over, blinking wide yellow eyes, and I try not to move at all because I don't know how to coordinate my muscles to effectively gesture as a cat. Even a simple shrug might throw me off balance.

"Just watch where you're going, and you'll be fine," they say.

"Okay," I relent. "Let's just go."

They nod vigorously and face forward to stare down the trail. "Ready…"

I look down the trail myself and let out a breath as it appears somewhat less treacherous than I had imagined. It's at least eighteen inches wide for the most part, which should be safe enough given our smaller size, and seems decently well maintained. I'm not worried for Cassidy at all, but maybe a race like this will be a good crash course in feline movement—provided that James and I manage to survive.

"Set…"

I tense the muscles in my hind legs, readying my feline body to propel itself off the dusty sandstone. James and I exchange another glance. His posture is equally forced and awkward, but he tears his eyes away, returning his attention to the trail ahead.

I follow suit and plan my first move.

"Go!"

twenty-four

I hesitate as Cassidy and James kick off, leaving me a couple paces behind by the time I push my feet off the ground.

It's fine. I wasn't expecting to stand a chance, anyway, but I don't really care about the race. This is just practice. Something to help me adapt to processing my environment in feline form —thinking ahead to avoid tripping over rocks, exposed roots, or my own feet.

Paws. They're paws.

And I didn't want to disappoint Cassidy.

My gaze flicks up just long enough to check on the two ahead of me. They're almost neck and neck a few feet down the trail. Until James fumbles. He catches himself, cursing under his breath, and Cassidy cackles as they take the lead.

I feel the ground incline beneath my feet, and I spring off the top of a bump in the trail, nearly catching James' tail when I land. My cry as I hit the sandy ground with a tail in my face startles him, and he glances over his shoulder, losing even more speed.

I laugh. "Sorry."

He huffs and rolls his eyes before returning to the task at hand—*or...paw?*

Jeez. I suck at being a cat.

James' stride is longer than Cassidy's, so he quickly gains on them with some effort. They laugh as he catches up, then they veer sharply to the right, leaving the trail to half-run, half-slide along the steep, sandy cliff face toward a switchback further down.

"Hey! That's cheating," James calls, abandoning all sense of inhibition as he follows them off-trail and skids across the ground after Cassidy.

I watch for a second as I pass by, unsure whether to worry or lean into my exasperation. Either way, I have no intention of throwing myself down the cliff to catch up with them. I increase my pace as much as I can while also paying attention to my paws, and I eventually reach the bottom of the trail.

James is flopped on his side in the sand, chest heaving from exertion, fur dusty and ruffled with several burs caught in it. Cassidy stands beside him, practically weeping with laughter, their head down by their paws as their short tail twitches high in the air.

"Are you okay?" I ask once I catch my breath.

"I think he tripped and fell through a sticker bush," Cassidy says through their feline form's wheezing.

"I'm *fine*," he gasps as he pulls himself to his feet.

I glance him over, but he's standing and seems alright, so I suppress the flicker of fear that arose at the thought of his healing rib cage.

"Who won?" I ask.

"Me, of course," Cassidy says, looking up.

They morph, human form sitting cross-legged in the sand.

They pick a bur out of James' fur and pat his back. Cassidy's touch was gentle, but his ears lay flat against his head, and his tail thrashes. When he morphs, he's also sitting—and watching Cassidy with obvious malcontent.

"You cheated," he says, ruffling his hair to clear it of sand.

They grin. "I never said we had to stay *on* the trail."

As they argue back and forth, I hook a paw on the River Sapphire's cord and slip it off, miraculously returning to human form standing with the necklace still in my hand. I look myself over, but I seem untouched by the sand I was just racing through.

Okay, that's pretty cool.

I put the River Sapphire away and offer a hand to help James off the ground. He accepts without hesitation.

"That was fun, right?" I ask.

He drops my hand to look at his palms. They're a little scuffed up, but he meets my gaze with a smile. "It wasn't so bad."

The three of us stand around, chatting about the race until Matthew appears beside us. He hands over our backpacks. James puts his on, while I just sling mine over one shoulder.

"You should hang out for a minute," Matthew says. "At least grab drinks before disappearing on us."

James sighs. "You're drinking already? It's barely noon."

"There's soda too," he says with a shrug. "Cassidy made me buy a shit ton of Leninade."

James sighs as Cassidy giggles.

"I don't mind hanging out a bit," I say. "I don't think I've met everyone here yet."

"Ugh. Fine. But just for a minute."

We walk through the warm sand toward the group near the coolers. Cassidy scans the beach with heightened interest, but I find myself distracted by James' unenthused attitude. He didn't say exactly, but it seems like he stopped coming to these parties because he felt left out. If that's the case, intentionally avoiding everyone won't help. No one will even have a chance to include him if he doesn't at least *talk* to them.

"Who invited Paige and Claire?" he asks under his breath.

Matthew squints at him. "Jesse. He's dating Claire."

"No. You're kidding, right?"

"I am not," Matthew says mildly. "They've been a thing for a few months now. They both go to USF, so I figure they hooked up down there."

James mutters something I don't quite catch. Matthew laughs in response, and I look ahead again.

"The blonde girls?" I ask.

"Yeah."

They stand close to each other, holding glass bottles and talking with Jesse and two men I don't know. One sister has her long, platinum blonde hair in a tight, high ponytail that puts anything I've ever managed to do with my hair to shame, while the other wears her hair neatly curled with a wide headband stuck fighting the wind to keep it out of her face. Both sport matching metallic bikini tops—one rose gold and the other silver—and white sarongs tied at the hip.

Even from a distance, the women exude the same high-class aura that Ice did when we first met. Sexy. Confident. *More than a touch vain.* As far as first impressions go, I'm not sure how to feel about it.

James rubs his eyes. "I swear... If they say anything—"

"Dude, it'll be fine," Matthew says with a laugh. "Chillax. No one's gonna start shit with you, okay?"

Even further down the beach, Carmen is hanging out beside a sunshade with Lucas, Stephen, and a woman with short, dark hair. Now that I'm closer, I think it's Natalie—Carmen mentioned that she cut her hair short. But the group with the blonde Porter twins is between us and *my actual friend*, and, as we near them, they collectively turn to look at us.

Matthew and Cassidy, who want to meet up with Carmen, continue on, but Jesse and the two other guys stop us to greet James. As they chat, ponytail twin looks me over, entirely unimpressed judging by her raised brows, sharp blue eyes, tight frown, and the hand now planted on her hip.

I would acknowledge her, but I have a feeling saying anything would only get me in trouble.

"This your girlfriend?" smiling baseball cap guy asks.

James nods, clearly uneasy as he glances at me. "Yeah. Jayde, this is Nick and Parker—Jesse's friends."

Nick, the shirtless, hat-wearing earth immortal, seems friendly enough, in the sense that I'm not intimidated by him. The other, Parker, is a fire immortal with spiky, dark blond hair who gives off vaguely untouchable vibes, though not nearly to the same extent as the female twins.

Both men offer to shake my hand. I wasn't expecting *handshakes*, but their expressions seem genuine, so I go for it. Then a low scoff from ponytail twin diverts everyone's attention and leaves a pit in my stomach.

"So, this is the new human immortal girl, huh?" she asks with a short, condescending laugh. "Honestly, James?"

I drop Parker's hand and turn toward Jesse and the girls. Ponytail twin's gaze borders on hostile, but the other is now pointedly not paying me any attention at all, having turned away to talk to Jesse, though her smile is uncomfortably strained.

"You got a problem, Paige?" James asks, voice a bit tense.

Ponytail twin, Paige, bats her eyelashes through her rose-tinted glasses. "Oh, no; it's nothing, James. I merely find it so interesting to finally learn that the rumors I've heard are true."

Her cool eyes gloss over my arms and chest, and I *really* wish I'd thought to put that flannel on earlier as she takes a slow drink from her wine cooler and glances away. *At least I'm wearing the wristband...*

"She looks about as messed up as you," she says. "No surprise there, though. I imagine this is the best you can get."

Damaged goods.

Prickling, I smother my grimace and fold my arms over my chest in an attempt to hide the scars. But, now, I understand what James was going on about earlier.

Why'd Jesse invite this bitch?

"Cool it, Paige," Parker says, his tone frustratingly passive.

"Yeah," the other twin, Claire, agrees mildly. "I mean, she's no different than Taylor, right?"

Like that comparison makes me feel any better!

Paige shudders—like *visibly* shudders in disgust—so I can only assume she feels roughly the same about Taylor. But, before she has a chance to insult me further, I hear Carmen calling my name from the second group.

Thank god.

"Well, it was nice to meet you all," I say without caring if I sound standoffish.

Jesse flashes an apologetic smile as James takes my hand, and we promptly abscond to join the others.

Matthew stands with his hands on his hips, his expression more mild than usual. Carmen, her short hair now a sunset ombre, leans on Lucas' shoulder, trying and failing to restrain laughter. Natalie looks vaguely embarrassed from where she sits in the shade of a small day shelter a few feet away, but her eyes are obscured by mirrored sunglasses.

Cassidy seems to be the only one who didn't pay any attention to our confrontation with Paige. They're way off in the distance, taking photos with a small digital camera.

"Okay, yeah, that wasn't so great," Matthew says with a sigh. "Sorry, man. I haven't talked to Paige in ages, but I guess she hasn't changed a bit."

"You thought she would have?" Lucas asks.

"Oh, hush," Carmen says, still laughing as she pushes her sunglasses up like a headband. "Never mind Paige Porter. She's just a bitch. All bark, no bite. But I'm happy to help you guys avoid them if you want."

James frowns, and there's a beat of quiet. Then he looks to Matthew and asks a question about a video game I've never heard of, and the younger Stephen pops out from behind Natalie to join the discussion with enthusiasm.

Uninterested in video game talk, I wave to Natalie and walk past the guys. She smooths the sheer fabric of her summer dress and smiles mildly.

"It's been a while," she says, her tone cordial.

I force a smile. "Yeah. I, um… I like your hair."

She thanks me, reminding me of Night even more with her new haircut. *Speaking of*—

"Have you heard anything from Night yet?" I ask.

The video game talk quiets as James pauses in the middle of a sentence, and Carmen and Natalie jump into discussing Night. She hasn't responded to messages or calls in weeks, and Carmen never got around to visiting Westbrooke in person, so they don't have any news. They don't seem too *worried*, though.

Then Natalie asks how I've been, and Stephen asks James a question that draws him back into his own conversation. I glance from James to Natalie with a sigh before briefly and vaguely explaining what I've been up to over the past week—a bunch of *nothing* in a hot bedroom—and conclude that I'm doing alright. She seems satisfied with my answer, and doesn't ask about my few extremely visible scars, so the conversation remains tolerable.

After a while of talking about the beach and the weather, and what everyone has been up to since they got here, James taps my shoulder.

"Hey, I wanna show you something real fast."

I nod, but Carmen stops us from leaving.

"Want a drink before you take off?" She pops open the nearest cooler and peeks inside. "We got, uh…light beer and wine coolers—a few different flavors."

"Maybe later," James says. "Jayde?"

"I probably shouldn't."

With a shrug, she pulls one bottle out and closes the cooler. "Suit yourselves."

Matthew, having apparently foreseen this outcome, offers me two water bottles from the cooler he brought. I stick them in the side pockets of James' backpack.

"See ya around," Carmen says with a small salute, open bottle in hand.

I wave before walking with James back along the beach to the south. When we pass by the group with Jesse and the Porter twins, Paige glances at me with narrowed eyes.

twenty-five

"You're thinking about drinking later?" I ask once I'm sure we're far enough away that no one else can hear.

"Well…" James laughs and scratches his collarbone. "It's my party, right? I'm almost twenty-one, and everyone bothered buying all this alcohol, so I figure I can have a couple drinks. I just have to watch myself. I mean, I guess I turn into a complete dumbass when I drink too much."

That makes two of us.

"Remember the Fourth of July?" I ask.

"The Fourth of July? Oh, uh—" The color drains from his cheeks, and I remember too late that *a lot* happened on the Fourth. "I got smashed at Matt's party, okay? I never would've— I mean, I never meant— God, I am so fucking sorry I did that. Ugh. What a mess."

But I laugh. Because, somehow, what James did that night was less upsetting than— *Well…* I don't want to talk about that either, so I'm not entirely sure *where* I was going with my question.

"It's alright," I say. "I drank more than I should have too. I probably wouldn't have fainted at all if it weren't for the alcohol… But it feels like all that happened so long ago, doesn't it?"

He flashes a brief, sad smile and glances away.

I cough. "Anyway, where are we going?"

"Oh!" He looks ahead and points in the general direction of *south*. "It's a spot further down the beach. I thought we could set up camp there—at least drop our bags off for now."

As we near the *spot*, he says it might be more fun to make it a surprise and suggests I cover my eyes. It's random—kinda cute, if suspicious—but I humor him. I close my eyes and cover them with one hand while he holds my other hand to guide me down the beach.

We continue through the warm sand for some time before we finally stop, and he lets go of my hand.

"Okay, now turn ninety degrees—to, uh, your left."

I turn. He sets a hand on my shoulder and adjusts my position slightly.

"Perfect," he says. "Now you can look."

I drop my hand to my hip and open my eyes.

"Aah— This *is* cool."

We're standing in front of a natural cave carved into the sandstone cliff. The opening is about ten feet tall and fifteen feet wide, and I head inside to get a better look. After five feet or so, the floor drops a few inches, and I step into a flat, sandy area. The cave goes back at least another fifteen feet before the ceiling abruptly slopes down and closes off at the end. It feels larger on the inside, and most of the inner sanctum offers more than enough headspace to stand comfortably.

I've never seen anything quite like it—not that I've seen many caves before.

We could have easily set up a tent here, had James decided to bring one. But no. I guess we're just gonna lay a tarp and sleeping bag out on the ground and hope for the best. To his credit, though, the cave does a great job of cutting off the wind.

"We're camping here, right?" I ask, just to be sure.

"This is where I always stay when I come here overnight," he says, not really looking at me or anything in particular. "When I was a kid, I liked to pretend it was an old pirate cave."

I laugh. "I can see that."

After leaving my bag on the packed sand floor, I approach the nearest wall. *It's decorated.* Small hollows are cut into the rough sandstone in several places around the cave, a few still containing the remains of candles burnt nearly to the base. But what really catches my attention are the numerous dates, words, names, and other doodles etched into the wall.

James. Jesse. Matt. Stick figures. A boat—*or ship?* Some kind of sea monster? A poorly rendered shark chasing a school of fish. Some accompanying dates go back over a decade. Other things are scratched out, obscured by large, pale scars in the reddish stone, to the point I can't make out any distinguishing details.

Hm...

"This is fine, right?" James asks from somewhere behind me.

"Yeah... This should work."

"Good. Plan B was the car."

He laughs, and I glance over my shoulder. He left his back-pack against the opposite wall and is now wandering toward the mouth of the cave with a water bottle in one hand.

I examine the wall carvings a moment longer. I run my fingers over one of the damaged sections. Dust flakes off. But I still can't work out what any of them used to be, so I give up.

I step away from the wall and follow James.

Standing just out of reach of the sun overhead, the air holds a mild but comfortable chill. We're both quiet. I watch the water across the expanse of white sand wash up onto the beach in calm waves. The weather is ideal. Perfect. I forgot how nice the beach can be during summer.

"We should check out the water," I say.

I pull my shirt off, toss it aside, and fix my hair. Then I look to James, who seems moderately embarrassed, eyes wide and ears flushed red. He's seen me wear this bikini top before—and I'm almost certain he's peeked at me while changing at least once— so I'm not sure why a bit of skin is suddenly a big deal.

I roll my eyes and grab his hand. "Come on. Let's go."

"A–ah… Fine."

We leave our shoes and phones near the mouth of the cave and slowly walk across the beach toward the water. The sand is warm and soft under my bare feet. The sun is almost hot on my back. And I feel *good* being here on the coast with James, miles away from Riverview.

Then he stops just before the line where the dry sand meets the wet and gazes out over the ocean. With a soft frown, he drops my hand and sighs heavily before reaching behind his shoulder, grasping the back of his t-shirt, and pulling it off over his head. He holds it in his hand, his jaw set nervously, eyes on the sand at our feet.

I almost ask what's wrong, but I catch myself.

Oh—

The small, pink stab wound and scabbed-over incision down his sternum are nothing new, and they never seemed to bother him much. *But those aren't his only scars.* Dozens of others hatch his arms above his defined t-shirt tan lines. Old but still clearly visible. Tiny, straight lines. Small, faint circles. Pale, faded, and slightly raised from the surrounding skin. Scars always kept hidden beneath the sleeves of a t-shirt.

Ah...

I see.

Stifling a rush of gut-wrenching sadness, I don't let my eyes linger on his shoulders for long—though I'm sure my expression shifted in an obvious way. Maybe that's why he's not looking.

He didn't want to see my reaction.

"Sorry." He flashes a contrite smile and drops his shirt to the dry sand before meeting my gaze. "It'd be weird if I never took my shirt off, right? Now, at least, I don't have to worry about catching you off guard."

He was worried I'd find out by accident? Why? Did he think I'd be *upset* or something?

"Hope I didn't kill the mood," he says.

I purse my lips. "James—"

He glances away again. "I've been meaning to tell you—if only because I thought knowing you're not the only person with a bunch of scars they hate might make you feel better—but, uh… It's not so easy to admit you have a problem, is it?"

He's talking about the self-harm scars, right? That's what it sounds like, but his downcast eyes are locked on the straight surgical scars on his left hand as he flexes his fingers.

"No, I totally get it," I say, biting back a handful of questions that don't feel appropriate. "But I'm glad you trust me enough to tell me now."

"It's not that I didn't trust you before," he says hastily. "I just... It's not something I wanna advertise, y'know?" He forces a smile as his hand moves to itch the scars near his shoulder. "I mean, I'm sure most people would see all this and think, '*wow, check out this angsty loser who cuts himself.*' You know?"

I feel my lip twitch, but he reaches out and pulls me closer with a surprisingly easy laugh. His thumb brushes the long scar on my side, and my breath catches at the warmth of his hands on my hips. I almost forgot the scar was there until he touched it.

My eyes flick up to meet his.

It's not *nothing*, and it's not like my scars don't bother me, but his look old—how old exactly, I can't be sure, but they're certainly older than any of mine. I'm sure it was years ago. Back in high school, probably. He's fine now, right? He wouldn't still do this to himself, would he?

A dark room. A roll of distant thunder. Blue light reflecting off a mirror, highlighting a tragic face. The heavy, gnawing pit in my stomach when I realized...just how wrong *everything was.*

"Anyway," James says with a fleeting grin and no sign of lingering darkness in his amber eyes. "I bet the water's cold, but I'm down to get in if you are."

He is fine, right?

Either way, he doesn't want to dwell on it right now. We're supposed to be having fun. I swore we'd have a good time here.

I want to have a good time.

So, with a sigh, I shake off the nagging discomfort, hold James' hand again, and continue toward the water. And we're in luck. The ocean isn't too cold. It's actually warmer than the creek where we went swimming with Rose.

We wade in hip deep. James dunks his head under to soak himself, then we retreat to the shallows, where we sit with the water up to our waists. The waves crash into our sides as we watch the distant group off to the north. It looks like they're gathering driftwood for the bonfire, but none have wandered too far in our direction.

"What's the real reason you stopped coming to these parties?"

"Besides the fact I don't like parties?"

I hit him with a blank look, but he's not fazed.

"I don't care for parties either," I say, "but I can't tell you how many Rose has dragged me to, and I never had a *bad* time. At worst, it was awkward or kinda boring. But it seems like Matthew organized this one especially for you."

He laughs and scratches the back of his head. "Yeah, I dunno. I guess I just don't like being around so many people. I mean, Matt was surprised I went to his Fourth of July party this year after how Memorial Day weekend went, but... To be honest, I only wanted to go because I was curious about you. I knew Carmen would be there, and I knew she met you a couple times, so I thought I might hear something I hadn't before. And I did. She slipped that you were hanging out with Ice and Night at their house, and, well... We both know how that turned out."

"Yeah..." I glance away, lost in thought.

I knew about Matthew's party.

When we worked out our Fourth of July plans, Ice mentioned that Night invited him to a house party, but he wanted to avoid it—probably because he figured James would be there. *Still...*

How would things be different if we *had* gone to the party instead of celebrating at his house?

There was clearly alcohol at Matthew's party too, but I doubt I would've been comfortable drinking nearly as much in an unfamiliar house surrounded by tons of people I didn't know. Would I have run into James, though? I would've recognized him from the mall, but would I have *talked* to him? Even if I did, would he dare talk to me, knowing I was there with Ice? Would they have clashed at all during the party, or would Ice have ignored him and played it off to avoid causing a scene in public? *If we went to that party together, would I still be with him now?*

I sigh and look back to James. "So, you only decided to come this year because I wanted to go?"

"Sort of," he admits. "Not that I blame you for wanting to come. Even if they whisper about us behind our backs the entire time, it's better than being stuck in town. At least I can relax for real out here."

Sure, but...

I point at his chest. "Does that hurt anymore?"

"No?" He sets a hand over his sternum. His fingers run down, along the healing incision. The stitches are gone, replaced by a thin scab and pink scar tissue. "I mean, it's still kinda sore, but I'm fine. This isn't what's bothering me, anyway—my ribs are worse."

His eyes flick up again. "Yours don't hurt, right?"

"No."

"Good," he says.

But I look at my arms. Without my shirt and the knit band I left with my shoes, every wound Ice left on my body is visible. Spending all my time with James makes it easy to forget.

After the way Paige looked at me earlier, I don't think I'll rejoin the others wearing only a bikini top. *But I imagine James won't go back without his shirt either.*

I force a smile. "Anyway, as I was saying, Rose took me to parties with lots of people and alcohol all the time—in high school and since. I usually planted myself near the food and only talked to anyone if they talked to me first. And I wasn't even the subject of crazy rumors back then, so... I get not wanting to hang out with everyone the whole time. That would be exhausting. But it seems like Paige is the main problem here."

"Paige. Yeah." He picks up a handful of waterlogged sand and watches it drip between his fingers. "She can't talk shit about me being defective anymore since the news is out that I can morph, but me dating a human and you *being* human, on top of whatever bullshit rumors she's heard, is more than enough ammo. I mean, she always thought I was a creep, and she's never been afraid to express that publicly."

"You never know," I say with a laugh. "She might get so sick of looking at us that she leaves. But, anyway, I don't care what anyone is saying—especially not someone like her."

His eyes narrow, and he dunks his hand back into the water. "You don't wonder what everyone's been saying about you?"

"Of course, I wonder," I mutter, watching the sea foam and sandy water swirling in my lap. "I thought about asking Carmen what she's heard, but it honestly doesn't matter. I feel like I can't ask without explaining the truth, anyway, and I'm not ready to deal with that right now either."

We look up at the same time and end up staring at each other. Cool waves lap at my side, their force lessened after hitting James first. In our silence, the ocean drowns out all other sound. He seems to be considering something quite deeply as more wet sand oozes between his fingers and falls into the water, but another minute passes without a word.

"Have you asked Matt what people are saying?" I ask.

He shakes his head.

"See? The rumors don't matter."

twenty-six

We sit in the path of the waves, existing in the moment, until I voice concern over our risk of sunburn. My shoulders are warm, but I'm more worried about the fair, freckled skin on James' back—since I assume it rarely has a chance to see the sun.

He laughs at me but agrees, so we rinse off the sand and leave the water. We wander further down the beach, toward the rockier end of the cove.

"How are the tidepools?" I ask.

He shrugs. "They're alright. Better at low tide."

"Is it high tide?" I ask with a glance at the water—like I have any idea how to tell the difference.

"Eh… It's kind of in between right now. Going out, though, so just give it a few hours."

How do you know?

I stare down the beach, but there are too many sandstone out-croppings between us and the tidepools. I can't make out much of anything.

"That's fine," I say mildly. "I'm getting hungry, anyway. But I wanna check them out later, okay?"

He flashes a smile. "Sure. You wanna head back now, then?

I'm sure someone brought food."

Right? We sure didn't.

We loop back to the cave to put our shirts on. We leave our shoes, but I grab my phone and the wristband I left on top of my flip-flops. Then we head north, collecting several pieces of dry-enough driftwood along the way.

As we near the main group, it's clear they've been busy, having amassed a few decently sized piles of firewood. The bundles of chopped logs and kindling bound with plastic ties were obviously brought in from elsewhere, but most is sandy driftwood taken from around the beach. Matthew and Jesse are digging a shallow pit several yards south of the coolers and sunshades. Seems like everyone else split into a few distinct groups since we left. I drop my armful of wood onto a driftwood pile, and we pass by the guys digging and a circle of people sitting several yards closer to the cliffside without incident.

Then Cassidy appears as if out of nowhere, racing up to meet us in feline form. They morph and skid to a stop in the sand a few feet ahead. Before they have a chance to say anything, James says he'll find something for us to eat and continues toward the coolers without me. *Which is fine. I guess.*

"You swam already?" Cassidy asks, pushing the brim of their hat up and out of their face. "Is the water cold?"

"No, it's not too cold."

"Sweet!"

Flashing a grin, they turn and take off in the direction of the water. *Children...*

I keep walking, and, as I approach James and the collection

of coolers planted in the sand, I notice a few new faces. One of the newcomers, a petite woman with short brown hair, looks up from her phone. Her expression shifts when she sees James—a look of surprise, I think—and she waves to him.

"It's so good to see you," she says, smiling as she steps away from her friends. "Happy birthday, James."

He freezes in apparent alarm before greeting her properly and gesturing at the *six* coolers beneath the sunshades.

"Where's the food?" he asks.

"Blue cooler right there," she says. "The sandwiches are fair game, but don't touch the cake yet."

"Obviously."

She looks past James as he moves to check out the cooler and notices me having awkwardly stopped some distance away. She offers me a smile, and I drift closer. Her pleasant expression feels genuine even as she looks me over.

"You're Jayde, right?" she asks.

I nod, and James absentmindedly introduces her as April while still shuffling through the large, blue cooler. She seems friendly—same as everyone else I've met today, with Paige being the one exception.

"Do you remember me?" she asks. "I cut your hair a while back. You came in with Night, and Carmen wouldn't shut up about wanting to give you an asymmetrical bob."

Oh!

"Yeah, I remember."

I can't believe I didn't recognize her. She was super nice to me back then too, but I guess I was too distracted to commit her face to memory.

"I hear you're the one who convinced James to come," she says. "I'm glad. I feel like I haven't seen him in ages."

I force a smile and nod, but I can't believe she's not asking about Ice. I'm pretty sure we talked about him a lot during that salon visit. Why is she not asking about him now? *Does it have something to do with the rumors? What has everyone been saying?*

James taps my arm, snapping me out of my panic. I glance over, and he hands me a small, plastic-wrapped sub sandwich. Holding the cold sandwich in both hands makes me feel better.

April turns back to get the attention of the three she was hanging out with before our arrival distracted her. Two women relaxing on a blanket beneath a sunshade and a man standing nearby, all smoking marijuana as far as I can tell.

The man is a tanned fire immortal with spiky, strawberry-blond hair. The girl nearest to me is wearing a rainbow striped bikini top, hipster glasses with tinted lenses, and has short, choppy hair dyed a vibrant purple. The other is wearing a short, white dress that contrasts her deep brown skin and dark, coiled hair. She removes her floppy hat to look up at me with emerald green eyes and a curious smile. Both girls wave, the guy nods in passive acknowledgment, and I accept that literally everyone here already has some idea of who I am.

Jayde, James' new girlfriend.

The human girl who was with Ice Monroe in June.

I follow April and James closer to the others, and I struggle to not look uncomfortable as they all inevitably glance over the scars on my arms. It's only natural for them to notice. The injuries aren't *that* well healed. Thankfully, though, I don't get the feeling anyone intends to mention them.

"Jayde, this is my husband, Tyler," April says, dragging the strawberry-blond man to her side.

"You guys are *married*?" James asks.

She laughs but doesn't answer, instead introducing the two women as Hannah and Mina—Hannah in the dress and Mina with the purple hair.

"Fair warning," Hannah says, "Paige has been talking up a wicked shit storm about you two ever since we showed up. We shut her down earlier, but she's still lurking."

James doesn't look surprised.

I glance back to scan the beach. Paige and Claire must be in the circle, where most everyone who isn't busy with something else is hanging out. *Yep. There she is.* But they're all well out of earshot and don't seem to be paying us any attention. I can barely even make out their faces from here.

"It was uncalled for," April mutters. "I hate confrontation, but it drives me crazy when immortals act like that—like they're better than everyone else. We're all adults here, but I swear she thinks we're still in high school. And, every time I see her, she pulls something like this. If it's not James, she'll go after some-one else. Mina. Dawn. Lucas. Anyone she thinks she can sink her teeth into. Who invited her, anyway?"

"I hear Jesse is dating Claire," James says, coming across more casually than he has with anyone other than me or Matthew since we got here. "The Porter girls have always been a package deal."

Mina shrugs. "This grade school drama is stupid. We've all been through it with her, so don't let it get to you. But it's good to see you, dude. Feels like it's been years."

That's almost exactly what April said!

"Yeah..." James grimaces and itches his arm.

"Is there a reason she hates you specifically?" I ask.

James glances aside and takes a bite of his sandwich, avoiding the question, but Hannah sits up and laughs.

"Honestly, girl, that's just how Paige is," she says. "She has it out for anyone outside her narrow definition of *normal*. Makes me wonder why she ever bothers coming to Matt's parties."

Mina cackles, slapping Hannah's thigh. "No kidding. You'd think she'd be too disgusted to come and just go around telling her boring cishet friends we have weird gay orgies at all of his parties."

Hannah shoves her back, grinning. "Oh, you wish we did!"

James sighs, and April's husband, Tyler, offers a lit joint to him. He stares at it for a long second before averting his eyes.

"Nah, man, I quit smoking," he says.

"That's cool," Tyler says with a shrug.

He sighs *again*. "Thanks, though."

When the joint is offered to me next, I smile and shake my head. *I have never smoked weed in my life, and it's probably not a great idea to start now, miles from civilization on a beach with a bunch of people I hardly know.*

In an attempt to calm my nerves, I unwrap my sandwich and take a bite. It's good—fancy sliced turkey with smoked cheese and baby lettuce—and I find the group's continued conversation more entertaining than expected. Maybe there's a reason immortals have such a deep rumor mill. They all seem to lead eventful lives.

"Yo, James," a distant voice calls, heavily muffled by the wind and crashing waves. It takes a second to recognize it as Matthew's voice, but I quickly spot him standing among the circle of people sitting in the sand. "Bro! Get your ass over here!"

James reacts to the summons with visible relief followed by fleeting dread, but I offer him my hand, and we leave the relative safety of April's small group together.

twenty-seven

I was right.

The larger group contains almost everyone else on the beach. They're all gathered in a rough approximation of a circle near two large coolers, one of which I'm pretty sure is full of light beer and wine coolers. A few different conversations are going on at once, and everyone looks to have an open drink, except for Stephen and Natalie. Cassidy is a few yards further down the beach, burying themself in sand.

Upon noticing us, Paige sets her drink down, twisting the bottle's base into the soft sand beside her.

I ignore her and sit next to Carmen, clear across the circle from Jesse and the blonde twins. James takes the space between me and Matthew, and I chat with Carmen while James attends to whatever he was called over for. Though, I can't pay much attention to the details of their conversation. Holding my own while also working on my sandwich *and* carefully keeping an eye on Paige in my periphery is turning out to be quite the task.

I catch her glancing at me with sharp, critical eyes as her sister goes on about something that sounds in no way related to me—I think it has something to do with school or San Francisco in general. But Claire finishes her train of thought, probably catching on that her sister isn't paying attention and has instead been watching me long enough that both James and I had time to finish our sandwiches.

Then Paige clears her throat. Bracing myself, I jam the plastic sandwich wrap into my pocket.

"So, James," she says, her voice unnecessarily loud. "We're all dying to hear how you met your girlfriend."

I keep my mouth shut, glancing at James as he slowly turns to face her. He's not mad—*yet*—but I know he doesn't want to deal with her any more than I do.

"Long story," he says.

"Oh?"

Beside her, Claire frowns. Her shoulders rise in discomfort as she looks from us to her sister to Jesse. She sets a hand on his arm and whispers something to him, and irritation flickers over his face. It looks like they want nothing to do with whatever Paige is so obviously trying to start—*though neither one speaks up in our defense*.

Paige's eyes dart aside, toward her sister, for an instant before landing on me and James again.

"We have all day," she says with a toxic smile, "so let's hear it. How many of the rumors are true? Do you even know what I've heard about her? About you?"

"I don't know about any rumors."

"Uh-huh…" Paige raises one perfectly manicured eyebrow, regarding James with acute skepticism.

Claire drags Jesse to his feet, and they *leave* the circle, heading toward the sandstone cliffs. *Seriously—you're just bailing?*

Paige doesn't even seem to care. She doesn't spare a glance in their direction. Beyond the space they left empty, Cassidy looks up, their expression unreadable from so far away.

To my right, Carmen lets out a short, dry laugh. "Oh, get the fuck over yourself, girlfriend. You seriously wanna do this now?"

Paige ignores her too. She looks me over again, her attention pausing on each visible scar for an uncomfortable second, and her eyes narrow before flicking back to stare James down.

"I heard you were arrested by RPD in July," she says. "That girl—Jayde, right? She didn't have these scars before that, did she? While she was with Ice Monroe, I mean? So, is it true that you sliced her up because she refused to break up with him?"

Static. Ringing in my ears.

Hands at my chest, a pit in my stomach, mouth dry. The ocean wind suddenly feels twice as cold. But, through the overwhelming static, I can't find words to combat the accusation or defend James. All I can do is sit, frozen in the sand, as a few in the circle mumble to each other.

What the hell have they been saying about me all this time? I haven't shared any pictures showing the scars online. How does anyone here know *anything? Who spread these rumors?*

"That is *not* what happened," James says, voice stilted.

I tear my attention from Paige to check on him. His eyes are wide, his face pale, but our reaction only seems to embolden her. She laughs and stands, folding her arms over her chest as she sneers down at us from across the circle.

What's the point of doing this? It feels so petty, and I—

"Is it true that she slept with Ice just so he'd—"

My heart stops.

But she doesn't have time to finish her question as James sputters something and scrambles to his feet. I realize I'm standing too—though I'm not sure at what point I stood up. It feels like I lost a couple seconds there. *Maybe I did.*

"Shut up," James growls. Eyes burning with anger, his voice carries a hint of danger even as his mouth quirks up on one side. "I mean it. You think you're *so* much better than me, but you're not. I'm not intimidated by you. I've seen worse. Way worse. You're just a spoiled brat."

Her expression blanks, smile slipping as her cheeks flush, but she stands her ground and recovers quickly. She scoffs, flashes a pained, bitter smile, and steps closer.

James says he's not intimidated, *but I am.*

Her easy conceit and the disdain in her sharp, blue eyes remind me of Ice. It's like I'm back in that hallway in West-brooke, a deer in the headlights paralyzed by fear even as every muscle in my body begs me to step back—*to run.*

"How dare you speak to me that way?" Her eyes narrow as her voice rises. "You think just because you and your freak girl-friend can turn into cats now, you can just—"

"No. I'm sick of your shit, Paige. Say whatever you want about me—*I don't give a fuck*—but I'm telling you right now; you better leave Jayde out of it."

Her eyes snap open wide, self-righteous arrogance shifting to pure rage, but James doesn't give her a chance to respond.

"I'd bet anything you made up half those fucked rumors for attention. But look around you; no one's impressed. You're only embarrassing yourself."

She does not look around. Her wild eyes don't leave him for a second. Instead, she bares her teeth, steps forward, and slaps him across the face.

He hardly reacts, but my blood boils at the *smack* of her hand striking his cheek, eradicating the chill I felt before. Even if she's not the one who spread rumors that James attacked me or that I slept with Ice *for any reason*, this is too much.

She's taking it too far.

"What difference does it make?" she cries. "I bet it's all true, anyway. You're insane—you both are!—and there's no way it's a coincidence that four people disappeared off the face of the Earth at the same time. I bet you brainwashed that girl to like you. Maybe you killed the Monroes too, huh?"

A hint of deep, agonized darkness flashes in James' eyes. And I watch helplessly. Unable to move. Unable to speak. Mind racing, trapped in a body I can't control.

It's exactly the same…as that rainy morning in July.

"You have no fucking idea what you're talking about! Shut up already, you unhinged rich bitch."

Paige recoils, her smirk twisting into an enraged grimace. Then her hand draws back like she's about to hit him again. That's all I see, really. Just her hand. Long lavender nails. A silver ring on her index finger.

And time slows to a crawl.

My mind is blank—a tumultuous, buzzing mess of nothing

—but I feel myself move. My chin lifts. Teeth click as my jaw sets. Right hand balls into a tight fist. My feet move too. They put me between Paige and James. One arm moves to push him out of the way, so I can get to her.

And my knuckles contact her perfect cheekbone.

Time returns to normal, and I realize what I've done as Paige shrieks like a wounded animal. A jolt of fear that she might retaliate makes me freeze, but she merely glares at me, too-blue eyes watering as she holds a hand to her face. Then she turns on her heels, morphs into a sleek silver cat, and races off.

My heart pounds, chest heaving with each heavy breath, but I can't seem to move. And no one speaks. But I feel everyone's eyes on me.

What just happened?

"Holy shit," Carmen breathes, breaking the heavy silence.

Finally, I regain control.

I glance over my shoulder.

Carmen is still sitting in the sand, biting her fist rather than holding a beer bottle. Matthew also has a fist to his mouth, but he looks like he's trying not to laugh as he slips a phone into his pocket. Natalie and Stephen are both pale and silent. Cassidy, still half-buried in sand several yards away, stares into the distance, where Paige—back in her human form—met up with Claire, Jesse, and...*Parker?*

Lucas, who I don't think has uttered a single word since I joined the circle, turns to open the cooler behind him and grab another beer. James stops the lid from closing. He fishes two purple wine coolers out of the ice, sticks them in his pockets, and takes ahold of my hand.

Being touched is like an electric shock. I suck in a sharp breath and once again feel present. Once again hear the waves crashing on the beach and feel the hot sun on my shoulders.

I meet James' gaze for a second before he looks away, but I can't tell what he's thinking. I don't even know what I'm thinking. My head is still buzzing. Swirling. But he starts walking, and I follow. We're both very quiet and very tense as we leave everyone behind, heading south along the beach.

Neither of us say a word. James walks, and I trail behind, watching his back and trying to think of what to say as my heart beats far too fast, and I start to feel like I might throw up.

Once I'm certain we're far enough away that no one can hear—and no one can see us clearly—I stop.

I just stop walking.

My knuckles ache as James holds my hand. But I look away, and my eyes lock onto my left instead. The grey sweatband. It seems, almost, like it's all I can see at the end of a long, dark tunnel. And I can perfectly picture the scar underneath.

Six short lines that form an angular heart.

I pull my hand out of James' grip, and my hands ball into fists at my sides as I meet his gaze. He doesn't look nearly as angry or upset as I still feel. But I have to say *something*.

"I…" *Ugh.* "I never slept with Ice."

"I know," he says.

"I'm serious! I can't believe she would even say something like that. I never would have—"

My trembling voice cuts off mid-thought. My hands relax,

and my eyes grow wide as tears prick the corners. I look down, quickly, to the white sand between us.

Is that true?

I used to *really* like Ice. I was desperate for his attention. In June—*and half of July, even*—I probably would've done anything if I thought it might make him like me more. How do I know that I, back then, wouldn't have had sex with Ice if he ever initiated anything? I might have even *wanted* it.

I can't imagine it now. The thought makes me feel sick to my stomach. *But what was Paige going to imply I slept with him for?*

Just to get him to like me? In exchange for him sponsoring me or enrolling me in the Human Immortal Program? *For the River Sapphire? For money? Just because all immortals are hot, and she thinks I'm a slut?*

What the hell was she gonna say?

Why do I care so much? Damn it...

My breath catches as my chest grows tighter, and I cover my face. I press my palms to my eye sockets so hard it hurts.

"Whoa. Hey—" James' hands settle on my shoulders. "What's wrong?"

God... I'm seriously crying over this?

How pathetic can I get?

I force a deep breath to take in *some* oxygen. Then I shake my head and wipe my eyes with the back of my hand. My mascara left grey streaks on my skin, and my knuckles are kinda red. They still hurt a little, too.

"I'm fine," I insist despite sounding absolutely miserable. "It's not like it was a secret that I was with him or anything. I mean, we were never…technically dating, and I did not *ever* have sex with him for *any* reason, but it must have looked weird to everyone who knew or heard about it—whatever *it* was—since I'm human, and Ice is, well…*Ice*. And then, for you and me to be together all of a sudden…"

"Jayde, I never heard rumors that you were dating."

When I look up from my hands, he winces.

"Okay, that's a lie," he admits hastily. "Before we met, there was a rumor going around that you guys were dating. Carmen told Matt and a few other guys that Ice confirmed it, but I didn't buy that. Ice doesn't date. Everyone knows that."

I sigh, disappointed by how many times I've heard this story. Obviously, Carmen didn't mean any harm by telling her friends that Ice insinuated we were dating, but it's still annoying.

"And I never once thought that you slept with him."

"Really?"

He nods. I stare him down for a moment, but his expression doesn't change, and I feel bad when I notice the faint, red mark on his cheek. Paige must look worse, though. I may be human, but my brain shut off back there, and I hit her way harder than I should have. *Not that I* should have *hit her*.

Oh god…

"Sorry," I say mildly. "I guess I just never expected the rumors would have so much to do with…*before*, you know? It caught me off guard. I… I panicked."

"Hey, you know I don't care about whatever happened before, right?"

Ugh... Nothing *happened*, but why'd she have to bring it up?

"And then, for her to say in front of everyone that *you* hurt me? Or even *killed* Ice and Night? How am I supposed to react to that?"

"Jayde..." He forces a smile. "I don't care what anyone says about me, but no one believes that shit anyway."

My eyes water, this time in frustration, and I glance at the sand again. *There's no way he doesn't care.* After what Paige said about us in front of everyone? *And then they all watched me punch her!* How are we supposed to bounce back from this? What if everyone hates me now? What if *anyone* believes what she said?

Maybe we should leave before things get worse...

James steps closer. I look up, ready to apologize again, and he pulls me into a tight hug. After a second's hesitation, I hug him back. My hands ball in the fabric of his shirt, and the floodgates finally burst.

He kisses the side of my head. My cheek. My neck. And he whispers in my ear that *everything will be alright.* Forget about Paige—*she's a bitch, anyway.* Forget about Ice. Forget about everyone and everything. The rumors are stupid—*all of them.* It doesn't matter what they're saying if we know none of it's true. They have no idea what they're talking about—*no idea what we're going through. No idea what we've been dealing with.* I shouldn't let it get to me.

He's right, obviously. I know he's right. Deep down, I do. And I manage to stop *sobbing*, but nothing he says makes me feel any better about myself. None of it makes me feel better about anything that happened in the past either.

This sucks. It all sucks.

"I love you," he says. "I love you so much, Jayde. More than anything."

"I know," I mumble into his warm shoulder. "I love you too."

"Don't worry about anyone else."

He's right. I shouldn't worry about it—at least not right now.

But it still sucks.

twenty-eight

It takes forever, but I eventually manage to get over myself —or at least stop crying. Either way, I no longer feel like I'll sink into the sand and disappear if James let go of me, so I take another calming breath before relaxing my hands and stepping back.

He still looks worried, though.

"I'm sorry for freaking out," I say, sniffling while trying to smear the rest of the melted mascara off my face.

"It's okay. You feel any better?"

"Yeah, I'll be fine."

James averts his eyes, scratching the back of his neck. "Good. Sorry for causing a scene back there, though."

Paige started it.

He was only trying to defend me by calling her out, and she *hit* him. No one deserves to be treated like that, especially at their own party. But I can't bring myself to say there's no need to apologize.

"We can leave if you want," he says.

"No way! I wanna stay. I won't let her ruin this for us."

He blinks. "Okay."

Okay.

With that, we make our way further south.

Once we reach the cave, I clean my face using water from the bottle I forgot I had and a corner of my beach towel. Then we sit in the shade just inside the entrance.

James opens a mixed berry wine cooler and offers it to me. The drink is surprisingly sweet, almost like Kool-Aid. I barely taste the alcohol, but the label says it only contains five percent.

I set the bottle aside, hug my knees to my chest and dig my toes into the warm sand in the sun beyond the shadow cast by the sandstone cliff above. After getting away from everyone else and talking and crying it out, I feel better—*more or less*—and James seems alright too.

Even if we have resorted to drinking.

"You got her pretty good, huh?" James says with a soft laugh.

I frown, staring at my toes. "Better me than you, I guess."

"I wasn't gonna hit her," he says sharply. "But, uh… I guess you're not wrong."

I look up to check, and *he actually looks concerned.* Gazing out over the beach, brows furrowed, one finger tapping the side of his bottle and everything. But I don't honestly think he would've hit her. He's more the type to stand there and take the abuse.

Ugh.

"She was about to slap you again," I say. "I was so mad. I just snapped. But I had to do something, and I didn't want her to hit *me*."

James meets my gaze with a hint of surprise. I crack a smile and massage my sore knuckles. Then he mirrors my smile, relaxing again. He leans back and drapes his arm over my shoulder.

I hold my wine cooler to my lips. "And I can't say she didn't deserve it."

"Think she'll leave now?" he asks.

As I laugh, I wonder if it's worth feeling guilty at all considering what she said. *Can't be worse than nearly stabbing a man with his own knife, anyway.*

We sit together, drinking our wine coolers as the sun creeps closer. I lean on James' shoulder and watch the waves. It's nice. I like this. It's easy to imagine we're the only ones here. *Does he feel the same way?* Does he also wish we had the whole beach to ourselves? I want to ask if, maybe, we can come back some time in the future—just us. But the soothing illusion of solitude withers as I hear distant voices over the crashing waves.

Carmen and Cassidy.

I don't mind seeing them, though, and I push myself up off the ground to greet them as they approach.

"Jayde, that was fucking *wild*," Carmen says, violet eyes wide and glittering. "I had a front-row seat, and I still can't believe you decked Paige Porter in the face."

I force a smile, scratching my arm. "Yeah... My body just kinda went for it. I think my fight or flight response is broken."

"No. I'm serious." She plants her hands on her hips, still grinning. "I figured you've been through some shit, but I wasn't expecting you to suddenly be a total badass."

That's a bit of an exaggeration, I think.

James stands and brushes off the back of his shorts. Carmen looks to him, her expression mellowing as she asks if he's alright. He frowns, rubs his cheek, and half-shrugs.

"No one buys those insane rumors, right?" he asks. "Have you heard them before?"

She hesitates. "Which ones?"

He gestures vaguely, she averts her eyes, and I suddenly wish I were deaf. My curiosity is a force to be reckoned with at times, but I no longer want to know anything about whatever rumors have been circulating about me, James, or Ice. I've heard enough to know it's worse than I thought.

Cassidy looks between the three of us before flashing an apologetic smile. They drop their tote bag and hat in the sand, turn and morph, and race toward the water in feline form. After watching them for a moment, Carmen returns her attention to us with a sigh and folds her arms over her chest.

"I never heard rumors that Jayde slept with Ice for favors," she says dryly. "You're probably right that she made it up just to get under your skin, but some crazy shit has been going around town, James. I heard the one that you attacked Jayde, but—"

"Does anyone believe it?"

She glances between us. Uncertainty creeps into her expression as her eyes pass over my scars again, but she shakes her head and looks back to James.

"Matt cleared up the rumor that you hurt Jayde a while back —not that I ever believed it since I was one of the first to know you guys were hanging out—but that only leaves a couple possibilities, if you know what I mean?" She frowns more seriously. "I don't know you too well, James, and we haven't always gotten along, but I doubt you murdered anyone. You get what I'm saying, right?"

He doesn't respond.

Neither do I. Faced with her conclusion, as vague and round-about as it was, I can't even bring myself to meet her eyes.

"Anyway," she says. "I've corrected a few wayward gossipers myself the past couple weeks, but I don't know what actually happened. And I can't say for sure what anyone else believes."

James doesn't look entirely convinced.

I take a breath. "No one else has accused you of hurting anyone. No one else has even looked at you weird. Everyone besides Paige seems cool with both of us."

"Paige is screwed in the head for real," Carmen agrees. "It blows my mind that she thought it was remotely okay to say those things here—especially to your face. No joke, she got what was coming to her. I'm *glad* you punched her."

There's a moment of quiet. Seagull cries and waves crashing. But I honestly can't tell if Carmen's approval makes me feel more justified or not.

Then James sighs. "I should talk to Jesse."

He looks past Carmen to scan the group in the distance. It seems the circle of people has completely split up since we took off. I hope we haven't created a huge schism among everyone...

"Feel free," Carmen says with a shrug. "If it helps, I'm happy to stick with Jayde and the kid for a while."

"Yeah, thanks."

James kisses my head before he leaves—morphing to run up the beach in feline form. He seems to have the hang of it now. Carmen watches after him for a moment, then turns to me again.

"He really can morph now, huh?" When I nod, she flashes a

soft smile. "Good for him. Maybe it'll help him loosen up."

We can hope.

She glances down, and I follow her gaze to the empty wine coolers discarded in the sand beside my flip-flops.

"You're drinking?" she asks.

"A little."

"Are you okay? Badass or not, that was hard to watch."

I sit down again. She sits next to me, and I watch Cassidy's small feline form run and splash in the shallow waves across the beach.

"Hear me out a sec," Carmen says, her voice casual. "A few years back, most girls would've *killed* to sleep with Ice Monroe. Maybe she was just projecting her own sexually repressed teenage disappointment onto you."

"You think?"

She laughs and leans back, gazing into the blue sky. "A few girls spread similar rumors about Night when we were in high school—just because they were jealous of how close they were, right? So, honestly, I wouldn't put it past Paige to make up that sort of shit now since she's apparently still living in a Mean Girls fantasy land."

"Wait— It was a real rumor?"

"Of course, folks wondered if you were sleeping with Ice," she says, puzzled by my surprise. "I mean, I never heard that you were trading sex for favors. Knowing him—and you—that's fucking hysterical. But most everyone I talked to was curious what he got out of dating you. Immortals don't often date humans, you know? And, as far as I'm aware, Ice has never really dated anyone, so it was extra strange."

It's great to know that just about *everyone* has been speculating about my nonexistent sex life all summer.

She pats my back, laughing again. "I'll take that to mean there was no sex."

I can't bring myself to respond. I just hug my knees, feeling sorry for myself for entirely too many reasons. *For one: why am I so embarrassed that she knows I never slept with Ice? What the heck is up with that, huh?*

"Sorry," she says with a sigh. "Anyway, don't stress yourself out over Paige. I'm more worried about what she said about Ice and Night."

"No one murdered anyone," I mutter. "I'm sure Ice and Night are fine."

"Have you seen them lately?"

"Not in a while."

The waves lap on the beach. I hear Cassidy's laughter, carried on the wind. Then Carmen clears her throat, and I look to find her smiling. The emotion behind it is odd and difficult to pin down, though—wistful, maybe?

"Hey," she says. "You wanna sunbathe with me for a few? I gotta take a nap if I wanna keep drinking."

"Um... Sure. I mean, it's not like I'm busy, right?"

"Sweet. Thanks."

She stands, strips down to her red bikini, and fluffs her short hair up a bit. *Wow. Carmen is super pretty.* She has more tattoos than I thought too. I wonder if Lucas did them all.

My eyes dart to the side, and I hesitate before pulling my own shirt off. I do *not* look to catch her initial reaction to seeing the rest of my scars, but her expression is still passively pleasant when I finally have the nerve.

"You got sunscreen and towels around here, right?" she asks, glancing over her shoulder to check out the cave behind us.

"Yeah, one second."

Carmen follows me into the cave and looks around while I locate both beach towels and dig the sunscreen lotion out of my backpack. I meet her in the sun outside, then we spread the towels on the sand and apply sunscreen to each other's backs. All the while, I weigh the pros and cons of taking a nap in direct sunlight too. Even a short one seems like a bad idea, but the adrenaline rush and all that crying wore me out.

Cassidy runs up the beach toward us. They're in human form again, sopping wet. They stop to grab a plush towel from their tote bag, which they promptly lay next to mine.

"I can hang out with you guys, right?" they ask.

"Not a problem, kid," Carmen says.

She tosses the bottle of sunscreen to me, plops down on the towel I let her borrow, and fishes a phone out of the shorts she left on the ground. I rub sunscreen onto Cassidy's back and hand over the bottle when I'm done. Then I sit on the towel I nabbed from James' bag and turn to Carmen, who is still messing around on her phone.

"Do you have service out here?" I ask.

"Nah, but I've been taking tons of pictures."

She drops her sunglasses from her hair to her eyes, purses her lips, and takes a few selfies. When finished, she pushes the sunglasses back up and waves me in.

"Here, I'll tag you on FaceSpace later," she says.

Cassidy laughs at us as we lean in close just long enough for Carmen to snap a decent photo of us smiling and flashing peace signs. I watch her slap a gradient filter and a few strategically placed fire emoji stickers on the image before turning her phone to show me the final result. We look silly, but it seems I managed to clear the smudged mascara from my face earlier. My scars aren't too noticeable either—most being covered by stickers—so I agree it's fine to share.

I should take some pictures with James when he gets back.

"We have to leave early tomorrow," she says, "so the album will probably be up before you guys get back into town. Keep an eye out for the clip of you decking Paige too."

The WHAT?

"Matt showed it to me earlier, and it is—*muah*, chef's kiss—pure cinematic gold."

"Oh, no." I feel my stomach drop. "He's not planning to share that online, is he?"

She laughs, shaking her head. "Nah. Don't worry. He said he won't post it anywhere. But, honestly, I kinda think he should. Maybe some good, old-fashioned public humiliation would take her down a notch."

"Mm…"

Why'd he record it, anyway?

Cassidy taps my shoulder. "Hey. Can I add you on FaceSpace later?"

"Yeah, of course."

They grin, and the three of us chat for a while before Carmen, who is apparently a little bubbly after however much she's already had to drink, rolls onto her stomach and falls quiet. Then Cassidy puts their large headphones on, and we follow Carmen's lead in getting comfortable on our towels.

Lying on my stomach with my arms folded and cradling my head, I close my eyes and listen to the water. The sun is warm, but the cool ocean breeze cuts the heat, so it's refreshing. It's *nice*—so much better than being stuck in James' small, stuffy bedroom.

I think, right now, I'd rather be here, resting on the beach, than anywhere in Riverview.

twenty-nine

I must have nodded off because I went from thinking about the sun on my back to James' voice rousing me from the brink of sleep in what felt like two minutes.

"Yikes," Matthew says. "I hope y'all haven't been sleeping out here very long."

Carmen groans. "What time is it?"

"It hasn't even been an hour," James says.

I sit up and touch my back—it's hot but seems fine—before looking up at James and Matthew. Jesse is with them too.

"How's it going?" Carmen asks with a yawn. "Paige still a raging bitch?"

Matthew shrugs. "She bailed with Claire and Parker right after you took off. I tried talking her down, but she wouldn't have any of it, so I said she should leave. And she did."

No one looks upset. Even Jesse, who is supposedly dating Claire, doesn't seem concerned that his girlfriend left because his brother's girlfriend punched her sister.

What a mess...

"Did she have a black eye or what?" Carmen asks while wriggling back into her shorts.

"Maybe she did. Maybe she didn't."

"Nice."

I almost feel bad thinking I might have *given her a black eye*, and I almost feel bad that she got into it with Matthew and left the beach because of me. *Almost.* I still can't believe she picked a fight like that, right in front of everyone, and I can't get what she said out of my head. It's annoying, but I'm glad she's gone.

That's one less thing to worry about.

I pull my shirt on.

Cassidy is still fast asleep with their headphones leaking music and drowning out the world, so I gently wake them up. They look at me for a second, groggy and tired and rubbing their eyes. Then they notice the three who joined us, pop up to a seated position, and take the headphones off.

"How long was I asleep?" they ask.

"Maybe twenty, thirty minutes," I say, trying to shake the sand out of my towel without getting it on anyone else. "We just woke up too."

They nod, stand and read the room, and nod a second time. "I guess Paige went home? Well, that's good, right? Now you guys can relax and have more fun, right?"

"Yeah," James agrees lamely.

"I shouldn't have invited them." Jesse sighs, his mild, awkward expression reminding me an awful lot of James. "I know Paige can be a lot to handle, but I wasn't expecting...*that*. I'm sorry, guys."

I doubt any of us blame him.

"Did Claire break up with you over it?" Carmen asks.

Jesse shrugs. "Paige didn't give us much time to talk before she dragged her off after Matt asked her to leave. But Claire was real upset about the whole thing."

"Hm… Maybe she's not a total beta twin anymore," she mutters. "Anyway, now that it's safe to be weird without fear of persecution, I should get back to it."

"Yes, good," Matthew agrees, his relief exaggerated.

We talk as a group for a few minutes. The bonfire won't be lit until close to sunset, and we won't be doing cake or other organized party activities until after dark, so we're free to do whatever we want in the meantime. Then Carmen, Matthew, and Jesse leave, returning to the main group—to carry on drinking, I imagine.

Cassidy stays with me and James, and we work out what to do next. James wants to party responsibly and avoid the alcohol for as long as possible, so he asks me to decide.

I mention the tidepools, Cassidy excitedly seconds the idea, and that's that. Our decision is made. They grab a camera from their bag, and the three of us set off toward the rockiest section of the beach.

"I'm gonna poke an anemone!" Cassidy cries.

They dash ahead and scramble up onto the uneven sandstone. Their awed gasp is audible over the crashing waves.

"Don't fall in," James calls after them. "I won't save you."

They glare over their shoulder and stick out their tongue before continuing forward and dropping into a kneel a moment later. I step up onto the water-worn rock and survey the tidepools carved into the stone ground between the frothing ocean and tall cliffs. Cassidy is sitting in front of a small pool, their hand in the water. The marine tang in the air is stronger here than on the sandy stretch of beach behind us.

I drop James' hand and lean over a pool of clear water in a

shallow depression. There's nothing but barnacles and a tiny fish inside. The fish swims in circles with nowhere to go. It's trapped. *Like me.*

The fish is in luck, though. High tide will free it soon enough.

I stand and look to James, but I don't know what to say when he asks if I'm alright. I just shake the unease off, force a smile, and move on to check out another tidepool.

This one is large, formed in a wide split in the stone. It's several feet long, and some sections are easily three or four feet deep. I kneel at the crevice's edge and lean out over the water to get a clearer view of the animals living inside.

"Look." I point at a purple starfish with one bumpy arm poking out of the water.

"Mm-hm."

He didn't look. He seems distracted, watching the waves crash against the rocky shore a few yards away. His eyes hold a thoughtful distance.

I sigh and poke a large sea anemone anchored on my side of the pool. As it tries to suck my finger into itself, another sea creature catches my eye, and I pull my hand back.

"Hey. James."

"What's up?"

"There's a huge crab in here."

"Oh?" Finally, he kneels beside me and peers into the water. "What kind of crab? Where?"

I point out the brown, fist-sized crab as it crawls along a narrow shelf not far from the anemone. He watches it for a moment before looking to me again, thoroughly unimpressed.

"It's a rock crab," he says. "But it's not very big. They can get twice that size."

"Oh? Should I catch it?"

He looks at me like I've said something outrageous, and I laugh. It's been years since I last messed around tidepools like this, but I remember catching hermit crabs when I was younger. Even if I was never very good at it, it was always fun.

"You wanna catch it, then?" I ask.

"What?" He pales almost imperceptibly before laughing. "Why would I?"

I hold a hand over my mouth to hide my smile. "Oh, no. Don't tell me you're scared of this little crab."

"I'm not scared. You catch it if you want it."

"Okay, fine."

I dip my hand into the cool water and carefully position it over the crab, still trying to work out the best way to catch the thing without taking damage. With my thumb on one side and my index finger on the other, I grab the shell and quickly pull it out of the water. This startles the crab, justifiably, and it manages to twist its big claw around just enough to pinch me.

The pinch is not painful, but it is surprising, and I squeak. I drop the crab, retract my hand to rub my pinched middle finger, and watch the creature dart into a patch of seaweed well out of reach.

"Nice," James says dryly.

"Hey, at least I tried."

I stop pestering the wildlife and sit on the cool, damp rock with my feet over the edge, submerged in a deeper part of the tidepool. James hesitates a moment before following suit. *And, for some reason, I think about the carvings in the sandstone cave.*

"You used to come here a lot, right?" I ask.

"Yeah…" He glances aside to watch the ocean. "We used to drive out here several times a year, no matter the season. Then my mom died when I was nine, and, uh… Things slowed down after that, but we still made it out here once or twice during the summer until we were maybe thirteen or fourteen. Now, I can come whenever I want, but I… I rarely do."

"Why? You said you like the beach."

"Yeah, I do," he says mildly. "This place is awesome. A whole private beach? There's never anyone else here—literally, I've only caught someone trespassing once—and it's quiet in a cool, noisy way. But, uh, I guess it's been kinda ruined for me."

"Did something happen?"

"Here? Not really, but it's a long story. Probably shouldn't get into it now if we're supposed to be having a good time."

I sigh. "Because that's going well so far."

"Right?" he says with a short laugh. "To be honest, I have no idea how to act around a few of the guys who showed up. Guess I can't complain, though, since most of them at least pretend to be nice to me now."

"You think they're pretending?"

"Maybe they're not." He looks into the water. "I don't know how to tell. But, even after what Paige did, I'm glad you convinced me to come."

I dip my hand into the cool water.

"Does that mean you're having a good time?"

He laughs again. "I mean, this is better than being at my dad's house, isn't it? Better than Riverview. I'm not *stuck* here. I can breathe. I can think. And it's not so fucking hot all the time."

"Are you happy here?"

I feel myself frown as I watch the light shimmering on my hand through the water. Somehow, the rippling light highlights the pink scar on my palm. Somehow, I think I forgot I had a scar there at all for a while.

"I'm happy that you're here with me," he says.

I turn my hand over, draw it out of the water, and rest it in my lap. Then, finally, I look to James again. I'm not sure how long he's been watching me. Or if he understands how I feel—about him or about anything else.

"You know I love you, right?" I ask.

He laughs again, the sound richer as his expression warms.

"So you've said," he agrees.

Looking at him now, I don't think Paige slapped him very hard. His cheeks are rosy from the heat of the day—I don't think he's put any sunscreen on, which might be an issue later—but there is a tiny bruise, surely left by a ring she was wearing.

Maybe I overreacted by punching her.

I touch the mark and ask if it hurts, but he didn't seem to realize there was a mark there at all. I take my phone out and launch the camera to show him. The skin isn't broken, but a thin red line is clearly visible on his cheek beneath his left eye.

He rubs the mark as though that'll make it go away—it doesn't—and then sighs. "And here I was, thinking I should get a few pictures of us while we're here."

Ah—

"We still can," I say a bit too eagerly. "But I was just thinking that earlier—that we should take some pictures, I mean. You can barely even see that mark through the camera."

And everyone knows how you got it, anyway.

He laughs and rolls his eyes before taking his phone from

his pocket. I scoot closer.

"I just need one decent one," he says.

I grin. "Sure. Then I'll take a bunch of less decent ones."

Phrasing.

After taking one admittedly good photo with his phone, we switch to my phone and spend a few minutes taking a variety of questionably cute, stupid, and downright cringe selfies. Pictures while hugging or kissing. Pictures of one or both of us mid-laugh with our eyes closed. I swoop in to lick his cheek, but he dodges, so I end up licking his eye instead, and I snap a couple pictures of him hiding his face in his hands while I'm dying laughing mostly out of frame.

"The hell was that?" he asks, fighting laughter as he wipes my saliva off his face.

"Sorry," I wheeze. "I just wanted to see what you'd do."

"Oh, yeah?" he asks, turning on me with feigned seriousness.

Before I can react, he sandwiches my face in his hands, and I scream as he licks me back. Once I dry my cheek, and we both stop laughing, I take a picture of our feet in the water to complete the set.

As we sort through the thirty-odd photos I took and delete the ones that are horribly out of focus or so unflattering they're not even funny anymore, Cassidy runs up in feline form. They stop at the edge of the far side of the tidepool, sopping wet, coppery fur plastered to their slight frame, but laughing.

James sighs. "Let me guess; you fell in?"

"I did," they exclaim. "But I did not drown."

"I see that."

They morph, returning to human form. Their hair and skin is visibly wet, but their t-shirt and thin jacket appear dry until both begin to wick moisture from underneath.

Interesting. How does morphing work, exactly?

Cassidy looks to me with a curious smile. "As far as I know, no one really understands how it works. They teach in school that science can't properly explain any of it—turning into cats, our weird powers, anything. Basically, immortals are magic."

"It's seriously magic?" I ask.

James groans. "No. Magic is such a cop-out answer. Just because science still hasn't worked out the exact mechanics behind it doesn't mean it's *magic*. Scientists couldn't explain electricity two hundred years ago, but it wasn't magic back then, and it sure as hell isn't magic now."

"Electricity isn't magic, but *creating* electricity with your bare hands totally is." Cassidy grins, a hint of deviousness in their wide, golden eyes. "Last year, a boy in my class got suspended for a week because he kept shocking kids with his magical powers."

"They have a point," I admit. "Nothing about immortals makes any sense."

"That doesn't make it magic," James insists, seemingly surprised that I'd side with a child over him.

"We turn into cats," Cassidy says.

"So? Morphing is probably tied to the metabolic system…or *metabolism*? Or whatever—you know what I'm trying to say."

I nod. After all, that lines up with what I heard while James was in the hospital. Maybe more is known than Cassidy thinks.

"Matthew can teleport," they argue, glancing from me to James again. "How do you explain that, huh?"

"Wormholes," he says.

"I can literally read minds, though."

"Electromagnetic radiation given off by brain waves."

His snap explanations make me even more curious and seem to give Cassidy genuine pause. They stand still for a moment, then drop to sit on the rock opposite from us.

"Okay, fine," they agree. "Maybe it has to do with, um... *metabolism*, you said? But why *are* my clothes dry after I swim as a cat even though my hair is still wet when I turn back?"

James thinks it over before nodding in apparent understanding. "Pocket dimensions. Whatever you're wearing or holding goes into one when you take feline form. Jayde asked something similar a few days ago, so I've been thinking about it, and that's what makes the most sense to me."

Cassidy frowns and stares into the water between us. Seems they ran out of things to say.

"What is a pocket dimension?" I ask.

"It's a concept in theoretical physics." He flashes an inexplicably nervous smile. "Essentially, it's a small pocket of space that's attached to the dimension we exist in but isn't technically part of it. My current theory is that morphing creates a temporary pocket dimension to store whatever doesn't carry over into feline form until you morph back."

"Wouldn't that be measurable?" Cassidy asks. "Also, aren't pocket dimensions a D&D thing?"

"Yeah, sure," he mutters. "I first heard of pocket dimensions while playing D&D, but that's not the point. It's a real concept, okay? Anyway, as far as I know, they've never been proven to exist—by immortals or anyone else. But, after what I've seen this summer, I don't trust the publicly available information that comes out of scientific research into immortals. Or if what they do tell us in school is everything they know."

"Sounds like a conspiracy theory," Cassidy says dryly.

They flash an impish smile, to which James rolls his eyes but says nothing further to defend his argument. *Is he right?* Night said something similar about Human-Immortal Affairs—about not trusting them. And they certainly haven't done anything to help me. Maybe the immortal government agencies shouldn't be trusted at all.

"What about my separate forms?" I ask, if only to distract myself. "Do you think my whole human body ends up in a pocket dimension when I morph? What do you think happens to it in there, without my consciousness inside it?"

"No idea," he says with a mild laugh. "That's too complex for me."

"But you honestly believe it can all be explained by science?"

"Of course! We just need to develop technology capable of detecting and measuring it properly."

Cassidy glares at him. "You're no fun. Wouldn't it be so cool if we were magic?"

"Personally, I think it'd be way cooler to know exactly how it works. Plus, I've read a ton of science fiction lately, so it's been on my mind, anyway."

"I don't know," they mumble, looking into the tidepool again.

I pat James on the shoulder. "For what it's worth, I like your theories."

"Thanks." He laughs, scratching the back of his neck. "I made most of them up on the spot."

Cassidy gasps. "Oh, look, a crab!"

thirty

We check out a few more tidepools, including one with a small octopus inside, before we leave the rocky area. Cassidy races past me and James, continuing north, when we stop at the sandstone cave to pick up our empty bottles.

"Don't let me forget to grab the sleeping bag from the trunk," James says. "Sometime before it gets dark, alright?"

I agree, and we make our way up the beach toward party central. The attendees are once again split into a few groups of varying size. Carmen, Lucas, and Natalie are with several others, mostly girls, while Matthew and Jesse are with a smaller group of guys. The last clearly defined group looks to be the smoker's circle from earlier, a bit further up the beach than before, away from most of the coolers. And Cassidy is far off in the distance, not far from the cliff, setting up a small, neon yellow tent.

After some thought and James' confirmation that he doesn't care what we do next, I decide to stick close to Carmen unless someone calls me away. Aside from James, I know her best out of everyone here. Matthew's small group is nearby, and I imagine James usually does the same—stick to the people he knows best; in this case, Matthew—so it should work out for both of us.

Carmen has obviously had more to drink since we last saw her. She almost looks how I imagine I must have looked to a sober person on the Fourth of July. Cheeks flushed as she laughs with a wine cooler in hand. Though, she sounds perfectly coherent as she calls us over.

"Hey," she says, voice a bit loud. "Remember how Taylor blew us off when Night tried to introduce you guys? Well, you will never guess who's here."

She gestures toward a girl I don't recognize. An air immortal with soft violet eyes and wavy, light brown hair who looks to be about the same age as me. She's with Alex, the muscular guy James and Matthew played HORSE with last week, and she was minding her own business before Carmen caught her attention by singling her out.

"Who's this?" she asks, though it only takes a second for grim understanding to wash over her. "Oh. The human girl everyone's talking about? Right."

I wave awkwardly.

"Dawn Corel," Carmen says. "She has the misfortune of being Taylor's sister."

Dawn laughs. "Misfortune is right."

I'm not sure what to say.

Not only is this girl Taylor's adoptive sister, *she's Dr. Corel's daughter.* Has he mentioned me or my situation to his family? Does she know anything more substantial than what the local rumor mill has churned out? Taylor mentioned reading my patient file. Did *he* say anything to her? *Does she even talk to him?*

"It's nice to meet you," I stammer.

She glances between me and James, who distracted himself by talking to Matthew the moment we got here and isn't paying attention to us. When her eyes land on me again, she frowns.

"Have you met Taylor?" she asks.

Oh, thank god. She doesn't know anything.

"Yeah. He gave me a ride from the hospital a while back."

"The hospital, huh?" she asks with an unabashed grimace. "That blows. I can't stand being around him at all—forget being trapped alone in a car with him. He's crazy. Seriously insane."

I avert my eyes. "It was…a long ten minutes."

"He didn't do anything weird, did he?"

"It was kinda awkward, but still better than walking."

"Really? You think so?" For whatever reason, she seems surprised. "I mean, I can't believe—"

Carmen interrupts by popping in to hand me an unopened bottle of pale red liquid. I take it, and she hands me another, and I suddenly have two bottles of hard cherry-lime soda—one for me and one for James, apparently. I thank her, and she returns to laughing at something Lucas said.

"Anyway," Dawn says slowly as she looks back to me, "he doesn't know where you live, right?"

"Taylor?" *Why ask? Now I'm nervous.* "No. He just gave me a ride from Riverview General to Centennial Memorial."

"Oh, good. Well, I hope things are going better for you now."

"Ah… How much have you heard?"

She shrugs. "Not much, but I've heard enough—the same as anyone else, I suppose. And you literally just said that *Taylor* gave you a ride from one hospital to *another* hospital."

"Yeah…" I sigh and drop my fake smile. "Good point. I'm fine now, though."

I want to ask if Dr. Corel has mentioned me at all, but that seems like too much. We just met. We're complete strangers. Even if she's heard the rumors or her dad told her anything specific regarding what happened to me, I'm sure it's nothing she'd care to repeat with so many people around.

I thank her and disengage to find James. He's now well incorporated into the group with Matthew, Jesse, Stephen, and Nick. They're talking about a game or TV show or *something*— I stumbled into the middle of it and honestly can't tell.

"James." I tap his shoulder and hold out one of the hard sodas. "You want this?"

He looks at the bottle in my hand, back up at me, and then at the bottle again before finally accepting it.

"Thanks," he says with a hint of uncertainty.

I twist the cap off mine and take a drink. As it says on the label, it's carbonated cherry limeade with a mealy aftertaste like beer. The sweet berry wine cooler was superior, but this is still palatable.

With nothing better to do, and Carmen now busy making out with Lucas, I hang around James and listen in on his conversation with the other guys. They're talking about some kind of…*card game*? But I hardly understand a word they're saying, so I leave to join Natalie beneath a sunshade instead. She's watching the water across the sand and has an open wine cooler in hand.

"Carmen told me you don't drink," I say.

"I don't drink *often*, but the wine coolers Nick brought are alright." Her expression shifts slightly, then she meets my gaze with a more pronounced frown. "Sorry. You're okay, right? After what Paige said, I mean?"

I scratch my cheek. "Oh, um… Yeah, I'm fine. I just wasn't expecting it."

"None of us were," she says, gazing out over the beach again as she takes a drink. "I hope she learned a lesson today."

Eventually, our small group and most everyone else converge some distance from the driftwood piles, forming a more disjointed version of the previous circle—the one I accidentally turned into a fight ring. The alcohol might be getting to me, as I made the mistake of asking about the friend group. Like how everyone here knows each other. But half of them laugh, and I receive the same answer Carmen gave before—most of them met through Matthew at some point during high school.

"I met Matt in my sophomore year," James says, though it seems like he has to think quite hard about it. "We had a PE class together, and he let me be on his team every time there was some stupid team activity. Then, out of nowhere, he started asking me to hang out outside of PE."

Matthew laughs. "Honestly, dude, I think I had a lil baby crush on you freshman year." Then he sighs rather dramatically. "Alas, it turns out you're the token straight friend."

James rolls his eyes.

April sighs in exasperation. "He is *not* your only straight friend. I'm straight, and so are Tyler, Nick, and, uh…Parker, I think."

"And me," Stephen says sharply.

"Me too," Natalie says, raising a hand before glancing away. "Mostly."

Carmen snickers, nudging Lucas in the ribs, but they don't comment. As I look around the group—most are laughing or joking around or talking to one another about Matthew or their sexuality or whatever—Mina's eyes lock onto mine.

"What about you, new girl?" she asks with a curious smirk. "Straight, queer, bi?"

Ah. I avert my eyes and down a gulp of hard soda to buy time. "Well, um… I mean, I've only dated guys before, but I… I've never really thought too hard about it. I guess?"

Am I straight?

I don't know. I feel like hanging around so many immortals has made it hard to tell. Literally everyone here is so stupidly attractive, and I'm not *blind*. But I'm not sure I'd date any of the girls I've met. *Probably.*

Somehow her smile widens, and she looks to James. "Would you feel threatened at all if you learned your girlfriend's bi? I mean, you'd suddenly have twice the competition, right?"

"No," he says without hesitation. "I'm not worried Jayde will ditch me to join your stupid harem."

"Having a stable polycule would be nice, though," Hannah says, her drink held to her lips.

Polycule?

Mina bursts out laughing. "Maybe *she's* the one you should be worried about. You always gotta watch out for the quiet queers."

"You're all weird as hell," Tyler says through laughter.

Wait— Tyler and Mina are twins, right?

Natalie pats my shoulder. "Don't mind Mina. Being straight is no worse than being queer."

"Pft—!" Mina is still laughing. "Yeah, I guess someone has to keep the earth populated."

"Girl, no." Carmen groans, leaning on Lucas. "We sure as hell aren't straight, but we wanna have kids."

Lucas sighs before clarifying that they've *talked about it a few times*. And, as I try to keep up with several people talking and arguing and laughing over each other, I swear my head starts spinning.

"When did we stop talking about me?" Matthew asks.

The circle falls quiet for a moment, then Mina gasps.

"Oh, shit; that's right," she says, golden eyes wide as she flashes a less conniving smile. "So, anyway, in our sophomore year, we used to call him SnacPac 'cause he randomly started coming to school with this lame rolling backpack full of cans of Mountain Dew and those Halloween-size candies—like Reese's cups and Sour Patch Kids and shit."

"No kidding," I say, trying to pretend I'm not reeling from the abrupt change in conversation topic.

Matthew nods. If I weren't convinced it was impossible, I'd almost think he looks self-conscious as Mina and a few others laugh.

"For real," she insists. "And he'd sell this shit to other kids at insanely high prices—like one dollar for a goddamn Reese's cup. Legit highway robbery. But he always managed to sell his entire stock every single day for like two years. No joke. I even saw teachers buy from him a few times before administration shut the whole operation down."

"I met him as SnacPac," Alex says.

Mina grins again. "Now we just call him *gay*."

"I'm not gay," Matthew says with a laugh. "I'm bisexual. There *is* a difference. But, yeah, the SnacPac gig landed me the treasurer position in the QSA junior year."

"Bro," she says, *still* laughing. "Forget Wisteria's lame QSA. When's the last time you even kissed a girl?"

His smile hitches up, and his eyes narrow. "Bet."

"Eat ass, Mina," Carmen says hotly. "I liked the QSA."

Wow.

I glance at James. He flashes an embarrassed, apologetic smile before averting his eyes and chugging half his drink. But I can't remember the last time I laughed this hard, and, after everything I've dealt with lately, it feels amazing.

thirty-one

Within an hour, the group splits as Matthew, James, Cassidy, and a few others leave to start piling wood into the shallow depression they dug and Mina, Hannah, April, Tyler, Dawn, and Lucas head to the north with the intention of smoking.

Natalie stays with me near the coolers, and we sit beneath a sunshade. I think about turning it around, since the sun's low angle renders the shelter mostly useless, but I want to see the water. James joins us some time later—honestly, I lost track of him for a while—and sits beside me.

It's just after 6PM, still a good two and a half hours before sunset, but I'm starting to feel strangely sleepy.

I blame the alcohol.

"Is she seriously taking another nap?" he asks with a glance at Carmen, who is passed out on a towel on Natalie's other side.

Natalie and I nod at the same time. But she's...*mostly* in the shade, so she should be fine.

"Is it true that someone brought liquor?" Natalie asks.

"Yeah." James sighs. "I guess Nick picked up tequila and fireball on his beer run, but it sounds like we're saving it for after dark."

She blinks. "There's already been a beer run?"

Oh, boy...

"You only turn twenty-one once, right?" he asks dryly.

"Ugh. Keep me away from the fireball, will ya, Jayde?"

"I'll try," I agree.

How much has everyone had to drink?

I drank two bottles with a couple hours in between, but I'm human. If the Fourth of July was any indication, immortals have a higher alcohol tolerance in general.

As I scan the beach, everyone seems fine. No one's stumbling or sick or passed out—except for Carmen—and, with Paige gone, the mood is casual and fun. Kinda impressive, considering I know a few started drinking *before* we got here.

Sure, I still feel alienated, but that's not anyone's fault. I'm new and human—the girl Ice Monroe sponsored in June. I don't blame these guys if they find me strange and hard to relate to.

Only three people on this beach know exactly what happened after James and I dropped off the radar. I'm sure the others are too nervous or polite to ask directly, but they must be curious. They must wonder how much of what they've heard is true. And I'm sure James looks at them and worries about the same thing after Paige accused him of giving me these scars in front of everyone.

And James... He's in a good mood now, and he's been hanging out with his friends more since then, but...

Ugh. I can't stop thinking about it.

I itch beneath the edge of the wristband. The knit fabric is still damp from messing around in the tidepools. I want to take it off. I'm not used to wearing it all day anymore—especially not while it's wet—but I don't want anyone to know.

I don't mind if everyone has seen the others, *but this one...*

James pats my arm. "Let's see what Matt's up to," he says as he stands.

I agree, and we head toward Matthew's group and the wood-pile they've amassed. The unlit bonfire is at least half my height with plenty of wood piled a few yards away to feed the fire as the night goes on.

"I've never been to a bonfire before," I admit under my breath.

"Trust me, it's not as impressive as it sounds."

Cassidy notices us, tosses an armful of wood onto the pile, and runs over. They beam at me, bouncing from one foot to the other.

"We brought hot dogs and marshmallows," they say. "Wanna make s'mores with me later?"

"Bonfire s'mores?" James asks.

They think about it before shrugging. "Maybe, once it's dark, we can build a small fire over by my tent instead?"

Matthew appears behind Cassidy, having teleported from the far side of the woodpile. He tries to spook them. They don't react, but he doesn't seem even the slightest bit disappointed.

"A small fire's for the best," he says casually. "You'd need a long-ass stick to roast a marshmallow over a bonfire."

"You're not gonna douse the wood with gasoline this year, are you?" James asks.

Matthew laughs. "No explosions this year, dude, I swear, but— Hey, speaking of; you know where Carmen's at?"

Explosions? Wait—

"She's passed out back there," James says, pointing a thumb toward the coolers and sunshades.

He sighs but doesn't appear particularly surprised. Cassidy volunteers to wake her up and runs off without waiting for a response. James watches them for a moment before looking to Matthew.

"You're seriously gonna let her light the fire?" he asks. "You do realize she's already drunk, right?"

"Better her than gasoline, right?"

"Barely!"

As James shakes his head, I ask what they mean, and Matthew explains that Carmen is pyrokinetic. She can create and control fire—sort of, according to James. Sounds like a flashy ability. I guess that explains why she kept it a secret when Natalie first showed off her ability to control water. Fire lacks the same level of subtlety.

"I'm sure she has more control over it now," Matthew says.

"She's passed out drunk, Matt."

"It'll be fiiiine."

"Are you sure immortals aren't magic?" I ask blankly.

"Ugh. No one here is magic!"

Matthew laughs again. "Seriously, man, it'll be fine. If anything goes wrong, Nat can put out the fire with your tears."

"Oh, shut up."

Matthew grins, and James stifles a laugh as he cuffs his friend on the arm. Then Cassidy returns with the Choi twins.

Carmen yawns and fluffs up her hair. "You called?"

"You wanna light the bonfire?" Matthew asks.

"Not the birthday boys?" She looks to James, who shrugs, so Matthew calls out to Jesse, who also shrugs. She thinks about it a moment longer, the sleep slowly clearing from her eyes, then flashes a smile and pats Natalie on the back. "Let Nat do it. She has a huge crush on you, y'know?"

"Seriously?" she hisses.

She doesn't seem embarrassed, exactly, but she hit Carmen with a razor-sharp look, so it's hard to say if what her sister said is true or not. Either way, Matthew laughs.

"I don't care who lights it, but James doesn't want me to pour gasoline on it again, so I'm trying to be a good boy."

Carmen's eyes grow wide, and she gasps before bursting into laughter. "Oh my god, I totally remember that!" She turns to me with a wild grin. "Okay, so, get this: Matt poured a whole can of gas on the driftwood—like five fucking gallons, right? He tossed a match in, and the fire was like *WHOOOSH*— Shot up like twenty feet in the air. And the whole thing exploded! And I mean *really* exploded. A huge bang and everything; like a bomb went off! My ears were ringing the whole fucking night, and wood flew *everywhere*. A splinter the size of my pinkie got stuck in my leg. It was sick as hell."

Natalie sighs. "You should be glad no one died."

"I teleported out of the way," Matthew says mildly. "But it was kinda cool."

"No, seriously, look!"

As Carmen shows off a small, white scar on her thigh, I try to imagine the scenario. A massive fireball as the bonfire exploded. A chunk of wood sticking out of her leg. James averts his eyes—I get the feeling his experience of the event was far from stellar—and her expression softens when she notices his reaction.

"Okay, fine," she says, looking to Matt. "You sold me. I'll do the honor of lighting the lovely mound of wood you've got going on here. And I promise I won't let it explode."

"Sweet. Thanks."

Matthew teleports to stand on top of a cooler between us and the smoker's circle, where he loudly announces that it's time for the bonfire lighting ceremony. There's still at least an hour before sunset, but I imagine lighting it now will up the energy of everyone here. And everyone seems excited as they drift our way and gather around the mound of wood.

Lucas hands Carmen a freshly opened beer bottle as she stands in front of the unlit bonfire, closer than anyone else. She takes a breath, and a drink, before holding her free hand out, low but away from her body. Then she swipes her arm up, as though throwing a ball underhand. An orb of yellow fire erupts in the center of the woodpile and quickly engulfs it, the flames licking several feet into the air.

The crowd cheers, whistling and applauding her performance and the burning pile. I clap too—*because honestly wow.*

Carmen steps back and watches the fire for a moment before turning to face everyone. Beaming, she takes a dramatic bow, then enters the crowd to meet up with Lucas.

I overhear her say that she hasn't played with fire in a while, but I think she did a good job. The heat from the roaring bonfire is intense even from some distance, and the flames appear to have caught even on the dampest pieces of driftwood. And it looked so easy for her.

James seriously doesn't think these abilities are magic?

"Right?" Cassidy exclaims. "It's totally magic. He's in denial!"

James opens his mouth to argue but changes his mind before saying anything—probably realizing there's no point.

Matthew ruffles his sibling's hair. "Cut James some slack, Cass. We can't all be true believers."

"It's sad," they say, nodding in solemn agreement.

I nod also, though I can't keep from smiling, and James rolls his eyes. Then Matthew asks if we want more drinks.

James and I exchange a glance.

I feel fine, so… *As long as we're both comfortable.*

We nod, and Matthew blinks out, reappearing near one of the coolers. He digs through it, removing several bottles. On his way back, he hands a wine cooler to Natalie.

thirty-two

The sun dips lower in the sky. And, as I squint at the golden sun barely a hand's width over the rippling horizon, I remember the sleeping bag and tarp still in the trunk of James' car.

Oops.

We've been hanging out with Matthew, Carmen, Natalie, and a few others in the sand not far from the bonfire. The sand is cool now, instead of warm.

Cassidy is off playing in the water again—capitalizing on the last of the day's heat before the sun goes down and the cold wind picks up. April and Tyler sit in the shallows too. Mina, Hannah, Dawn, and a handful of others are gathered in the distance, listening to EDM and smoking weed.

More tents have been set up around the beach since Carmen lit the fire, but the mythical cake and hard liquor have yet to make an appearance. Though, I spotted a bag of plastic shot glasses near the coolers earlier.

I have never done shots in my life. I still feel good. The tiniest bit warm and fuzzy, but I've been pacing myself and drinking water and snacking, and I feel *nothing* like how I did on the Fourth of July.

One or two shots in another hour or so should be safe, right?

Yeah, we should get the sleeping bag now.

I tap James' shoulder. "We should head up and grab the stuff from the car before it gets too late."

"Ah—" He glances toward the top of the cliff, where the cars are parked, and back at me with a hint of nerves. "Yeah, you're right."

He stands and helps me up. I dust the sand off my thighs with my free hand. As I take a step, ready to leave the circle with James, Carmen says my name. I glance back to find her beaming up at me from her spot on the ground.

"Don't get lost on your way to the car," she says, holding a hand beside her mouth as though it blocks the sound from reaching anyone else. "If you know what I mean."

"Um…"

My eyes flick back to James, who is pointedly ignoring her.

Is this heat from the alcohol or something else?

Natalie swipes Carmen over the back of the head before turning to Matthew on her other side. They laugh as they clink their bottles together—*I think she's drinking more than she meant to.* But Carmen just snorts and hides her face in Lucas' shoulder. He sighs and shakes his head as he rubs her back.

"This'll only take a minute," James says dryly.

We leave the group, holding hands, headed in the direction of the trailhead that leads up to the sandy turnout above.

"Get some, James Reid!" someone calls as we pass the smoker's circle—Mina, I think.

I swear half the beach laughs.

James' hand tightens around mine, and he walks a bit faster. My face is on fire, and he looks frustrated, but I can't help laughing too. Even if it's kind of awkward, the atmosphere on this beach is way different than any of the parties I went to with Rose.

Being with James is different.

As we get further away and the wind snuffs out the voices on the beach, he sighs, and his grip on my hand relaxes.

"It's weird, uh…" He chuckles. When I look up from our hands, he flashes a strange, mild smile. "With you here, even though you're human, everyone has been…so much nicer to me."

Nicer?

I stop a few feet from the trailhead and turn back to look out over the beach. The smokers sitting in the sand or dancing to music played on a bluetooth speaker. Matthew and Carmen in the large group near the bonfire. Cassidy, far away, splashing in the shallow waves.

Thanks to the rumor mill, we're the center of attention, but everyone here has treated James like a good friend they haven't seen in a while. They treat me like any decent person would treat a friend's new partner. But, unlike James, I don't know these people at all. From the sound of it, most of them have known him since high school—at least.

"They weren't always nice to you?"

He scans the beach too. After a moment, he shakes his head and frowns. "I… I honestly don't know anymore. It wasn't like this before. I thought…for sure…that a few of these guys *hated* me, but…"

"It's been years since you went to one of these parties, right?"

"Sure," he says slowly. "But I still see them around. There are other parties. Other things and places. You know?"

I get that, but…

"People change," I say. "Or maybe they never hated you to begin with."

He sighs and glances at the sand between us. "I don't feel like I've changed at all, though. Everyone else is different from what I remember, but I feel exactly the same. I haven't done anything with myself. Until now. For three years, I just…"

James…

Fighting my instinct to hesitate, I reach up. I pat the top of his head, and his eyes flick up from the ground. *Tired. Sad.* I offer a smile.

"I don't care what you've been doing the past three years," I say—and I mean it. "You're here with me now. And we're stuck on this beach overnight, so we need to grab the sleeping bag before it gets dark."

His expression softens. Then he kisses my forehead, and we resume our trek.

Navigating the trail is surprisingly more difficult in human form than it was in feline form. The path is dusty and narrow, and we have to walk in single file, so it's a good thing I kept an eye on my alcohol intake. If I were actually drunk, I might not be able to make it back down.

We reach the top of the cliff safely, but my lungs burn. I stop to catch my breath. James checks on me to make sure I'm not about to pass out or anything—I'll be fine—before walking ahead. Spending most of the summer indoors, in various states of injury, and deliberately hiding from reality seems to have left me a bit out of shape.

My side hasn't bothered me like this in a while, though.

Once I recover, I catch up with James at the car as he pops the trunk and pulls out a red sleeping bag. It's the cheap polyester kind, missing the original storage bag and instead rolled up and bound tightly with old shoelaces. He stares at it for a few seconds, then grabs a small drawstring bag that must contain the tarp.

"Maybe I should've brought a tent," he says before slamming the trunk shut.

"It'll be fine. We make your tiny bed work, so sharing a sleeping bag in feline form will be nothing."

He glances away, scratching his jaw. "Yeah, I guess..."

I look back toward the beach. The sun has already sunk well below the cliff and will set over the water soon. We probably shouldn't stay here much longer. The trail will be more difficult to navigate in the dark. But it's been a while since I went out of my way to watch a sunset, and I've never seen the sun set over the ocean before.

When will I get another chance?

So I ask, "Will you watch the sunset with me?"

"Up here?" When I nod, he glances past me, to the top of the ridge. "Oh. Sure. We can hang out for a minute if you want."

We walk up the path cut in the scrubby grass, and I search for a place to sit that isn't covered by dry, prickly-looking plants.

"There's a good spot over here," James says.

He points off to the right of the trailhead, indicating a flat slab of reddish stone half-buried in the sand only a couple feet from the edge of the cliff. He steps onto the rock, shifting his weight to test its stability. It doesn't wobble, so it looks good to me too. He drops the sleeping bag and tarp off to one side, and we sit close enough that our thighs touch.

The whole cove is visible from up here.

The bonfire burns brightly on the sandy beach, orange and blue-tipped flames licking the air. Most everyone has gathered to form a single, large group in the vicinity of the bonfire—with the exception of Cassidy, still playing in the surf, and Carmen, who seems to be struggling to set up a tent alone not far from Cassidy's yellow tent. The distant voices of the chatty, laughing partygoers are muffled by the wind and waves, little more than a murmur on the salty breeze.

The sky is light blue and dotted by soft, lavender clouds. The sun nearly touches the horizon, casting a golden glow over the water, and the wind carries a fresh chill.

The world is still beautiful. Sometimes.

"Hey, Jayde, ah…" James' expression is mild, but he flashes a smile as our eyes meet. "Why do you like me?"

"Why?" I echo.

"Yeah." He looks out over the beach, the line of his mouth more serious. "It's kinda fucked up, isn't it? How we got together, I mean?"

Oh?

"For a while, I thought you were only staying with me because you were scared of being alone—just scared of Ice, you know?

Or because you had no other option. 'Cause Rose was out of town and you don't have family around here or whatever. But… that's stupid, isn't it?"

"It's not stupid," I say slowly.

"No?"

"No."

He sighs. "For a while, I think I wanted to be with you so bad because *I* was desperate. *I* didn't want to be alone. I was terrified of being left alone—still am, to be honest. But, now that I've had some time to think about it, I… I feel like I have no idea what we're doing." He laughs, clasping his hands in his lap. "Ah… Sorry if it seems like this is coming out of nowhere."

"It's fine," I say as a creeping unease settles in my mind. "I get what you mean."

I think.

He glances over, a hint of tension in his wary smile. "So, why do you like me? What is there to like?"

"Oh—"

I *do* understand. I've worried about the same thing.

Were we only together because we were both afraid of being alone? Was James a shallow rebound at first? A shield I could hide behind? Or an outlet for the emotions I had to suppress while I was with Ice?

For a while, I didn't know. I wasn't sure, and it scared me.

But the past month has relieved that uncertainty. My feelings for James are real. How could I doubt that after the gut-wrenching fear I felt, thinking he might die? Considering the lengths I was willing to go to just to improve our situation in any way…

And the longing I feel every time I look at him.

"I don't know why I like you," I admit.

His expression shifts, eyes flicking toward the horizon, and I start laughing as my cheeks flush hot.

"No, wait a second! Hear me out," I say, struggling to crush my laughter. Thankfully, he meets my gaze, vaguely humored, and I take a deep breath. "Right. Anyway, this summer has been insane, for sure. But we get along, don't we? You're sweet, and you're funny, and I know I can count on you to be there for me. I really like you. And I want to be with you. So, even if I don't know exactly *why* I feel the way I do, I think it's fine. Don't you?"

"Yeah, I... I guess that's fine." He flashes a timid smile, then leans back to watch the sky. "You know, uh... If it makes you feel better, I doubt what I felt in...most of July was real. It wasn't like this at all. During that storm... I was in a bad place. A real bad place. Ah... I was jealous—of what, who fucking knows anymore. But I was pissed and desperate and *tired*. I mean, I'm sure you could tell. I was pretty fucked up. But it's not like that anymore. Now, I *know* how I feel. I know I'm in love with *you*, and not just the idea of you. Or whatever it was before."

My heart quickens.

James' eyes reflect the yellow light of the sun. The shadows beneath them seem lighter than when we first met. For once, he truly does look *okay*. No lingering darkness hiding behind his soft smile. No distant melancholy in his eyes.

And I have never felt like this before.

Not with Ice. Not with anyone.

"I love you," I say.

His smile widens, crinkling his eyes. He tucks a strand of loose hair that must have escaped from my bun behind my ear. When he kisses me, my breath catches. But I'm done being scared. I'm done holding back. I throw my arms around him, pressing myself closer and deepening the kiss. He holds my face in his hands. His warmth all but erases the wind's chill, and I feel his heart beat fast through his shirt.

This is how it should be, right?

An actual relationship.

I shouldn't have to wonder how the other person feels. I should *know*. Because they should tell me, and I should be able to feel it myself. And, with James, I do. I know how he feels about me, and I know how I feel about him, and we're okay.

In this moment, *we are okay.*

He hugs me, nuzzling his face in my neck. I comb my fingers through his short, messy hair. And the sun touches the horizon, setting the sky and sea on fire. I watch the color change over the top of James' head and wish we could stay out here forever. I wish we could just hold each other on the beach and never go back to Riverview, even after everyone else leaves.

But...we can't.

James sighs and kisses my neck once more before sitting up. And my heart seizes when I notice the tear tracks glistening on his cheeks in the warm light.

"Are you okay?"

He laughs and wipes his face with his arm. "Yeah, I'm fine. I just— No, I'm fine."

I touch his face to remove the last trace of dampness with my thumb, and his hands raise to hold my wrist. I hold my breath as he holds my arm in one hand and slips the wristband off with the other. The loop of grey fabric falls to the rock between us. My eyes lock onto the raised, heart-shaped scar. Then he lifts my wrist to his lips and gently kisses the marred skin.

"Everything will be okay, Jayde."

"I know."

Does he really believe that, though?

His eyes flick up to meet mine. "You honestly believe that?"

Jinx.

"I have to believe it," I say. "What else can I do?"

He returns my hand, smiling again, and looks out over the edge of the cliff. "I'll keep trying. To see things the way you do, I mean. I'm sick of living like this—just…surviving. Barely. I wanna enjoy the little things too, so…"

I feel myself frown as I massage the scar on my wrist. Maybe hiding it is silly at this point. Maybe I should let it go. Carmen already guessed that my scars have something to do with Ice. Maybe the others have too. Either way, what difference does it make if anyone sees it? What could anyone possibly say about me that's any worse than what Paige said earlier?

The damn thing itches, and it's getting dark, anyway.

I stuff the knit sweatband into my pocket and check out the sky again. Only a sliver of sun pokes out from the glowing, red horizon, and the sky above is growing darker.

This feels familiar, somehow.

"Should we head back?" James asks with a mild laugh. "It's

almost dark. They might start wondering what happened to us."

"Not yet. I wanna stay here a little longer."

"Okay."

Something...

I lean on James' shoulder and watch the beach. Everyone's hanging out near the bonfire now. The bright flames cast long, dancing shadows behind them. I'm sure they are waiting for us to come back. Holding off on cake and shots for us.

After all, the party is for James' birthday.

"Are you cold?" he asks.

I say *no*, but he slings an arm over my shoulder and pulls me close. I don't mind. He's warm and comfortable, and the wind's starting to pick up.

He's right, though. We should head back soon. It's almost dark. Everyone's waiting.

But I'm not ready to let this moment end.

I turn to watch the sky again. Ahead, there's a touch of pink and orange, but the sky directly overhead is navy blue. The faint pinprick of stars appear in droves.

Even if we should leave, I still don't want to.

And, right now, I don't have to.

"Anyway," James says slowly. "Ready to find out how stupid I get when I drink?"

I laugh, but I shake my head. "As fun as that sounds, I think I want one more minute of this."

"Just one more?" he asks, his voice humored.

I don't have a better excuse, so I look back to the sky without answering. Clouds are starting to blow in from over the ocean, but the sky inland is clear, and, though the moon is almost full, the stars are bright. The Big Dipper. The silvery stripe of the Milky Way. I've never seen anything like it in Riverview.

"The stars are out," I say.

"So they are."

As I stare at the sky—at the twinkling stars—the curious sense of familiarity strikes again. This time, it hits me more like a train.

Because I have seen this before. Weeks ago. In my dreamscape.

Right.

I glance at James. The same as in the dream, he's watching me with warm, glittering eyes. I'm not sure he ever stopped to look at the stars.

"You're beautiful," he says.

I don't know why it makes me laugh.

Then a sound—*a faint, high-pitched whistle*—stops my heart. I look out over the beach and catch sight of the ember not even a second before the shell explodes a hundred feet above us and blooms into a huge multicolored flower. The group near the bonfire cheers, and the colorful sparks flicker out as they fall to the sand.

Fireworks.

I turn to James, who seems far less surprised than me that a skyrocket was just set off on the beach.

"They're getting impatient," he says. "We should head down before Matt decides to come up here himself."

"Oh, um… He brought the fireworks?"

"He makes the fireworks. He does it every year since he picked up the hobby in high school."

Right. I knew that. I have several questions about James' past and how everyone else ties into it, but this is absolutely *not* the time or place to bring Ice up *again*.

"Well, um…" I sigh. "I guess we should go, huh?"

Without waiting for a response, I stand and peer further over the edge. Everyone has gone back to hanging out near the bonfire, not seeming to do much of anything. Just waiting for us, I guess.

"If anyone asks why we took so long getting back, just blame it on me. Since staying up here was my idea."

He laughs. "Ah, man… It doesn't matter what we tell them. You know what they'll think."

They seriously think we'd stop and have sex in his car or something? *I mean, I guess we could have done that, but—*

James steps down and walks ahead, the sleeping bag tucked under one arm, but I hang behind. Still standing on the sandstone slab, I indulge in one last look up. The darkened, starry sky is the same as the one from my dream. This spot in the sand is the same too. *And the way James looked at me…*

If that dream was prophetic, at least it was something pleasant. Nothing of consequence. *Nothing bad.* But what does that mean for the others?

"You coming?" James calls from near the trailhead.

His soft smile is clearly visible in the fading light. I push my concerns to the back of my mind—*I'll worry about my dreams later.* Then I nod, step down from the rock, and run to meet up with him. His smile warms. I reach for his free hand, and, as we start down the trail, I can only hope…*that we will be fine.*

thirty-three

Carmen and Cassidy meet us at the bottom of the trail. Cassidy looks somewhat less energetic than earlier, and Carmen looks plain drunk.

"God," she groans. "Took you guys long enough. Just grabbing a sleeping bag? It'll only be a minute? Uh-huh. It's been like half an hour at least."

James groans. "The kid can read your mind, you know?"

Carmen blinks and glances at Cassidy. They avert their eyes, and she looks back to James with a shrug.

"Anyway," she says, "Cass here wanted your girlfriend's help to build a fire. A small one over there. I said I'd do it, but they insist it *has* to be Jayde."

"You can light the fire," Cassidy says. "I was just waiting for Jayde, so we could all make s'mores together."

"S'mores sound good," I agree.

James looks past them, toward those hanging out in the light cast by the raging bonfire. Some are sitting, some are standing, and someone—might be Hannah—is playing ukulele, but I can't hear if anyone is singing along over the wind and waves. Either way, no one seems bothered by our absence or excited by our return despite James' suggestion that Matthew only launched that skyrocket to get our attention.

"I'm sure we can spare a few minutes," he says.

Cassidy grins. "Alright, let's go!"

They take off down the beach toward their tent, morphing after several paces. The rest of us remain in human form and walk.

"I remember being that age," Carmen says. "Still thinking that running around as a cat was the coolest thing ever. Nat and I, we'd chase other kids on the playground and bite their ankles."

James sort of averts his gaze and doesn't say anything. I hold his free hand, but I am curious.

"Can immortals morph from birth?" I ask.

"No," he says. "Kids usually start around age four or five."

Carmen cackles, slapping her bare thigh as she nearly doubles over. "Can you imagine, though? A woman walking around with her baby, and the fuckin' baby turns into a kitten in the middle of the grocery store? Normies would freak."

We laugh along with her, but I can't help picturing James' younger self realizing that he still can't morph when his peers—including his identical twin—could years earlier. He probably can't relate to Carmen's perspective of a *normal* immortal childhood at all.

We meet Cassidy near their tent, where they already have several chunks of driftwood carefully arranged inside a ring of smooth stones. They kneel in front of the makeshift fire pit and shove a handful of paper napkins into the woodpile.

"Okay," they say. "It's ready if you wanna light it."

"Sure thing, kid."

Carmen drops to sit in the sand across from Cassidy. She holds a closed fist in front of the driftwood piled inside the circle of stones. When she opens her hand, a small fireball engulfs the paper in the center and licks at the wood around it.

Cassidy's face lights up in the fire's glow. "Wow! It's just as cool as before."

"Thanks," Carmen says. She leans back, planting her hands in the sand. "I don't get to use it often. No fireplace at home, you know?"

James makes a soft noise, and I glance over in time to catch him rolling his eyes.

Once it looks like the flames caught and have no intention of going out, Cassidy jumps up and dips into their tent. A moment later, they return with a cloth shopping bag and pass out s'mores ingredients and forked marshmallow roasting sticks.

We settle around the fire and chat as we roast marshmallows. James' catches fire, and he tries to convince us it was intentional —something Cassidy points out isn't true. Carmen gets melted marshmallow goo all over her fingers while trying to construct her s'more. But we all manage to eat one, and it was fun.

I wouldn't mind sticking around a while longer, but it's after 9PM. We've been away from the main party long enough.

I thank Cassidy for the snack, and they smile brightly as James, Carmen, and I stand and brush the sand off our legs. They stare into the smoldering fire for a long moment before looking up again.

"Thanks for hanging out with me," they say. "I'm almost ready for bed, so it's okay that you can't stick around."

"Don't forget to put your fire out," James says. "Just to be safe, you gotta douse the coals with water."

They nod and flash a grin. "I won't forget. Have fun!"

We exchange goodnights before leaving Cassidy and their tent behind. James drops the sleeping bag with the tarp stuffed inside beneath an abandoned sunshade on our way to the crowd gathered around the bonfire. We make it close enough to feel the warmth before Jesse and a few others passively acknowledge our return.

I expected Matthew to fuss over James for being gone so long, but he's busy—*busy* as in sitting in the sand several feet away from everyone else and making out with Natalie.

Somehow, this does not actually surprise me.

Carmen snickers. "They've been on each other like that for a while now. But I wasn't lying when I said she has a crush on him. I was trying to do her a favor. Guess it worked."

"Guess so," James says dryly.

When they eventually stop to breathe, Matthew spots us. He pops up from the sand and disappears, reappearing in the center of the crowd, where he says something to Tyler.

In response, Tyler raises his half-empty beer bottle over his head. "Y'all ready for cake and shots?"

Several cheer, including Carmen, who breaks away from us to meet up with Lucas and collect Natalie from the ground.

"Oh, great," James mutters.

While Tyler digs through a small drink cooler beside Mina and Hannah—who are preoccupied with each other in their own right—Matthew and April start passing out plastic shot glasses.

"We'll be fine," I say as I accept one of the tiny red cups.

Matthew gives one to James before moving on. Soon enough, everyone who is drinking has a shot glass. Then Tyler and Mina make the rounds with bottles of liquor, and Matthew and April pass out slices of cake on small paper plates—without utensils, apparently. I accept a plate from April and hold out my cup as Mina comes by with a bottle of tequila.

She flashes a smile, either uncaring or unaware of the perfectly formed red lipstick stain on her cheek. "Wait until everyone's ready," she says. "For this first shot, we're all gonna go at the same time."

We agree, and Mina fills our shot glasses. I stare at the golden liquid in the tiny cup. The surface reflects the bonfire's chaotic, dancing light. *It's kinda dizzying.*

"You sure you're cool with this?" James asks. "We don't have to drink if it bothers you, you know? I don't mind."

I nod.

He doesn't know what I did on the Fourth of July. I mean, he knew I was at Ice's house, and I mentioned drinking too much, but I never told him that I kissed Ice. He doesn't know I was so embarrassed I couldn't face anyone after.

James has *no idea* that a stupid, drunk kiss is the only reason I was alone at the house while he happened to be sneaking around. He's never asked, but it's bad enough that he knows Ice and I kissed once.

"It's fine," I assure him. "I'm having fun."

Our eyes meet, and he smiles.

We mingle with the others for a few minutes. Then Matthew

stands in front of the bonfire, a dark silhouette with reflective eyes against the near-blinding light.

He claps to get everyone's attention, the crowd falls relatively quiet, and he speaks, "As I'm sure you all know, I threw this party for my dear friends, James and Jesse. They turn twenty-one this week, so, in their honor, we're gonna get lit tonight."

Several in the crowd cheer.

"Now, let's get the birthday boys up here." Matthew has to stop to laugh as Carmen, who is surely already lit, whistles loudly. "Come on, guys!"

James hesitates, glancing at me rather than moving. I flash a smile, and he exhales deeply before mirroring it. Then he steps away to join Matthew and Jesse in front of the fire. Jesse passes a shot glass to Matthew, who stands between the two. James blinks, awkward as usual, as Matthew drapes an arm over his shoulder and raises his tiny cup into the air.

"It's your birthday, so you go first," Matthew says, his voice barely audible over the wind and crackling fire. "Cheers!"

The twins "clink" their plastic cups together before downing the shots in unison. James' nose wrinkles as he looks up to face the crowd with some uncertainty, while Jesse pumps his arm into the air and cheers. Matthew pats James on the back and tells everyone to have fun before taking his own shot.

As several call out *Happy Birthday!* and start drinking, Natalie catches my attention, and we down our tequila together. The cold liquid is smooth at first, but the burn hits right after. I cough to clear my throat.

Natalie coughs too, holding a loose fist to her lips, but quickly recovers as James and Matthew pick us out of the crowd.

"How's it going, ladies?" Matthew asks.

"We're good, right?" she asks with a glance at me.

I nod, amazed by the tequila's lingering warmth as it settles in my stomach. The taste isn't as harsh as Night's spiked strawberry lemonade, but I'm not sure how to feel about that considering the shot was straight liquor.

"Perfect. Glad to hear it." Matthew grins. "I can expedite the next shot if you want?"

Natalie thinks about it for a second before smiling. She gives her plastic cup to him. Her cheeks are flushed, but it's hard to say whether the alcohol, our proximity to the bonfire, or her previous one-on-one time with Matthew is to blame. Either way, it's kind of funny. *And cute.*

Wait— *Didn't she tell me to keep her away from the liquor?*

"James?" Matthew asks.

"Maybe one more," he says.

He looks to me. I shrug, so we hand over our shot glasses, and Matthew teleports off to wherever the booze is hiding.

While we wait, I try to eat my cake without the help of any utensils—since asking around never produced any. I resort to carefully nibbling a bite off the top. Rich chocolate cake with white buttercream frosting. It tastes homemade.

April brought the cake, right? Did she bake it herself?

"So much for not drinking today," Natalie says with a sigh.

James laughs and grimaces at the same time. "Right? I wasn't expecting to get so into it either."

"It's your birthday. You deserve to have fun."

"Yeah, I guess," he agrees. He picks up his slice of cake with his bare hands to take a bite. "But I was worried Jayde might feel left out if I drank much."

"I'm having fun," I say. *And I'm drinking too, so I'm not being left out at all.*

Matthew reappears with our refilled shot glasses and passes them out. Somehow, I can already smell the pungent cinnamon over the ocean and smoke. I've seen fireball whiskey at several parties. Everyone always made a big deal out of it, like it's a fun drink, but I never had the nerve to try it. *How many shots can I handle? Maybe I should stop after this…*

"Cheers," Matthew says.

The four of us tap our tiny cups together and down them at the same time. It's like drinking a handful of red-hot candies dissolved in nail polish remover—spicy cinnamon and sickly sweet syrup with a powerful alcoholic kick.

It's…*not bad.* This is kinda fun.

Matthew asks if we want anything else, listing off all of the drink options he knows of.

James shrugs. "Whatever's fine with me."

I missed half of what Matthew said, but I acknowledge my weak human nature and opt to forgo the hard liquor moving forward.

Natalie sides with me, so, as the guys go for tequila mixed into half-empty cans of Mountain Dew, we accept wine coolers. We talk and laugh, and Matthew regales us with several stories of past bonfires that I can only assume are slightly exaggerated. Hanging out with them is fun. *It's a lot of fun.* But, eventually, we all finish our cake, and Matthew and Natalie excuse themselves to carry on with their business elsewhere.

James and I toss our paper plates into the bonfire. We watch them burn and turn to ash and crumble to nothing in the flames. Then Jesse, Alex, and Stephen find us. They ask if they can borrow James. He hesitates, but—

This is his party.

"Go," I say with a smile. "I'll be fine here until you're done."

He nods, and the guys leave, heading to the south, while I stay by the bonfire.

Standing too close to the flames is uncomfortably hot. But the air is cold now, and the wind is even colder. It takes a few minutes to find the perfect spot to stand. Then I look around. It feels less crowded all of a sudden. Several people seem to have left the area entirely—to set up tents or change into warmer clothes, I think. I'd go change clothes too, but I'd have to walk to the cave, and James went that way, and I don't want to distract him from hanging out with his friends the whole time we're here.

Aah...

I spot Hannah and Mina off to the left. They're taking a selfie with the bonfire in the background, one girl kissing the other's cheek.

Hey, that's a good idea.

I move further back, just into the *a bit too cool* zone, and pull my phone from my pocket. I open the camera app, switch the facecam on, and adjust the exposure until the flames don't wash out the image. Then I hold my arm out and struggle to steady my hand long enough for the camera to focus on my face.

And I hear it. Somehow, over the crackling bonfire and chatty partygoers and wind and crashing ocean waves, I hear a faint, whistling *ziiiiiip*, and my chest grows tight.

BANG!

I flinch, dropping my phone as a smattering of color reflects off the sand, even brighter than the light cast by the bonfire.

Ugh.

As I retrieve my phone, an image flashes through my mind. *The Fourth of July. Metal sparklers and strawberry lemonade. A warm arm slung over my shoulder. A selfie on my phone.*

Frustrated, I back out of the camera and open my photo library. It takes a bit of scrolling, but both the selfie I took with Ice and the candid photo that Night took of us on the edge of the patio are there. The stupid emoji sticker hides his face in her photo. But, in the photo he let me take, he's smiling.

We look like a totally normal couple.

I forgot about these pictures. I forgot, but seeing them now makes me *so angry. Why lead me on if you didn't give a shit?*

As I stare at the soft warmth in his expression, my eyes flood with moisture. My thumb hovers over the delete button—the tiny, blue trash can in the corner—but the screen dims and locks before I convince myself to tap it. My teeth grit. My grip on the phone tightens. The yellow flames behind me reflect off the black screen.

I wanna throw it.

I want to turn around and chuck my stupid phone into the raging bonfire. I wanna watch the screen warp and the metal buckle and the battery pop. I want to buy a new phone and change my number and never think about Ice Monroe ever again.

But I don't do it.

I don't turn. I don't throw my phone.

Instead, I take a deep breath. I wipe my eyes. Then I unlock my phone and take the cute bonfire selfie I wanted to take. And it turns out good. I look good. My bun is mostly intact, and the fire looks cool in the background.

As I'm touching up the photo's contrast, I hear Carmen. Hardly a second later, she's throwing an arm over my shoulder.

"Jayde," she croons, pressing her warm cheek to mine. "Why are you out here all alone, huh? Where the hell'd your dumbass boyfriend go? You need help finding him or something?"

"He left with a few guys," I mumble. "They might be setting off fireworks?"

She steps back and blinks. "Hey, were you taking pictures just now? Can I take more with you?"

I smile. "Sure."

thirty-four

After taking a series of admittedly fun selfies with Carmen, Natalie approaches us. She's alone and has nothing better to do, so we take a few more pictures as a trio before resolving to look for James and Matthew—who left Natalie around the same time James took off with Jesse and the others.

The energy around the bonfire is steadily growing more mellow even as April continues feeding driftwood to the fire. At least half the group is missing from the immediate area, and a few seem to have already turned in for the night.

"James went that way," I say, pointing to the south. I can't see much of anything down there, but it's the direction the sky-rocket was set off from.

The three of us head out, leaving the bonfire and its warmth behind. The beach is cold now. Windy and dark and kinda creepy, with the only real light coming from the moon. I hug my arms to reserve heat. But Natalie soon points out the silhouette of a group in the distance, halfway between the bonfire and sandstone cave, and Carmen grabs my hand to lead me through the dark, and I feel better—if still cold.

As we make our way closer, I see a spark of light. The tiny

flame of a lighter, held low to the ground. A few seconds pass, and then—

Ziiiiiip—

I track the firework's path into the sky.

BANG!

The blast reverberates in my chest as it explodes into an orb of yellow and red sparks that consumes the entire sky for a moment. Then a chunk of smoldering cardboard lands in the sand with a thud, and I hear the guys laughing over the howling wind.

Carmen drops my hand to run ahead. "Hey, losers!"

Natalie and I do not run. But I was right. James is with them. Matthew is too, along with the three James left the bonfire with.

"How many fireworks did ya bring, anyway?" Carmen asks, hands on her hips.

"I only got a couple big ones left," Matthew says with a glance at a cardboard box on the sand. "But I bet Alex fifty bucks that he couldn't catch one of the spent shells as they fall."

She grins. "Oh, yeah? You catch one yet?"

Alex shakes his head, and both Carmen and Matthew laugh.

"Might lose your hand if you did," Jesse says.

"But it'd be sick as hell!"

These guys are insane. I could barely handle standing a hundred feet from a skyrocket being set off, but they're hanging out *right there* like it's nothing.

James steps around the metal plate they've been launching the fireworks from and looks me over with no discernible unease, which is both comforting and a surprise.

"You good?" he asks.

"Yeah, I'm fine. But Carmen accused you of abandoning me, so I thought I should at least check on you."

His smile hitches up on one side as he glances at her. She's still excitedly chatting up Matthew and Alex about the fireworks while Natalie hangs a couple steps away.

"Oh, yeah? Where's Lucas?"

"No clue. She was alone when she caught me."

He sighs before turning to everyone. "Hey, Matt. I'm gonna head back to the bonfire, if that's cool with you."

"Yeah, it's cool," Matthew says, not paying us much mind.

I wave to Natalie, who waves back, and we head north again.

We reach the bonfire, where we warm up and hang out for a while. We take a few pictures in the same vein as the ones I took with Carmen and Natalie—James laughs when I show off the funniest ones. We grab new drinks and another slice of cake to share. We sit in the sand and talk with Mina, Hannah, and April about the cake. She did bake it herself.

Then James and I head to the small, pop-up day shelter we left the sleeping bag under. We're a good distance away from everyone else now. We're alone.

I stand and listen to the wind. The waves. The crackling fire, and the voices of those still gathered around it. Faint ukulele notes. And I watch the dark line where the sky meets the sea. The pale, ghostly glow of the waves washing over the sand.

This is what it's like?

The beach at night.

Goosebumps prickle my arms. I look back to James, and we dip into the shelter and out of the cold wind. As he sits in the sand, I carefully let my hair out of the bun it's been confined to all day. My hair is wavy as hell thanks to the humidity and misty breeze, but I tease it out as best I can. Then I sit in James' lap and continue watching the dark horizon while he combs his fingers through my hair, working out more tangles.

It's quiet. For a few minutes, it's like I'm not really *thinking* about anything. I'm just existing. On the beach. In this weird, surreal moment in the dark.

Then James asks, "How do you feel?"

"What do you mean?"

"Drinking so much, I guess," he says slowly. "I dunno."

"Hm..."

I feel the familiar warmth swirling in my chest. A fuzziness in the back of my head. A curious, artificial drowsiness. All similar to the Fourth. It's been a long day, though, so maybe I am just tired.

"I feel okay," I say. "You?"

"I'm feeling the alcohol now."

"You had fun, though?"

"Some."

"Oh?" I ask sharply, turning in his lap to plant my hands on his shoulders. "Only some?"

After a beat spent staring with wide eyes, he sucks in a breath through his teeth. Then he glances aside, chuckles, and drinks from his soda can. Only then does he meet my gaze again.

"There were a couple rough patches," he says mildly. "But you made it...tolerable."

Mm...

Maybe I drank a bit more than I should have. But it's fine. I meant what I said earlier. I'm having fun. And I feel safe here. I love James, and I know he feels the same way. He'll look out for me. But I'm not *that* drunk. And I'm not worried either.

When I kiss him, I'm not afraid he might reject me. He doesn't tense at my touch—not even for a second. His hands move to my back, and he reciprocates the kiss, and *it's what I want.*

It's not embarrassing. Or frustrating. Or confusing.

Our eyes meet again. Half his face is illuminated by the distant bonfire, flickering light reflected in one eye as he watches me, our faces hardly an inch apart.

Then he flashes a broad smile that crinkles the corners of his eyes. "You'll still be here when I wake up, right?"

"Of course," I say with a laugh. "You're my ride. Where would I go?"

"Hm… I feel like we've had this conversation before."

"Something like it. Maybe."

Soft rain pattering on the roof, collecting in puddles in the gravel. The end of a storm. The start of something far worse.

His smile softens, and he kisses my cheek. As he leans back, all I can bring myself to do is stare at him. He does seem different here. Softer. Calmer. Maybe it's the alcohol. Maybe it's the change of scenery. The noisy sort of quiet the beach provides. I'm not sure what it is, but he hardly seems like the same guy who begged me to stay *just one night* at Reid Manor.

"Can I…" His expression shifts, and he sighs before looking at me more seriously. "Can I ask you something?"

"Go for it."

"I feel kinda weird asking now, but—" He laughs with a hint of unease. "Why did Ice kiss you? That day, when— Well, you know the one?"

"Oh."

Alarm flashes over his face, and he downs another gulp of his spiked soda. "Oh, ah— I'm sorry. You don't have to answer that. I'm just curious, but it's okay if you don't want—"

"No, it's fine," I mumble.

He rubs his nose. I glance away, toward the fire, and try to work out what to say. The question wasn't one I expected—I don't know exactly what I was expecting him to ask—but I understand why he might be curious. And this is hardly the *most* upsetting thing we could talk about when it comes to Ice.

It's awkward that we were both thinking about him, though.

I force a smile. "I, um… I was finally trying to tell him how I felt about him, you know? But, even though we'd been practically dating for weeks, he said he didn't feel the same way. I really liked him. He told me about immortals. He was my sponsor. We spent a lot of time together, and I really liked him, so it… It hurt to hear that. I almost left. I just wanted to go home, but then…"

"He kissed you? After saying that?" he asks sharply. When I nod, he thinks about it for a moment before grimacing. "Fuck. Sorry. I mean, yeah, that does sound like something he'd do, but come on…"

"Yeah? Well, I fell for it." I don't bother masking the disdain that slips into my voice. "I stayed with him, even after what he did to you. Even after he came inside with blood on his hands. But I… I couldn't stop thinking about it."

He brushes my hair out of my face. I place a hand over his as it rests on my cheek.

This is frustrating, though.

I want to ask about his history with Ice too. I know there's so much more to it than anyone has told me, but I don't think James would explain now. He's never wanted to talk about it before. Surely, it's too much to discuss at a party where we're supposed to be having a good time.

"You know I don't care what happened between you and Ice, right?" he asks.

You keep saying that, but—

"Nothing happened between us," I mutter. "He kissed me *one* time, but it was nothing like this." *I don't care what Night thinks.* "Ice never cared about me."

"I care about you," James says.

I laugh despite myself. "I know you do."

He kisses me again, and I feel a little bit better.

thirty-five

"Ready to go?" James asks.

"Back to the cave? Are you tired?"

He shrugs, but I agree to head back, so we help each other up off the sand. My legs are unsteady, but I get the hang of walking as I step out of the shelter and into the ocean wind. Cold, moist air prickles the hair on my bare arms and legs, and I shiver.

It's damn cold now, and most stars are hidden by low clouds, but the beach itself is gorgeous at night.

James tucks the sleeping bag under one arm, so he can still hold my hand, and we set off.

As we approach the bonfire, Matthew pops up out of nowhere, having teleported to meet us. He's slightly disheveled, wearing a tracksuit with the jacket unzipped rather than the tank top and swim trunks he was wearing earlier, but it looks like he's having a fantastic evening. Though, I find myself wishing I had a jacket too.

"Sup?" he asks. "Need more drinks?"

"Nah."

I stopped drinking alcohol after the last wine cooler and still have a water bottle in my free hand, and James hasn't finished his drink yet. But Matthew doesn't seem to mind.

He pats James on the back and leans in to loudly whisper, "So, you see any action yet? I hear ya took forever grabbing that sleeping bag earlier."

Ha...

"Uh-huh," James mutters. "The most action I've seen today is you all over Natalie Choi."

We all glance at Natalie, standing several yards away. She awkwardly adjusts the bikini top beneath her unbuttoned cardigan and waves at us. Matthew returns the wave before turning back to James.

"Fair enough," he says more mildly. "Well, even if you don't get laid, I'm glad you showed up. Thanks for hanging out with us."

"Yeah, okay. No problem. But she's right here, dude."

I take a drink of water in an attempt to keep from laughing. Matthew notices, and his smile cracks a bit wider.

"Jayde seems cool," he says. "Less of a square than you, anyway. Were you even watching when she gave Paige that sick black eye?"

"What does that have to do with anything?"

James' grip on my hand tightens, but Matthew laughs as though he said something terribly funny. To be fair, this is silly, and he clearly doesn't mean anything by it. There's no reason to get defensive.

"Never mind; never mind," Matthew relents, recovering from his laughing fit. "See ya in the morning, dude. Don't get too carried away."

James sighs again. "Yeah, whatever. Goodnight, man."

"Goodnight," I say.

Matthew salutes with a grin and teleports back to Natalie. He says something to her, and they both laugh, leaning on each other for support. I look to James, who meets my gaze, tired and frustrated. I hold a hand over my mouth, but the laughter finally bubbles over.

"What is so funny?" he asks, eyes wide.

"It's nothing; just that Matthew reminds me so much of Rose. She doesn't have a filter or know when to shut up either, especially when she drinks."

"Told you they were similar," he says dryly.

Ah... I miss her.

I warm my hands near the bonfire, then we continue past it. A few stragglers take notice and call out *goodnight* to us. I wave to Mina and Hannah before walking into the dark with James.

There's still a group of guys gathered around the makeshift firework launch pad. Two have phone flashlights on, beams aimed down like they're looking for something in the sand. Jesse calls out to us, and James drops my hand as we approach the group.

Jesse looks as tipsy as most everyone else does. Alex and Stephen are here, but Carmen isn't. She might have gone to bed already.

"What's up?" James asks.

"Alex lost the lighter," Stephen calls from several feet away, where he's shining light on the sand.

Jesse sighs, ignoring the others, and looks to James. "You having a good time?" When James nods, Jesse points out the sleeping bag under his arm. "Heading in for the night now?"

"Guess so. It's getting late."

"I'm glad you made it this year, James." His expression grows surprisingly serious. "You look like you're doing better."

James smiles. "Yeah. I'm good."

Jesse holds out an arm, prompting a hug, and James hesitates before moving to accept it. Their brief side-hug is awkward to watch—since they're both holding open drinks, and James has a sleeping bag under one arm—but Jesse doesn't seem to notice. He beams at us, looking a bit sleepy, as he steps back.

"I'll see you around," he says.

"Yeah," James says with a nod. "Goodnight."

I offer a small wave, and James watches as Jesse turns away to regroup with his friends, who are still scanning the sand on the far side of the metal plate.

"Where the hell'd you drop the lighter?" Stephen asks loudly.

"Dunno. I swear I had it in my pocket."

Jesse stops atop the metal plate, glances down for a second, and plants his hands on his hips. "Bro, how fucked up are you right now? Valdez! It's here in the box."

With a sigh, James takes my hand again, and we keep walking. Darkness creeps in and the air gets even colder the further south we go. With only faint moonlight filtered through clouds illuminating the beach, I can barely see. I stick close to James and listen to the wind and the waves. I can't hear the bonfire anymore. I can't make out any voices behind us.

BANG!

The sound and bright flash of colorful light in my periphery make me jump, but it's only a skyrocket set off too close for comfort. Then I get the hiccups, and I feel compelled to say *something*, so the only sounds aren't the ocean and my stupid hiccuping.

"Can you see in the dark better now?"

"Uh... I mean—" James laughs. "Sorta? I know where I'm going, at least."

"Okay, good. I can't see anything."

Despite the dark, we reach the cave in one piece. I don't miss the wind, and the air inside feels at least ten degrees warmer.

I turn my phone's flashlight on while James digs a small metal flashlight out of his backpack. Then he places it on the ground near the center of the cave, pointed at the ceiling. Somehow, that single light is enough to light up the entire space and cast long, dramatic shadows on the walls.

James gets to work arranging the tarp and sleeping bag on the cave floor, so I step away to dig through my own bag.

"You never told me if you're actually tired," I say.

"Oh, well... I'm not *that* tired, but I could tell you were getting cold. I thought we should come back, so you could put something warmer on, you know?"

I guess we were on the same page.

"So, you want to hang out here, then?"

"That's up to you," he says. "Whether you wanna stay here and hang out or go to sleep or grab a coat and head back to the bonfire. Mina's practically a vampire, so I'm sure she'll keep it going a few more hours."

Am I tired? Hm...

"Let's stay here," I decide aloud. "It's warmer anyway."

"Sounds good."

I finally find my fleece-lined leggings and the lightweight hoodie I stole from James a few days back, and he makes a point of not peeking while I change into them. I feel cozier already, but I pull the small fleece blanket out of my bag too. By the time I turn around, James is lying flat on his back on the sleeping bag. Staring at the rough sandstone ceiling. He changed into sweatpants but isn't wearing anything over his t-shirt.

He sits up as I join him on the ground.

"Is that my coat?"

"Maybe."

He tips his head, lips pursed. "You wearing anything under it?"

"Um... No."

My cheeks catch fire, but I laugh, and his face turns red. He looks away and downs the rest of his drink, judging by the hollow, metallic clink the can makes when he sets it down.

"What? Did you think I'd sleep in my swimsuit?" I ask, still laughing.

"No, I guess not." He scratches his neck. "Wasn't thinking at all, to be honest."

I glance over my shoulder to find my water bottle lying on its side near the head of the sleeping bag. It's probably a good thing I stopped drinking when I did. Those two shots packed more of a punch than I expected.

"Are you worried about what everyone's been saying?" I ask.

"Oh, uh—" He sighs and looks from his lap to the cave's

dark mouth. "I'm trying not to take it too seriously, but, for what it's worth, I never—" He laughs. "I didn't come here thinking we'd *do* anything, you know? And, after what Paige said about Ice... It doesn't seem right. You know? I don't wanna...push you into anything or make you uncomfortable..."

HAHAHA— Oh, James...

But I sigh too.

I came here hoping to escape the drama, but I knew there were rumors. I should've known it would follow us here too. If it wasn't Paige, someone else would have brought it up—the scars or my relationship with Ice. Even the most innocent question or well-intentioned comment could have haunted us for the rest of the day.

James clears his throat. "Maybe I should ask, though. I mean, you didn't come here expecting sex, did you?"

Today? Here? UH—

I hide my face in my blanket. "I guess it never really crossed my mind until Carmen said something, so... There's no rush."

I guess??

"Okay," he says with a laugh. "Just making sure I don't disappoint you or anything."

"No. It's totally fine."

Lowering my blanket, I flash a smile. He returns it with a hint of uncertainty, until I lean closer to ruffle his windswept hair. And he grins and grabs my arm and pulls me into a kiss. I nearly fall onto him, and we're both laughing, and I...

I wish we didn't have to leave tomorrow.

thirty-six

~ ∞ ~

What?

How'd I get here?

I'm at the top of the cliff, overlooking the cove. It's daytime, but the sky is overcast with dark clouds that desaturate the world, and the salty wind carries an uncomfortable chill.

I'm sitting on the flat, reddish stone, wearing sweatpants and an oversized sweatshirt. My loose hair, cut just below my shoulder, is carelessly blown about in the wind. I don't do a thing to tame it, but I raise an arm to wipe my eyes with the sleeve of the sweatshirt my hand is tucked inside.

Something isn't right.

I mean… Obviously, this isn't right.

But I'm also not in my body.

Of course.

This isn't real.

I'm asleep.

Looking more closely, only a few yards surrounding the spot where my dream-self sits near the top of the ridge are properly formed in any direction besides straight ahead. Even that image wavers, like the mirage buildings in Night's urban dreamscape.

But why am I here? Why am I alone? What am I even looking at? And, most concerning, if this dream reflects the future in any way, *when* is this?

I step forward, pausing as I realize I'm still in feline form.

No wonder I can't see over the edge.

I shake the River Sapphire off and return to human form sitting on the cool, sandy ground. The strong, freezing wind buffets my hair into my eyes. I tuck the necklace in my pocket and stuff most of my wild hair into the back of my hoodie, pulling the hood over my head before finally standing.

I walk until I'm right beside the other Jayde. She doesn't seem to see me at all, so I look over the edge of the cliff. A large bonfire burns on the grey beach below, but there are only a handful of people in attendance—Matthew, Cassidy, *Carmen?*, and a few others, all bundled in cool-weather clothing. Among those in the group, I spot someone who looks remarkably like Rose, hugging her arms as she stands a couple yards from the flames.

If that is her, why is she here?

What's going on?

I scan the beach a second time, then check the half-formed sandy turnout. The ghost of Matthew's red BMW and Rose's dark coupe are parked in the lot, but I don't see James or his car.

So I look back to the girl on the ground beside me.

Her nose and cheeks are red from the cold. Eyes puffy from crying, she sniffles and hugs her knees tighter to her chest.

Why are you alone?

I turn and stumble past myself, toward the trailhead that

should take me to the beach. But my first step down the partially formed trail sends me falling.

I didn't trip.

There was simply no ground to support my weight. My foot passed right through the earth, and my body followed it. I fell out of the illusionary world my dreamscape created and into the empty void I'm more familiar with.

My feet eventually contact the ground, the landing unusually gentle considering how often my dreamscape likes to drop me like a lead weight.

Ugh.

I look around, hoping to see something—any clarification or context for the scene it showed me. But there's nothing. My dreamscape is dark and cold, and, tonight, even the soft firefly lights are absent.

God, I hate this place.

~ ∞ ~

thirty-seven

I'm warm and cozy, but the outside chill soaks through the blanket and nips at my toes, as my feet—*or paws, I guess*—found their way out from underneath me at some point during the night. My fur coat and James' feline body molded against my back are likely the only reasons I'm not freezing.

James' breath still has the rhythm of deep, peaceful sleep. It's soothing. Kind of a relief, feeling his chest rise and fall against my back. Knowing he's here and safe and perfectly fine.

But I remain unsettled.

What the hell was that dream?

I open my eyes to find pinpricks of light filtering in through the thin fleece. It's morning, but it's hard to say how early if it's still this cold.

Should I wake James up or let him sleep in a bit?

I listen to the waves crashing against the beach for a while. The seagulls cry, and wind whistles as it passes the cave entrance, but we're too far from the bonfire or any of the tents set up last night to hear anyone—assuming anyone else is awake.

For all I know, it could be 6AM. I left my phone in my backpack, so I can't easily check.

Ah...

My feline limbs don't have the same range of motion as my human ones, so I resort to wiggling around until I can nudge James' shoulder with my nose. He shifts slightly when I whisper his name.

"Mm...?" He lifts his head, eyes shut as his jaw unhinges in a sleepy, feline yawn. "Is it morning?" he asks, the words unaffected despite being said mid-yawn. Then his jaw snaps shut, and he opens his wide, yellow eyes. "Did you sleep alright?"

"I slept... Well, yeah; alright is a decent way to put it."

His head tips almost ninety degrees, but I shake mine.

"Just a weird dream," I say. "I'm fine."

He shrugs it off and asks for the time.

I slip out from underneath my blanket and shake the River Sapphire off. The cool air shocks my warm cheeks. The edge of the plastic tarp beneath my hand is cold to the touch. I take a second to orient myself before standing.

But I lose my balance almost immediately.

Wait—

I manage to catch and steady myself, so I don't actually fall back to the sand, but I quickly realize the problem.

I'm unsteady on my feet. Trying to stand left me slightly dazed and queasy. My cheeks are too warm, and my vision seems to lag behind as I look from the bright cave entrance to my hands planted on my knees.

Great. Just...great.

"Hey," I say slowly.

"What's up?"

"Remember what I said about my separate forms yesterday?" He makes a soft noise, but I get the feeling he has no idea what I mean. "Yeah, um… I'm definitely still a bit tipsy right now."

He laughs, and I glance back to find him still covered by the purple throw blanket. Then the small feline shape becomes a larger humanoid one, and James shrugs the blanket off. He smiles up at me from the middle of the unzipped sleeping bag.

"That sucks," he says brightly. "I feel great."

I sigh and carefully make my way across the cave to my backpack. "Dr. Corel said there's not much reliable information about separate forms or how they work, but I wasn't expecting *this*. For some reason."

Somehow, I feel worse than I did last night. I thought I was totally *fine* then, but now my stomach grumbles unhappily, and my head aches. Maybe it's because I was used to the whole malaise of intoxication in the moment, but it hit me all at once after I morphed back? Or maybe I'm just hungry and dehydrated. I honestly can't tell.

I groan as I drop to sit in front of my bag.

"Have any fun theories?" I ask.

I take my phone from the front pocket—it's just after 8AM; *not bad*—and turn back to James after relaying the time. He doesn't seem bothered by how early it is either, and instead looks to be seriously thinking my question through.

After a moment, he looks up from his lap. "It does sound like it could be some kind of pocket dimension. Only, instead of just your clothes and phone or whatever going in there when you morph, like most immortals, maybe your entire human body stays there until you turn back."

I pull my hairbrush out of my bag and work on my hair. As the brush immediately catches on a tangle, I regret not brushing it at all last night.

"Okay, but why am I still drunk?"

"Dunno." He frowns, holding a hand to his chin. "Maybe time doesn't pass there? It's a separate dimension, right? It doesn't have to follow our dimension's rules. So, if time doesn't pass in the pocket dimension, you wouldn't metabolize the alcohol at all since you slept in feline form."

"Makes sense... I mean, I didn't bleed to death after I morphed the first time, so it seems like my human body didn't lose any blood while I was a cat."

He glances away. I tug a bit too hard on my hair.

Ugh.

I can't blame him for not wanting to talk about it—for not wanting to believe I was crazy enough to meet with Ice and let him nearly kill me. But the way James feels about it doesn't change the fact that neither of us would have morphed if it weren't for him.

At least I can accept that. *Even if I hate him for everything else.*

I slip the hair tie off my wrist and carefully work my hair into *something* of a ponytail, but I'm sure I look like a hot mess.

"Do you seriously believe the pocket dimension thing?" I ask.

"Sure. Why not?" His voice is soft and mild. "You can't prove that immortals aren't associated with pocket dimensions."

I crack a smile and turn to face him. "I'm not sure you can

prove they exist in the first place."

He laughs before standing. When he looks to me on his way over, he seems to have recovered from my tactless mention of almost bleeding to death. He helps me up off the floor, and I dust the sand off my leggings.

"Let's pack up a bit and see if anyone else is awake," I say. "Carmen said she has to leave early, but I have no idea what she considers early."

He nods, flashing a smile, and we get to work.

thirty-eight

"Jayde!" Cassidy calls from several yards away.

They run to meet us before we make it to a small fire burning just to the south of the blackened, ash-filled pit where the bonfire was last night. Roughly half the partygoers are awake and present —Matthew, Jesse, Carmen, Natalie, Dawn, and Alex included.

Good. I'm not too late.

"You didn't drink too much, did you?" Cassidy asks. "Natalie got super sick."

"I'm fine," I say, and it's mostly true.

I look past Cassidy. Carmen and a few others are roasting hot dogs while Natalie hugs her knees and stares into the flames. Matthew pats her back with his free hand, and she sighs heavily. She must have drank more than I did. I hate to admit I stopped paying much attention to her alcohol intake after the shots.

"Jayde's separate forms?" Cassidy asks curiously. Before I answer, their eyes widen, and they glance between me and James. "Oh! Sorry. Is it rude to ask?"

Did he think about how I'm still sort of drunk?

It's whatever.

Once I confirm the information, James explains how it lends

credence to his pocket dimension theory.

Cassidy listens for a moment, frowning with arms folded over their chest, before groaning. "I swear, James, you are no fun at all. But you're welcome for the s'mores last night!"

With that, they turn and run the few yards back to their spot near the fire. James gives me a look, but I shrug. If Cassidy really wants to believe that immortals are magic and impossible to scientifically quantify, there's not much point in trying to convince them otherwise.

James sighs and says he'll find something for us to eat, so I sit in the sand beside Carmen. She looks great considering how much she drank yesterday.

"You guys leaving soon?" I ask.

She nods. "Still got a few hours before we *have* to leave, but I wanna make sure Nat won't throw up in the car before we go."

"I won't throw up again," Natalie mutters.

Matthew laughs from her other side, where he's roasting two hot dogs on a single stick. "Sorry. Guess it's my fault."

Carmen snorts. "Yeah, it totally is your fault, dude. You know she can't hold her liquor worth shit. She wasn't planning to drink anything at all, you know?"

Uh-huh... Not that you tried to stop her either.

James returns with two water bottles and hot dogs skewered on metal roasting sticks. He hands me one of each, and I take a drink before positioning my hot dog over the fire. My hand is unsteady, so the hot dog wavers in and out of the yellow flames.

This is so dumb.

I should've slept the alcohol off like everyone else. But no luck, I guess. Instead, I'll have to deal with *this* for hours and probably suffer a hangover in the middle of the day too.

When I complain about my separate forms, Carmen bursts out laughing. "Wait, so, you're still drunk right now? That's wild. And…shitty?"

"Definitely shitty," I agree.

"Do you need help?" James asks.

"No, I'm fine."

I can roast my own hot dog. I'm not *that* messed up—just buzzed enough for it to make life slightly more difficult. *Definitely not as bad as the Fourth of July, anyway.*

Carmen frowns. "But you had fun, right? No regrets?"

"I had fun," I say, glancing at James.

He shrugs. "I had a good time—considering everything."

"Good!" She grins and removes her bubbly hot dog from the fire. As she leans back, her eyes flick to me. "I, for one, certainly do not regret being here to witness you pop Paige Porter in her smug, bitchy face. That was truly legendary."

I smother a grimace.

"Hold up," Alex says from the far side of the fire pit. "She *hit* Paige? Is that why Parker bailed before we got here?"

"Hell yeah." Carmen nods, a bit smug as she puts together her hot dog without looking at it. "Paige was all up in James' face, right? Spouting some crazy shit—like he murdered Night Monroe and gave Jayde her scars or whatever. Anyway, Paige slapped him after he called her out on her bullshit, but she wouldn't back down, so Jayde straight-up decked her. Right in the face. She left with a black eye, ugly crying 'cause she didn't have makeup to hide the bruise before everyone saw it."

That seems…*slightly exaggerated*, but Alex appears to take Carmen's version of events at face value. Sitting beside Alex, Dawn tips her head and frowns more skeptically.

"You're serious?" she asks.

Matthew shrugs before passing Natalie a perfectly roasted hot dog in a bun. She offers him a weak smile and takes a bite, holding the hot dog in both hands.

"That's basically what happened," Matthew says. "I caught the whole thing on video if you wanna see."

Alex laughs. "A video? You're fucking with me, man."

"I am not."

"Was she seriously crying when she left?" I ask, annoyed by the fleeting sense of guilt that hit me when Carmen said that.

But she repeats Matthew—*That is basically what happened.* And that confirmation, dramatized or not, doesn't make me feel better about the whole thing, since I didn't really *mean* to hurt her.

"So," Dawn says slowly. Her lavender eyes flick to watch me over the yellow flames, and something in her passive expression worries me. "What actually happened—with you, I mean?"

"With me?" I echo, nearly dunking my poor hot dog into the coals at the base of the fire.

"Ice Monroe is your sponsor, right? I heard you were dating him in June, but no one knew anything about you before then, so he must have been the first to tell you about immortals. Why would he do that?"

"I don't know," I admit.

"You don't have to tell me anything, obviously, but Paige isn't the only one talking about you. I've heard rumors too, and some of it's real fucked. Don't you want to clear all that up?"

"Oh, you're right!" Carmen perks up sharply and takes a bite of her hot dog. "I know a ton of people—like, no joke, I know most of the immortals our age in town. We could totally set the record straight for you."

Well...

"Exactly," Dawn agrees. "But that's kinda hard to do if no one knows what actually happened."

I chew on my cheek.

The offer is tempting, but I don't know Dawn Corel at all. I hardly know anyone here, even Carmen. Can I trust them? Is the truth better than the rumors I've heard so far?

"Um... Ah—"

My hot dog is burning.

It hasn't quite caught fire yet, but the bottom half is turning black, and most everyone else seems to have finished roasting or eating theirs already. I pull mine off, and James, who has been uncomfortably quiet since Dawn mentioned Ice, passes a bun to me. I put my hot dog on the bun, plant the metal stick in the sand, and hold the hot dog in my lap.

"James." Even trying to sound normal, my voice feels low and distant. "What do you think? Should we tell them?"

He sighs. "I... I don't know enough about the rumors."

"Dude, that's such bullshit," Matthew says sharply. "I fed you rumors all summer. Even before you ghosted us, you knew what was going around about her and Ice. I told you what people were saying about you after you disappeared. You never responded, but I know you read them. And, now that we're talking again, you still won't explain a thing about whatever went down. How the hell is anyone supposed to defend you?"

What?

I turn on James, my chest tight. "You knew about the rumors this whole time? You said—"

He groans. "I know what I said. But is this really the best time to explain—?"

"Why not now?" Matthew glances between us, more confused than frustrated. "The rumor mill has been out of control since July. Someone sees you in town with a black eye, but you won't respond to messages. Someone's worried you're in trouble since no one's seen you in weeks, still no response. I can only do so much when I have no idea what's going on with you. They come to me since I'm your best friend, but I don't know what to say to anyone."

"I almost died, Matt," James cries. "How many people know about that, huh? How many of your other friends did you tell?"

Matthew recoils, eyes wide and jaw set.

Yikes.

I hold my breath as everyone falls silent and stares at us with pale faces. And Cassidy leaves, surely overwhelmed by our racing thoughts.

The fire crackles. Seagulls cry. Waves crash on the sand.

Then Matthew laughs once, his expression dark. "I didn't say shit about what you told me in the hospital. At all. To anyone. You seriously thought I would?"

What did *James tell him?*

"I—" He looks away, hands balled into fists in his lap as panic replaces his anger. "I don't know what to think anymore. Sorry, man. I just— *Fuck.* I don't know where those rumors came from. I don't understand how anyone knows about any of this in the first place."

Matthew doesn't respond, but his expression shifts, and he looks slightly less upset—at least outwardly.

I force myself to drink water. My hot dog is probably getting cold, so I take a bite of it too. The char and ash from accidentally dunking it into the coals doesn't exactly complement the cheap hot dog flavor. *It's kinda sad.*

"Dude, you almost died?" Alex asks, breaking the heavy quiet.

James cracks a weak smile and shrugs. "Why do you think I can morph all of a sudden? Some kind of miracle? Yeah, right. The only miracle here is that I didn't bleed to death."

"What happened?" Carmen asks, more serious than I've *ever* heard.

He hits her with a sharp look, like he suspects she's one of the people who initially spread shady rumors about him. Then he takes a deep breath and massages his temples. He's still clearly annoyed, but he looks marginally calmer.

Meanwhile, I desperately try to not think *at all.*

"You guys want the truth?" he asks. "Fine. A couple weeks back, Ice broke into Jayde's house and stabbed me."

"Ice Monroe *stabbed* you?" she exclaims. Her shock fades quickly, and she glances away with wide eyes and a hand over her mouth. "So, it really is him?"

"It's always been him," I say under my breath.

"What the hell happened?"

Carmen tries to meet my gaze, but I avoid it. I stare into the crackling fire and take another bite of my hot dog. My stomach hurts. I want to blame it on this conversation—on talking about Ice. But it probably is the alcohol.

Or the hunger. I can't tell.

"I heard rumors that he'd done something," she admits. "You all up and vanished around the same time, you know? But I had a hard time believing anything I heard until I saw you again— with James all of a sudden. I was sure you wouldn't be with him if he hurt you, but, I mean, you and Ice were dating just a few weeks earlier. It was weird, sure, but you seemed pretty happy about the whole thing when we first met."

My mouth feels dry.

I don't want to talk about it, but they're right. The truth needs to come out eventually. I don't want people thinking that I slept with Ice or that James did this to me or hurt *anyone*. I don't want the rumors to be the only thing anyone knows.

Besides, Ice doesn't deserve anonymity. And, at this point, I don't care what Human-Immortal Affairs or anyone else thinks about me for speaking out against him.

What do I really have to lose?

I take a deep breath and force myself to meet Carmen's gaze. "I honestly couldn't tell you what went wrong, but Ice and I… Ugh. We were never…*dating*. Even if I thought we were, and it looked like we were, and he said we were, I don't think he ever really saw it that way."

"For real? But I saw you guys together." She glances around like she isn't sure what to say. "You seemed totally fine. Everything seemed fine. I teased Ice about dating you, and he laughed it off. You were fine, right?"

"Oh, yeah," I say quickly. "I was fine. Things weren't always like this. Everything was normal, mostly, until—"

James sort of laughs. "Until I came along and fucked it all up for ya."

I glance at him as everyone falls awkwardly quiet again. He stares into the flames with narrowed eyes, worrying his hands in his lap, frustrated and uneasy.

"Maybe...we shouldn't do this right now," I say, looking back to Carmen. "Maybe, for now, it's enough to say that Ice is the one who hurt me and leave it at that. He sponsored me in June, yes, but I never once had sex with him, and he's the one who gave me these scars. James did nothing wrong."

"I did nothing wrong?" he asks with another short, dark laugh. "Right."

"In comparison," I mutter.

James doesn't go further, *thank god*, but everyone watches us, hungry for details and context or *any reasonable explanation for what either of us have said.* Jesse looks sort of peeved, and both Carmen and Dawn look even more confused than before.

"Do the police know?" Carmen asks.

"I heard James was arrested last month," Alex says.

Carmen claims to have heard the same. Matthew averts his gaze, leading me to believe that he might have known about it already.

"That one's true," James says. "But only because Ice called RPD after he attacked Jayde out of fucking nowhere and pinned it on me. He had me arrested by *human police* while she was stuck in the hospital."

"*Why*, though?" Carmen asks. "Why would he do that?"

"Which thing?"

I finish my cold hot dog and stare at my hands. Right now, the scarred heart is hidden by the sleeve of James' hoodie. *How much do I want them to know?* Will revealing the full story help at all? Will the information get back to Ice somehow? Will this destroy his reputation? Will it piss him off? Do I want that?

Do I want to risk it?

Do I care what Ice thinks?

I push my sleeve up to show Carmen. She grabs my trembling arm to steady it, and she stares at the heart-shaped scar for a long, quiet moment. She seems puzzled at first. Then surprised. And, then, as her grip tightens ever so slightly, anger creeps into her expression.

"What the fuck?" She drops my arm and looks up, violet eyes narrow and dangerous as she searches my face. "You're telling me Ice did this to you? Does Night know about this?"

She does.

But I have no idea what Night is dealing with at home. Ice doesn't know that we've been talking, and it seems like she's trying to work damage control on her end as best as she can. Telling Carmen might compromise whatever she has going on.

"I don't know," I say. "I've messaged her a few times, but she hasn't responded since I left their house."

Carmen bites her lip and glances away, her concern so deep she hardly resembles herself. "Is she okay? What if Ice hurt her too? Do you think—?"

"He wouldn't hurt her," James says before I have a chance to say anything. *I mean, according to what Night has told me, he's probably right, but—*

"How do you know that?" she asks, turning on him. "No one has heard from her in *weeks*. She won't answer the phone, doesn't read texts, and hasn't been online in over a month. Even Smoke refuses to talk about her or meet up with anyone, so how can you say that Ice wouldn't hurt her after what you're suggesting he did to Jayde? And to you? What the hell do *you* know, huh?"

He averts his gaze and drinks some water. "Ice won't hurt Night," he says again, his voice low. "You don't have to worry about her. I'm sure she's fine."

Carmen opens her mouth to argue.

But Dawn speaks first, "I don't get it."

Carmen's jaw snaps shut as she looks across the fire to watch Dawn, whose attention is on me rather than James.

"Human-Immortal Affairs knows about this, right?" she asks. "They know that Ice Monroe, the guy *they* designated to be responsible for you, hurt you like this?"

It's a good question, but the answer sucks.

"Oh, they know," I say. "They know that Ice has sent me to the hospital three times, and they know he stabbed James. They know everything—more than I do, I'm sure—but they don't care about me. They only care about their stupid program. Ice is my sponsor, and...it really is like he said. He can do whatever he wants because of that."

She shakes her head. "There's no way. If what you're saying is true, it sounds like Ice literally tried to *murder* James. There's no way they're cool with that."

"Yeah, that's insane," Alex agrees.

"As far as they're concerned, I'm the one in the wrong here," James says with a dry sort of distaste. "RSP talked to me while I was in the hospital. Jayde has zero agency in any of this. If Ice wanted, he could press kidnapping charges against me just 'cause she's staying with me."

Kidnapping charges? Is that true?

Dawn stares at him with marked disbelief before looking to me again. "Okay, but you just…let him do whatever he wants?"

"No, of course not," I say, the words almost slurring together as I speak too quickly. "But there's no real solution here. Human-Immortal Affairs doesn't care about me—I can't even get ahold of them—but I can't just ignore Ice either. I tried that already, and James almost died. Ice ambushed us. He held a knife to my throat. He stabbed James and left him to die in my kitchen. My roommate found out about immortals because of it. And nobody cared. No one. There's nothing either of us can do."

I wipe my damp eyes, and the circle falls quiet again. The fire crackles. Waves crash. Seagulls cry. My heart pounds. *And, for the first time since coming here, I just wanna go home.*

James sighs and takes another drink. He looks pissed. Jaded and defensive, like he might snap if he hears one more thing he doesn't like.

My own anger ebbs, and I drink some water too. But my head

throbs worse than before. And the hot dog did nothing to settle my stomach. *Ugh.*

Then Jesse clears his throat. I watch as he looks up from his lap, his expression unreadable. I can't tell if he's mad or upset or what. He's barely said a word since we sat down, and he's said nothing since Ice was brought up. He just...*listened.* And James looks terribly nervous considering the bombshell we dropped on everyone.

But all Jesse says is, "We'll talk later."

James winces, and I feel the intensity of his reaction in my gut as his eyes snap down to the bottle in his hands. His fingers drum against the thin, crinkly plastic. *He really told Jesse nothing. Even less than he told Matthew.*

"Maybe we should...take a walk," I say lamely.

"Yeah, okay," he mumbles.

I stand, careful to keep my balance, and offer James a hand. He looks up at me, scared and miserable and tired, but he takes my hand, and I help him up. Then I move to leave. I take the first step, but he stops me and turns back to the circle of people around the fire.

"I hope this helped," he says, a tremor in his voice. "I hope you're able to set the record straight."

They all avert their eyes.

thirty-nine

I let go of James' hand and sit just out of reach of the highest waves. I kick my flip-flops off, dig my toes into the cool sand, and stare out over the ocean while James remains standing nearby. *I don't know how to feel. About anything, really.*

Maybe I shouldn't be so surprised that he knew about the rumors. Maybe it's stupid to be upset about that while I'm still keeping plenty of things secret from him, but…

The way he accused Matthew of talking about us behind our backs. The sour disappointment on Jesse's face before we left.

Either way, some version of the truth is out there now. We're not the only ones who know what Ice did. But telling the truth was rough. *Was it worth it?* Will our situation improve? Or was ruining everyone's morning the only thing we accomplished?

Maybe James was right. Maybe the timing was off. What if the rumors only get worse?

Ugh…

Behind me, he sighs. "Look, I— I'm sorry. I didn't mean to blow up on Matt. I just… I hate talking about this. About Ice and everything else. After what Paige said… I should've told you or done something about it sooner, but…"

"It's kinda late for that," I mumble. "I would've been upset either way, though, so it's whatever."

"No. It's not *whatever*, Jayde. The rumors have always been about you—the moment someone saw you with me in town and weeks before that—and you deserved to know. I shouldn't have ignored Matt, and I really screwed up by not telling you."

"I don't wanna know, anyway. If what Paige said is only half of it, I honestly don't want to hear anything more."

"You sure? I can show you the texts if you want. I still have everything Matt sent me."

"I said I don't want to know!"

My nails dig into my calves through my leggings, and tears prick my eyes. But I mean it. I *don't* want to know.

What difference does it make? They thought that James sliced me up and forced me to stay with him or murdered Ice and Night because he was jealous. They probably think I slept with Ice to get sponsored and only joined the Human Immortal Program for attention. They don't know that I never had a real choice—that Ice manipulated me from the start. He stalked me before we met and took advantage of my feelings for him. He *lied* to me. The moment he realized I stopped trusting him, he turned on me. And, even now, he just *won't let it go*.

That's what I'm dealing with. That's my reality. What does it matter what anyone else thinks about me? I don't know what they really believe. But I don't care, and I don't want to find out. I've heard enough already.

I've heard more than enough.

I want to go home. *My* home. I know James is scared, and I

know he doesn't think it's safe, but I don't want to leave here just to sit in his small, stuffy bedroom. I hate having to sneak around the first floor, hoping that James' father isn't home or doesn't wake up and harass us.

I hate it. I wish none of this happened. None of it!

I look up from the sand at my feet. Over the water. To the clear, blue sky. *Is that really how I feel?*

Maybe not.

Sometimes, I can't tell if I wish I never met Ice or if I just wish summer would end already. If things calmed down, even a little, maybe life could return to some sort of normal. Maybe James would finally feel safe. Maybe we could be happy for more than five minutes. *But what will that take?*

James sits beside me. He asks if he can hug me.

Permission granted.

For once, I'm not crying. There are no tears. But I am upset, so a hug is nice even if I am, in part, upset because of him.

What will it take for this nightmare to end?

"There's something I need to tell you," I mumble. "I didn't say anything earlier because... I guess I didn't want to over-whelm you."

He leans back, planting his hands in the sand, watching the horizon instead of me. He's clearly listening, though, so... I watch the water too.

"Last time I was in the hospital, after—well, you know." I laugh and cough at the same time. "Ice was there when I woke up. It was the middle of the night, but we talked before he left."

I glance at James again. He meets my gaze for an instant,

but he doesn't seem particularly surprised to hear that Ice was there or particularly upset that I kept it to myself until now. His expression doesn't reveal much of anything.

"What did he say?" he asks.

"He seemed relieved that I survived," I admit. "I mean, he was only there because Human-Immortal Affairs made him stay, but... Anyway, he thinks someone has to die—one of us."

"One of us, huh? That's what he thinks?"

"Yeah. I don't know why, but, um... It didn't seem like he was joking either."

His eyes narrow. "Sounds like he still has it out for me. Guess I shouldn't be surprised, since his previous attempts at killing me failed."

"James..."

When he looks to me again, his jaw is set, and his amber eyes burn with resolve. *Damn it. I should've known he wouldn't take it well.*

"You're right that we can't ignore him," he says, "but if he's so certain that one of us has to die, I'll be damned if it's you."

"I already told you; he doesn't want that."

He laughs, raking a hand through his hair. "Uh-huh. Of course, he doesn't."

I don't like...the hint of wildness in his eyes.

But I don't say anything. I just stare and listen to the waves.

Then he says, "I bet I could kill him."

"What? *No*. That's insane." I hug my arms and glare at my half-buried toes. "Don't even joke about it. I don't want anyone to try killing anyone else."

"What? You think we can just talk our way out of this?" His voice rises, but I still don't look. "You *just* said he thinks someone has to die. Do you seriously think he'll listen to anything either of us have to say? You think he won't start shit again?"

I hold my head in my hands. "I don't know. I just—"

"He *stabbed* me, Jayde! You said it yourself. You just told *everyone*. He held a knife to your throat. He left me to die in your kitchen!"

"I know, but—"

I force myself to look up from the sand. But James looks away sharply. He's obviously as upset and frustrated as I am. *Why are we arguing about this?*

"Never mind." He takes a breath, and his anger tempers to general dissatisfaction. "I'm no match for Ice, anyway. He'd win even in a fair fight."

Is that true?

After a second's hesitation, I pat his back.

"We'll figure it out," I say. "Maybe something *has* changed. Or…maybe he'll back off once it gets back to him that we told people what really happened."

"Maybe…"

For several minutes, we sit. Quiet. Watching the waves wash up on the sand hardly a foot from our toes. Not looking at each other for more than a second. But I'm tired of being miserable. I shouldn't worry about the rumors, and I can't let what Ice said worm into my brain and drive me crazy. I have to believe we'll be fine. I have to believe no one will die.

Ice doesn't know where we are.

He doesn't know we're out here, on the beach, miles from Riverview. He doesn't know that we're staying with James' father. And, even if he did, it might not matter. He was calm and reasonable the last time we spoke.

And I'm not so afraid to stand up to him anymore.

I can't be afraid.

I can't...afford to be.

So I look to James with a smile. "Wanna swim?"

He sighs again. I'm sure neither of us *want* to swim—it's still cool out, with the sun just beginning to warm my back through the thin sweatshirt material—but the shock of cold water might be enough to get our minds off *everything* for a minute.

He nods, so we head back to the cave.

When I turn away from my bag after changing into my swimsuit, James is still standing near the opposite wall. He changed out of his sweats and t-shirt, but he seems distracted—still upset about any number of things, probably. *Can't really blame him for that.*

"Ready to go?" I ask, stepping closer.

"Ah…"

His frown grows more pronounced. He itches the long scar on his chest and glances down at the sandstone floor.

"Are you…happy with me?" he asks. I go to answer—to say *yes*—but he raises a hand to stop me. "What I mean is; do you ever wish you were still with him?"

With…Ice?

"What?" I laugh, but I feel my smile crumble as a chill creeps up my spine. "Why would you even ask me that?"

He averts his eyes again. As his hands ball into fists at his sides, a heavy pit settles in my stomach. I shake my head, hands over my chest, and I force myself to move, ending up near the center of the cave as the tangled mess of emotions I've repressed for *weeks* unfurl, spilling over and turning into words.

"I already told you; I was never *with* Ice. He never loved me. I don't even know if he ever saw me as a friend, or if I was just an object—an…*accessory*—to him the whole time. He said to my face that he wasn't attracted to me, and he kissed me anyway. Just to keep me from asking questions. Why the hell would I want that over what I have with you now?"

"I don't know," he says, eyes wide as he stares at the floor.

But I…can't stop.

"You think I still want Ice just because he's hotter than you? Or maybe because he's smarter than you? Or has more money? What does any of that matter? Do you seriously think I care about that stuff more than I care about being treated like a *person*?"

His hand slides up his arm, and he scratches the faint scars near his shoulder. "Of course not. I just…"

He looks…really upset.

My hands fall back to my sides, and I bite my lip.

Is he seriously worried about this? Does some part of him honestly believe that, after everything, I would still prefer Ice over him? Does he feel like he ruined whatever *thing* we had going on in June by showing up when he did? Does he think I'm upset about that?

How long has this bothered him?

Why is it just coming up now?

"I don't love Ice," I say, struggling to keep my voice level. "I don't want him, James. Maybe I used to—I guess I'd be a liar if I said I didn't—but the person I thought I liked… I hate even thinking about it now. I'm sure it's too much to ask, but I hope I never see him again."

After a second's hesitation, I walk the last few steps to stand in front of James. And he finally looks up again. His face is flushed, eyes glistening like he's desperately trying not to cry.

I hate this.

I hate knowing that he feels somehow *inadequate* compared to Ice. And I hate Ice all the more for having caused it.

"I'm sorry." He covers his eyes with one hand. "I don't know why I'm like this. I just— It's so hard to believe that— *Ugh.* I always do this. Goddammit…"

I touch his arm. My fingers brush over several thin scars, and he freezes, breath catching.

"Look at me," my voice says.

He takes a deep, shaky breath. His hand falls away from his face, but he doesn't look directly at me, and he's still clearly fighting back tears. It's like a punch to the gut. Seeing him like this and being able to relate but having no idea what to do.

"I'm sorry," he mumbles again. "I ruined the party. You just wanted to have a good time. You just wanted to help—everyone did. But I—"

"Stop."

I hold his face in my hands, and his wide eyes finally track up to meet mine. He starts to say my name, but I kiss him first. I move faster and more forcefully than I meant to, and it catches him by surprise. His hands land on my waist as he steadies himself, the touch sending a jolt of hot electricity through my body. But I press closer, and he stumbles back against the cave wall.

"What are you doing?" he gasps, his hands moving to my shoulders as he breaks off the kiss. Panicked pain flashes in his eyes—a sense of conflict I also understand perfectly.

"I want you, James," I say. "*You.* That's all I want."

He laughs once, a hint of brightness in the smile he flashes as a tear slips down his cheek. I catch the tear with my thumb and kiss him again. His lips part. Warm hands slide down my body, the sensation shocking without a shirt as a barrier. As his hands settle on my hips, he melts into the kiss. Melts into me completely. A mix of sadness and anger and desperation.

My breath catches as I remember the first night in his bedroom. Hands inching up my shirt. A question in his eyes. And my mind fills with static.

What am *I doing?*

James seems into it—I mean, he clearly is. And I want to be here, doing this with him. I want to go further—as far as he'll let me take it—but… *Am I wrong for thinking about this right now? Am I just projecting my own insecurities onto him? Should we slow down? Should I stop?*

We're still on the beach. There are so many people here.

I pull away.

His eyes open. They're beautiful and wide and hesitant, and they search mine, holding the same question as before. The same question swirling in my own head.

Is this okay?

Then I realize we're both breathing heavily. His chest rises and falls against mine as my heart pounds. His hands on my hips. My face on fire. My mind is a disaster—a racing mess of longing and nerves and an unfamiliar ache that never really left after that night sparked it.

I don't know what to do next. I don't think he does either, but I can't even think of anything to say. I—

"You want me?" he asks.

I nod, and he lifts a hand to touch my cheek. His warm hand slides up my jawline to my ear, and his fingers comb through my hair. I meant to put my hair up into a bun before we left the cave, but I forgot. The sad look on his face distracted me, and now…

Now what?

"Do you want me?" I ask lamely.

He laughs. "Right now, Jayde, I want you more than I have ever wanted anything in my entire life."

James kisses me again, and we sink to the cool sandstone floor.

forty

We never got around to swimming.

Instead, I fell asleep cuddled up to James in the middle of the open sleeping bag. I don't know how long I've been out though, as approaching voices ring out over the dull murmur of ocean waves, and my eyes snap open.

Shit.

"Yo, James—" It's Matthew, and his voice cuts off abruptly. "Oh, ho, ho; what have we here?"

Ugh. At least I put my swimsuit back on before I passed out.

I roll onto my back, groan as I heft myself up to sit, and drag the thin fleece blanket into my lap. Head throbbing in dissent, I squint at the blinding cave opening through a mess of hair, where four silhouettes block some of the light, until my eyes adjust.

Matthew smirks, arms folded over his chest. Carmen looks to be trying her damnedest not to laugh while prodding an indifferent Lucas. And Natalie looks thoroughly embarrassed but less ill than earlier.

Faced with everyone in my current state, I should probably feel more mortified than I do. But I mostly just feel groggy as hell. And resigned. Though, I try to fix my hair.

I would insist it's not what it looks like, but this is exactly what it looks like. There's no point trying to deny it.

They all seemed to be expecting it, anyway.

Opting to say nothing, I look to James. He somehow managed to pull a shirt on already, and he props himself up with one arm, staring at the group in the cave's mouth.

"You guys mind?" he asks.

Matthew cackles and looks around. "The hell was I supposed to do, man? Knock? On what door?"

"*What door?*" Carmen wheezes, choking back laughter. "Oh my god, Matt— I'm *dying*."

James rolls his eyes. I think he's trying to play it off by feigning irritation, but his beet red face betrays the full extent of his embarrassment. I wasn't expecting to get "caught" either, but we should've seen it coming. Of course, someone would want to stop by and check on us after the way we left.

"So, did you—?"

"Shut up!"

But James cracks a smile. Then he grabs my half-empty water bottle and chucks it at Matthew, who effortlessly catches it and laughs even harder.

"Y'all are lucky Cass didn't tag along," he says.

Carmen spirals into another hysterical laughing fit, and Natalie mutters something of an apology before sidestepping out of view.

Ugh... We're not even naked. A bikini is hardly indecent, and James is fully clothed. Why is this so awkward? *On the bright side, at least this rumor won't be a bad one.*

"You need a minute?" James asks with a sigh.

Carmen gasps for air and breaks away from Lucas, who still looks like he couldn't care less about any of this. After another deep breath, she wipes her eyes and flashes a smile.

"Sorry," she says. "We gotta go, but I wanted to make sure we're all cool before we take off. No hard feelings, right?"

I shake my head, but I still can't bring myself to speak.

"Yeah, you're fine," James says mildly. "You guys didn't do anything wrong. I…overreacted, and I apologize for that."

"You gotta stop taking everything so personally, dude."

James casts a dirty look Matthew's way, but he responds with a grin, and James backs down. He sighs again and waves it off, muttering something about assuming things he shouldn't have while Matthew nods sagely.

"Sweet," Carmen says brightly, seeming to ignore the guys. "I'll upload those pictures as soon as I get home. I totally drank more than I should've yesterday, but I did not forget."

I offer a smile. "Okay, thanks."

Matthew points a thumb back toward the main beach. "Well, we should probably give you some space, huh?"

"See ya around, girl." Carmen's smile widens. "Hit me up if you ever feel like hanging out—or cutting your hair."

I wave. Then she takes Lucas by the arm, and they leave with Matthew in tow. James sits up straight beside me, and we stare at the mouth of the cave for at least a full minute before we look at each other again.

As I flash a nervous smile, he groans and drags his hands down his face. I laugh and try to fix his horribly messy hair.

"I'm sorry," he says. "I can't believe—"

"You can't believe Matt came looking for you after the way you freaked out on everyone earlier?" He responds with a pleading look, and I can't help but laugh again. "It's okay. If anything, it's my fault for falling asleep, right? I mean, we were supposed to go swimming."

His frown softens. "Do you feel better, at least?"

"Mm-hm. Do you?"

"Yeah, uh…" He lets out a short, soft laugh and scratches the back of his neck. "I'll be alright. Sorry if I worried you. Again."

I kiss his cheek and pick myself up off the ground. As I shake the sand out of my fleece blanket, James does the same with the cheap sleeping bag. Though, he seems to run into a bit of trouble when it comes time to roll it up. There is sand *everywhere*.

"Do you still wanna swim?" I ask.

He asks for the time, so I step away to dig my phone out of my backpack. It's almost noon.

"Later, maybe," he says. "Give it more time to get hot out."

I shrug in agreement, as I no longer feel a plunge in the cold ocean is necessary to get my mind off how screwed up my life has become. I've accepted it. I'm over it. I'm moving on. And I think James is fine for now.

Looking back to my bag, I consider forgoing my shirt—since everyone knows where my scars came from—but I'm not that brave yet. So I put a tank top and shorts on over my bikini.

"How late should we stay?" I ask.

"As late as possible," he says—exactly what I was hoping to hear.

I brush my disastrous mess of hair as best I can and fix it all into a haphazard bun on top of my head. Then, as I squint at the frustratingly indecipherable carvings on the stone wall *again*, I throw caution to the wind and ask if we can stop by my house on our way through town.

"Your house?" he echoes.

I turn to face him. He tips his head, still smoothing the front of his Arizona t-shirt.

"Just to decompress for a minute before we go back," I say. "We can shower there. And do a load of laundry too."

He thinks about it for a moment before agreeing. He doesn't look too confident in his decision, but any agreement at all is more than I expected, so I'll take it. I zip my backpack and leave it against the wall. Then James meets me near the center of the cave—his backpack and the rolled-up sleeping bag left against the wall behind him.

Our eyes meet. My heart beats faster just looking at him. My face warms, and my head aches, and I break eye contact to laugh.

"You don't happen to have Tylenol or anything, do you?"

He shakes his head, then smiles warmly and holds my hands in his. "Sorry, babe. I'm sure someone will have something you can take. Come on."

We make the walk of shame back to what's left of the party. The small fire has long since been reduced to ash, but there's still one colorful day shelter set up near the few remaining coolers. I only see Matthew, Cassidy, April, Tyler, Dawn, and Alex around. Cassidy and Matthew are playing in the shallow waves together, Tyler is dismantling a tent not far off, and the other three are hanging out near the coolers.

Returning is less immediately awkward since Matthew and Jesse aren't around, but Dawn and Alex both witnessed James' outburst over breakfast. Do the others already know what we said this morning? The whole point of saying anything at all was to clear up the rumors, right?

April offers me an unopened can of soda, and I accept it as James asks if Jesse already took off. Alex nods—he left not long after we did earlier.

"How pissed is he?" James asks, failing to smother a grimace.

Alex shrugs. "Dunno, man. I think he has something going on tonight."

"I doubt he left because of anything you said," Dawn says mildly. "If that's what you're asking, I mean. He was all packed up before you guys even came out."

James relaxes, but only slightly.

"Did something happen?" April asks.

Dawn sighs. "Just that stuff we told you about the rumors."

"Oh!"

April laughs nervously before clearing her throat. As if by instinct, I press a hand over my wrist. *I forgot the wristband in my bag. I didn't even think about it. But Carmen is the only one I've showed the scar to.*

"Right," April says. "Sorry."

I force a smile.

"Do you think Night is okay, though?" she asks.

My smile grows strained.

"Night is *fine*," James says, a hard edge to his voice.

Tyler drops a packed-up tent on top of a cooler and turns to us with marked disbelief. "You're telling me all that shit's true? Carmen said you told everyone Ice Monroe stabbed you. Matt said the same thing—said you spent a few days in the hospital?"

"What?" He flashes a wry smile. "You think I'm lying?"

Tyler shrugs.

James smothers another grimace, but he grabs the hem of his shirt and lifts it to expose his chest. He points out the stab wound and briefly explains how Ice picked a fight and pulled a knife on him. They listen, but his story and the small, pink line are greatly overshadowed by the partially healed surgical scar running the full length of his sternum, and his friends eat it up.

These guys *know* James and Ice, so their collective horror and morbid interest is more obvious now than it was when they could only judge my visible scars.

"That's wild," Alex says, taking a drink.

James, expression now hardened, lets his shirt fall back over his torso and steps away to dig through a cooler. Then everyone turns on me, and I freeze—*another thing I should've seen coming.*

"Are all of your scars from Ice?" April asks.

I nod. She's one of few immortals who saw me before I had them. *She's probably the most likely to believe what I say.* I hesitate, but I raise my left hand to reveal the heart on my wrist.

Only a few people knew about this, and now—

I hear a gasp, and I startle again as Dawn steps forward, bumping April aside to grab my arm and get a better look. Her face pales immediately. Then she drops my arm and meets my gaze, disgust and *anger* etched deeply into her soft features.

"This is completely *fucked*, is what it is," she says. "And you say Human-Immortal Affairs doesn't care at all?"

I shake my aching head, fighting against the static buzzing in the back of my mind. "Besides a couple letters, I haven't heard anything from them. I saw two agents when they took my roommate away after she learned about immortals. They knew who I was, but they wouldn't talk to me at all. Even after I morphed for the first time, and I was stuck in the hospital, they only left behind a questionnaire for me to fill out after I woke up. I never saw a single agent myself. No one talked to me. But I guess they swarmed the place while I was unconscious."

Her eyes snap open wide. "You were in the hospital after you morphed? At Riverview General, right? Was my dad there—Eric Corel?"

I hesitate again before nodding.

"Was he your attending?" When I admit that I saw him every time I went to the ER, she groans. "Why hasn't *he* done anything to help? And how the hell is my dad treating you not a conflict of interest?"

"Right?" James exclaims through a mouthful of *something*.

"What do you mean?" I ask.

Dawn glances past me—to look at James, I think. A flicker of confusion crosses her face, but she quickly shrugs and refocuses on me.

"Because he adopted a human kid," she says, her voice more level than before. "Not that his soft spot for humans seems to have done you any favors."

"He hasn't talked about me at all, has he?"

She sighs. "No. I love my dad, but we don't talk much these

days. I moved out the instant an opportunity presented itself just to get away from *you know who*."

Everyone knows exactly who she's referring to, and, the more I think about it, the less I blame them for not thinking too highly of Taylor Corel. I can't imagine having to go to school with him for years.

"Your dad seems like he wants to help," I say slowly, "but it also seems like there's not much anyone can do. Ice is my sponsor. I can't even get ahold of Human-Immortal Affairs without going through him, but there's no way he'd help me with that. He has all the power in this situation."

"That's…too bad."

The group falls quiet, and they all glance around like they aren't sure where to look. James drinks his water. I drink my soda and consider trading him for the water bottle. Standing around is kind of awkward. *Ugh.* My head still hurts.

"I hope everything works out," April says meekly.

The others nod in agreement.

Then Matthew and Cassidy return from the sea, soaking wet and laughing, and the mood lifts. The conversation we just had surely isn't lost on Cassidy, but their attitude doesn't shift as they walk through the group and retrieve a plush beach towel from on top of Matthew's red cooler. They bundle up before looking to me with a smile.

"Feeling better now?" they ask.

"Yes, but I still need Tylenol."

It was the first thing that came to mind, and it makes James laugh.

forty-one

April hugs me before stepping away to pick up her cooler from among the last few still on the beach. Water, ice, and loose drinks slosh around inside the cooler as she shifts her weight.

"Sorry you've had it so rough lately," she says. "But I hope things are going a bit better now? You and James seem happy together."

I glance over my shoulder. James is helping Matthew and Cassidy fill the bonfire pit with sand. I can't hear their conversation from here, but it looks like he's having a good time.

Still... I wonder how he used to act at parties if April seriously thinks our behavior the past twenty-four hours seemed *happy*. I punched someone I just met, James freaked out on everyone after being caught in a lie, and we dumped our trauma onto everyone else. *Do we really seem happy?*

It's not that I'm *not* happy—with James or whatever else. I just have some glaring concerns that have yet to be resolved, and I'm no closer to working out a way to resolve them than I was before.

"I think we'll be okay," I say.

She smiles, says she'll see me around, and begins her trek

across the beach to the trailhead. Tyler follows her, carrying the rest of their gear, but stops when he reaches Matthew and James. I hear nothing over the wind and waves, but Matthew laughs and James scratches the back of his head.

As Tyler continues past them, I turn back to Dawn. She's been quiet, looking frustratingly deep in thought for a while now, but I'm too nervous to ask—since I can only imagine what's on her mind after everything she's heard.

She meets my gaze, and I start slightly upon being caught watching. But she merely sighs. "I'm still trying to figure out why Ice would do it. I didn't know him well in school—he was two grades above me—but he was popular and seemed at least halfway decent."

Ice in school, huh?

"He wanted to hurt James," I say, suppressing many swirling questions. "As far as I know, that's the only reason he ever hurt me too— Well, except for last time, when he thought it might activate my necklace."

"Ugh." She grimaces, another flicker of disgust, before looking past me toward the group further down the beach. "What is it about James, though? What did he do to Ice to make him take it this far?"

"In July, James told me that Ice said some nasty things about me behind my back. Ice never denied it when I confronted him, but that's when he first attacked me. After that, I decided to stay with James because I didn't want to be alone, and I'm sure that pissed him off too."

"Hm…" She looks to Alex. "Hey, you were in the same grade

as Ice and James, right?"

He nods, and Dawn holds a fist to her mouth, brows furrowing deeper. Her lavender eyes search the sand at her feet as though she might find an answer there.

"I'm trying to remember," she mumbles. "Were they…*friends* in middle school? Or something like that?"

"Ah…" Alex glances aside, also frowning, but he shrugs as he looks to her again. "I honestly don't remember much of Ice before high school. I'd never even seen him before…sixth grade, maybe? I don't think he went to Wisteria in elementary."

Ah—

"He was adopted when he was eleven," I say.

"Right," Alex says. His eyes widen slightly, as though something suddenly clicked for him, and he looks from Dawn to me. "Ice did hang around James in middle school. It was just them and the Monroe twins, I think. He got into a lot of fights—a lot of black eyes and busted lips—but that's about all I remember."

"James did?"

He laughs. "No. Ice did. Now that I think about it, he was a creepy kid—totally different from how he was in high school. Pretty sure we got into it once over something stupid too, but I forgot all about it. It might've been seventh grade? But, yeah, I remember his face now—like he was pissed, but there was nothing going on behind his eyes. Super fuckin' creepy."

Creepy, huh?

"Anyway, I wasn't friends with Ice or James in high school. I didn't even start hanging out with Matt and them until senior year, and James already transferred out of Wisteria by then."

"Wait—"

But Dawn turns to me before I managed to say anything, eyes glittering with curiosity. "That's right! I totally spaced it. Did you know him in high school? He went to RHS his senior year."

James...went to RHS?

"I had no idea," I say. "He never mentioned going to RHS. But I think I would've only been a sophomore then, so..."

"Oh." Her expression blanks for an instant. "I guess we're the same age, huh? I thought, maybe, you were a bit older."

You are probably the first person to ever think that.

"It makes me wonder, though," she says, hand dropping to her hip. "When we were younger—I was maybe...twelve or thirteen—Taylor told me that Ice threatened him with a knife. I didn't believe him. No one did. Not even my dad. But maybe he wasn't making shit up after all."

Oh.

Her gaze flicks past me again. She straightens up, smoothing over her uneasy expression, and I glance back too. James and Matthew are heading this way—without Cassidy, who is running back to the water. *Guess she's done talking about it for now.* But, as the guys join us, I realize I can't let it go.

"Why didn't you tell me you went to RHS?"

It's an innocent question—I'm not *mad* that he never mentioned it; just confused—but sharp surprise flickers across his face, and he quickly averts his gaze.

"It was one year," he mumbles. "I barely even remember it."

"I'm only curious," I admit, hoping I didn't sound too upset or accusatory by mistake. "It's just that one immortal would stand out in a crowd of humans, so I can't believe I don't remember seeing you around at all. Did you ever see me?"

He frowns but looks up, brows still furrowed. "I didn't talk to anyone if I could avoid it. I just wanted to graduate and get the hell out, so I don't know if I ever saw you. Doubt I'd remember even if I did. Anyway, I spent most of this time trying to *forget*. High school was easily the worst four years of my life."

Worse than this?

"Hey!" Matthew cries, feigning distress. "You met me in high school, man. I thought we had some good times together."

"We did, but it still sucked."

"High school sucks for everyone," Dawn says dryly. "You're not special because you were bullied, you know?"

"I never said I was." He sighs. "I don't think I'm special, and I'm sure it sucked for you too, growing up with Taylor and all, but not everyone has such a shitty time in school, and you know it."

Dawn frowns, seemingly unable to argue, while Matthew and Alex nod and say some variation of, "I always liked school," at roughly the same time.

Everyone looks to me to be the tiebreaker.

"Um…" I laugh, nerves slipping through. "School was okay, I guess. I didn't have many friends—just Rose—but I always did alright academically, and I wasn't bullied. Maybe a few small things here and there, but that happens to everyone, doesn't it?"

"Sounds like you had the average school experience," Dawn agrees, clearly unimpressed. "School was hell for me. Taylor was angry and dramatic and a total asshole all the time for no reason, and everyone knew I was his *little sister*—" She shudders. "—so no one liked me for *years* after my dad adopted him. Things were better in high school, but Taylor was still a shitty person, and, yeah, I had to deal with that at home too."

"That's rough. My parents argued a lot before their divorce, but I think I had a pretty typical home life too. I always got along with my brother, and I never got into trouble or anything."

"Aah…" Dawn pulls a conflicted grimace and presses a hand to her forehead. "You sound so *normal*. James, how the hell did a weird, depressing recluse like you pull such a normal girl?"

He prickles, taking offense to what I assumed was a joke. *I mean, she was joking, right?* But he doesn't answer.

I force a smile. "Well, I guess I was normal up until a few months ago. Now, I feel like I might be the weirdest one here."

A moment of quiet. Then Matthew bursts into laughter.

"It's so true," he exclaims, turning to James with a grin. "Dude, now that you can morph, your girlfriend totally has you beat in the weirdness department."

Alex nods, a smirk slipping through his otherwise thoughtful expression. "A human chick in with immortals—who can morph, no less. Plus, she has a psycho, knife-wielding stalker. And she wants to date James Reid. Yeah, I'd call that weird, for sure."

"Hey!" James protests, his ears turning red.

"I'm kidding, man," Alex says with a laugh. "None of us give a shit that your girlfriend is human."

"For real," Dawn agrees. "Who cares?"

Matthew nudges James' shoulder. "See, dude? You're good."

As James smiles and seems to relax, I breathe easier too.

forty-two

I wave to Dawn and Alex, and they set off across the sand, leaving me, James, Matthew, and Cassidy as the only ones on the long, empty stretch of beach. Cassidy returns from wherever they ran off to, and, after a quick snack, we all head to the tidepools.

Cassidy shows off the small, hot pink sea creatures they discovered during a previous solo adventure around the cove. James seems to know a bit about the animals—they're some kind of tidal sea slug—but I've never seen anything like them before, so I take a few pictures.

"I'll scout ahead and look for more cool stuff," Cassidy says with a grin.

Without waiting for a response, they morph and dash along the sandstone toward the south end of the cove, much farther than I went yesterday. We don't follow, opting to stay closer to the sandy beach after Matthew reasons that they'll surely come back if they discover anything interesting.

We sit along one side of a wide, deep tidepool worn into the reddish stone, and I peruse the sea life inside—a few small fish, a bright orange starfish, and several decently sized anemones. Then, in the corner of my vision, I catch Matthew leaning back.

He looks out over the beach, blocking the early afternoon sun from his eyes with one hand.

"So, uh... How'd sleeping in the cave work out for ya?"

"I slept fine," James says. "But I'm pretty sure that's not what you're asking."

I look up from the clear water as Matthew's inquisitive eyes bore into James. He's a lot more like Rose than I thought. Generous and supportive but terribly nosy when it comes to the personal affairs of others and lacking something when it comes to tact.

But Matthew laughs like James' mild irritation is the funniest thing. "Dude, are you seriously embarrassed right now? You're a whole-ass adult, you know? You're allowed to have sex with your girlfriend at your birthday party. Literally no one cares."

"Then why are you asking about it?"

"Okay, okay. Fine. I won't ask you." He looks to me instead, and I blink in anticipation. "Alright, Jayde, I'm dying to know; was it your first time?"

Before I can respond, James gasps and sputters something like *"What difference does it make?"* and *"You do* not *have to answer that."* His face is flushed, but he looks more scandalized than upset or angry, and Matthew laughs easily. I can't help but laugh too, though I at least try to restrain myself and hold a hand over my mouth to hide my smile.

"It was," I admit. "But maybe we should be a little nicer to him—since it's almost his birthday and everything?"

"Honestly, you're lucky to have him," Matthew says with a hint of questionable wistfulness as he blatantly ignores my suggestion. "James is a great friend—you know, when he's not totally ignoring you—and I bet he's super nice in bed. *Nice* as in *kind*, I mean. But he could be great at sex too. I wouldn't know."

I'm dying.

James groans and hides his face in his hands. "Dude. Matt. Please. *Shut up.* Or I swear I'll push you in."

I almost feel bad for laughing so hard. But it is *really* funny.

Matthew's expression softens, but none of the humor leaves it even as he pats James on the back and apologizes for being an ass. James does not respond in any meaningful way, his face still almost entirely covered by his hands.

"I'm teasing you, man," Matthew says, some sympathy slipping through. "Seriously. I'm happy you finally found a decent girl, and I hope you get that shit with Ice worked out soon."

James sighs heavily. He dips his hands into the tidepool and splashes seawater onto his cheeks. When he opens his eyes again, he looks to Matthew, more collected but unimpressed.

"How about you and Natalie?" he asks. "Did you guys hook up last night or what?"

Matthew grins, a finger to his lips. "Now, that's none of your business."

"Ha. Ha." James rolls his eyes. "But isn't it kinda weird, since you dated Carmen and all?"

"Weird?" He tips his head, a flicker of genuine confusion in his golden eyes. "Nah. We're all good friends, so it's not a big deal. Besides, Carmen practically set us up."

I got that vibe too.

James sighs again, peering into the tidepool. "I don't get it. Feels like you just hooked up with her to win a bet with Mina."

"It has nothing to do with any bet, man," he says with a glance at the sky. "Nat's cool. Actually, I was thinking of asking her out. I know it's been a couple years since I've really *dated* anyone, but I have more free time now, and she was talking about going to some design school down in SoCal next year, so it might even work out long-term."

Oh?

"You should," I say—without really thinking. "Natalie likes you, so, if you like her too, you should definitely ask her out. I'm sure she'd say yes."

He flashes a crooked smile, eyes flicking in my direction. "You think? I mean, I *know* she likes me. Last night, we—"

"Hey!" James knocks Matthew off balance and into the water. "What happened to *it's none of your business*?"

He rights himself in the large tidepool and spits out a mouthful of seawater before laughing and raising his phone over his head. "Fucking hell, James. You're lucky this thing's waterproof."

"Good luck with Natalie, Matt."

The water is up to his waist, but Matthew sets his phone on the sandstone where he was sitting before and folds his arms over the edge instead of climbing out. He watches James, who is still a bit flustered, for a second. Then he looks to me.

"You saw the carvings back in that cave, right?" When I nod, he smiles. "I remember the first time I came here. I was like fifteen, and one of the first things James did was show it off to me. But it's pretty sick, right? The doodles and whatever from when he was a kid? He got all embarrassed about it—you know how he is—but I managed to talk him into making more with me."

James sighs heavily again. It almost looks like he wants to dunk Matthew under the water a second time, but his eyes flick away, and his loose fist taps against the damp sandstone near his thigh. I pat his shoulder, but I really want to hear this story.

"I drew our characters from Wisteria's pop culture club D&D campaign," Matthew continues with a laugh. "We're both shit at drawing, but it was fun." He looks to James. "Hey. You should have Jayde put something up on the wall too. Even just her name, you know? That'll really consummate your relationship."

James grimaces, glancing between us with some uncertainty. "I... I don't have a knife or anything."

"I gotchu, bro. I keep a box cutter in my glove compartment."

"Oh, uh..." His frown grows more pronounced as he itches his arm. "Well..."

"I'll carve my name on the wall," I say.

James looks at me in surprise—like, perhaps, he thought I wouldn't want to. *But why wouldn't I?* I've never carved my name into anything before, but I wouldn't mind leaving a piece of myself behind. Plus, I lost my virginity in that cave, and it would be funny to carve the date into the wall.

"Alright," he agrees. "We can if you want."

"Now?" Matthew asks.

Another sigh. "Yeah, I guess."

"Let's do it."

I stand, and James helps Matthew out of the tidepool. Matthew then peels his soaking wet tank top off to wring water out of it. After stuffing it into a pocket, he attempts to squeeze some of the water from his shorts too.

"Look; I scraped my leg, you dick."

We look, and he points out a pink graze on his shin that I wouldn't have noticed if he hadn't pointed it out. The wound isn't bleeding or anything, but he pouts about it all the same.

Once again, James is not impressed. They bicker more playfully than before, and I scan the rocky stretch of beach to the south.

As if sensing me, a head topped with bright red hair pops up from the ground in the distance. I can't quite make out their expression, but they wave exuberantly. I gesture for them to join us, and they sprint across the uneven ground without trouble. When they tackle Matthew on approach, he nearly falls into the water again.

"Ah! You're wet," they cry.

"I know. Can you believe James tried to drown me?"

"I totally can."

Matthew lets out a wail of feigned betrayal while his sibling nods in solemn understanding. James groans—I get the feeling he deals with this kind of thing a lot. But my laughter seems to break Cassidy, who grins between stifled laughter of their own.

"Can we go swimming?" they ask, looking between the three of us. "I'm kinda scared of going in too deep alone."

"Might as well since I'm already soaked," Matthew says with a shrug, having dropped his bitter act. He flashes a smile as he turns to me and James. "How about you?"

I still have my swimsuit on, so...

"We were planning to go swimming earlier," I admit. "You guys can go ahead of us, though. I'm supposed to carve my name on the wall in James' cave."

"Oooh!" Cassidy looks from me to Matthew. "That sounds fun. I wanna find something to carve *my* name on too. Can I borrow the box cutter when they're done?"

"Only if you swear you won't tell Mom—or run with a knife in your hand."

"Deal!"

They take off in the direction of the sandy beach.

Matthew watches them go for a moment before offering us an easy smile. "I'll grab the box cutter and meet you by the cave."

He flashes a thumbs-up and vanishes. James glances to the north, toward the sandy turnout at the top of the cliff where the last two cars are parked far out of sight. Then he sighs and meets my gaze with a passive, sheepish smile.

"Sorry about Matt," he says, taking my hand to begin the trek out of the tidepools. "Even before I met you and got into it with Ice again, I was having…problems—I mean, with my dad and couch-surfing and everything, y'know? He's a lot, but he's just relieved to see me in a good mood. And getting out at all, I guess. I was kind of a shut-in for a while there."

"I don't mind Matt," I say. "But, if it makes you feel better, I've always been kind of a shut-in too. I get nervous around so many people. I feel like I never know what to say. Most the time, I just sit in the background and…listen to everyone else."

"We don't have to go to things like this if you don't want to."

"I don't mind," I admit. "Parties, hanging out with a bunch of people, whatever. It can be fun if I'm with someone I like."

I drop James' hand, step up onto a rock, and jump off, landing in the soft sand on the other side. Our eyes meet as I glance over my shoulder. And, suddenly, I can't help but remember the way his hands explored me earlier, trailing warmth in their wake. The love and adoration in his eyes. *The relief.*

And I smile as I turn away again. "Matt's right, you know? We're adults, and we can do whatever we want even if I'm human, and you're an immortal."

"Oh, ah— I don't think it's so simple. For that exact reason."

"Mm..." I hesitate, looking back as he steps down from the rocky outcropping. "I mean, it's not *illegal* or anything, is it?"

He laughs. "It's not illegal, but we should still be careful."

Careful? Careful...?

Matthew's reappearance a good hundred yards ahead, near the mouth of the cave, distracts me. He looks around and waves as he spots us coming. When we meet up with him, he grins and hands a folded utility knife to James. It's a well-loved box cutter, the handle plastered with rainbow duct tape.

"Thanks..." James looks to me with a muted frown. "We'll meet you at the water in a few."

"A'ight."

Matthew drops his wet tank top in the sand, turns toward the ocean, and yells Cassidy's name. They were splashing about in the shallowest waves in feline form, but they freeze and look up just as their brother morphs and races across the sand as a rust-colored cat.

"I'll get you!" he calls, garnering a squeal from Cassidy, who takes off running further to the north along the beach.

James lets out a breath. Then he turns and steps inside the cave ahead of me. I follow close behind, scanning the sandstone walls.

"Where do you want to put it?" he asks.

It sounds like he just wants to get it over with, which is kind of lame. But I drape my shirt over my backpack and study the wall behind it—the one with the majority of destroyed carvings. *Surely, these were things James wanted to forget.* None of the inscriptions I've seen include dates more recent than three years ago. But most of the dated ones still visible on this wall are *old* —going back ten or eleven years, with some even older.

There's plenty of room here, but…

I turn and point to the opposite wall. "Over there is fine."

He glances over his shoulder to see where I'm pointing. Then he nods. As I cross the cave, he kicks the sleeping bag out of the way, and we stand in front of the wall together.

There aren't as many carvings on this side, and most are more recent, including the ones Matthew mentioned. Stick figures with swords and horns and pointed ears. I press my palm to the gritty, red sandstone. It's rough and solid. *Wow, I kinda feel bad for pushing him up against this earlier.* But sandstone is a fairly soft stone—compared to other stones, anyway. *I think.*

"Is it hard to carve into the wall?" I ask.

He shakes his head and looks from me to the box cutter in his hand. I follow his gaze, and we're quiet for an uncomfortably long moment. Long enough for it to finally sink in—the realization that he's holding a *knife*.

Then he flips it open.

It's not a pocket knife. It's just a utility knife with a small, angled razor blade meant for slicing boxes open. I used a similar one while working at CoffeeStar last summer—to cut those thick plastic ties and open boxes full of lids and cups and flavor syrup. But the sight of silvery metal triggers something in the deepest recesses of my mind, and my heartbeat quickens.

"Look," James says. His voice is level, but his brows are furrowed as he holds the blade to the cave wall. "Even with something as shitty as this, you don't have to press too hard."

I watch closely. The sound of the thin blade scratching the stone is grating, but he doesn't seem to have any trouble carving his name into the wall.

JAMES REID // 20

The marks the knife left behind are thin and shallow but far lighter in color than the weathered stone around them, the contrast making the letters stand out. There's something incredibly cool about the process—or...*I don't know*—and I find myself asking for the knife more eagerly than I thought I would.

My lack of hesitance seems to bother James, but he steps aside and holds the unfolded box cutter out for me.

I take his place and accept the knife, and...*nothing happens*. No jolt of fear. No stolen breath. No shiver up my spine or flash of unwanted memory. *Nothing*. Somehow, that startles me more than I imagine any of those other things would have.

My hand trembles ever so slightly as I raise the knife to the wall, but the trembling stops once the blade touches stone, and I carve my name just below his. One line at a time. One letter at a time. Something about the act of writing my name into the wall of an ancient sandstone cave with a busboy's utility knife is oddly surreal. The obvious resistance of rough stone. The blade skipping over a piece of harder grit. Retracing the line with more force. Thin scrapes left behind in a brighter shade of whitish red. *A long, pink scar on my forearm.*

JAYDE PALMER-19

"Here, um…" I look to James with a smile that feels off in a way I can't quite pinpoint myself. "Can you do the date for me?"

Concern flickers in his eyes, and I'm beginning to understand his hesitance when Matthew first suggested the idea. Holding a knife is a necessary part of carving words into stone. *Duh.*

I return the box cutter and step away from the wall. He takes my place to finish the engraving, and I clasp my hands together just so they have somewhere to be. I look down at them. At the heart on my wrist. At my feet. At the sand below.

Last time I held a knife…

"I tried to stab him," I whisper. James makes a soft noise, but the scraping of metal against stone only pauses for a second, so I don't look up. "When I met with Ice. The knife was in my pocket. I don't remember, but I must have grabbed it from the floor before we left for the hospital. Anyway, he realized I had it, and, when he asked for it back, I just…went for it. But the hinge was messed up, and I was too slow. He caught my arm. It freaked me out, but he just laughed at me like it was nothing."

A beat of silence.

"What would you have done if he didn't stop you?"

"I—"

I look up, but James' narrow-eyed attention is on the wall.

"I don't know," I admit. "I mean, maybe it's stupid, but, in that moment, I felt like I was no better than he was. Like trying to hurt him in retaliation or revenge or whatever meant stooping to the same level and losing myself."

"You still think we can get out of this peacefully." It's not a question, and the frustration leaking into his mild voice isn't lost on me.

"I don't know, but I have to try. I don't want to die. I don't want you to die. And I don't want us either of to live with the guilt of hurting anyone else."

"What guilt? What's one more thing to feel bad about?"

Without thinking, I hug him from behind. My cheek rests in the space between his shoulder blades as I stare at the bright cave entrance with wide eyes. He sighs, chest rising and falling beneath my hands.

"Sorry," he says softly. "Anyway, I'm done. Now your name will be recorded in stone forever."

Forever?

I free James and step back, turning to face the opposite wall. "What about those ones?"

"Which ones—? Oh. *Those* ones." He sighs again. "Yeah. Well, whatever happens, I won't scratch your name off. Even if you end up hating me someday."

I bite my tongue to keep from asking more questions. Instead, I look back to see how our wall carving turned out. It's just our names, ages, and today's date. I almost want to add a heart, *but it'd probably turn out like the one on my wrist.*

James tosses the folded utility knife toward the mouth of the cave. It lands a couple feet from the tank top Matthew left in the sand.

"You still feel like swimming?" he asks.

When I nod, he doesn't hesitate to pull his shirt off.

forty-three

We relax on beach towels and eat the sandwiches April left behind. The mood is comfortable and easygoing, and it truly seems that Matthew is over the mess we made this morning. I'm sure they'll talk about it more later, but they're best friends. It's nothing that can't wait. Still, James' smile falters when Matthew suggests the three of us hang out on his birthday.

"And do what?" he asks as though he can't think of a single thing we could do on his birthday of all days.

Matthew seems equally confused. "I have the day off, so we can do whatever you want. Hang out at my place or the mall— Actually, the mall might be better. I think there's a tournament that day. Could be fun, right?"

"Magic?" James asks. Matthew nods, and he glances aside. After a moment of quiet thought, he looks to me. "It'll probably be boring for you, but I wouldn't mind going."

"I'll go," I say without hesitation.

Even if I have no idea what the actual plan is, hanging out with Matthew sounds better than staying at James' dad's house or sitting around by ourselves somewhere in town the whole day.

"Alright, we'll go," he agrees.

Cassidy perks up. "Can I come too?"

James shrugs, though he seems less bothered by the idea now than he was when it came to them attending the bonfire or riding here with us. Their easy smile all but confirms that they've successfully secured James' trust—at least in part.

"I don't mind hanging out with Cassidy while you do your tournament or whatever," I say. "I mean, we spend so much time together already; it's only fair I give Matt a chance to hang out with you too."

"Aah—" Matthew swoons against James' shoulder, only to be pushed back into sitting up, though being rebuffed has no effect on his dramatics. "See, James? She understands. You know, I almost thought you were dead for a while there. I was worried! But, now that I know you're fine—*mostly*—I just wanna hang out. You're my best friend."

James' expression softens as he looks away. "Whatever, man. It's not like I was trying to worry anyone."

He looks the slightest bit embarrassed, while Matthew's concern appears mostly exaggerated—even if I can only imagine how deep his concern must have been previously. Though, I have a feeling they banter like this a lot.

I miss Rose. I feel like I've barely seen her all summer. And, now, I can't even talk to her.

Cassidy taps my arm, and I glance over. Their large amber eyes are the most feline of any immortal's eyes I've seen. Wide but unconcerned. Focused and inquisitive. More intense than you'd expect from a twelve-year-old.

Then they flash a toothy grin, broad and crinkling the corners of their eyes. "If you and your friend are anything like Matt and James, you'll be fine."

They sound so confident, I almost believe it.

"What's that?" Matthew catches my attention and frowns. "You and your roommate not getting along again?"

I force a smile and look at my hands. "Rose was there when Ice stabbed James. I mean, neither of us saw it happen—I wasn't lying when I said I wasn't in the room—but she saw the aftermath. The...blood. And she saw him morph."

"Oh."

Yeah.

"Anyway, Human-Immortal Affairs took her away before you met up with me at the hospital, and I haven't heard from her since. Pretty sure she's ignoring me."

"Well," Matthew says, his voice light again. "Cass is right. I'm sure she just needs time, and you'll be talking again real soon. I mean, James has put up with me for, what, almost six years now?"

"*I* put up with *you*?" James asks in surprise.

He laughs. "Yeah, man. I'm hella annoying, right?"

"What? And I'm not? Disappearing for weeks just to show up with all sorts of trouble?"

"Not even kidding, you're one of my least annoying friends," he says with a passive shrug. "And one of the most trustworthy. Seriously. I feel like I can tell you just about anything."

"Whaaat? You're joking."

Matthew's laughter is easy and warm, but James is puzzled. Soft frown. Furrowed brows. Head slightly askew. He's looked at me like that before. Like he can't understand why anyone genuinely wants him around. Like he can't comprehend how anyone can laugh at all considering the circumstances. Like there's no time for brevity.

"James," I say. Matthew's laughter stops, and both men look to me. "It's okay to let our guard down too sometimes. If I've learned anything from what happened with Rose, it's that we have to trust our friends. That's the only way we'll feel okay to focus on ourselves. And what we have to do."

He stares at me for a moment. Then he sighs and glances away with the faintest smile.

"What we have to do, huh?"

* * * * *

It's just after 5PM when we start packing up and gathering the last of our things from around the beach. Together, we hike up the narrow trail to the top of the cliff. Matthew groans as he drops his cooler once we're all back on flat ground.

"You could've teleported," Cassidy says with a laugh.

"I'm trying to be a good friend," he argues—though he doesn't sound winded, and I know for a fact that the cooler isn't heavy because I moved it earlier.

James stifles a groan and holds a hand over his left side. "If you wanted to be such a good friend, you should've teleported me up here."

Matthew purses his lips and lifts the cooler without a hint of effort. I take the sleeping bag from James and look him over. He seems more out of breath than me despite having carried so little.

"You okay?" I ask. "Good to drive?"

"Mm… My ribs are acting up a little." He flashes a tired but otherwise warm smile. "Maybe you were right about taking it easy. But, as much as I'd like to hide out here another night with you, we're out of food. We'd starve."

"We can eat the crab from the tidepool."

He laughs, straightening up with a fleeting wince. "I wish, babe. But we gotta head back to town."

Back to town. To Riverview. Closer to Ice.

But I have to agree.

We follow Matthew and Cassidy down to the sandy turnout —to the red convertible. The cooler and their bags go into the trunk. Cassidy gives me a tight hug before hopping into the passenger seat and donning a pair of sunglasses. Matthew hugs James, then rounds to the driver's side of his car.

"See ya in a few," he says. "And let me know if you need anything, okay?" James nods, and Matthew's upbeat expression grows a bit strained. "I mean it, James. *Anything*. Just text me, and I'll pop in no questions asked."

James nods a second time, his smile mild. "Thanks, man. We'll see you in a few days."

"See you later," I say.

Cassidy waves, Matthew offers a two-finger salute, and they drive off. The car leaves a cloud of dust hanging in the air over the turnout, but the ocean breeze quickly blows it away.

Now, without anyone left to impress, James looks exhausted.

"Ready to go?" he asks.

"Um…"

I look from him to his off-white car to the top of the ridge. The beach isn't visible from here, but the spot where we sat last night is. Short, scrubby bushes and yellow grass shift in the refreshing coastal wind. The sky beyond the cliff is bright blue with only a few wispy clouds far above the ocean.

This place feels welcoming. Safe.

I don't want to leave.

Maybe I wouldn't mind living on the beach. We could build a wall out of driftwood to block the sandstone cave off from the cold. We could eat nothing but fish, crab, and wild berries. I'd almost rather do that than go back to whatever's waiting for me in Riverview.

But, obviously, we can't stay here.

"You good?" James asks.

I look back with a smile. "Yeah, I'm good. Let's go."

He mirrors my pathetic smile, and I walk around the car to the passenger side. We toss everything into the backseat, and the car rumbles to life as I buckle my seatbelt. Then I stare out the rolled-down window as the car backs up in the sand.

The stone slab at the top of the ridge. Where we sat and talked last night. Where I sat alone, crying in my dreamscape. Sky overcast and dark. Hair cut short, buffeted by cold wind.

And James…

But I catch myself. Is the dream worth worrying about? I don't have proof that every lucid dream means something or reflects the future. It could just be a random nightmare, a manifestation of my anxiety. It's not like I've never had nightmares before.

Night said I shouldn't trust the dreamscape, anyway.

I tear my gaze from the scenery outside. "We're still going to my house first, right?"

"Sure." He sounds surprisingly unaffected, so he must have come to terms with it already. "I could use a long shower."

"Me too," I say with a laugh. I have sand in some *unexpected places*, and not having to worry about running out of hot water while trying to rinse it all off would be great.

God, I hate his dad's house.

I sigh. "Anyway, you had a good time this year, right? Despite everything?"

"Ha." He glances at me, flashing a hesitant smile as his grip on the steering wheel tightens ever so slightly, then returns his attention to the road ahead. "Yeah... Somehow, this year's bonfire was better and worse than I imagined."

I laugh again. "It was...definitely a lot."

"But I'm glad we came. Thanks for talking me into it."

"Of course." I look at my lap. My hands. "At first, I thought I messed up—by deciding to tell everyone the truth. It was hard on you, I know, and I'm sorry. But the rumors would never go away if we didn't do something about it ourselves. And I couldn't get what Paige said out of my head. I didn't want anyone to think any part of it was true, so..."

He sighs. "Jayde. You didn't mess anything up. You were right. I should've trusted you. And Matt. And...everyone else. Instead, I lost it. I was a real jerk. And I'm sorry for that. And for lying to you."

"I don't like talking about Ice either."

"I know."

But, even if it was the right thing to do, it wasn't easy. Knowing that so many people know what he did isn't easy.

The car falls quiet—well, it would be quiet if not for the air pouring in through the open windows now that we're back on the highway. I turn the radio on and cycle through channels of static until I find something that *almost* resembles music. We don't talk much, and I check my phone periodically until cell service returns.

Several notifications appear on my lock screen in quick succession. A few FaceSpace notifications are first on the list, but the app won't load because my reception sucks, so I back out to the home screen. There are a few notification bubbles on random apps. And two new text messages.

Please be Rose. PLEASE be Rose.

Ice Monroe

Attachment: 1 Image

Ugh— Of course.

Whatever it is, it was sent yesterday. I don't want to open it. I really don't. But I also don't want the notification to remain there indefinitely, and I need to know if it's anything important. So I tap to open them. Both messages were sent at 8:47PM. The attachment looks like a picture of *drawers*. A dresser? It's familiar. That alone leaves a pit in my stomach, *but the text...*

Ice: Dust accumulates in your absence.

What? I tap to expand the thumbnail, and— *Yep. That's what*

I thought. The picture is of a white chest of drawers, wider than it is tall. On top, the hand-painted jewelry box I picked up from a yard sale when I was thirteen. A Phoenix, Arizona snow globe —*it's ironic*, as Rose said when she gave it to me. The bottom of several photographs taped to the edge of a mirror. The calculus textbook I *still* haven't found a permanent home for partially covered by a folded, grey cardigan.

The moment I saw the full image, I knew it was taken from inside my bedroom. *But how the hell did Ice get inside if he doesn't have a key?* And *why* would he go there? What was he doing? Was he looking for me?

This is so annoying! How am I supposed to convince James to stay at my house if Ice keeps breaking into it?

"Um… James?"

"What's up?"

I look up and hesitate. Will he still agree to stop by today if he knows that Ice was there while we were gone?

Oh, shut up. You promised *to tell James if he contacted you.*

I take a deep breath. "Don't freak out—because everything is totally fine—but I got another text from Ice."

"Oh?" Irritation flickers across his face as he looks back to the road. "What'd he say?"

"Well… I mean, it was sent yesterday. Last night. And, um, it's a picture of the dresser…in my bedroom."

"At your house?"

That's where my bedroom is.

"The text says, *Dust accumulates in your absence.*"

He groans, thumb tapping the steering wheel. "And that's it?

How the hell did he get inside?"

"That's it," I say slowly. "But I'm not sure how he got in. Maybe we forgot to lock a window? Anyway, I bet this means he has no idea where we've been staying. That's good, right?"

James is quiet for a long moment. Then he groans again. His shoulders fall as he glances aside to meet my gaze with a clear mix of frustration and grim disappointment.

"Lemme guess; you still want to go?"

I force a smile. "Just to shower?"

"Fine," he huffs, adjusting his grip on the steering wheel. "But only to shower. We can do laundry at my dad's—save five bucks that way, anyway."

Who cares about five dollars?

With a sigh, I back out of Ice's messages and tap Rose's name further down the list. I'm met with the depressing series of unread and unanswered texts I've sent. But I type out another.

Me: Just wanted to let you know I'm back from the coast. I hope you're doing alright.

If we weren't in the middle of...*whatever this is*, I'm sure she'd be dying to know how my trip went, considering I went with my *boyfriend*. She'd have a million questions. And, this time, the answers might surprise her. *For more than one reason.* But I have no idea when I'll be able to talk to her about anything —let alone this.

I almost put my phone down. I'm tired. Today was *a lot*. But, even if I don't actually want to know *why* Ice was in my house last night, I return to the conversation and stare at the small photo of my dresser. I read the accompanying text again and again, my thumb hovering over the text-input box. And I finally decide that I need to know.

> **Me:** How did you get in? Did you lie to me?
> Do you still have a key??

Then I lock my phone and look out the passenger window.

forty-four

When we arrive, the front door is locked.

James unlocks it using his key and steps inside ahead of me to search the first floor. I'm fairly certain we're the only ones here, but that doesn't stop me from locking the door behind me.

"First floor's clear," James says.

"Okay."

As he heads upstairs, I take a moment to look around for myself. I'm still not sure how I feel about the couch facing away from the door, but the only other off thing I've noticed is a pile of mail on the bookcase shelf I usually leave my purse on.

Hm.

I peek through the blinds beside the door. Ice's silver Porsche is nowhere to be seen, and the window is securely locked. Then I step aside and shuffle through the envelopes. The pile contains things addressed to me and Rose mixed together. None are opened, but none look especially important either.

Did she stop by and check the mail, or…?

This definitely wasn't here last time we stopped by, but the mail key is where we always leave it, hanging on the small hook on the side of the bookcase.

Ice was here, but why? What was he doing?

"House is clear," James says, coming back down the stairs.

"Okay, one last thing—" I cross to Rose's bedroom door, push it open, and step inside. "Ice said he got in through here. He said the window was cracked open."

The room is empty and looks the same as I remember from last week, but, sure enough, the window on the wall opposite the door is unlocked. The window screen was left on the dresser beside the window, propped up against the wall.

I open the window and pop the screen back into the frame. Nothing seems to have been damaged, and the window locks fine, so I think Ice was telling the truth. Rose must have left it unlocked at some point. Honestly, I don't remember checking this window either time we were here.

"The rest of the windows should still be locked," I say as we leave the bedroom. "I can double-check if you want, but no one can get inside without breaking a window now."

"You're sure?" he asks.

I nod. "I don't trust Ice—obviously, I'm not stupid—but I'm sure we'll be fine for a couple hours."

"Alright," he agrees, glancing away.

"Now, go take that shower."

He frowns. "Will you stay upstairs?"

"If it makes you feel better."

"It will."

I sigh, but I follow James upstairs and kiss him before locking myself in my bedroom as promised. I have no idea what he thinks this would accomplish on the off chance Ice does show up and try to break in. I wouldn't be able to hear any commotion downstairs over the sound of the shower running in the other room.

But it's fine. Because Ice isn't going to show up.

I slide open my dresser's top drawer. I was planning to put together an outfit to change into after my shower. But grey fabric folded on top of the dresser distracts me, and I close the drawer without removing anything.

I pick up the cardigan instead. The cardigan I noticed in the photo Ice sent. The one I threw on the ground and abandoned the night we met in the woods.

It smells like the sweet, heavily scented fabric softener used in the Monroe house. *Ugh.* I can't believe he picked it up—let alone bothered washing and returning it—but I put it away. Then I look through my jewelry box and move a few things around to make sure nothing was disturbed or taken. Everything is accounted for, the photo collage on the wall is fine, and the mirror itself is too. The *stupid* calculus textbook—

Oh.

Lifting the textbook revealed something hidden underneath. Only the corner was visible before—just a bit of white paper—so I thought nothing of it, figuring it was old class notes or something. *But—*

I set the textbook aside and pick up the envelope. It looks like the type of envelope a greeting card might come in. I turn it over and immediately recognize the handwriting on the back. My name, *Jayde Nicole Palmer*, written in pretentiously fancy script.

What a pain…

Should I wait for James before I open it?

I stand around for at least a full minute, listening to the shower through the wall. I look at the privacy lock on the door. I move to the window and scan the empty expanse of short, dry grass between my house and the trees of Windsor Park.

And I look again at the envelope in my hand.

Opening it now should be fine.

It's just paper. No matter what it says, the note itself is harmless. If it contains anything important—or *dangerous*—I can show James once he's out of the shower. Right?

Right. Yeah, this is fine.

I open the envelope, remove the contents, and unfold the paper. The letter takes up the entire page and is neatly written in black ink on cream stationary.

My dear Jayde,

I recently received a check for $1500 and a certificate from Human-Immortal Affairs with your name on it. I took the liberty of depositing $750 into your bank account this morning, but the other half went into my personal account as compensation for my trouble. You can expect your payments to be garnished in a similar fashion for the foreseeable future. As for the certificate, I think it looks quite nice on my desk.

Rude, but whatever.

I guess those are the checks James mentioned—*SIP, right?* Or something similar? I didn't realize Human-Immortal Affairs would issue payments to me, though…

And $1,500 seems like a lot…

On an unrelated note, I find my current difficulty in locating you rather vexing. Your cottage has been quiet for some time, yet Reid Manor also lies empty. Wherever have you been staying? You haven't skipped town on me, have you? I'm certain you know by now that nothing good will come from ignoring me.

If it comes down to it, Fayde, I can and will find you.

A cool shiver runs down my spine as I chew the tip of my thumbnail.

This is just gross.

All discourse aside, I hope you find the pocket change useful. Feel free to splurge. Spoil yourself. Replace the clothes you've lost. Or buy more cookies. Your favorite is M+M, right?

Double gross!

Best regards.
Ice Monroe

Best regards?

Yeah, right. His writing is pretentious as usual, but the sarcastic tone contrasts our last encounter so much that I can't take any of it seriously.

Showing this vapid garbage to James would only upset him more. I mean, Ice probably only wrote it to rub in the fact that I'm barely in control of my own life anymore. Even the threat —*if you can call it that*—feels empty.

Nothing about the letter strikes me as particularly dangerous.

I already know I can't ignore Ice, and I'm sure he *could* find me if he tried. But I wasn't planning to ignore him or leave town for more than a day or two until I'm sure this is over.

No. If anything, this letter is good news.

He doesn't know where we've been staying. James was right in thinking Ice wouldn't check his father's house.

I crumple the letter and drop it into the wastebasket beside my desk. Then I check my bank account. Sure enough, I'm $750 richer than before, as of yesterday. *Nice.* I wanted to buy a birthday present for James, and now I have plenty of cash to spare.

With a final glance at my name written on the back of the envelope, I drop it into the trash too.

* * * * *

Convincing James to stay a while longer after my shower was surprisingly easy. All I had to do was ask nicely, turn on the TV, and offer to order pizza, and he caved. Obviously, he's not thrilled about going back to his dad's house either.

And everything is fine. The house is secure, and the person who delivers the pizza is not Ice. I feel great.

I browse the internet for gifts while James is distracted by his phone. Eventually, I settle on a "good used quality" GameStation X, three highly rated video games that look interesting, and a $20 gift card. The purchase takes a decent bite out of the $750, but I have a fair amount left over. Maybe we can go to dinner after hanging out with Matthew.

Either way, I don't regret spending the money. The main issue is that the packages will be delivered *here* in a few days—because I couldn't remember his dad's address and didn't want to elicit suspicion by asking.

But that is a problem for future me.

I open FaceSpace to get on top of the notifications that bombarded my phone earlier. Rose doesn't look to have been online at all while I was gone, but I have friend requests from Matthew, Cassidy, and Dawn Corel. I wasn't expecting a friend request from Dawn, but I accept all three. Interestingly, both Matthew and Dawn are mutual friends with Night.

Back on my newsfeed, I find a ton of photos from the beach.

Cassidy uploaded over one hundred images. I scroll through the album, which contains dozens of landscape photos and macro images—the seascape, the sandstone cliffs, close-ups of plants and tiny crustaceans, vague impressions of fossils, and random textures—along with a handful of selfies, far-off shots of the party crowd and bonfire at night, various food items, and other random pictures. There's one of me and James, taken from behind while we were crouched over a tidepool. I tag myself in the photo before saving it to my phone.

Matthew posted less than his sibling, but still a fair amount. Most are selfies with his friends, including a few with James. In one solo selfie taken well after nightfall, he's wearing...*Carmen's sunglasses?* Wait, no. I think the Choi twins wore matching pairs, so they're probably Natalie's. *Yeah, that makes more sense.*

I show the photo to James. He grimaces, and I laugh.

Carmen's uploads are mostly selfies too. Some alone, some with others, and some with a half-empty wine cooler in her hand. Many have interesting filters and stickers on them. I find the one she took of us before sunbathing. It's just as cringy as I remember, but I save it anyway—along with the ones we took in front of the bonfire, in which she looks *plastered.*

James uploaded one photo—the *decent* selfie he took of us at the tidepool. The tiny red mark from Paige's ring is faintly visible below his eye, but he looks really happy. We both look happy. He didn't tag me or include a caption, but it's his profile picture now.

I spent half the ride here sorting through and touching up the photos I took, so they're easy to upload. Pictures of the ocean. Selfies with James. A few more with Carmen and/or Natalie. One with Cassidy. A couple alone.

After tagging everyone involved, I close FaceSpace and open the messenger app. Rose still hasn't read any texts *or* FaceSpace messages I've sent, and her *last active* status looks to have been shut off, so I can't even tell if she's been lurking.

Ugh... Well, if she happens to see the photos, at least she'll know I'm doing alright. I guess.

With a sigh, I lock my phone and snuggle closer to James.

Then the movie ends, the sun dips low in the sky, and it's time to leave. James doesn't want to stay after dark. I still don't want to go at all, but I don't argue.

So, here we are, sitting in the car, parked on the curb outside his father's house. The beat-up truck is parked in the driveway, and neither of us want to go inside and deal with his dad. At least the temperature is more tolerable today.

"Maybe he's asleep," I say.

"With my luck?"

I frown. "Well, we can't stay out here forever."

We exchange a look, and James groans, dragging his hands down his face. I get it. Completely. I wish we could climb in through his bedroom window to avoid going through the first floor. It's not realistic, but he laughs at the suggestion.

"I've done it," he says.

"Seriously?"

"Seriously!" He laughs again before resting his chin on arms crossed over the steering wheel. His expression mellows as he looks out the windshield. "We had a big fight. I don't remember what it was about, but it was pretty bad, and he kicked me out. I didn't have a car yet—I was only fourteen or fifteen—and it was the middle of winter. So I took a ladder from a neighbor's yard and used it to climb back into my bedroom through the window."

"Oh."

"Jesse snuck me food while I skipped school, and our dad waited three days to call and ask where I was and why I wasn't in class. When I walked downstairs with the phone in my hand, he wasn't even mad to see me again. He couldn't remember the fight at all. He was too drunk, I guess—same as Memorial Day weekend."

"*Oh*."

He sighs. "Yeah. Pissed me off."

I pat his shoulder, and he glances over. He looks tired, but he leans across the center console to kiss me. And, one mutually half-assed pep talk later, we're finally out of the car with our backpacks on.

Still holding my hand, James steps through the unlocked front door ahead of me. We make it through the kitchen, then a throat clears. Eyes lock onto us from across the dimly lit room, where Jonathan Reid sits at the couch. James freezes, his grip on my hand tight, as his father looks both curious and annoyed to see us again.

"Where'd you run off to this time?" he asks.

"My birthday party—out on the beach."

"Did ya see Jesse?"

James winces. "Yeah? He was there. He's been in town for a couple weeks now. Why?"

The staircase looks extremely attractive right now. I hate being in the middle of this. *I hate it.* I wish James would just ignore his dad and keep walking. He shouldn't have to put up with this either.

"That girl—" Jonathan says. I look back to find him vaguely gesturing at me with the tall beer can in his hand. "She's over eighteen, right?"

"What the *fuck*, Dad?"

Okay, that's it— I adjust my grip on James' hand and drag him toward the stairs. He resists for a second, then he turns away from his dad, and we make it to the bedroom without much of a fuss.

James turns the privacy lock and stands with his back to the door. "Sorry. He's usually not this annoying."

"Are you okay?"

He nods. His cheeks are a touch pink, so it must have been embarrassing, but it's hardly the worst thing I've witnessed since we started staying here. *And not the first time his father has asked about my age.*

I leave my bag beside the door, and, as I turn to face the small, stuffy bedroom, I feel like summer couldn't end soon enough.

forty-five

Aah… This sucks…

Riverview must be twenty degrees hotter than the coast during the hottest part of the day. The refreshing ocean wind spoiled me. I almost forgot how hot it was here. It's so bad, I've resorted to sprawling out on the bed in feline form. The room is still too hot, but lounging around this way is more comfortable. At the very least, I don't sweat as a cat, and the air *almost* feels cool on my damp nose.

The documentary that was playing on my phone ended a few minutes ago. When I first put it on, I thought I might take a catnap to kill time, but my mind won't stop wandering.

And now the room is quiet. Just the buzzing fan.

I open my eyes and look past the River Sapphire and my phone's dark screen to James, who is sitting on the edge of the bed in human form. He was reading on his phone when I last checked, and he's still reading now. His messy, orange hair flutters in the fan's breeze.

For a moment, it's hard to believe I'm here. Staying in James' childhood bedroom. Lying around in feline form.

A strange, fleeting sense of unrealness. A disconnect.

"Hey," I say, if only to break the silence.

James doesn't look up from his phone, but he acknowledges me with a small sound, and I hesitate. I'm not sure what I wanted to say. I just wanted to talk—to say anything to break the silence.

"Um…" *Think of something… Something interesting… Oh!* "Do immortals have a higher body temperature than humans?"

"What?"

He laughs and glances over his shoulder, his smile blank and brows furrowed—like my admittedly random question was the last thing he expected. It's something I've wondered about for a while but never thought to ask. Though, all I can do in my feline form is tip my head and blink at him.

"Do you know?"

"Hm…" He glances aside, frowning thoughtfully. "Pretty sure we do. Average human body temperature is something like ninety-eight degrees, right?"

"Mm-hm. They used to say it was ninety-eight-point-six— that's what they taught us in elementary school, anyway—but Rose learned a couple terms ago that the average is actually something more like ninety-seven-point-five."

"Yeah. Immortal body temperature is a bit higher, then. We usually run somewhere between one hundred and one-hundred-and-one degrees, which is closer to a cat's average body temp. I think."

"All cats aren't immortals, right?"

"No way," he says through poorly stifled laughter. "Regular domestic cats exist too. Did you think they didn't this whole time?"

"No," I say. But I feel my tail flick, betraying my offense. "It was a joke. Obviously."

"Right."

I fail to keep from laughing. "I'm serious! I'm not dumb, you know. It was just too quiet in here. I wanted to hear you laugh."

He rolls his eyes and looks back to his phone.

He can tease me all he wants, but knowing that immortals run hotter than humans makes a lot of sense.

I crawl closer, careful to keep my claws from catching on the bedsheet, and roll onto my back with all four feline limbs tucked close to my body. I lean against James' thigh and stare up at him. He watches me with a curious, vaguely uneasy expression.

"It's weird seeing me like this?" I ask.

"Absolutely."

"Oh? You don't like it?"

He shrugs without answering.

With another laugh, I roll back onto my stomach and sit up. Then I catch the River Sapphire's cord with one paw and pull it off over my head. The necklace falls to the mattress, and I return to human form sitting on my knees. Our faces ended up closer than I expected—though the real surprise is that he doesn't immediately kiss me. *Which is fine. I guess.*

"I prefer you like this," he says.

I smile. "So, if you're a few degrees warmer than me, do I feel cold to you?"

"Cold?"

He drops his phone and cups my face in his hands. His hands are warm even compared to the surrounding hot air, and his expression is serious and focused. Several seconds of relative quiet pass as we search each other's eyes.

I wonder what he's thinking, but I don't ask.

Then his hands fall away, and he shakes his head. "You're not cold. But there is some difference, I think."

Some difference?

He smiles faintly, and, for some reason, my first reaction is to hug him. His hands move to my back, pulling me closer. He kisses the side of my head, and, as much as I wish it didn't, even a hug borders on uncomfortable in this heat.

"You feel especially warm to me," I admit. With a sigh, I lean back and out of the hug. "You're like a radiator or something. It sucks because it makes you harder to cuddle at night."

"Doesn't seem to stop you," he says dryly.

"It's worth it." I fall across his lap and stare at the ceiling, trying to ignore the heat seeping through my camisole and into my back. "But I bet those few extra degrees will really come in handy during the winter."

As I meet his gaze, his smile falters. "You think we'll still be together in the winter?"

"I hope so. I really like you, you know?"

"Yeah," he says quietly, glancing away again. "I know."

"Hey."

"What?" He doesn't look at me.

"I was thinking… Maybe, once Rose is talking to me again, we can look into adding you to the lease."

A flicker of surprise. Then he takes a deep breath. "Maybe…"

"What?" I feel my smile slip. "You don't wanna move in

with me?"

"Of course I do." His expression softens. A warm hand comes to rest on my stomach, but he's still looking at nothing in particular. "That would be amazing. Seriously. Getting out of here and never coming back sounds like a dream. But, with the way things have been lately, it's hard to imagine."

"It won't always be like this."

"No?"

"No. Summer will end, and Ice will go back to Palo Alto, where he can't bother us." I look past James to the window. The spinning fan blades. "He's supposed to graduate from *Stanford* next year. I don't think he'd mess up his entire future just because he's mad at us."

"You think he cares about school?"

The humor forced into his voice failed to mask his contempt, and I sit up. I feel bad for mentioning Ice since we were having a decent time, but James is still listening, and he doesn't look *upset*.

He tucks a few stray hairs behind my ear. His fingers linger on my jaw for a second before falling away.

"You think Ice cares about anything?" he asks more seriously.

"I think he cares about the way people see him."

"Well, yeah," he agrees. "But his reputation's gonna be fucked once everything we said at the beach gets out. There's no way he won't hear about it."

"All the more reason for him to want to leave, right?"

He doesn't answer. I ignore the slight tension in my jaw.

"I'll stay with you even if he doesn't," I say. "Even if we

have to stay in a motel. Even if we have to stay here."

He sighs, hands balled in his lap. "Jayde… You don't have to promise anything like that."

"I'm not just saying it to make you feel better. We've been through this already—tons of times, right? I'm not here because I'm scared of Ice or because I pity you or whatever. I'm with you because I want to be. Because I love you."

"I know." Shoulders falling, he looks from his hands to me to the half-empty closet across the room. "I'm sorry."

Why is it still so hard for James to believe that I genuinely care about him? Or that, one day soon, we'll be back in my air-conditioned living room, free to do whatever we want without having to worry about Ice? He wants that too, right?

I glance aside.

Damn it... I never know what to say when this happens. When it feels like there's something I *should* say, but it also feels like nothing I could say would make any difference. Because I don't have a real solution besides sit and wait and hope for the best as fall term approaches. And I know we both hate that.

"You're still scared, though, aren't you?" he asks.

"Me? Um—"

I look up to find him watching me with a murky and vaguely nervous but otherwise unreadable expression.

Why am I hesitating?

The answer is obvious, right?

I should be scared, right?

Ice almost killed us both. He hurt me. Tormented me. Ruined my life. But, honestly, I'm not sure if I am scared of Ice anymore

—at least when it comes to myself. Of course, I'm still worried about James, and I'm concerned for Rose's safety. But, now, when I think about Ice, I'm just...*frustrated*. Why do I feel so differently now? Meeting with him before was terrifying.

I don't get it.

"Sure," I say slowly. "I want everything to go back to normal, and I don't want anyone to get hurt. So I guess I'm scared it's not over yet—whatever that really means—but I won't give up no matter what. Not even if Ice tries anything again."

He sighs. "How long do you figure I have to stay with you before your senseless optimism rubs off on me?"

"At least a few more months."

"You're crazy. Seriously crazy."

"Oh, whatever." I laugh. "Well, if I'm right—if Ice leaves at the end of September, and we're still alive—you owe me. One-third of the cottage's rent is four hundred dollars, utilities included. You can afford that, right?"

He cracks a weary smile. "You want me to move in that badly, huh?"

"Maybe I do."

His smile falters. We stare at each other for a long moment.

I intentionally kept my tone lighthearted, but I'm serious. He deserves better than this. Better than staying here or squatting at Reid Manor or sleeping in his car. And I happen to be renting a perfectly livable house with more than enough room for a third person. I want him to stay with me.

Finally, he glances away.

"Okay," he says.

"Okay?"

"Yeah. If we survive the next month. If Ice leaves Riverview." He looks to me with the ghost of a smile and a hint of darkness in his golden eyes. "If you still want me when this is over, I'll move in with you. I'll do anything you want."

"You don't think it'll work out?" I ask sharply.

He shrugs. "I don't know. How could I know?"

Now, it's my turn to tear my eyes away. I look at my lap. At my clasped hands. The pink scars on my arms.

What does James think?

Does he think Ice won't leave for fall term—that he'd throw away his entire college career over *me*? Or does he think someone will die? *Who? Why?* Or, maybe, he's worried I'll change my mind—that I'll…come to my senses and ditch him the moment we're in the clear?

Ouch. If that's how I felt, why would I still be here?

Maybe I'm reading too much into it.

Maybe he's just nervous.

Maybe it doesn't *mean* anything.

"I love you," he says. "And I hope you're right. I really do. Because I want to stay with you."

"We'll be fine," I say.

"Fine, huh?"

"You told me the same thing, and I want to believe it."

"Mm…"

I have to believe we'll be fine. No one has to die. We just have to get through another month. One more month. Surely, we can manage that much.

The room falls quiet and feels a touch colder.

I listen to the fan in the window behind me. I stare at my hands—at my nails. I almost want to paint them again. I haven't painted my nails in a while. *Not since June.* Maybe I would if I brought any nail polish with me.

God... I just want to go home.

But I won't leave without James. I can't leave him here.

I don't know how much time passes.

A few minutes.

Several minutes.

Then James sighs. He leaves the bed and takes a couple steps before I glance up. He's standing near the middle of the room with his back to me, his posture slightly tense. What could he be thinking now, after such a long, awkward silence?

"Are you okay?" I ask.

"Oh. Yeah, I just..." He shifts his weight and clears his throat. When he finally glances over his shoulder to look at me, he flashes an off smile. "Are you hungry?"

Yeah, okay, so maybe he's not totally fine.

"I could eat," I say.

He continues across the room to the mini-fridge in the closet. I move my phone and the River Sapphire to the dresser, sit on the edge of the bed, and watch James carefully. But I don't even know what I'm looking for.

"We need to go shopping soon," he says. "There's enough for today, I think, but... I'll go pick up something to eat now. If that's okay."

"Sure."

He walks toward the bookcase, closer to the door. His expression is more or less unreadable, like he's intentionally trying to keep his emotions off his face. But his eyes remain sharp.

Why do I feel so weird about this?

"Want me to go with you?" I ask, resisting the urge to stand.

"Nah. It's fine." *He sounds fine, but—* "It won't take long."

"You sure?"

"Yeah," he says without hesitation.

He doesn't want me to go? He wants to be alone?

"Is your dad home?"

"Yeah." He glances at me again, but I *still* can't work out what he might be thinking—or feeling. "But I'm gonna head out through the window, so it doesn't matter."

"The window?" When he nods, I crack a smile. "You sure you don't want me to come? I bet I could nail a jump from the second floor now."

He laughs but shakes his head. "It's fine, Jayde. I can handle a fifteen-foot drop easy, even without a feline form to help stick the landing, but I'd rather you not risk it. Like I said, I won't be gone long. Less than an hour, I'm sure."

"Alright."

I didn't want to jump out the window, anyway.

Though, I'm curious what it's like. Ice made a fall from the third floor look easy, and he went out of a broken window backward in human form.

James grabs his backpack from the foot of the bed. As he stands, he hesitates. He looks at the bag in his hand. The locked door. And, finally, at me again. For a second, his face holds the slightest hint of familiar despondence. Then he takes a deep breath, puts his backpack on, and approaches me.

"I'm okay," he says with a mild smile. "Don't worry, alright? I'll be right back."

The words feel like a punch to the gut. I don't even know why—I can't pinpoint what feels so wrong—but *I have to trust him.* So I nod.

"I'll be here," I say.

He kisses my cheek and looks past me, to the window. As he steps aside and sets a hand on the edge of the bed in preparation for climbing up, the sight of his uneasy profile sends my heart racing. I stand from the bed, and he stops to look at me. His eyes are wide, confused. But I'm confused too. I'm not sure what came over me.

"I love you," I stammer.

He smiles, head tipped to one side. "I love you too?"

My face on fire, I step back and watch as James climbs onto the bed and pops the box fan out of the open window. He props the fan against the wall before glancing back to check on me. He looks more relaxed now. He doesn't look nearly as anxious.

He looks fine. Maybe I am overthinking it.

"Be careful," I say more softly.

"Sure. See ya in a few."

I look down, at my hands, so I don't freak myself out by watching him leave through the window. But I hear the soft thud as he lands, and I crawl across the bed to make sure he's okay.

He's already standing, dusting himself off. When he glances up and notices me in the window, he grins and offers a thumbs-up. *He totally dropped down in human form, didn't he?* Then he turns away and walks around the side of the house, toward the street.

I hold a hand to my chest. My heart's still beating a bit fast, but I think I'll be alright, so I return the fan to the window and sit in the middle of the bed, facing the empty room.

What is wrong with me lately?

With a sigh, I grab my phone and stretch out on the bed. I don't have any new notifications. Rose is still ghosting the world, but I give calling a go anyway. The same as yesterday, the call is sent straight to voicemail.

I hang up and drop my face to the pillow.

forty-six

True to his word, James returns within an hour. He brought Taco Bell and one cloth grocery bag, and he looks *fine*. If he talked to his dad on his way through the living room, it couldn't have been too bad. Maybe he was asleep. Either way, I'm not asking.

He drops his backpack beside the bookcase, hands the food to me, and crosses back to the closet.

This smells good. I guess I was hungry.

"I picked up more snacks," he says, kneeling in front of the mini-fridge. "Not much—granola bars, chips, whatever... But it should be enough to hold us over until tomorrow."

"Or we could just—"

He stands, having finished whatever he was doing, and I lose my train of thought as my eyes lock onto the black handgun tucked in the waistline of his jeans.

"Just what?" he asks, looking back at me.

Oh, um... I was about to suggest we go shopping today instead of waiting until tomorrow. It's still early, not even 5PM, and I wouldn't mind getting out for a while. But—

"Why do you have that?" I ask, my voice surprisingly cold.

"What?" Confusion flickers across his face. Then he glances down at the gun and laughs. "Oh, this? Something you said earlier reminded me of it, so I grabbed it before I came in."

Grabbed it? "From where?"

"My car. It's been in the glove compartment since, uh... Well, ever since we stopped staying at Reid Manor last month. Anyway, I kinda forgot about it until now. Why?"

Why?

I haven't seen James' black handgun since the day I fell out of the crawlspace. The day I landed on Ice and *his* gun, the cause of my second hospital stay of the summer. *The day we left Reid Manor for good.* I wasn't expecting to see it again. Maybe I forgot about it too. Maybe I just didn't want to think about it. *I didn't want to think about James constantly carrying a gun around. Or the piercing sound of a gunshot. Or the three small, circular holes punched into a wooden door inches from my hands. I don't want to remember how time slowed to a crawl as Ice cracked a smile and aimed his loaded gun at James.*

I don't want—

My heart races, and I shake my head in a desperate attempt to curb the thoughts from completely overwhelming me.

"I don't know," I say. "I just— Do we really need it now?"

"You never know, I guess."

"I guess..."

James stands there, a few feet from the bed, glancing around like he isn't sure what to do with himself. So I leave him to it and turn my attention to the paper bag in my lap. My stomach grumbles just looking at the colorful wrappers inside.

Maybe I haven't been eating enough...

I look up from the food again.

James is messing around on his phone. He seems a bit flustered but otherwise fine. He doesn't look particularly stressed or upset even after my reaction to seeing the gun.

Ugh.

He notices me watching and pockets his phone, and I continue staring, frustrated by how intensely uncomfortable I feel as he steps closer to stand in front of me. I don't move. I can't. All I can do is watch while he removes the gun from his waistline. As he stares at the weapon in his hand, my heart starts to feel like it might give out on me.

All I see, as James holds that gun, *is the same gun aimed at me. All I see is Ice knelt in front of me, frowning like I disappointed him, as he brings the gun to my forehead and presses the cold, hard tip between my eyes. Until the back of my head knocks against the wall.*

The paper bag in my lap crinkles as my grip on it tightens ever so slightly. My chest hurts. I tear my eyes from the gun, my mouth suddenly dry.

Why do I feel like this?

"Here," James says.

The word shocks me back to the present, and I look up from my lap. But it takes a second to register what he said even as he holds the gun out, flat on its side, in his hand.

He's...*offering it to me? Why?*

"You should hold onto it," he says. When I look from the gun to his face, he flashes a strange, sad, vaguely apologetic sort of smile. *Muddy.* "For safekeeping."

"Me? Ah…"

I clear my throat and set the Taco Bell bag on the dresser. He glances away like he knows I'm having a hard time, *but he still doesn't know what Ice did while he had me alone with that gun in the third-floor bedroom. He never saw Ice hold it against my head. He didn't get there until it was already over.*

He doesn't know. I never told him.

And, until now, I didn't think it had affected me this much.

I don't want to take the gun. I don't even want to *touch* it, but… *Ah…* Maybe it's better if James doesn't have it. At least I know I don't have the guts to use it.

"Alright," I agree.

I raise a hand to accept the gun, but I hesitate again. Our eyes meet as my fingers finally touch the plastic grip.

"It's loaded," he says. "The safety's on, but you still gotta be careful with it."

I nod and take the gun into my hand. *It's…heavier than I expected.* I stare at it, the black shape in my hand that my brain almost refuses to process as a real object, before looking up again.

What do you expect me to do with this?

His hand brushes my cheek, and he offers a more reassuring, if tired, smile. I force a smile in return, but I probably look a bit sick. I certainly *feel* a bit sick.

"I'll be right back," he says.

He steps away and heads for the door.

For some reason… *Even though he didn't look the same, all I saw in the second before he turned away was the vacant, glassy darkness that filled his eyes in July.*

The privacy lock clicks unlocked.

James' hand closes around the doorknob.

I jump to my feet. Heart pounding, still cradling the gun in both hands, I call his name—*James, wait.* He stops. He freezes. Then he glances back at me, his expression blank.

"Why do you have this, anyway?" I ask. My voice sounds too loud in the small room. "You never actually told me."

"I've had it for a long time," he says as though that explains *anything.*

"But *why?*"

He stares at me for a moment before sighing and turning back to the door. "It was years ago," he says, voice low. "But, uh... I thought I was in danger, so I picked up the gun just in case—to protect myself, I guess. I bought it from some...shady-ass guy; I dunno." He laughs softly, the sound off. "But I've never had to use it. Last month was the closest I ever came to firing it."

Danger...?

He opens the door and steps out, then pauses and turns to face me again. I'm uncomfortable, no thanks to the gun in my hand or our conversation or whatever, and I'm sure it shows on my face. I'm sure he knows, but he merely shakes his head and smiles.

"But I don't really want it anymore," he says. "I don't want that...responsibility hanging over my head all the time. So, I think it's better if you hold onto it for me. At least for a while, okay?"

I don't feel any closer to understanding, but...

"Okay," I say lamely. "I'll take care of it for you."

His smile brightens. "Thanks, babe."

And he leaves, closing the door.

I stand still for a moment. A long moment. My eyes drift from the door to the black handgun. *I think James is okay—mostly.* But I'm more out of my element than ever.

Knowing what this is capable of... How could Ice aim it at me like it was nothing? How could he switch the safety off and do that to another person and laugh about it? I can barely hold it pointing at the floor without freaking out.

Smothering a grimace, I look up from the gun.

I'm fine. It's just a gun. An inanimate object, harmless on its own. And James just wants me to hold onto it for a while. For safekeeping. *That's all. It's not a big deal. I can do this.*

I walk around to the foot of the bed and sit on the floor in front of my duffel bag. *He said he doesn't want the responsibility anymore.* What does that even mean? *Maybe he just doesn't want to know where it is...* I think I can work with that.

I unzip my bag and hide the gun at the bottom, wrapped in a camisole and buried beneath the rest of my clothes. I close the bag, certain it looks about the same as before I stuck the gun inside. Then I return to my spot on the bed and unwrap a soft taco. It's cooled to room temperature, but it's fine.

When James returns, he sits beside me. He doesn't mention the gun. He just smiles and asks for a taco, and everything seems normal.

He seems fine.

And I decide to be fine too.

forty-seven

~ ∞ ~

I open my eyes, and—

Goddammit.

The inky, swirling darkness and soft, flickering firefly lights give my dreamscape away. It's quiet, but the silence isn't overtly threatening, and I don't see anything of note in the abyss. Just me, illuminated in that strange but familiar way.

So I step forward.

The sound echoes through the void like a heavy footstep on the floor of an empty warehouse, and I freeze, eyes locked on my expensive leather boots. The air cools several degrees in an instant. Goosebumps prickle my skin as the cold settles in my bones. I hug my arms and look around. I turn a full circle, each cautious step ringing out as loudly as the first, but I see nothing. No Night. No mirage-like scenery in the distance. No creepy nightmare version of myself. *Thank god.*

"Hello?" I call, just in case. "Is someone there?"

My voice echoes the same as my footsteps, but I receive no answer. I'm alone? *Is that good or bad? What is happening? This feeling... I'm gonna be sick.* Still scouring my surroundings, still seeing nothing, I take a slow step back. And the firefly lights blink out, plunging me into an even more impossible darkness.

I raise my hands to suppress a gasp, but nothing happens. I don't gasp. I don't have hands. It's like, the instant the lights went out, I stopped existing. Now, only the oppressive void and deep, unsettling silence remain.

No. Oh, no no no... Not this kind of dream.

If it's gonna be bad...

Please, Jayde—wake up!

Out of the silence, a new sound.

It's...vaguely musical. Light and bright. A soft tinkling. Like ice cubes against the side of a glass. Or a wind chime, maybe. In any other context, it might be nostalgic, but I know my dreamscape better than that. I don't trust the gentle sound.

I don't want to know. I don't want to see. Whatever this dream wants to show me, I—

The musical tinkling slowly fades out.

The crushing weight of dread quickly replaces it.

Loud, painful static floods my disembodied mind. The sinking in my gut as panic seizes my chest and muscles. I can't think. I can't breathe. Even without my physical body. *Even without it, I feel everything.* Heart racing. Cold sweat beading on my forehead. Mouth parched as bitter bile rises in my throat.

This is a fear I've felt before.

The fear of death.

The mind-numbing resignation that washes over you as far too much hot blood slips through your fingers. The dark inside of your eyelids once you can no longer keep your eyes open.

An image of a black hole.

BANG—!

This time, I recognize the sound. It's not a skyrocket. *It's a gunshot.* And it leaves me reeling as my dreamscape flashes pure, blinding white for an instant. Just long enough to catch the dark silhouette of someone falling. *Collapsing.*

The body hits the floor with a sick thud.

And I'm once again plunged into darkness.

It's quiet too.

For a moment, I feel nothing. *Nothing.* My mind is a vacuum, one with the surrounding void. And I'm a blank slate. Listening. Waiting. *Waiting for what?*

Slowly, the surreal nothingness builds. Surprise. Confusion. Fear filling my lungs with concrete. The uncomfortable pressure of holding my breath. An unbearable, burning tightness in my chest.

Then a shrill, blood-curdling scream shatters the silence, and a torrent of frantic thoughts hit me at once. Disbelief. Horror. Pleading words spoken between sobs. *No, no... This can't be happening. This can't be real. Please get up... Get up!*

The sound—*my voice*—cuts out.

My knees buckle. I clutch my shirt, knuckles against my racing heart. I cough. Again and again, near dry-heaving, as I try to catch my breath. Just as breathing grows easier, the floor vanishes from underneath me. And I fall.

I cover my face with my hands as I fall further and further. Down, down, down. And I pray the landing will be enough to jolt me out of this hell.

When I finally hit the ground, the solid surface knocks the air from my lungs. It doesn't *hurt*, really, but it doesn't wake me either. I lie in the fetal position on the smooth, cold ground for a while. Hugging my dissenting stomach. Eyes squeezed shut.

Aah... I hate when it does this.

Eventually, my stomach calms, and, after coughing a few more times, I drag myself up to sit. I look around, but falling and landing doesn't seem to have changed much. It's still dark and cold and empty. It feels like I'm back where I started.

I stand. A speck of color in the endless void.

"What do you want from me?"

My voice echoes. As it fades after an honestly unreasonable length of time, something lands on the ground behind me. A soft pat. Like a book falling from a low table onto carpet. I turn to look, and my heart damn near stops.

The black handgun.

I step closer. Harsh light glints off the metallic components, making it stand out against the darker ground. With James' gun at my feet, I glance around again. I'm still alone. It's still quiet. But I don't like this. I don't like anything about this.

Why am I here?

I look back to the gun.

Why is this here?

I kneel to pick it up. It's cold and heavy, but nothing happens. No jarring sound. No foreign light. No cheap horror movie jump-scare. But, as I stand again, cool fear crashes over me. The warmth drains from my cheeks. My hands tremble. Stomach churns. Heart races. Chest locks up. It's the same as before, only worse, as my physical body is along for the ride.

I stare at the gun in my trembling hand. Taut muscles scream for me to run. But I can't move. I'm frozen in place. Glued to the floor. Trapped by the weight of a crushing terror I can't begin to comprehend.

Why is the gun here?

For several tense seconds, my quick, shallow breaths are the only sound in the dark. My eyes trained on the gun. Sinking anticipation. Then the small safety switch clicks into the off position on its own.

My mind reels.

A flash of wild blue eyes.

Blood—

I drop the gun.

~ ∞ ~

forty-eight

I lie awake. The room is hot and stuffy, and the air blown in by the fan does little to clear it. I stare at the open closet, the contents faintly lit by the neighbor's floodlight. I roll onto my back and stare at the popcorn ceiling for a moment. Then I carefully turn the rest of the way onto my other side.

James' eyes are closed.

He breathes softly, evenly. I set a hand on his chest. He doesn't move. He doesn't even shift. But heat soaks into my palm through his shirt. His heart beats in a steady rhythm.

He's here. He's alive. Warm. Fine.

Relief settles me a little, but frustration wells in my chest.

I hate this place.

But, deep down, I know James is right. His dad is annoying, but he's not dangerous—not the way Ice is. As long as we're here, we're safe. And James, who cares for my safety above all else, knows that. That's why he wants to stay here.

Everything will be fine as long as we're here together.

That's what he thinks.

But my dreams... The gunshot. The body.

I shouldn't take it at face value, right? It could mean anything.

Or nothing at all. Like Night said, dreams aren't simple, and that's doubly true for dreamscape visions. The future isn't set in stone. A single decision could change everything.

But, who knows; maybe I only had a nightmare about the gun because I spent the whole evening thinking about it. Maybe it was just a manifestation of my anxiety. Even if it's not, I'm sure…

It'll be fine. No one has to die. I won't let that future come to pass. This time around, I'll make better decisions. The right ones. I won't let Ice walk all over me. I won't hide in the crawlspace. Or the bathroom. I won't ignore the things I'm afraid of.

This time, I'll face my fears directly.

And everything will be okay.

* * * * *

I open my eyes to an unobstructed view of the wall. The open window with the box fan. The sky above the neighboring house is a cloudless blue. I must've fallen asleep again.

What time is it? Where's—?

I roll over to face the room and immediately feel better.

James is sitting on the floor. He's going through trading cards, taking them from a shoe box and sorting them into piles arranged around his open notebook. He drops a card and scribbles something in the notebook. After a moment spent chewing on the back of his pen while scrolling on his phone, he notices me watching and looks up with a smile.

I push my hair out of my face and smile back.

Tendrils of darkness, remnants of my dream, lurk in the back of my mind, but it's nothing James needs to worry about.

The dreamscape is my problem.

I crawl out of bed and sit beside him. As I look over the cards stacked on the carpet, he asks if I've ever played Magic. I shake my head and try to keep up with his rambling explanation.

Basically, it's a collectible battle card game, and each card represents a different character or item or whatever. Like Yu-Gi-Oh, I guess. But I'd never heard of Magic before it was mentioned a few times at the beach.

I admit that, and James laughs.

"Matt told me to bring a deck," he says. "No way am I touching that tournament, though."

"Is it hard to play?"

"No. But I haven't played in a couple years." He thinks about it for a moment. "Anyway, Magic's one of those things you never really escape, you know? I bought a few booster packs yesterday, but I'm not even sure what color deck I wanna build yet. I don't know shit about the current meta or what decks any of Matt's friends use. I think his main is still red/white, but..."

Out of curiosity, I pick up a card.

Adlein, Goddess of the Blue Flame

The character art is dynamic and fun—a busty, scantily clad woman wearing loose robes fashioned from neon blue flames—but the text below the artwork that details the card's abilities may as well be written in a foreign language. This doesn't seem like the type of game I'd be too interested in, though. I don't mind Uno and some of the other party games I've been roped into playing over the years, but this seems more...*involved?*

I return the card to its pile.

James sighs. "They added dinosaurs to the game. *Dinosaurs.* I don't know how to feel about that."

I watch him sort cards and write in his notebook for a while. As he goes on about strategy and potential deck matchups, talking mostly to himself, I find myself far more intrigued by the various creature designs than I expected when I first looked them over. But I eventually convince myself to get up and get dressed.

"Wanna go to the park later?" I ask.

"Oh? Is something going on today?"

"Not that I know of. I just wanna get out for a few hours and do more than just grocery shopping. It's too hot in here, you know? And I'm super bored."

"Yeah. I know." He looks up from the card in his hand and flashes a smile. "We can go. Let me know when you're ready."

I drop to the floor in front of my duffel and dig a hairbrush out of the toiletry bag on top. Then, ignoring the fact that *there's a loaded gun hidden barely six inches away*, I get to work on my hair.

Evening showers are a mistake when you sleep somewhere like this, squished on a twin-size mattress with another adult. *Another adult with an above-human body temperature.* James doesn't like sleeping in feline form—I'm not convinced he cares much for his feline form in general—but I have half a mind to do it myself. Cats don't sweat at all, so I'd probably be more comfortable.

Though, I agree that being a cat is strange.

I change clothes, pull my hair up into a ponytail, and apply mascara with the help of my phone's front-facing camera. Sure, I *could* sneak down the hall and do this in the bathroom, but I slept like shit and don't feel like it. As I pack everything back up, I spot the grey knit sweatband near the top of the clothing piled inside.

One look at the scar on my wrist, and I slip the band on.

I don't care if it's tacky and only draws more attention to the area; I'm still sore over what Paige said. The other scars are what-ever. They don't hurt or itch anymore, and I don't care if anyone looks at me and wonders how I got them. But it's probably better for my sanity if the heart isn't on full display yet.

Yeah... It's fine...

I sit on the edge of the bed and tie my shoes, which seems to signal to James that I'm almost ready without me having to say anything. He puts his cards away, returning them to the shoe box in neat stacks. Then he slips his shoes on, and we're ready to get the hell out of here.

Jonathan is nowhere to be seen downstairs, so we leave happy and undisturbed. And relief washes over me the instant I buckle myself into the passenger seat of James' car. I don't even mind the lack of AC.

He laughs before looking away and turning the key in the ignition. "You seriously hate it here, huh?"

"Um. Yeah." But I force a wry smile. "I've been saying that ever since you first brought me here."

"Don't worry. We might not stick around much longer."

"Wait. Does that mean we can go back to my house?"

"I've thought about it," he says. "Or a motel. But, as long as we're careful—"

I gasp. "I will be *so* careful. I swear!"

He laughs again but doesn't respond one way or the other as he returns his attention to the road. With nothing better to do, I watch him drive. His eyes ahead. Hands relaxed on the steering wheel. He doesn't look nearly as tired or stressed as he used to. I'm glad—for him, I'm happy—but I'm ready to go home. Even a motel would be a million times better than this. *And have air conditioning.*

I spend the rest of the drive fantasizing about sprawling out on a queen-size bed in a cool room and pop back into reality as James parks in Riverside Park's overflow lot. The lot is half dirt now, the dry grass worn away by so many cars driving over it.

The park isn't crowded, but the weather's perfect—not *too* hot—so there are still a lot of people around. Children on the playground while their parents watch from benches in the shade of trees. Joggers and dog-walkers on the paved paths. Several teenagers hanging out in the pavilion near the restrooms.

We meander along the walking path, through the park and down the hill toward the river, where the air is slightly cooler. We follow the trail under the bridge, past where the pavement ends, before heading into the trees that border the riverbank. I vaguely remember the path from the last time we ventured back here, but James knows exactly where he's going, and we soon pop out onto the secluded, pebbly beach.

My eyes glaze over the shimmering water and land on the rock where James was sitting when I kissed him for the first time.

I sit on a boulder in the shade, keeping close to the trees, while

James walks out into the sunlight. He talks about how he and Jesse used to catch tadpoles here when they were kids. The park isn't too far from his house, so they came down here a lot. It's a *secret place*—or that's how he felt about it as a kid, anyway.

It seems like he used to have a lot of secret places. Places he could go to escape reality, even if only for a few hours. Places like this small stretch of riverbank and Reid Manor and the sandstone cave.

He kneels to pick up a rock, and, after standing and drawing his arm back, he throws it. The flat stone skips across the water's surface three times before sinking.

Then he looks back to me, his expression hard to read. "You've lived in Riverview your whole life, right?"

"Yeah. My parents moved up here a few months before I was born. They bought a house—a lot easier to do here than in LA, I guess. Anyway, I lived there until I moved in with Rose last summer."

"Both my parents grew up here," he says. "Their parents too. And theirs, probably."

James abandons the water's edge to sit beside me. His fingertips are an inch from mine on the grey stone. Our eyes meet for a second, then he glances aside with a frown.

"Do you ever think about leaving?" he asks.

"Once I'm done at RCC, maybe."

His laugh holds a touch of nerves, but he smiles. "Oh. That's right. I forgot. What are you studying, again?"

"Just general education. It's a transfer degree, but I'm not sure what I wanna do with it yet. I don't even know which universities I should apply to. Or if I want to go to university at all anymore."

"You have time," he says mildly.

I *know* I have time. And I know James is the wrong person to complain about my college prospects to, but I should've enrolled in fall classes weeks ago—or at least looked into what I need to take. I have some idea, but the end of spring term feels like *forever* ago.

"Anyway—" I force a smile. "You want to leave Riverview? Where do you wanna go?"

He searches my eyes carefully. I'm not sure what he's looking for in my expression, but the guarded edge eventually leaves his, and he leans back to gaze out over the river.

"Somewhere big," he says with a broad gesture and a small, wistful smile. "Somewhere I can disappear—just blend in, one in a crowd of a million different faces. Somewhere no one knows me. Away from my dad, and away from my past and everything else I can't stand anymore. Maybe I could start over in a big city, but…"

"But what?"

He glances at his hands, balled in his lap, with a hint of tension in his jaw. "Would you come with me?"

Oh.

"Robbie goes to UCLA," I say slowly. "I've visited a couple times, and the city isn't awful. So, maybe…if you can wait until next summer? I mean, I don't know what *I* want to do yet, so—"

"What?"

He turns to me with wide eyes. *Disbelief.* But I don't blame him for wanting to leave. It sounds like this town has treated him poorly his whole life. *And, after the past couple summers…*

"I like Riverview, but Rose and school are the only things really keeping me here. Well, and the fact that I can't drive, I guess."

"I can drive."

I laugh. "I know you can drive."

"We can go," he says. A desperate warmth floods his voice as he takes my hands in his. "I'm serious, Jayde. I can wait—what's one more year?—and then we can go anywhere. Doesn't have to be LA, either. Pick whatever school you want. Just say the word, and we're outta here. I can get a job, so you can focus on your classes, and—" He pauses, face flushing red as his eyes dart away. "Ah— I mean…"

He drops my hands, but I thought it was cute. I like seeing him get excited, and I loved listening to him imagine a future with me. *It seemed like he was really feeling it.*

I laugh again, and he stops stammering. He clears his throat and stares at me. Mouth closed. Wide eyes flicking between mine as he waits for me to say something.

"I'll have to look into schools," I say.

"Yeah. Okay." He rakes a hand through his hair and flashes a weak smile. "Sorry, it's just… I feel like I've never had much to look forward to like that before—something I really want that seems like it might…actually happen, you know? So…"

My smile comes easily. "You don't have to apologize. Once this is over, we can be together without worrying about it. We won't have to be afraid of anything."

"You think so?"

"Of course."

I have to believe that. I can't believe everything I see in my dreamscape. I can't accept that future, whatever it was.

We stare at each other for a calm, quiet moment. He seems to have recovered for the most part. But my cheeks still feel hot, and the fleeting image of his warm hands on my hips sends my heart racing.

This isn't...exactly how I thought hanging out at the park would go. I wasn't expecting James to suggest running away, and I wasn't expecting to think it might be a good idea. *But I wasn't expecting to fall in love with him at all.*

Compared to the guy I first tripped over in June, he seems like a completely different person. He's still nervous. Still insecure. But he's so much more than that. He has some small confidence. Some drive. He doesn't seem nearly as tired. He's less...*empty*. His eyes sparkle in the natural light. His smile is genuine and warm. He says he loves me, *and I believe it*, and he kisses me without hesitation.

And, god, do I wish we could run away and never come back.

forty-nine

James is twenty-one years old, and we're on our way to meet Matthew and Cassidy at Century Plaza Mall. I feel better after a night free from dreamscape nonsense. I'm wearing a dress for the first time in weeks, and I don't care that my outfit leaves most of my scars visible.

James is in a great mood too.

We meander through the mall and, after some messaging on James' end, find the red-headed siblings loitering beside a vendor's stall near the food court. Cassidy notices us first and runs up with a huge smile. They wish James a happy birthday, and we meet up with Matthew at the kiosk, where he's checking out a display of novelty phone cases.

"I was thinking of buying you one," he says, skipping over any sort of actual greeting. "Your naked phone freaks me out every time I see it."

"Shut up, man."

Matthew laughs. "I'm serious! Not even a screen protector? It's a miracle you haven't killed it yet. So, you like any of these? Pick whatever you want."

With a heavy sigh, James looks over the kiosk. Bulky silicone cases with 3D designs modeled after cartoon characters and retro game consoles. Hard plastic cases with colorful printed designs. Cases with glitter and charms suspended in liquid. Eventually, he points out a case that looks more practical than most: a red and black case with a built-in screen protector and silicone bumpers on each corner.

"For real?" Matthew asks dryly. "What's the point of putting a drop-proof case on a phone that's already cracked to shit? How old's your phone, anyway? What if I just buy you a new one?"

"What? No!" He looks scandalized for a second, then starts laughing. "My phone's fine, dude. Shut up."

"You telling me that thing doesn't slice your fingers up?"

"So what if it does?"

Matthew snickers, but he buys the bumper case.

James works his phone into its new case on our way to the food court. We order smoothies and Chinese lunch plates and settle at a tall, round table. After some idle conversation, Matthew mentions the Magic tournament.

"I put a deck together," James says with a sigh, "but I'm not entering the tournament. I haven't played in forever, never mind competitively."

Matthew shrugs. "Never said you had to join the tournament. I just thought you'd have more fun if you didn't have to borrow a deck to play casual while *I* participate in the tournament."

"Uh-huh."

Last night, James played a few rounds against himself to test the decks he made. He had to double-check random rules on the internet more than once. After watching him play, I've decided the game isn't as complicated as I first thought, but winning still relies more on tactics and strategy than sheer luck of the draw.

"I don't really get the whole Magic thing either," Cassidy says. "I mean, I know how to play, but no one likes playing against me. For reasons. You know?"

I stuff my face with rice, so I don't have to say anything, and they laugh. But James frowns and tips his head, catching Cassidy's attention.

"I'll play against you," he says. "I don't play the long game, and I don't care about winning, so it doesn't matter if you know my hand or whatever."

They gasp. "For real? I thought you hated me." But they laugh again before he can protest. "Kidding! But, if you wanna play against me, maybe I can use your second deck, so you know all the cards too at least?"

"Sure. It might give me a slight advantage."

Matthew snickers. "Told you he doesn't hate you, Cass."

"I literally just said that! I know *everything* James thinks about me, and, right now, he thinks I'm perfectly adequate. I'm *relatable* because we're both weird."

"Don't push your luck, kid."

Cassidy apologizes with a smile, James rolls his eyes, and we carry on eating and chatting about this or that. When I mention RCC—since it's been on my mind lately—Matthew perks up. He completed his transfer degree this year, but his end goal is a degree in graphic design from CalArts. I guess it's a tough school to get into, so he's taking a gap year to put together a portfolio.

After hearing him out, I feel obligated to explain my general education transfer degree for the second time in twenty-four hours—not that Matthew seems to think any less of me for it.

An education is an education, I guess.

"Where are you gonna transfer to?" he asks.

"I'm thinking somewhere in LA," I say slowly. "I doubt UCLA would accept me, but Cal State might... Anyway, I still need to look into it more. I'm not even sure what I want to major in yet."

"CalArts is close to LA." Matthew glances at James, who immediately breaks eye contact, then looks back to me with a cheeky grin. "Y'know, I was planning to force James to room with me in Santa Clarita, but maybe he should stay with you instead—if you're still together next year."

"Hey!"

He laughs at whatever offense James took to his comment, and I can't help but laugh too.

"We were just talking about this yesterday," I admit, smiling more easily. "And I think that's the plan. I mean, I have no idea what I want to do, and I have to pick *some* school."

"Nice! A fresh start would do you guys some good, huh?"

James glances at his plate. "Yeah. I'm thinking about it..."

"You should go to a trade school, dude," Matthew says. "There are tons down there, and most programs only last a year or two. I mean, I could see you as an electrician or something. And they make decent money, you know?"

"I can look into it..."

As he trails off, frowning, Cassidy chokes. Their cheeks pale, and their eyes snap open wide as they turn to stare at him.

Surprise. Concern. James winces. And I can only imagine what he might have thought to catch them so off guard.

"Ah— It's not like that." He forces a smile and gestures in a desperately pacifying way, but his voice is taut. "I'm fine, Cassidy, so just...don't worry about it. Okay? I'm one-hundred-percent fine. I swear."

They frown, brows furrowed, before flashing an equally forced smile. "Sure. I've heard worse things in school, you know?"

"Sorry."

There's a moment of silence.

I want to ask. I'm curious. But do I *really* want to ask?

Would he even tell me whatever awful thing crossed his mind? While we're all sitting around a food court table in the crowded mall?

On his birthday?

Cassidy glances at me, mirroring my uncertainty, while James stares intently at the near-empty paper plate in front of him. Then Matthew sighs and pats him on the back.

"The tournament starts soon," he says. "You wanna head to the backroom now?"

I can take a hint, so I announce that I would like to look around the mall a little. They can go to wherever the tournament is being held, and we can meet up later—in an hour or so. James frowns, but Cassidy offers him a bright smile.

"I'll stay with Jayde," they say. "There's something I wanna check out too, but we can play a few rounds once we all meet up again."

"Good idea," Matthew agrees.

James looks to me with an even more pronounced frown. "You sure?"

"Yeah. Go with Matt. Watch the tournament and play cards or whatever. I'll be fine with Cassidy."

He hesitates. I hold his gaze for a long moment. Just when I think he might refuse, he takes a deep breath and smiles.

"Alright," he says. "Text me if you need anything."

"Okay. Have fun."

After a bit more waffling, James leaves with Matthew, and Cassidy and I continue sitting in the food court despite having both finished eating.

I check my phone.

A few minutes pass.

It's kinda awkward—though, I'm sure me thinking that only makes it even more awkward for them. But I can't decide what to do from here. There's nothing I really need to buy. No specific shops I care to check out.

Cassidy sighs, resting their chin in their hands. "I didn't have a plan either, but I realized you were right. Maybe James and Matt should hang out without us. Maybe I shouldn't have asked to come at all. It's just...I don't have many friends, you know?"

"Yeah... I know how that is."

They smile faintly but glance aside with shadowed eyes. "Everyone has thoughts they don't want anyone to know about. It's not like I'm trying to listen in on them—I don't wanna hear any of it—but a lot of people avoid me once they know I do."

"I'm sorry."

"You don't have to feel sorry for me," they say, seemingly

surprised. "I get why they feel that way. Because I've heard all the things they're trying to hide. Everything they don't want anyone else to know they think about."

When I avert my gaze, they laugh. "Yeah, just like that! Anyway, I feel like I have no right to complain. I know everyone else's problems, but my life is amazing and comfortable. My family loves me, and there are plenty of people who understand me—like you and Carmen, and even James. He never trusted me before, but he feels bad about it now. I'm lucky."

"That's one way to look at it, I guess."

"Well, how do *you* do it?" they ask, golden eyes intensely curious. "I get picked on a lot, but nothing like what happened to you. How do you keep going?"

"Ah—" I feel my face adopt a strange blankness. My mind too. "I think I just…try not to think about it."

They sigh. "Yeah. Most people are like that. And they all suck at not thinking about it."

"Is James like that?"

"Oh, um…" They glance around before meeting my gaze with a hint of frustration. "I only hear thoughts on a…surface level? Like, if you focus on something super distracting, that's all I hear. James usually thinks about books and music and weird science crap when I'm around to keep his deeper thoughts private. But that's hard to do while you're talking. Plus he has pretty bad anxiety and everything. So, if anything reminds him of whatever he's trying to avoid thinking about, those deeper thoughts pop to the surface where I can hear them. Sometimes, there's nothing you can do to stop it."

I want to ask. I *really* want to ask. But I won't.

It was probably just something to do with Ice, anyway. If that's the case, though, Cassidy's careful expression doesn't give it away.

"He feels bad being around you because of it," I say.

"Because I'm only twelve, I know." They smile. "But I really have heard worse things from my classmates. Middle schoolers' brains suck, and some kids have it real bad at home. They think about dying and hurting others and being hurt and hurting them-selves. Even 'normal' kids do. Everyone gets intrusive thoughts like that sometimes. It just surprised me, the way something like *that* slipped through during such a totally normal conversation. I guess. But he says he's fine, so…"

They trail off, looking aside with a mild, thoughtful expression. And I sigh. We shouldn't be so serious, right? Today is James' birthday. We're at the mall. We're in public. We're safe.

Everything is fine.

I ask Cassidy about the pictures they took during the bonfire, and they perk up like nothing happened.

fifty

We leave the food court and aimlessly wander the mall, checking out window displays and walking through a few stores. I'm not too interested in buying anything, and Cassidy doesn't seem to be either. We're just wasting time so James and Matthew can do whatever they're interested in for a while.

Watching Cassidy is fun, though.

For a long moment, they check out a hot pink beret on a child-sized mannequin, hands pressed to the glass, staring through the window with such intensity I'm convinced they're considering a purchase. Then they step back and turn to me with a muted smile. Before I say anything, they point to a corner shop on the opposite side of the building. A bakery with a glass counter full of baked goods on display.

"Have you ever tried those giant cookies?" they ask. When I shrug—I've had a few—they grin. "Baking is the owner's number one passion in life. Like, no joke, I know he runs a bakery and all, but baking is basically all he ever thinks about."

"I guess you would know, huh?"

They laugh. "Yeah, I would. You wanna get one?"

"Oh. Sure."

"Awesome. I can pay," they say, walking ahead.

I jog a couple steps to catch up, ready to protest. *What kind of person would I be if I accepted handouts from a literal child?*

Cassidy laughs even louder. "It's fine. Trust me. You would not believe my allowance."

Allowance? *Right.*

I still have a couple hundred left over myself. It's not a lot, but it's money I didn't have before. *And Ice did suggest I buy cookies with it. Such a dick move…*

"I'll pay for them," I say.

Cassidy glances back at me in mild confusion. "Oh? You get Supplemental Income now?"

I can't hide it, so I smile and raise a finger to my lips. "Don't tell James, but I'd have more if *someone* wasn't embezzling it."

They search my eyes, soaking in the information. The texts. The letter Ice left on my dresser. Half of my stipend deposited into my checking account.

And they frown. "Ice doesn't seem like a very good person."

"No." With a sigh, I dig my wallet out of my purse as we make our way to the bakery counter. "And he's been weirdly polite about it lately, which is super annoying."

I get a sugar cookie that's arguably more frosting than cookie, intentionally passing on the giant M&M cookie out of spite, and Cassidy chooses a snickerdoodle. Then we head to a small table in a quiet corner of the food court. Cassidy snaps a picture of their cookie, seemingly thrilled, but the longer I stare at the nine-inch-diameter cookie in my hands, the more I doubt I'll be able to eat the whole thing in a single sitting without getting sick.

Maybe just a piece.

I peel the plastic wrap away and break off a chunk roughly the size of a normal cookie. When I look up, Cassidy has their cookie unwrapped and is already chowing down.

"I saw the pictures you shared from the beach," they say between bites. "Do you like photography too?"

"A little…"

As they talk about their photography Snapgram at length, my phone goes off inside my purse. Just a notification or text or something—I didn't quite make out the sound. I wait for Cassidy to finish their tangent before I check my phone.

Ugh. Great.

This is absolutely not what I needed today.

Ice Monroe   now

Hey, have you considered the fragility of this world at all?

There's another image too.

All I can really make out in the tiny thumbnail is green, so I bite the bullet and unlock my phone to see whatever dumb thing he sent this time. *An oak tree.* A photo of the underside of the canopy, taken from near the base of the tree's trunk. Grey-green leaves and brown branches with a few specks of blue sky peeking through the foliage.

Is this…?

Studying the photo, it really could be any oak tree. Who's to say it's the massive oak at Riverside Park—the one we sat under in June? I remember picking at the grass and looking up into the branches because I was too nervous to look at him for more than a few seconds at a time. Because he was so handsome, and I was too shy. I couldn't understand why he wanted to hang out with me.

Then he asked that stupid question: *Do you ever consider the fragility of this world?*

I just went to Riverside with James yesterday.

Is Ice there, sitting beneath that same tree, right now?

"Everything okay?" Cassidy asks.

"Yeah. Everything's fine." I lock my phone and drop it into my purse. "It's just a dumb text. They've all been like this since I last saw him."

"Why don't you ask *why* he's texting you?"

I laugh. "Should I? Do you think he'd answer?"

"You never know unless you try."

We've exchanged several harmless texts recently, so it's not like I'm *scared* of responding or anything, but I don't want to entertain a whole conversation right now. I'm mostly just annoyed that he'd reference something from *before*.

It's the same as the letter he left in my bedroom.

I'm not *worried*, but I don't want to engage. He's probably only texting to get under my skin, anyway. Maybe he knows it's James' birthday. Maybe he's *trying* to ruin my day.

Either way...

I sigh. "I should tell James before I do anything. I promised to tell him whenever Ice messages me."

Cassidy pops the last piece of their cookie into their mouth and nods thoughtfully as they chew. *I can't believe they ate the whole thing.* The rest of my cookie is safely tucked away in my purse. I'll share it with James later.

"You wanna go find the guys now?" they ask.

"Sure. You know where they went, right?"

They grin. "Of course! Matt goes there all the time."

Cassidy stands from the table, brushes the crumbs off their shirt, and starts across the food court with purpose. I hop out of my chair to follow, and they slow somewhat to walk beside me.

"The place is sort of hidden and out of the way." Flashing a wry smile, they cup a hand over their mouth and lower their voice. "Only immortals can get inside."

"Oh. Will they let me in since I'm—?"

They wave off my question. "You're with me, so it's fine."

I can't tell if they're joking or being serious.

"What kind of place is this?" I ask. "I figured it was a game shop or something, but it almost sounds more like…a club?"

"A nerd club, maybe." They snicker. "One of Matt's friend's uncles—or whatever; I forget, but it's not important. Anyway, one of Matt's friends knows the guy who owns this bookstore, and a bunch of their friends use the back room to play Smash Bros and D&D and stuff like that. That's why it's called *The Backroom*."

They point out a shop just up ahead.

It's the small indie bookstore that James disappeared into the day we met. I've been there a few times, including once with Night in July.

Stepping inside, it looks like any other bookstore. A few

rotating displays of bookmarks, greeting cards, tarot decks, and small novelty items near the front. Head-height shelves lined with new and secondhand books, meticulously organized by genre with flashy signs indicating where each section begins.

I follow Cassidy through the store until we reach a door on the back wall. A red *Employees Only* sign is taped to it, but I hear muffled music, conversation, and laughter coming from the other side.

"Not very subtle, is it?" I ask dryly.

They laugh. "No. It's not."

fifty-one

Cassidy tries the door, but it's locked, so they knock instead. A few seconds pass before someone inside yells something about the door. Another few seconds, and the lock clicks. The noise loses its muffled quality as the door opens a crack.

"What do you want?" a voice asks through the unnecessarily narrow gap in the door.

"We want in," Cassidy says brightly.

The door opens a bit wider to reveal Stephen as the one who answered it. He glances us over, but he looks confused.

"Cass and..." He points at me. "Who's this?"

Cassidy groans. "You seriously don't recognize Jayde? She's James' girlfriend. You guys met twice. She was at the beach."

"Jayde, huh? Yeah, I guess you can come in." He opens the door the rest of the way and glances over his shoulder. "James, come here a sec; your girlfriend's here!"

"Is Matt still playing?" Cassidy asks as they slip past Stephen and into the room.

Stephen doesn't answer, too busy looking me over again, but I ignore his attention and scan the surprisingly large game room behind him. There are a good dozen people inside, hanging out at plastic tables and plush couches. James steps away from a square table at the far end of the room and hefts his backpack over one shoulder.

"Right," Stephen exclaims. "Everyone's been talking about you guys since the bonfire. I still think it's weird that he hooked up with a human, but I guess you're pretty hot."

"Um… Thanks."

Aren't you like sixteen?

Still frowning, I look to James, who absolutely overheard our exchange considering he's hardly a foot from the door.

Stephen glances back, following my gaze, and immediately prickles. He stammers an awkward apology and slinks back into the room, heading for a large table where Cassidy, Matthew, and a few others are gathered.

I sigh. "Well. That just happened."

But James laughs and takes Stephen's place in holding the door open. "Yeah. That kid's an idiot, but he's alright. Anyway, did you wanna come in?"

"Mm…"

He promised to play a few rounds of Magic with Cassidy, but I'd feel weird sitting around while everyone plays a game I don't fully understand. I only know a few people here, and I don't want to cause a scene by existing in an immortal-only space in light of the news I'm sure is actively circulating about me right now.

Besides…

"Maybe another time. I need to talk to you." I hesitate as his expression shifts, but I force a smile. "It's nothing serious, really, but we should probably go somewhere…quieter."

He shrugs. "Alright. The tournament should be on for another hour, so we've got plenty of time."

"Thanks."

He calls back to let his friends know we're leaving. I wave to Matthew and Cassidy, neither of whom complain or look bothered. Then James steps out and closes the door. The sound inside the room falls quiet, and I let out my breath.

"Everything okay?" he asks, more curious than concerned.

I nod, suppressing a faint stitch of unease. "Everything's fine. I just feel weird talking to everyone—especially people I don't know very well—now that they all...*know*. You know?"

"Oh. Yeah, I get that." He glances aside. "They know. And it is weird."

With a sigh, he takes my hand, and we walk through the bookstore and back out into the mall. We pass the clothing boutique outside which I first bumped into him. When I mention it, he cringes, and I can't help but laugh.

"It was my fault," I say. "I was so lost in my own head, I didn't notice you until we smacked right into each other. But now it's kinda funny."

"I guess. I still feel stupid thinking about it."

"Why'd you stop to talk, anyway? Just because you recognized me from the pictures Carmen shared?"

He frowns pointedly. As I laugh again, his expression softens.

"To be honest, I didn't recognize you right away. I just felt bad for knocking you over, and you were pretty nice to me considering that, so..."

He thought I was being nice? Because I mostly remember

feeling embarrassed and frustrated. *But it's whatever, I guess.*

Our eyes meet, and he glances away. "I thought you looked familiar, but I didn't realize why until you mentioned Night. Then I saw the necklace and remembered the pictures Matt showed me, and I panicked. I knew you were with Ice, and I didn't wanna get mixed up in that."

"Maybe I shouldn't have mentioned you to them."

"Nah." He sighs. "Don't feel bad. You had no idea who I was, and I was acting weird as hell. I don't blame you for telling them about it."

"I guess. But, honestly, I'm glad I met you, even if it turned out like this."

Like this... Another sigh makes me realize we shouldn't be talking about this right now. The decisions we made months ago don't matter much, even if they're what led us to this point.

"Where should we go?" I ask. "Back to the food court?"

He seems to relax the moment I change gears, and he pauses —literally stops walking—to think about it. We're coming up to the food court now, so it seemed like the obvious choice. But he shakes his head.

"Matt wants froyo before they take off," he says. "We can just wait for him there."

Froyo, huh?

I haven't had frozen yogurt since my first date with Ice. *Ugh.* I hate even thinking about it like that. And I still don't understand how he's the least bit comfortable wearing that leather jacket all the time, especially now that I know immortals have a higher body temperature than humans.

"Works for me," I agree.

I already have to talk about Ice, so I'd rather not also explain why I don't particularly want to sit in the frozen yogurt shop. It won't kill me to hang out there for an hour, anyway.

We walk into One Scoop, Two Scoops together.

The layout is the same as I remember, and I immediately zero in on the round, window-side table where I sat in June. I feel my jaw set. Ice never showed it, but I bet he thought I was a complete idiot. A hopeless, nervous, squirrelly virgin. I bet he was ashamed to be seen in public with someone like me.

Ugh. Stop. Who cares what Ice thinks?

After a calming breath, I pick a table in the far corner of the shop. James sits beside me, and I offer up a chunk of my giant sugar cookie. He takes it without hesitation, and, for some reason, I feel better.

"Were you able to play any Magic?" I ask.

"A few rounds." He smiles. "I lost three, but I got lucky and won the last one. Stephen sucks at Magic, though."

"But you had fun?"

He nods, glancing aside. "They all asked…less questions than I expected. I get the feeling Matt told everyone to keep their mouths shut in advance. Either that, or they're scared to talk to me now. Who knows."

"Yeah… That's the main reason I didn't want to go in…"

"Anyway, you said you needed to talk? What's up?"

"Um…" I dig my phone out of my purse and set it on the table. "Ice messaged me earlier—while I was with Cassidy."

"Oh?"

His air of mild interest doesn't falter. As unavoidable as the topic has been lately, I'm sure he didn't wanna talk about Ice on his birthday either, but I'm relieved that hearing from him won't be enough to ruin his whole day.

I unlock my phone and reread the text before showing it to James. He steadies my hand with his and reads the message at least twice.

"What does that even mean—*the fragility of this world?*"

"Right?" I exclaim. "I don't get it either."

Frowning, he taps the photo to enlarge it.

"A tree, huh?" He tips his head, squinting at the screen. Then his hand falls away, and he looks up in obvious confusion. "Why would he send this to you?"

"Well..."

Begrudgingly, I explain how Ice invited me to Riverside Park before I knew about immortals. How we sat in the shade under the large oak tree just off the walking path at the top of the hill. He asked that same question as he stared up into the leaves. I don't mention how nervous I was or how hot I thought Ice looked or how Night showed up and gave me my first taste of jealousy in years, but that doesn't stop me from remembering those details and hating myself for it.

I study the picture message again.

Surely, it's the same tree.

Ice went back to Riverside, and he sat under that tree, and he thought about me. Then he took this picture and sent it to me. And I hate him for that too. I hate knowing he thinks about me at all.

"I guess he didn't forget what he said," I say.

James sighs. "Honestly, when you first said he messaged you, I was worried it'd have something to do with my birthday. But I'm sure he doesn't care about it—assuming he remembers."

I don't know what to say.

Talking about Ice with Cassidy was easy, but... Sitting in One Scoops, Two Scoops and telling James about the afternoon I spent with Ice at Riverside? I feel bad, like *guilty* bad, and I don't like it.

"Cassidy thinks I should ask why he keeps texting me."

James' eyes narrow as he stares at his hands on the edge of the table. "Sounds like a waste of time. Just tell him to knock it off."

"Is that okay?"

"How many times has it been now?" he asks, his voice low. "Twice? Three times? It's annoying as hell, and I can tell it makes you upset. Something like this? These stupid texts? He's just doing it to be a dick, and you don't need to deal with that on top of everything else."

Does it upset me?

Sure, it's annoying, but, as I scroll through our text history, I'm not sure how to feel. *Is James right?* Is Ice only doing this to get under my skin? I know that was his intention with the letter planted in my room, but none of these photos or the accompanying texts give me the same feeling. I just don't know *what* this feeling is, and the fact that he responds normally whenever I text him is not helping me work it out.

The photo messages are extra weird. Annoying and confusing,

for sure. And, I suppose, even a bit upsetting—in the sense that I *hate* seeing his name pop up on my phone when I'd much rather see Rose's. Even so, if there *is* a reason why he's been texting me, I want to know. *Assuming he'd tell me.* Can't hurt to ask, anyway. *Probably.*

"Maybe it's worth a shot," I say with a sigh.

"You're gonna respond?"

"Just to ask…"

I waffle for a moment and reread what I typed several times before tapping send.

Me: Why do you keep texting me?

I watch my screen with wide eyes, unsure what to expect.

Several seconds pass before the read indicator appears beneath my text. He's typing already… *How will he react? Will he be mad? Was responding at all a bad idea? Whatever you do, please don't call me…*

Ice: I'll take that as a no. lmao

What?

The casual inanity of his response leaves me at a loss. Reeling, yet strangely relieved. I let out the breath I was holding as the tension leaves my shoulders. Then I realize he started typing again.

Oh, god.

After a few seconds, a picture appears on my screen. Curious, I tap the thumbnail to reveal the full photo—a tan shield bug on dark tree bark. *A bug? What the hell…?*

I back out to read the accompanying text.

Ice: This little guy reminds me of James.

Chest tight, I feel my face flush hot.

Me: That is NOT funny

Ice: idk I found it funny

I stare at the screen, my thumbs hovering over the keyboard. *But I can't believe—*

"Hey," James says warily. "You okay? What'd he say?"

I glance over, and he looks about as worried as he sounded. This text is absolutely meant to piss me off. I don't want to show James—it's sure to upset him too—but I *promised.*

"It's stupid," I mutter. "Really stupid, but—"

I force myself to angle my phone, so he can see, though I keep my eyes on the screen rather than his face. A few quiet seconds pass.

Then he sighs. "Well, at least it's not about my birthday."

"Sorry," I say as my anger shifts to regret. "I guess you were right. I shouldn't have asked."

"Jayde…"

The typing indicator appears again, and I hold my breath.

Ice: You with him right now?

My heart races.

James groans. "Babe, come on; he's clearly fucking with you. Just tell him to cut the shit already."

He's right. Ice is just trying to upset me, taking advantage of the fact I responded. I bet he's laughing his ass off imagining my reaction to these stupid texts. *I know James is right, but that doesn't make me any less mad.*

I take a deep breath and bring my phone back to the space in front of me to reread the messages.

"Okay," I agree.

> **Me:** None of your business. Leave me alone.

Typing...

> **Ice:** boring (-_-);;

Oh my god—

> **Me:** I'm serious. Unless it's important, please
> don't text me again.
>
> **Ice:** k

"Ugh!"

I lock my phone and drop my face to the table. It's cold, which is nice considering I must look like a tomato right now.

James rubs my back. "Sorry."

"It's not your fault," I mumble into my arm. "You tried to warn me. I should've known he'd pull something like that."

"Just ignore him. Trying to talk to Ice is a waste of time."

"Yeah... I'm starting to think you're right."

When I finally calm down enough to sit up and check on James, he seems frustrated but otherwise in a decent mood.

I feel like talking about Ice usually doesn't go over this well. *But he sat through me having an actual text conversation with*

Ice, and he even compared him to a bug!

What's so different about today? Is it just because we're in public? Because it's his birthday? Because he knows I'd only be more upset if he let himself get worked up over it too?

The fragility of this world?

I don't understand what Ice meant in June or why he'd bring it up again now, but I have at least considered the fragility of life. How a single action can be the determining factor between survival and death. How the slightest movement of a finger can so easily end a life.

The weight of a loaded handgun. Staring down the black hole at the end of the barrel. The cold, sinking pain of wondering if a loved one will ever wake up again.

Would knowing that it haunts me satisfy Ice?

Would he laugh at me for being pathetic?

Can he relate at all?

After our conversation at Riverview General, I have no idea what to think.

fifty-two

I feel better by the time Matthew and Cassidy join us, but I stay at the table while everyone else gets froyo. I'm not hungry. Because I ate too much for lunch along with part of that massive sugar cookie—*not* because texting Ice put me off eating.

As they make their way back to the table, Matthew is in the middle of telling James about the last half of the tournament. Seems he made third place out of the seven participants. I'm not sure how impressive that's meant to be, but he doesn't seem disappointed. I assume he only plays for fun, anyway.

James sits beside me, and— *Oh my god.* His cup totally looks like mine did in June. It's such a mess of fruit and candy, I can't make out the color of the actual yogurt underneath.

It's not that funny, but I laugh. *Hard.* He looks at me in mild alarm, but I wave off his confusion with a smile.

"What flavor did you get?"

"Oh, uh…" He glances at his cup. "It's lemon meringue."

"Oh! That's my favorite. Well, I mean, my actual favorite is watermelon, but they stopped serving it here months ago."

He laughs. "Want some?"

I nod, figuring I can stomach a single bite. The taste of lemon frozen yogurt topped with a strawberry slice is more refreshing than I expected. I almost wish I got a tiny cup for myself even if I really don't need one.

James kisses the side of my head before going to town on his froyo. Matthew is still talking about Magic, though I think James stopped paying attention, and Cassidy looks to be zoning him out.

Once they're all done with their froyo, we loiter in the corner of the shop for at least another half hour.

James and Cassidy play a round of Magic—Cassidy wins, but I think it was close—and the four of us talk about this and that and nothing of consequence, and it feels so *normal*. We're joking around and laughing easily, and it feels *good*. This is exactly how I wanted today to go, and I hope that, with Ice's annoying texts out of the way, we can keep the momentum going.

Matthew yawns, stretching his arms over his head.

"So, you guys wanna hang out at my place later?" he asks. "You'd have to supply the booze, now that you're a real adult and all, but I don't work tomorrow."

"Oh, uh…" James glances at me, then looks back to Matthew with a faint smile. "Nah. We've got plans tonight. Sorry, man."

"Ah." Matthew sighs and nods. "Secret birthday plans? I see."

"Dinner plans!" we protest in unison.

James' face turns red as he stares at his cackling friend. I don't fare much better, as I can't stop the memory of being woken up by Matthew and Carmen after— *Think of something else! Uh… Going on a nature walk. Windsor Park's wildlife pond. Cute ducks!* Despite my best efforts, my cheeks are far warmer than they should be, and I'm certain at least a few other customers are watching us.

"Guys, stop," Cassidy says through stifled laughter, hiding their face in their hands. "This is too much information."

James suddenly looks downright mortified, which only makes Matthew laugh even harder. Cassidy smacks his arm a few times, still partially shielding their face. Matthew does little to fend them off, but their glancing blows appear intentionally soft.

Once the embarrassment wears off, I can't help but laugh too.

* * * * *

The blue truck is still missing when we get back to the house, so we remain in good spirits as we step into the bedroom. Sure, I'd rather have gone somewhere else—even to Matthew's house in Westbrooke—but James wanted to change before we head to the restaurant.

It's silly. After all, a t-shirt and jeans won't offend anyone at *Applebee's*. But I stand around while he changes into a nicer pair of pants and digs through a box in the closet that's full of clothes he previously said he'd probably never wear again.

"Why change, anyway?"

He shrugs without looking up from the box. "Dunno. Aren't you curious to see how I dress up?"

"I—"

I've never seen James wear anything besides super casual clothing—a relatively small selection of t-shirts; jeans, sweats, or gym shorts; and hooded jackets. Now that he's said it, I'm curious what he has in mind.

But this cotton sundress is the nicest thing I brought from home. I'd rather not end up horrifically underdressed compared to my date. *Again.*

"How dressed up are we talking?" I ask.

"Well... How dressed up to you want me to be?"

"Aah—" An inexplicable current of electricity shoots up my spine, bringing a wave of warmth with it. Cheeks on fire, I tear my eyes from his bare back and look at my hands instead. "Doesn't matter to me. Wear whatever you want."

He laughs. "Alright."

James eventually finds what he was looking for and throws an undershirt on before shrugging into the brick-red dress shirt and buttoning it up. It doesn't quite fit him properly, and the fabric is wrinkled from being balled up in a cardboard box for god knows how long, but his awkwardness alone is adorable.

"I guess I lost some weight," he says mildly. He picks at the loose fabric before looking to me again. "I haven't worn this since graduation. Should I tuck it in or what?"

I would tell him to just wear a t-shirt instead, but...

"You could try tossing it in the dryer for a few minutes?"

"Good idea. I'll be right back."

He dips out of the room, and I sit on the edge of the bed.

I go through the motions of checking FaceSpace, but I don't have any important notifications. Rose hasn't posted anything new either. It sucks but is hardly unexpected, so it's...*fine.* I won't let it get me down.

We will have a good time tonight if it kills me.

To distract myself, I pull my hair out of its ponytail, brush it, and put it back up into the neatest bun I can manage without the help of a mirror. As I check myself out using my phone, I realize my hair doesn't hold a candle to what Carmen can do, but I look slightly more put-together than before.

When James returns, I leave the bed to look him over now that the shirt has gone through the dryer. It's still slightly too large, but the fabric is warm to the touch, and the wrinkles are mostly gone.

"Better?" he asks. I nod, and relief washes over him. "Cool. So, uh, should I tuck it in or not?"

"Maybe you could…"

I move to tuck the shirt's hem into the waistline of his jeans. He sucks in a sharp breath at my touch, but I carefully avoid meeting his eyes until I finish. The moment my hands fall away, he releases the same breath and glances aside.

"Sorry if it's…disappointing," he says.

What?

Eyes downcast. Frowning with his jaw set. Hands balled into loose fists at his sides. He's totally serious. Totally nervous.

I laugh. "James, *no.*"

He looks up in surprise, and I cup his warm face in my hands. This only seems to confuse him more, but I flash a smile.

"You look great," I assure him. "I mean, I still think dressing up at all is silly, but I am not disappointed."

He mirrors my smile with some hesitance, and I kiss him. He pulls me closer, enveloping me in warmth. *It's easy now.* And I imagine it must be a little easier for him too.

fifty-three

It's almost 8PM.

We've been at Applebee's for nearly two hours. We're done eating and have been for a while, but James must have seriously considered what Matthew said earlier because he's on his third tall, fancy alcoholic birthday drink.

The conversation is good, though.

Not sure if it's the alcohol or just how painless the day has been in general, but I can't get over how happy he looks. Talking about books and Magic and dumb shit he did with Matthew as a teenager. Anything that comes to mind. Laughing between drinks and bites of the complimentary double chocolate brownie ice cream sundae our server brought by after I mentioned that it's his birthday.

How much alcohol do the bartenders put into the drinks here? Until now, I figured they'd be pretty weak. But our server is an immortal. Maybe they slipped him extra...

I bring up something he said to Matthew earlier—about video games. He groans, kicking himself over having sold his Game-Station *again*, but I ask a few questions, and he eventually mentions two of the games I ordered by name while going off on a tangent.

Perfect.

The packages should be delivered tomorrow. Now, I just have to figure out how to bring up stopping by my house to get them before anyone has a chance to swipe them off the porch.

Sounds like another problem for future me.

How long does he want to hang out here? Maybe I can convince him to stay at the cottage tonight? My house is closer than his dad's—plus it's nicer, and we could be *alone* there.

"You know, this is probably the best birthday I've had since I was like eight," he says. His smile mellows as he glances down, into the neon blue liquid in his half-empty glass. Then he looks up again. "Thanks. For making me get out more, I mean."

"Of course! I think I needed to get out more too."

He reaches across the table to hold my hand, and he grins. Cheeks rosy. Eyes crinkled at the corners. I *still* can't decide if it's the mood or the alcohol, but it's so cute I can't help but smile too. After a moment, he glances down with a softer expression.

"I wish every day could be like this."

I squeeze his hand. "It can be—one day. I already told you."

"Mm..." He drinks from his glass, still avoiding my gaze. "You say that like you can see the future."

"Did I?" I ask with a laugh.

James, who didn't seem to notice the anxiety leeching into my voice, laughs too. Then he retracts his hand to take another bite of his dessert.

"Almost makes me believe it," he says.

I prop my chin in my hand, elbow resting on the cool tabletop.

Hm... Maybe I should tell him about my dreams. Maybe he should know that, while I have no idea what might actually happen in the future, I saw...*something.*

I believe what I said about Ice leaving for Palo Alto soon, but I don't want to risk freaking James out by saying anything. I don't want imagery from my dreams to worm into his head the way it wormed into mine. Besides, it's his *birthday*. He's been drinking. We're having a good time. I don't want to screw that up by bringing up things I don't understand. *Just because...someone gets shot in a dream...*

No one will die. I would do anything to stop that future.

Though, we might want to get a ride back to wherever we go from here. Most immortals have a high tolerance for alcohol, but James seems to be on the less tolerant end of the spectrum.

I ask what he thinks—if he's okay to drive—and he looks at his fancy drink glass with his head tipped.

"I can drive fine," he says slowly. "Three drinks isn't much unless they're half alcohol, but I doubt it. These are real sweet. Probably a shot or two in each one, tops."

Potentially six shots? Even if he's right, that's still a lot.

"You don't think you're even a little drunk right now?"

He glances aside, and I take a sip of water as he thinks it over for a curiously long moment. When he meets my gaze again, he flashes a sheepish smile.

"I feel fine, but we can call a cab if you want."

"I want to go home—to my house."

His smile falters, and his eyes flick to his drink again. I feel bad for dropping it on him out of nowhere, but it's the truth. I'm ready to go home. I do not want to go back to his dad's house.

"I know," he says slowly. "I know that. And I… Honestly, I liked it there. A lot. But I can't…" He clears his throat and looks up. "I think we should stay at my dad's a few more days. Then… I dunno about your house. But a motel, maybe…"

A few days? *Until September, maybe?*

Does SIP come in at the beginning of the month?

If mine works the same, and Ice keeps his word, I can help pay for a room. At the very least, I'm glad James doesn't intend to hide out at his dad's until fall term. I'd lose my mind.

"It's fine," I agree. "I don't want to go now if it'll only stress you out more."

"Thanks. I know this sucks and all, but I'm trying to play it smart this time. Mitigating risks or whatever, y'know?" He sighs, and the frown that was creeping onto his face smooths itself out. "Anyway, about calling a cab… Yes? No?"

"Yes, please."

He laughs more easily. "Good to know you trust me."

"Oh, no, it's not that I don't…"

I trail off as he shakes his head, still laughing, and raises a hand to cover his eyes.

"Nah, it's fine," he says. "I'm kidding. I get it. Just means I'll have to ask someone to help pick up the car in the morning." Eyes averted, he nurses his drink. "Matt or…Jesse, maybe. I, uh… I guess I could walk, but it's kinda far. And we should… probably talk about what went down at the beach."

Oh.

"Yeah," he says dryly.

My face must have said it all. *Oops.*

"You should talk to him," I say. "He seemed upset, so…"

James chuckles. "You know, I called him after RPD took me in. I didn't tell him *why* I was arrested or ask him to do anything about it. I didn't even mention it was RPD. But, uh… Well, let's just say that wasn't the first time I've called him from jail. He's been in the Bay Area, though, so I guess he missed out on most of the gossip."

I keep quiet, and his expression shifts again, seeming less wry and more disappointed. Or maybe he's tired, it's hard to say.

"But he was there when I first woke up—at the hospital, you know? He asked what happened, and about your scars, and I…" He sighs, scratching the back of his neck. "He was worried. I haven't landed myself in the hospital like that in years. He wanted to know about the fight—or whatever you told him—but you weren't there. No one had seen you in *hours*. I couldn't think about anything else. I didn't know what to say to Jesse. I didn't care what he thought, about me or anything, so I just said it was an accident. More dumb shit I got myself into. I asked him not to tell our dad how bad it was, and that was it, basically. Then Matt came in, and he took off to meet up with someone, so… We barely talked about it then."

What should I say?

Obviously, I wish he told Jesse the truth earlier, but I did the same thing with Rose. She didn't know what was going on until I had no choice but to stop hiding it. And Robbie still has no idea I've been hurt at all. He thinks I've been totally fine. He doesn't even know that Ice exists. He liked my photos of the beach and teased me for being too embarrassed to admit that James was my boyfriend. And I *still* haven't said anything. I don't have the right to judge James for avoiding it until the last possible moment.

"Will you guys be okay?" I ask.

"Yeah."

He holds his empty drink glass in both hands, staring into the blue-tinted ice chips left inside. The mood isn't dead—just a bit uneasy—but I feel bad even if I wasn't the one who brought it up. *For once.*

The server saves the day by stopping by. They smile and take James' empty dessert plate. As they ask about our meal and make sure we don't need anything else, we play happy until they set the check tray on the table and move on.

James picks up the receipt and sighs. "Those drinks cost more than my actual meal. Wild. Anyway, you ready to head out?"

"Yeah. I'm ready."

He pays in cash, leaving a generous tip, and we head outside. The sun has already set, the sky just beginning to darken. After we move the car to the back corner of the parking lot, James calls the taxi service, and we loiter beside his locked car rather than take up one of the benches outside the restaurant doors.

"I miss the beach already," he says. "Next time we go, it'll just be you and me. Okay? No one else allowed. Won't even tell 'em we're going. I love Matt, but *damn*. Why's everyone so obsessed with my sex life, y'know?"

I laugh, tugging at a strand of hair that escaped my bun. "Rose is the same way. She's always trying to hook me up with some friend of a friend or whatever. I shouldn't have to deal with that anymore, but, um… I wouldn't mind going back to the beach. Even with everyone there, it was fun. Mostly."

"Mostly," he agrees. He hefts himself up onto the hood of his car and watches the sky. "Still… It'd be better with just you."

"Maybe. It'd be more peaceful, at least."

I watch him for a moment before looking to the sky too. The sunset pinks and purples are slowly shifting to deep, navy blue. It's pretty, but the view in town is nothing compared to the view at the beach. Here, I can only make out a handful of stars.

I banish a flicker of another dream I don't care to think about. Then I toss my purse onto the hood of the car and climb up too. As I settle beside James, he glances over. He looks happy, if sleepy, his cheeks still tinged pink. It's probably a good thing we called a cab.

"Honestly, babe," he says mildly, "this summer has been a total shitshow—one disaster after another. But…" With a laugh, he flashes a warm smile that forces his eyes shut for a second. "There have been a few good days."

Yeah.

There have been a few.

fifty-four

When the taxi arrived, I asked if we could go back to my house instead. I asked, just to see if James might change his mind, but he shook his head and gave the driver his father's address.

And, now, I really wish he had listened to me.

I wish we didn't come back here.

Because I know— The instant I see that blue pickup truck in the driveway. The instant the taxi drops us off on the curb, and I catch the grim look on James' face as it drives away. The instant we step through the front door and into the kitchen. The instant James' father mutes the TV and stands from the couch, and we freeze three steps into the living room.

I know.

Our good day is over.

I want to turn back. I want to take James' hand and drag him out of the house and leave. I don't mind walking clear across town in the middle of the night if it meant avoiding whatever *this* is bound to turn into. Maybe we should've known we could only avoid another confrontation for so long.

But why now? Of all nights, why tonight?

"Where the hell were you all day?" Jonathan asks—rather

ironic considering we never saw him at any point while we *were* here today.

"Out."

His eyes land on me. "With her?"

"And Matt," James says lamely. "It's my birthday."

"Yeah? No shit. Why'd you ignore my call earlier?"

"Uh…"

He glances between his father, who stands near the corner of the TV stand a few feet away, and the staircase on the opposite side of the room. Then he adjusts his grip on my hands and takes a step toward the stairs.

"Don't walk away from me."

James freezes. Head held low, his grip on my hand tightens. "I know you don't give a shit about me or anything I do. There's no point acting like you care now."

"I do *give a shit*, boy. And that's exactly why I have to nip this little fantasy life of yours in the bud."

"Fantasy life?" James asks with a choked laugh.

He glances over his shoulder. Our eyes meet for only half a second before he returns his attention to his father, but I do *not* like what I saw. *Frantic, upset panic. Anger. Regret.* He drops my hand, and his hands become fists. Tension crackles the stuffy air. And, as if by instinct, I slip around to James' other side, closer to the stairs.

"What do you know about my life?" he asks, voice rising. "Honestly, Dad? You don't know the first fucking thing about what I've had to deal with these past few months—or, hell, the last few *years*, even!"

"I know you've been messing around with this human girl since you up and disappeared." He hardly reacted to the severity of James' response. *I can't believe it.* He doesn't seem impressed or offended or anything. His tone didn't change at all.

James throws an arm out to the side. "Who cares? Who cares if she's human? Who *cares* that I'm with her?"

"It's wrong, son. Not only that, but I heard the Monroe boy owns her—"

"Fuck that! Ice is just her *sponsor*. Nobody owns anyone!" He glances back to me with misty, pleading eyes. "Jayde. Please, go."

"But—"

I don't want to leave him to deal with this alone. He drank too much. He's already super upset. I know I'm not in *danger* if I stay, and this is—

"Go," he begs, voice breaking.

But—

I look past James, to his father. The man stares me down, distaste oozing off him in waves. Distaste for me, the human girl hanging around his son—the same son he treats like garbage every time they speak.

James seriously wants to deal with this alone? There's no way. He just doesn't want me around to witness whatever comes next. But saying what I think would probably make things even worse.

There's nothing I can do.

A heavy sickness settles deep in my chest as I tear my eyes away and take the first step. I cross the room and start up the stairs with no one speaking up to stop me. But I pause just out of sight after the turn in the staircase. I stand against the wall. And I listen. Because I just can't bring myself to lock myself away in the bedroom while James—

Damn it... I should've convinced him to come up with me.

"How'd you meet that girl, James?"

"Doesn't matter. You know it doesn't. And it's none of your business, anyway. Whether you like it or not, I'm an adult now too. I can make my own decisions."

"What would your mother think?"

"Don't you *dare* bring Mom into this! She'd be happy to know I found someone who actually cares about me. Someone who loves me for who I am and doesn't care if I'm a wreck or if I'm defective or whatever. Someone who isn't embarrassed to be seen with me in public. Someone who doesn't think I'm nothing but a failure the way I know *you* have for years!"

James...

I stare at my feet, biting my cheek so hard I taste blood. Wide eyes bore into the wall opposite me as my hands ball into tight fists. My right hand tingles, a twinge of discomfort, for the first time in weeks. But I ignore it.

"She's human, son."

"Yeah? And?"

"Are you fucking her?"

"*What?*"

"Are you fucking that human girl?"

"*Am I*—? Dad. What the fuck is wrong with you?"

I should go down there.

I should stop this.

I should say something.

But I peel my back from the wall and drag myself the rest of the way to the second floor. *My head hurts. Chest hurts. Stomach hurts.* But I shut myself in James' bedroom. I cross the room, climb onto the bed, and stare out the window through the spinning fan blades. The physical distance and buzz of the fan drowns out whatever nasty words they continue shouting back and forth.

We left the fan on all day. The sky is dark now. Outside, the temperature was almost comfortable, but it's still miserable in here. Still so hot. So stuffy.

God...

I guess it's true, though.

Some immortals can't stand the idea of us being together. Relationships like ours are taboo. I've known that for months, understood it on some level since I first learned of immortals. But, before James' father and Paige Porter, most of the *otherness* I felt was self-imposed. I felt different because *I* viewed myself as different, but none of James' friends have treated me like they think I'm different. My situation is unusual, sure. I mean, some random human girl who knows about immortals? And dates them? It's weird. I know it's weird. And they've all joked about it, but *this is...*

The door swings open behind me. The knob smacks against the rubber doorstop on the wall. I turn as the door slams shut again. And, in an instant, the temperature seems to drop several degrees.

James is okay, physically unharmed, but trembling. His back

is pressed to the door, his hands balled at his sides. Teeth grit. Face flushed red. He stares at the brown carpet, tears spilling from wide eyes.

Oh, no.

I'm already off the bed, closing the distance between us, before I even *think* I should move. But he doesn't look at me. I'm standing a foot away. But he doesn't look up from the floor. Tears drip from his chin.

I raise a hand to touch his face.

Our eyes meet.

A hand catches my wrist.

I flinch back, heart racing, and the remaining warmth drains from my cheeks as my foot settles on the floor. *Aah— Wait. You moved so fast.* I couldn't help it. My reaction was involuntary. *The flicker of fear was involuntary.* But my reaction wasn't lost on him, and his eyes fill with an unbearable pain.

He drops my arm and presses his palms over his eyes.

Shit.

"James…"

I glance at my arm. He didn't grab me roughly. I'm not hurt at all. It was just enough to stop my fingers from brushing his skin. *But I still…*

"I'm sorry," he gasps. "I didn't—"

"No, it's, ah…" My hands hover uselessly in the air between us. "I'm fine. It's okay."

"It is not," he moans. He pulls at his hair as his hands creep up his face. "Stop pretending that everything's okay. It's not okay. Nothing about this is okay. Everything is so fucked, and

I— Why did I think this was a good idea? Bringing you here? Coming back at all? Goddammit…"

As I watch, my mind fills with static. Frustrated and hurt and sad, frozen with no idea what to do. *How could I possibly salvage this?* But, even if he's right—even if everything is fucked—I have to do something.

Act, Jayde!

I shake the worst of the nerves off and plant my hands on his shoulders. He freezes long enough to catch his breath, then falls quiet. His shoulders are tense. He's still covering his eyes, still breathing too quickly.

The alcohol can't be helping.

Um… I glance over my shoulder. The fan in the window. The bed. Pillows. *Okay.* I look back to James, who hasn't moved at all but seems to be trembling less than before.

"We should sit," I say, keeping my voice soft. "Come on. James. Hey."

I carefully pry one of his hands away from his head. He stares at me with a wide amber eye leaking tears. But he doesn't protest, so I turn, still holding his hand, and walk to the bed. He follows sluggishly, but we make it, and he drops to sit on the edge when I release his hand. Though, he goes back to hiding his face as he lowers his head.

What now?

Nothing I say can make this better. I can't *fix* anything. I can't *change* the messed up reality of our situation. *I'm helpless again, but James has dealt with this far longer than I have.*

All I can really do is be here.

So I hug him. He starts crying again. I rub his back and fix his hair and tell him that I love him. Things are messed up right now, but it won't be like this forever.

Everything will be okay. Eventually.

Sometimes, though, it's better to cry. To let it all out instead of bottling it up. At least, tonight, I can be here for him when he needs someone. I can make sure he isn't alone.

James' breathing grows steadier with time. A few minutes. Several minutes. I don't know, but we've both been quiet for a while, and my back is starting to ache.

Then, with a tired groan, he shifts within my arms. I let go and sit beside him, and I watch as he wipes his eyes with his sleeve. He sniffles and glances up from his hands and looks at nothing in particular across the room. His breathing almost seems normal now.

"Of course," he says, voice rough as his mouth twists into a wry smile that quickly shatters. "Of course, he thinks everything's my fault. Getting kicked out. Spending a few nights in jail. Ending up in the hospital. You name it. It's *all* my fault, right? I did it all to myself. Everything. And what happened to you…"

Another tear slips from his eye.

After a second's hesitation, I reach out and gently nudge his cheek. He turns toward me but won't meet my gaze. His eyes narrow. Brows furrow. Jaw sets. He looks about as disgusted and pissed as he does upset.

Not great.

"None of what happened is your fault, James."

"He said, uh… Ha… He said it doesn't matter if I can morph

now. It's too late. I already let it go to my head and fucked my life beyond repair. Wasted it. And now I've ruined your life too. Just by meeting you, I—"

Oh, boy...

His eyes finally meet mine, and he flashes a weak smile. "Is that true?"

My lip quivers, moisture threatening the corners of my eyes, but I shake it off. *I can't break down. Not right now. I have to keep it together. For James. I have to. I have to be fine.*

I hold his warm, damp face in my hands and force a smile.

"No," I say firmly. "It's not true. It's not your fault, and my life isn't ruined. Remember what we talked about the other day? Next year, after I finish my degree, we can leave Riverview. We can pack up and go to LA or wherever you want, and you will never have to stay with your dad or see Ice or deal with *any of this* ever again. I swear."

"You sure?" he asks, eyes flooding with moisture again. "Can we really do that?"

"I swear. It won't always be like this."

He glances aside, seeming to think about it for a moment. Then his expression adopts an unsettling blankness as his eyes lock onto the heart-shaped scar on my wrist. Slowly, he lifts a hand out of his lap. Slowly, his fingers inch toward my arm.

He draws breath, as though preparing to speak.

And I panic. I do the only thing I can think of that I *know* will stop him from saying whatever nonsense he's thinking.

I kiss him.

He hesitates, but only for a second. Then his eyes close, and his hand—the one that *was* on a path toward my wrist—ends up on the back of my head. A hint of alcohol and sugar on his breath. He resists when I break the kiss. But I follow through. I lean back and let my hands fall away from his face.

Somehow, he looks more miserable than before as his hand returns to his lap. Bitter darkness flickers over his expression as tears spill from his eyes, and he averts his gaze.

"I should've died, y'know?" His voice is low. Hollow. And he shields his eyes with one arm. "If I just died, none of this would've happened."

I...can't move.

"If I died, you would've been fine, and—"

"Stop."

It was barely a whisper. Barely audible. But he freezes like I yelled at him. Slowly, he lowers his arm and turns to face me. His expression is about as blank as before, but it at least looks like he's breathing properly. *Sort of.*

Then he sniffles and wipes his nose. "But don't you ever wish you hadn't walked all the way out there to find me?"

At Reid Manor?

"No." My mouth feels dry. "Of course not."

Why does saying that now feel so disingenuous? Why does it leave a pit in my stomach?

I meant what I said. Obviously. I don't wish that at all. When I left Ice's house to look for him, I was more concerned than I'd ever been in my life previously—both about James and my own situation. The questions had gnawed at me for days by then, and seeing him that night was the final straw. I needed to ask him about what happened. I *wanted* to hear his side of the story and make sure he was okay.

But it doesn't matter. True or not, my words don't seem to comfort him. He doesn't look any less miserable. And an idle thought tickles the back of my mind.

"Do you wish I hadn't gone looking for you?"

His eyes snap open wide. They meet mine for a split second, and the blood seems to drain from his cheeks as he looks away again. He shakes his head, staring at his lap, and combs a trembling hand through his hair.

"No," he breathes.

His eyes fill with fresh tears, bringing tears to mine even as I can't seem to understand what's happening. It's like...I hear the words—I hear *what* he's saying—*but I just can't...*

"No," he says again, shaking his head, worrying his hands in his lap, tears spilling from wide eyes. "Being with you is— You are *everything* to me, Jayde, but I... Sometimes, I still wish..."

My breath hitches as the first tear breaks free and tracks down my cheek. But I hug him again, and I shush him, and he sobs while I stare at the blank wall behind him.

I don't like this, but I... I don't know what to do.

"It's not your fault." My head buzzes with uneasy static, but my voice remains steady. "Your dad doesn't know what he's talking about. Like you said, he has no idea what we've been through. And Ice is... He's just trying to hurt you. Whatever he's said..."

"Nothing Ice said about me is wrong," he mumbles into my shoulder. "He knows me better than you think. He was right to tell you to stay away from me."

"That's not true."

He sighs, and his hand brushes my side, fingers tracing almost perfectly over the scar through my dress. And my stomach turns.

"I could've stopped this a long time ago," he says.

"How?" I snap. I plant my hands on his shoulders and hold him at arm's length. "How, James? By getting yourself *killed*?"

He stares at me in alarm. But I want him to see the fire in my eyes. I need to make sure he understands clearly. *How pissed the thought makes me.*

He knows damn well how I felt about that before, and I feel the same now. I don't regret staying with him at Reid Manor in July. I don't regret taking the bullet Ice meant for him. I didn't regret either, even before I fell in love with him or knew about his *stupid deal* with Ice.

Knowing that, he can't seriously believe I'd be happier in a world where he left or died thinking it would protect me. It doesn't make sense. He *can't* believe that.

Yet, for some reason, he clearly does.

"I don't wanna give up." His voice is soft and fragile. "I don't want to die. I told you, right? But I don't know what to do anymore. I can't keep putting you through this shit."

My heart races.

A gun firing. A dark silhouette. Falling, in a dream.

Calm down. Snap out of it.

We're fine, safe in his miserable bedroom.

"No one is going to die, James."

"You can't say that," he whines, pushing against my hands.

"You don't know. You *can't*."

We seriously underestimated those Applebee's drinks.

I take a deep breath and *almost* feel functional again, so I relax my hold on James. I point to the pillows behind him and tell him to lay down.

He blinks at me, but I stand without waiting for a response and cross the room to turn off the light. As always, the room dims but remains illuminated by the neighbor's annoying floodlight.

And James did not lie down.

With a sigh, I return to the bed. He lifts his head out of his hands and stares up at me with glassy eyes. Upset and tired and confused. *This isn't his fault.* I comb my fingers through his short hair. It's still a mess. We're both a mess right now.

"We'll be alright," I say softly. "But it's late. We should try to get some sleep, okay?"

He's quiet for a moment. Eyes searching my face, expression still tense, hands loose in his lap. Then he takes a deep breath, and his shoulders dip, and exhaustion smooths his features.

"Fine," he says, almost sounding normal.

"Thank you."

I unbutton his shirt before stepping away to let my hair down and change out of my dress. When I check on James again, he's stripped down to boxers and his undershirt—the rest of his clothes discarded on the floor—and sitting on the far side of the bed. He stares out the window, one hand on top of the box fan.

"Sorry," he says as I crawl onto the bed. "Though, I guess I should've seen this coming after I ignored that stupid phone call."

"Did he say why he called?"

"No. Of course not." He laughs, finally glancing at me, but I still can't get a good read on him. "He didn't even leave a voicemail. But, knowing him, I bet it was just to…nag me…or ask me to pick up beer since I'm twenty-one now or some other dumb shit."

That is annoying.

He sighs. "Seriously though, why are you still here? Why put up with all this? With my dad? With me?"

"Because I care about you."

He flashes a pained smile, then looks back out the window and scratches the faint scars near his shoulder. "Ice or no Ice, all I ever do is cause trouble for everyone. I fight with Matt and Jesse and random guys outside of card shops and mini-marts, and I fight with my dad over the dumbest shit, and now you're stuck in the middle of it all. You never did anything wrong, you know? It's not fair to you."

"Well, um… In this case, I think I'm the one causing trouble for you—with Ice, your dad, Jesse, and everyone else. You know?"

"And I already told you; I'm *always* in trouble."

I sigh.

As things are, I doubt there's anything I can say to convince him otherwise. He's felt this way for a long time. It won't just go away, no matter what I do.

Though, getting him out of here surely wouldn't hurt.

I rub his back until he agrees to lie down. We end up facing each other on the small bed. His eyes are still wide, reflecting a hint of green in the low light, but he finally looks more tired than upset.

"Hey, um…" I trail off, but his eyes flick to mine, and I force a smile. "I got you something for your birthday. But we have to pick it up from my house tomorrow. Is that okay?"

He sighs heavily. "Yeah, uh… Yeah, that's fine. I was… thinking of going back, anyway."

"To stay?"

"Yeah. To stay." He rolls onto his back, rubbing his puffy eyes. "I have to get the fuck out of here, Jayde. This house and my dad… It's killing me. I forgot how bad it was, but I… I can't stay here another day. I can't do that to you. I— I'm really sorry. I shouldn't have brought you here in the first place."

"You were just trying to help."

"Sure, I thought I was, but I was wrong. I should've listened to you. You were right. Again."

"It's okay."

He grimaces. "It's really not. But I guess you can think whatever you want."

Fair.

With another sigh, he turns to face the wall. I wait a moment before shifting closer. He's so warm, and the room is hot as always, but he doesn't complain. I drape an arm over him, and our hands find each other, and his fingers interlace with mine. And I feel like maybe I wasn't *completely* talking out of my ass earlier when I said we'll be fine.

"You know, I…" He laughs softly. "This is gonna sound stupid, but I can't wait to be back in your bed."

"Oh, me either. It's not stupid." *With the air conditioning and the extra space*... I feel a real smile creep onto my face. "But, if you move in with me, it'll be your bed too, you know? *Our* bed."

"Mm… Our bed, huh? I… Yeah, I like that."

Part of me wishes he'd turn around and kiss me and pull me closer. Even if the heat borders on uncomfortable. Even if we're both still upset. I wish he'd turn around and creep a hand up my shirt. Maybe we could have the cliché birthday sex that Matthew teased him about. I'm down for it, but…

I missed out on most of what happened downstairs. I have no idea what else his father said, so I can only imagine how awful it was. *For him to come upstairs like this.* How painful it was, and how painful it must still be, having those things stuck in his head.

So I just squeeze his hand and kiss the nape of his neck. In response, he brings my hand to his mouth and presses his lips to my knuckles.

Maybe…he feels a little better?

"I love you," he breathes.

"I love you too."

fifty-five

James wakes up groggy, embarrassed, and complaining of a headache—hungover but otherwise okay. He kisses my face and brushes my bangs out of my eyes and apologizes for the tenth time.

I'm not upset, but I still double-check that he meant what he said about going back to the cottage today.

He did, so we get dressed and jump into packing.

While he texts Matthew to secure a ride, I shove my things into my duffel bag, including the hoodie I stole and claimed as my own last week.

Within the hour, Matthew texts to announce his arrival. *Finally.* We leave the bedroom with our bags packed and arms full of bedding, and I am not the least bit sad to leave this place. Nor am I sad that we don't run into James' father as we slip out of the house.

Matthew, wearing a hot pink snapback and easy grin, stands on the curb in front of James' idling car.

"Too much to drink last night, huh?" he asks.

"A bit," James says.

He sets everything he's carrying on the curb on his way to

the driver's side of the car. Then Matthew looks to me. His casually humored expression reminds me so much of Rose's cheekiness that it nearly kills me.

"You take shotgun," he says. "I'll sit in back."

The trunk pops open, and we stuff everything but my duffel bag inside. Then, after slamming the trunk like I mean it, I walk around to hop in the passenger seat. Matthew takes the center seat in back and does not buckle his seatbelt, much like Cassidy, but James says nothing before turning the key in the ignition.

"You said you're finally moving out?" Matthew asks.

"Something like that."

"Back to Jayde's place, where you were staying before, right?" When we both confirm, he smiles. "Nice. Mind if I hang out for a while?"

"Eh…"

"You can hang out," I say. James glances at me in surprise, but I shrug. "There's not much to do at the cottage, but I really don't mind."

"Cottage?" Matthew asks blankly.

I sigh. "It's less interesting than it sounds. More like a townhouse, but the buildings are all separate. Anyway, it's part of that new cottage cluster down by RCC. They're basically glorified apartments."

"Still sounds cool. So, I can come over, right? Or do you need privacy while you settle back into domestic life?"

"Shut up, man," James says with a laugh. "But, yeah, sure, whatever. You can hang out if you swear not to say dumb shit like that."

* * * * *

After breakfast and a quick grocery run, which is more entertaining than usual with Matthew around, we pull into the familiar Oakwood Cottages parking lot. Everything looks normal. Feels normal. The spaces in front of my house are empty, and James parks with the trunk facing the sidewalk.

When I leave the car, I am *so* relieved to find three packages on the concrete landing, partially hidden between the potted plant and short privacy wall. One reasonably large box and two smaller mailing envelopes.

That should be everything.

"You're right," Matthew says, carrying the two grocery bags. "It looks nothing like a cottage."

James, with his blanket and pillow, walks past Matthew and up the landing steps. He stops again when he notices the packages.

"This all for me?" he asks. "What the hell did you buy?"

"You'll see in a minute."

I unlock the front door and crack it open to peek inside. The living room is quiet and empty, and the air is hot and stuffy since I turned off the AC last time we left.

"I'll go first," James offers.

I'm confident the house is empty, but I agree, and he walks in ahead of me. Matthew follows with no hesitation. And I, mindful of the *loaded handgun* in my bag, carefully set my duffel and James' backpack just inside the front door. James does his thing, scoping out the place, while Matthew more casually snoops around the living room, having already abandoned the grocery bags on the kitchen table.

Ignoring them both, I step outside to scan the parking lot again. There's still nothing unusual—and certainly no flashy silver sports car—so I bring the packages inside and lock the door behind me.

"This your roommate?" Matthew asks.

He points out a framed photo on the bookcase by the stairs. I leave the packages on the couch on my way over to check.

Yeah. Our graduation photo.

"You know her?" I ask.

"Yeah, ah— Rose, right?" He looks over a few more photos, mild and curious. "I thought the name was familiar. She was in my speech class winter term. Seen her at a couple parties since. She seems cool."

"You really get around, don't you?" James asks dryly as he makes his way back downstairs.

He shrugs. "I get invited to tons of parties. Some are mixed-company."

"Everything look okay upstairs?" I ask.

"Yeah. All clear."

Good.

I step away from the bookcase to adjust the thermostat. Once the AC kicks on, I look around for myself, but everything seems fine. Nothing's out of place. The windows are still locked with the blinds drawn shut, and the mail left on the bookcase appears untouched, so I doubt Rose has stopped by either.

Even so, I lock the deadbolt for good measure.

As long as we keep the doors and windows locked, we should be fine. Even if Ice realizes we're back—assuming he's keeping tabs on the cottage—he doesn't have a key. He'd have to break something to get in.

Either way, we're better off here than with James' father.

"I see James is a wee bit paranoid," Matthew says.

"Hey!"

I force a smile. "He has a good reason to be."

"Yeah? You don't look worried."

"I'm just glad to be home."

When I check on James, he seems more comfortable than when we first arrived, but there's still a hint of strain behind his eyes.

I change the subject, and we move into the kitchen. Matthew spends more time checking best-by dates on various things in the cabinets than he spends helping, while James and I actually put the groceries away.

As we finish, James asks about the packages again.

"Yeah, um…" I laugh and follow him into the living room. "I came into some unexpected money a few days ago—now that I can morph and officially became a human immortal, I guess—so I may have gone a little overboard."

"How much did you spend?"

"I'm not telling."

He stops in front of the couch. Matthew teleports to his other side, watching with heightened interest, but James ignores him, sits by the packages, and picks up a grey bubble mailer. He should *probably* open the box first, but I resist the urge to stop him as he tears open the top of the plastic envelope.

When he pulls out a video game case, Matthew immediately says, "Nice," like it's a totally normal gift, but James' eyes go wide. He glances at the box beside him. Back at the game case in his hand. And then at me.

"You're kidding," he says lamely.

I shake my head and flash a shameless smile.

He removes the second video game and gift card, the latter of which elicits a chuckle from James and some light teasing from Matthew when I say it's meant for ebooks. The second bubble mailer contains only one game. He sets it with the others before hefting the box into his lap. I consider grabbing a pair of scissors, but he opens it no problem, unveiling the bubble-wrapped GameStation inside.

"Surprise," I say.

"You're crazy." He looks up with wide eyes. "This is a lot, Jayde. This is…too much."

But I flash another smile. "Just a little something to repay you for looking out for me the past couple months. Happy birthday."

"Ha… Thanks?"

"What happened to your old one?" Matthew asks.

"I sold it back in July 'cause I'm an idiot." James looks away and picks up one of the games. *QuarryKraft*. Then glances at me. "You wanna play?"

Me? I can't even remember the last time I played video games.

I laugh. "I made sure the system came with two controllers, so maybe later. For now, you should just play with Matt. I, um…

need to put all my stuff away while I still feel like doing it."

"Fair enough," he agrees, smile warming.

Matthew sighs and pats James on the shoulder. "Dude, this gift blows that lame phone case out of the water. But, yeah, I'm down to play some QuarryKraft."

"Sounds good." James starts unwrapping the plastic from the game case. "Do me a favor and set up the console?"

"Aye aye, captain."

Matthew marches off with the GameStation box, and James stands from the couch to close the distance between us. His fingers brush my arm, and the rest of his unease seems to have faded. He looks *happy*. As happy as he did at Riverside Park. Or last night at Applebee's before I accidentally made things awkward.

"Thanks, babe," he says.

He moves to kiss me, and, as I kiss him back, a rush of warmth blooms in my chest. *I almost wish I hadn't invited Matthew over.* But I think him being here is good for James, and we'll have the place to ourselves soon enough.

He breaks off the kiss, and his eyes flick aside—presumably to check on Matthew, who is busy working with the TV and GameStation and surely has no real interest in what we're doing at all.

But he's still worried what he thinks? Jeez...

I remind James that I need to go unpack, and Matthew distracts him by asking for help with something, so I slip away to retrieve my duffel. Though, I find myself hesitating as I reach for it. Light glints off the metal zipper, reminding me—

There's a gun inside.

What am I supposed to do with it?

With a sigh that no one seems to notice, I heft the strap over my shoulder, supporting the bag's weight with one arm, and head upstairs. I shut myself in my room, set the duffel on my bed, and stare at it for an uncomfortably long time *again*.

I don't know what to do.

There's no good place to stash a *gun* in my bedroom. I don't want it here. It's giving me nightmares, inviting my dreamscape to torment me more than usual. James barely knows how to use it, and I've only touched a gun once in my entire life.

Why keep it around at all?

Finally, I unzip the bag and put a few easy things away. My laptop on my desk. Purse and toiletry bag on the dresser. Leave my phone charger on the bed. Toss my shoes into the closet. Return a few articles of clean clothing to the appropriate drawers. As the bag deflates, all that's left inside are things I doubt I'll need right away. Some dirty clothes. My swimsuit. Whatever. The gun is still wrapped in a spare camisole near the bottom.

Mm...

Yeah. It can stay there for now.

I move the half-empty bag to the floor at the foot of my bed, half beneath the bed frame, where I intend to leave it until I come up with a better idea. Then I cross the room to take a long, hard look at myself in the mirror.

Who am I?

Anymore?

I look tired. I look tan, my shoulders slightly burned. My

eyes are too wide. And I'm still uncomfortably aware of the River Sapphire's absence, like I *miss* its cool, gentle weight against my skin.

I take the necklace from my pocket.

Rose, James, and Ice all thought it was weird that I wore it well into August—a gift from *an ex*, something that was *useless*—but I put it on every morning anyway. Whether it was out of habit or desperation, I'm honestly not sure anymore.

But, now that I can't wear the necklace, what should I do with it when I don't need it? Leave it in my wallet? A pocket? Keep it on my person 24/7? Is that what's expected of me? Is that what Human-Immortal Affairs wants me to do?

No thanks.

I open my jewelry box. As I hold the River Sapphire by the dark hemp cord, the pendant twists. Light reflects off the polished blue gemstone, flinging white sparkles on the wall.

This feels weird.

Why does it feel so weird?

But I ignore the feeling and carefully place the River Sapphire in the jewelry box. Then I close the lid and head downstairs without it.

fifty-six

Matthew sticks around a few hours before taking off. I guess he's running late for vague afternoon plans that may or may not involve Natalie.

Good for him.

It's still early in the day, though, so, with a basic understanding of how the QuarryKraft game works after some time spectating, I stick to my word and offer to play with James. He starts a new save file, and our characters appear in a field dotted with blocky hills and blocky trees. Taking his gameplay advice to heart, I manage to survive our first night, and I build a house out of dirt cubes. I keep accidentally pressing X instead of A, but the game is pretty simple, and it is fun.

Still, it turns out that video games consume a lot of brainpower when you're not used to playing them, so I pick a good stopping point after completing several in-game days. James thanks me for playing with him, then gets up to put in a different game—the recent release he mentioned over dinner yesterday.

He seems fine, and he doesn't stop me from leaving to check the mail alone. The parking lot and surrounding area is still clear. No silver sports car. No white cat slinking around. And I make it back inside in one piece.

Lock the door.

The deadbolt clicks. I leave the mail key on its hook, collect the mail left on the bookcase, and head for the dining table to go through everything. Nothing addressed to me is too important. A few pieces of junk mail. July's bank statement. Two letters and a fall term course catalog from Riverview Community College.

Right...

I still need to register for classes.

Annoyingly, there's nothing from Human-Immortal Affairs. No letter acknowledging my first successful feline transform-ation. No follow-up on the questionnaire I filled out at Riverview General. They sent that *one* letter about the River Sapphire in June, but it seems like everything since has gone to Ice instead —like my SIP payment and whatever certificate he mentioned.

I still have no idea how to contact those assholes in Seattle, but going through Ice can't be the only way.

After throwing most of my mail away, I leave Rose's on the desk in her bedroom. Then I settle on the couch next to James and watch him play for a while. This game is some kind of futuristic military-flavored drama—in space, by the looks of it. A lot is happening on-screen, but he seems to follow the action no problem.

I check my phone, opening FaceSpace.

Robbie shared a list of courses he's taking fall term at UCLA. A girl I haven't spoken with since graduation complained about the heat. I guess a heatwave is on the way. Highs forecasted over one hundred degrees for five days straight. It's a good thing we're back in my adequately climate-controlled cottage. We'd roast in a heatwave, stuck in the stuffy bedroom at his father's house. *Or Reid Manor.*

Rose hasn't posted anything new, but a question was left on her profile by a friend. A girl we went to high school with. I think they're in the nursing program together.

> **Abigail Marsh**
>
> Hey!! You're still in town right? We haven't heard from you in a while? What's up?

To my surprise, she replied:

> **Rose MacArthur**
>
> Yep, just taking a social media break rn.
> Sorry! <3

The post and her comment are from this morning.
Well, at least I know she's alive.

I back out of FaceSpace and try calling. The phone rings twice before sending me to voicemail. I don't leave a message, but the extent of my frustration annoys me.

She must feel bad for ghosting me like this. I felt awful the whole time I lied to her, and I avoided her for days after she found out about my scars. But what happened with Ice was insane and, from her perspective, came out of nowhere.

I convinced her that everything was fine, letting her assume that whoever hurt me was out of the picture. No one should have to witness what she did. *A strange man with a knife to your best friend's neck? Someone you'd been living with suddenly bleeding out in your kitchen?* I yelled at her while she panicked and cried. For a second, she thought James had *died.* Then she watched him turn into a cat and *still* drove us to the ER.

The whole thing was seriously messed up.

She has every right to be upset. To be mad. Or scared. I don't blame her. *I don't.* I just wanna know if she's okay. I need to make sure that Human-Immortal Affairs didn't traumatize her further or pressure her into doing anything she might regret.

So I switch to FaceSpace messenger and scroll down my friend list. *I can't message her mom; that's weird.* I could ask a mutual friend? Maybe one of the girls she went out to lunch with a few weeks back. I think we're friends on here... *But I don't think she's talking to anyone else right now either. Ugh...*

My finger pauses over Kyle MacArthur's image. Rose's older brother. He's online, and he should still be up from Fresno. If he's staying with their parents in town, and she's there too...

Sure, whatever. We never talk, but it's worth a shot.

> **Me:** Hey, sorry if this is random, but I haven't heard from Rose in a while. How is she?

I take a deep breath as the message appears as delivered. The *read* indicator pops up surprisingly fast, and he starts typing, so I distract myself by looking back to the TV. James pays me no mind, being deeply invested in whatever mission he's working to accomplish in the game. Which is fine by me.

My phone vibrates in my hand, and I glance down.

> **Kyle:** She's ok, been binging some ER show for the past week lol

It sounds like she's rewatching Night Hospital again. It's been her comfort show for *years*. She starts the series over from episode one fairly often, but she usually doesn't binge-watch unless she's upset. I'm not sure if Kyle knows that, though.

Either way, any confirmation that she's safe at home with her family is good enough for me.

> **Kyle:** Wait, you haven't been talking?

I sure as hell have tried.

> **Me:** Not since she left the cottage. She hasn't said anything about it?
>
> **Kyle:** Not much. You get in a fight or something?
>
> **Me:** No. She probably just wanted to spend more time with you before school starts up, since you don't get to visit very often anymore.

What am I even saying?

> **Kyle:** Sure. I can talk to her if you want?
>
> **Me:** No, it's fine. I just wanted to check in. Thanks though.
>
> **Kyle:** np

This is kinda sad, but it's a relief to know that Rose hasn't completely fallen apart. Sure, she's binging soap operas and avoiding her friends, but Kyle seems to think she's fine. She should be alright for a few more weeks—I hope.

I did the same thing for a while, anyway. I just sat around, wishing things were different, watching Netflix and feeling like I was wasting away. But I'm...*okay* now.

Ugh! I can't even convince myself that I'm fine.

Back on FaceSpace, I continue scrolling down my newsfeed. The final Music@ThePark of the year is next week. Considering the heatwave, I think I'll skip it. And...

No way.

Night tagged Carmen and Natalie in a post this morning. A photo of a porcelain teacup full of clear, red liquid with the caption, *it's nice to spend quality time with friends again*. The tagged location is The House of Tea, the same teahouse we visited in July.

A flicker of anxiety.

If they met up today, Carmen almost certainly relayed everything we said at the beach—or at least the gist of it. *Will the information get back to Ice?*

But this isn't *bad* news.

Even if they discussed our situation, I want to imagine they had a good time catching up. It couldn't have been *that* bad if Night felt comfortable posting about it. At the very least, I hope Carmen is less concerned for her safety now.

Maybe I should ask Night about Ice's texts.

Last time we spoke in the dreamscape, I'd only received one. I assumed it was a dumb, one-off thing—typical Ice nonsense—but it's only gotten worse and even weirder since. On the off chance they weren't *all* sent in an attempt to get under my skin,

I feel like I should mention them.

Maybe I just want an excuse to talk to her.

I tap to open our conversation and scroll up a bit. My previous messages remain unread. I have no real reason to think she'd respond to me just because she spoke with Carmen, but it can't hurt to try.

> **Me:** Hey, I've gotten a few weird texts from Ice since I left the hospital. I don't know if it means anything, but it's been bothering me. Just thought you should know.

Is that too obvious?

I'm guessing Ice still doesn't know we've talked at all since July, save for the two minutes we spoke when he last brought me to Westbrooke, but I've messaged her several times before, including about Ice. As long as I don't directly reference the dreamscape, it should be fine.

> **Me:** Anyway, I saw your post on FS. Carmen asked me about you last week, so it's good to see that you're talking again. Hope you're doing alright.

That should be enough.

James yawns and pauses his game before looking over with a comfortable, vaguely curious expression.

"You writing an essay or something?" he asks with a laugh.

"Oh. Um…"

Glancing down, I realize that Night read the messages. *For the first time, she actually looked.* I still don't expect her to answer, though, so I put my phone away. James saves and quits his game—it seems like he just wrapped up the lengthy tutorial —and offers me his full attention.

But I don't know what to say.

He doesn't know about the dreamscape at all, and, honestly, I doubt it would make any difference to try explaining it now.

"No," I say. "I messaged Rose's brother to ask about her. She's fine—at her parents' house like I figured. And then…I messaged Night to ask about the weird texts Ice keeps sending."

"Night, huh?" He averts his gaze, his smile fixed. "You talk to her much anymore? I mean, you were friends, right?"

Are we friends?

I still consider her one—I think. She says she wants to help, and I want to trust her. But, sometimes, I can't help questioning her intentions.

"I message her every once in a while just to keep her in the loop, but she hasn't responded since…" I sigh. "Well, since Ice attacked me that first time, you know?"

"Yeah? I bet anything he told her to stop talking to you."

"You think so?"

"Just a guess."

A guess? That's exactly what happened. *She admitted to it.*

Maybe it's not much of a stretch for James to guess that, but he has history with Ice *and* Night. Alex recalled all three of them hanging out back in middle school.

They were friends.

"Do you know her very well?" I ask.

He meets my gaze, eyes sharp. "Do you know her at all?

What kind of *friend* would ignore you for weeks, knowing damn well what her *brother* did to you? Because you know there's no way she doesn't know after all this time."

"I—"

"Wait." He blanks frowning more mildly. "Did you see her? When you went to Westbrooke while I was in the hospital?"

Yeah, I saw her. And I told her everything was fine while Ice held a knife to my brachial artery.

"For a second," I admit, glancing away.

"She saw your scars, and she's still ignoring you?"

I bite my cheek. *He has a point.* From his perspective, it must seem weird for me to still consider her a friend at all.

"She was worried about you," I mumble.

He makes a sound—a stifled gasp, maybe. His eyes are wide, and it looks like he isn't sure how to respond. Then he grits his teeth and glances away again.

"Of course she was," he mutters.

"I'm sure she's upset about all this too."

"Oh, yeah. I'm sure she's *real* upset." He scoffs—a short, bitter laugh with darkness in his eyes. "That's probably why she hasn't done shit to help."

The room falls quiet, save for the low hum of the central AC. James stares at his lap, massaging his scarred left hand. Anxiety creeps into his terse expression as he seems to realize how harsh his words were.

I understand where he's coming from. *I really do, but...*

"It sounds like you don't like her," I say.

"It's not that. It's just—" He sighs, and his eyes flick up from his lap. "It's complicated, alright? I've known them for years—Ice and Night both. Since we were kids. And it's been…a lot. I mean, it wasn't *all* bad, but it sure as hell wasn't all great. Some was… Well, it was nothing…quite…like this, but…"

Oh? This sounds familiar. *Why does this sound so familiar?*

He shakes his head and forces a smile. "Sorry. It's, uh… What happened with us was… Ugh. It's a whole mess. And it was *years* ago. I really don't wanna get into it right now."

* * * * *

James flops onto the bed. He pushes his throw blanket aside and stretches out before rolling over to look up at me. His eyes are bright, and he grins as he props his head up with one hand.

For the first time, he's not wearing a shirt to sleep.

"Your bed's bigger than I remember," he says. "We should've come back sooner."

"I tried to tell you that."

He laughs. "Yeah. Sorry."

"It's fine."

I turn away to find something to wear. Looking at myself in the mirror, I catch James still watching me from the bed. *This is weird.* Being back here is weird. Opening my own dresser. Having access to all of my clothes at once. *It's weird.* I won't have to wear the same three outfits over and over. I won't have to lock my bedroom door or risk an awkward confrontation just to get a drink of water at night.

Yeah, we definitely should've come back sooner.

I change into a loose tank top and cotton sleep shorts before returning to the bed. I sit near my pillow and set my phone up to charge on the bedside table. The bed shifts behind me as James sits up and scoots closer.

"Hey," he says. "Sorry if this is…out of nowhere, but, uh… Can I ask you something?"

"Oh? Sure."

His tone feels slightly off, but I glance over, and our eyes meet, and he looks fine. Pleasant expression, relaxed posture. But I still feel a twinge of concern.

"I thought about it before we left my dad's, but I felt weird about asking then…" He averts his eyes, a hint of uncertainty slipping through. "What'd you do with the gun?"

"The gun?" I echo.

I turn to face him properly, but he continues avoiding my gaze. Maybe I'm extra nervous thanks to the strange sense of disconnect I've been trying to ignore all day. Maybe the question just caught me off guard. I don't know, but… *Why ask about the gun now? Does he really think I'd tell him where it is?*

"I tossed it," I say.

His golden eyes flick up. "Huh? For real?"

"No." I laugh with surprising ease—the blank look on his face helped. "Don't worry. The gun's safe, just like you wanted."

"Alright," he agrees with a mild frown.

I kiss his cheek and fluff up his hair, and he scratches the back of his neck as I return my hands to my lap. He looks embarrassed now, but it's kinda cute.

"Relax," I say. "We don't need the gun, okay? As long as

we keep the front door locked, we'll be fine."

He nods, then looks around the room like he also can't believe he's here, back in my bedroom. When his eyes land on me again, his expression shifts, warming, and he laughs.

"So... This is our bed now, huh?"

That is what I said.

fifty-seven

~ ∞ ~

When I wake up, it's dark. Too dark. And I'm sitting on the couch with no idea how I got there. But the couch and my lap aren't cast in shadow. As I look around again, the fog of sleep leaves my mind.

The dark.

The soft, floating lights.

I'm in the dreamscape again.

The couch is new, though.

With a sigh, I stand to get a better look at what I'm dealing with. When I turn back, the couch is gone. *Weird.* But I'm alone, and nothing else seems out of the ordinary. No sign of Night. No mirage-like scenery, nightmarish images, or pinprick of light in the distance. No sound. Nothing.

I'm not sure whether to be frustrated or relieved.

All I can do is pick a direction and start walking. Maybe, if I walk far enough, I'll come across Night's dreamscape again. Maybe we can talk. I can ask about Ice's texts in person. *Or the deal with her and James. Or if Ice knows that what he's done is public knowledge.*

Ugh.

I walk and walk. One foot in front of the other. Enough time passes for my bored mind to wander. I think about Night. I hum a song. I keep walking. More time passes. But my pace falters as the surrounding air cools. The floating lights slow to a crawl. The tiny hairs on the nape of my neck prickle.

Aah... I don't like that.

I force myself to speed up again, but I only make it several steps before a sound stops me cold. A loud tap, like feet on pavement. Like someone jumped from the last step onto solid ground behind me. *It's been silent this whole time. My footsteps haven't made any sound—*

Someone chuckles. "What are you looking for?"

The voice is mine. Scathing and nasty, but definitely mine.

I spin to face her. *To face myself.*

The other Jayde stands a few feet away and, for some unfair reason, wears nothing but the long, black overcoat that Ice let me borrow on the Fourth of July. The coat is dusty, smeared with wet blood glistening red in the impossible light, and fastened only by the tightened waist strap, leaving the faded scar on her chest visible. Her expression is amused yet callous. A crooked smile, sharp eyes, and raised brows. The green in her left eye is crackled with water immortal blue, the same as my left eye in feline form.

Wait. Have I seen her before?

Before I have time to react—just as I reconcile what I'm seeing and process what she asked—she reaches inside the coat and draws a gun from an interior pocket. I freeze, and her smile widens as she aims the all-too-familiar black handgun at me.

"Dare me to pull the trigger?" Her voice is light and eager, but her eyes are wild.

I step back, shaking my head.

This isn't real. This is a dream. She can't hurt me. Nothing can hurt me here. The gun isn't real. She isn't real. None of this is real.

"You're scared?" She tips her head, lips pursed. "Wouldn't this fix everything, though?"

"No—"

I squeeze my eyes shut. Still backing away, I hold my head in my hands as an awful, buzzing static overwhelms me. But I cry out over it, demanding that the nightmare version of myself leave me alone. *Go away. I don't want to hear it. I'm sick of my dreamscape.* Ice was wrong. No one has to die. *No one.* I won't let anyone die. *I would die myself before I stood by and let Ice and James kill each other!*

My voice echoes around me before falling silent.

My chest heaves from the effort of shouting. My hands fall from my face, but I still can't bring myself to open my eyes. Then a light tap on my sternum—a small, cool circle against my skin—turns me to stone, silent and still.

I can't breathe, but my heart races.

Slowly, I look up.

The horrible dreamscape Jayde has the tip of James' gun held to my chest. Finger on the trigger. But she looks more like I should. Eyes wide and afraid, tears streak her flushed cheeks.

"You mean that?" she asks, her voice as unsteady as her

hands.

Wait—

I reach for the gun.

It goes off before I touch it.

The blast sends me reeling. There's no pain, but my ears ring. My vision flashes red and black and white. And I collapse. But, instead of hitting the floor, I pass right through it. I keep falling.

Down, down, down.

Eventually, my head quiets, and the sensation of floating in water replaces that of falling. When I open my eyes again—

I see the white halo around the supermassive black hole.

~ ∞ ~

fifty-eight

Before I asked, I almost expected James to refuse to go on a walk with me for any number of reasons, but he doesn't. He agrees to go—happily, with an easy smile. After we finish breakfast, I grab the half loaf of incredibly stale bread that Matthew missed yesterday, and we're off.

It's been ages since I last took bread to the wildlife pond. Hell, it's been weeks since I went out on the Windsor Park trails at all. The wildflowers are long gone now, even the late season blooms, and the grass is a golden yellow instead of green.

It's 10AM and already hot.

Oh, I totally forgot.

The last time I came out this way was to meet with Ice in the dead of night. James…knows that we met, but he doesn't know the details. He doesn't even know it was out here in the woods.

There's no point bringing it up now.

It's late August. Summer's almost over. In a few weeks' time, Ice will leave for Palo Alto to begin his final year of undergrad at Stanford. *Stanford.* There's no way he'd mess that up for himself. But, once he's out of Riverview, we should be fine.

I have to believe that.

We reach the end of the trail. I don't have to stop walking to catch my breath. I feel fine, like I always used to. And, somehow, we're the only ones here. Two people, alone in the center of the forested park. Though, there are a few dozen ducks around, resting on the muddy bank or aimlessly floating in the pond.

I take a slice of bread from the bag, break off a small piece, and throw it in. Several ducks scramble into action and converge on the crumb, dunking their heads beneath the green water. James asks for a slice. I hand one over, and we stand near the edge of the pond, tossing small bits of stale bread to the ducks.

For a while, we don't say much. A passing comment or light laugh here and there as we feed the ducks, who are *loving* it.

I offer James a third slice of bread. He takes it and stares at it for a moment. He looks up at the ducks in the water as they wait for more, then glances at me. His smile is strangely brooding, but he looks back to the ducks without saying anything, breaks off a chunk, and flicks it into the water.

"This isn't good for them, you know," he says.

"The bread?"

He nods, tossing another piece. "I read an article about it a few years back. Basically, this cheap white bread is like candy to ducks—it tastes good but has virtually no nutritional value."

"Oh." I glance at the bread in my hand. "I had no idea."

I count the remaining slices. Only three. We already fed them half a loaf, and James continues tossing bread into the water. The ducks frenzy after every piece and look to us with expectant beady eyes, quacking for more, each time they resurface.

But I frown. "Why didn't you say anything earlier?"

"Dunno," he says with an easy laugh. "I used to do stuff like this all the time as a kid. It's fun. But, uh... Mostly, I thought it was real cute how you wanted to feed the ducks instead of just throwing the bread out."

"But you know bread is bad for them. Why would you still feed it to them?"

He shrugs. "Because they like it, I guess."

Um... I don't know how to respond, so I say nothing and watch as he throws another piece to the birds.

"I mean, just look at them," he says, gesturing over the water as several ducks dive after the scrap of bread. "Ducks only live so long. They ought to enjoy themselves, don't you think?"

"Well... I guess..."

I purse my lips, unsure how to feel about what James just said, but he seems completely unaffected. He watches the ducks with a smile as the last few pop up and resume paddling on the pond's surface. Some watch us, eagerly awaiting the next crumb.

James tosses his last chunk of bread into the water. When he looks to me again, I catch a hint of seriousness in his eyes. A faint shadow behind his pleasant expression.

"Another slice," he says.

I give him mine.

* * * * *

It's great that James enjoys his birthday present, and I had fun playing QuarryKraft yesterday, but I still can't seem to wrap my head around the lasting appeal of video games. Maybe it's another distraction—something he can do to get his mind off whatever's haunting him for a while. And that's fine.

Honestly, I wish I had more things like that.

But, right now, I'm kind of bored.

There are tons of things I *could* be doing. Important things, like finally looking into fall term classes. Or less important things, like stalking Rose's FaceSpace profile for the third time today. But I'm not really in the mood to do…*anything.*

Now that I'm home, I feel kinda worn out.

I excuse myself from the couch and head upstairs to shower.

Last time I was here, I remember avoiding my reflection in the full-length mirror on the bathroom door. I haven't been too upset by my reflection in a while, but seeing the scars brings *Paige* to mind now. If it weren't for her picking a fight, I doubt I would've had the nerve to tell everyone the truth.

I'm glad I made that decision. But, in a way, I think the scars bother me slightly more than they did before *because* of it.

Whenever someone looks at me, the scars will be the first thing they see. Strange scars on a young woman, marking me as a *victim.* They might stare. They might avoid talking to me— too scared to ask how I got them but, oh, so curious about whatever tragic thing must have happened. And, if they already know, they might walk on eggshells around me. Like they think I can't handle the subject.

Maybe I'm wrong. Maybe, with more time, the scars will fade to the point they're hardly noticeable.

But how can I know?

Squeaky clean and wrapped in a towel, I step into my room

and look through the closet for something more interesting to wear. I never worry about hiding the scars when it's just me and James. There's no point. He's literally seen them all, and he doesn't seem to mind them—at least not when it comes to how they affect my appearance—but I have wondered how much could be covered up with makeup now that they've had more time to heal.

It shouldn't be difficult.

And there's an easy way to find out.

I grab a dress and return to the bathroom to change, after which I stare at myself in the mirror for a long time.

Why'd I pick this dress?

I bought the dress in June, using Ice's money. I haven't worn it since I tried it on in the boutique before buying it, but it still fits. A plum cocktail dress with a low, off-the-shoulder neckline. The hem falls several inches above my knees, and the silky fabric hugs my curves.

It's surprisingly comfortable, and I look damn good wearing it, but I don't know how to feel about it anymore. I mean, I originally bought it because I wanted to avoid ending up under-dressed compared to *Ice* again.

What a waste…

I blow-dry my hair, put it up into a messy bun, and start on the cover-up job. Concealer, foundation, finishing powder. The same routine as the week Rose spent in the dark about them. But, this time, with more patience. More careful blending. My forearms are easy. My wrist is too, with the scabbing long gone. My arms almost look like they did the first time I tried the dress on, but I can't do much about the scar near my shoulder—seems the bullet took a bit of my arm with it.

I give up. Just one more…

A knock on the open door frame startles me while I'm in the middle of applying concealer to the thin, diagonal scar on my chest. The makeup sponge falls from my hand, landing in the sink, and my other hand flies up to wipe my damp eyes.

I turn to face James and insist that I'm fine—*like I totally wasn't just crying*—but his expression silences me before I say a word. His eyes are wide but full of awe instead of the concern I expected. Head tipped to the side, he looks at me like he's literally never seen me before. I don't think he even noticed I was nearly crying a second ago.

"You're wearing a dress."

It's so random, I laugh. But, seriously, it's not like I've never worn a dress before. I wore one just the other day, and it wasn't a big deal then.

"Does it look bad?" I ask.

"No! It looks great. You look amazing."

Does he even realize I covered up the scars?

We watch each other for a long moment. Neither of us say anything. He doesn't move from the doorway, and I don't move from my spot in front of the sink.

Then he laughs, averts his eyes, and scratches the back of his neck. "You look amazing, but I'm kinda scared to touch you all of a sudden."

"Again? Why?"

"Dunno… I guess you seem…fragile," he says, still avoiding

my gaze. "I know better—it's dumb, obviously, like you said—but I get that feeling. For some reason. It's like…if something went wrong, you'd just…break."

I laugh again. "Like I'd break? Just because I'm wearing a dress?"

He shrugs, offering a halfhearted laugh that only seems to make him look more flustered. Then he meets my gaze again. His expression is nervous and mild, and his eyes search mine thoughtfully. Hesitantly. I consider asking if he's okay, but he takes a deep breath before I get around to it.

"Hey," he says. "Would you marry me?"

"What?"

I stare at him.

He stares back at me.

Then, after a moment of only the bathroom fan whirring, his eyes grow *wider*. His face and ears turn bright red, and he shakes his head, sputtering and gesturing wildly while all I can seem to do is stand in place.

"Oh, shit. Ah—!" His focus darts to the side as he blinks furiously, scratches at his arm, and forces a smile. "What?"

"James…"

My heart races, pounding against my ribs, but my face feels like a blank slate. Like I'm expressing no emotion at all. My mind is blank too. Nothing but static. I don't *feel* anything.

Why?

But he laughs, still not looking at me, and still scratching his arm. Fingers beneath the sleeve of his t-shirt.

"Is that stupid? Or crazy? Please tell me I'm crazy."

I shake my head, forcing myself to breathe. "Well, I mean, you're definitely crazy. But... Are you serious? Do you—?"

"No," he says sharply. "I mean, how could I be serious? I can't seriously marry you, right?" He cuts himself off, some of the color draining from his cheeks. "*I mean*— I was kidding! Sort of..."

"Sort of?"

He grimaces and turns around with his hands interlaced behind his head. "Just... Forget it. I don't know why I said that. Sorry if I freaked you out."

Sure, but...

"Are you okay?" I ask.

"Oh, yeah, I'm fine," he says with another laugh before glancing back with wide eyes and a taut smile. "Don't worry about it. Uh... You are so beautiful, though—like, for real."

"Thanks?"

Why'd I just say thanks?!

As I stand awkwardly, watching his back as the slippery dress fabric remains caught in my hands, James steps out of the doorway and carefully closes the door. I'm left staring at my reflection in the full-length mirror. I look pretty, I guess—I still think that—but I also look horribly confused.

What the hell was that? Did James seriously try to *propose* to me just now? Out of nowhere? *In the bathroom?*

Oh, god...

I turn to the mirror over the sink and search my pink face. Up close, my reflection looks even more lost. And my scars, hidden by makeup...

Who am I trying to impress by doing this?

It doesn't matter, does it?

No matter how much makeup I cake on myself. No matter how much I hate seeing them every goddamn day. They'll still be there. I'll still feel the raised scar in the rough shape of a heart when I touch my wrist. I'll still be able to make out the faint lines beneath the layers of concealer.

I will still know the scars are there.

The damage is already done.

So, what's the point?

I have to live with what happened to me every second of every day, whether the scars fade to almost nothing with time or not. If my scars make someone else uncomfortable...

That's their problem, not mine.

I turn the water on and rinse the makeup sponge in the sink. I wipe every trace of concealer from my body. I sneak back into my bedroom and strip out of the plum dress and toss it into the depths of my closet where I won't have to see it. Then I change back into a tank top and shorts.

On my way out, I pause in front of the mirror over my dresser. *Focused green eyes. A hint of nervous determination in the line of my mouth. Scars on both arms, one more peeking above the neckline of my shirt.*

I look fine this way too.

So I leave my bedroom and peek over the banister.

James is sitting on the couch, where I originally left him. But he's writing in his black spiral notebook instead of playing the game, which sounds like it's still running but might be paused.

I think about giving him a few minutes of privacy, but I'm too antsy, so I take a deep, calming breath and head downstairs. James shuts his notebook when he sees me. He tosses it and the pen aside before grabbing the controller from his lap. The game unpauses as I glance at the screen.

I sit beside him, but he doesn't look away from the screen. He seems...*fine*, save for the slight tension in his jaw, but he says nothing, and I get the feeling he's trying to avoid looking directly at me.

He's still embarrassed.

Hell, *I'm* still embarrassed.

It's fine if he doesn't want to discuss it now, but I refuse to let *this* remain brushed under the rug forever. I am not having a repeat of what happened with Ice after the Fourth of July. Good or bad or something in between, I won't pretend he never said what he did. Even if he begs me to forget it, I *refuse*.

But...*I can give him time.*

I clear my throat, and he finally glances over.

"Do you feel bad for the ducks at all?" I ask. When he squints at me, I flash a smile. "I mean, they don't understand that bread is bad for them—they couldn't possibly know that. But we know, and we let them eat half a loaf. Isn't that unfair?"

He shakes his head and looks back to the TV. "Nah. Even wild animals deserve a treat sometimes."

Ha...

Doesn't everyone?

fifty-nine

James sits on the edge of the bed.

The rest of the day was uneventful. Peaceful. But, even now, there's a hint of uncertain brooding in his eyes. And he hasn't mentioned what he said in the bathroom.

Though, neither have I.

I want to talk about it. *We need to talk about it.* But how am I supposed to bring it up without making things awkward?

Hey, do you really want to marry me?

Have you seriously considered that?

It is kind of crazy, isn't it?

I asked James to move into the cottage with me. I meant that. I want to live with him, and I like the idea of moving to LA together in the future. But marriage is…*a lot*, isn't it? I love him. I really do, but we've barely known each other for two months.

Sure, it feels like the longest two months of my life, but still…

I turn away from the bed and dig through my dresser. "The ducks are a metaphor, right?"

"A metaphor?"

"A metaphor." I glance over my shoulder, a smile tugging at my lips. "You read enough, you know what a metaphor is, right?"

His eyes narrow. It almost looks like he's pouting, which is both hilarious and entirely possible. I look back to my reflection to avoid laughing.

"No shit, I know what a metaphor is," he mutters. "The article I told you about is real—bread *is* bad for birds. Feeding them too much can cause malnutrition, wing deformities, and obesity, *and* it contributes to pollution of waterways or whatever. But, yeah, sure. I guess the ducks are a metaphor."

Well, obviously.

I didn't think he made the bread thing up, but I'm also not so oblivious that I can't recognize a metaphor when I hear one. I'm just trying to work out whether it's good or bad that James is suddenly introspective enough to spout off metaphors and randomly ask me to marry him.

After adjusting the hem of my silk camisole, I walk back to the bed. I stop in front of James and plant my hands on my hips. He watches me with a touch of longing, but he seems distracted.

"Alright," I say. "If you're the duck, what's the bread? Me?"

He purses his lips, glancing aside. "You think I had any idea where I was going with that when I said it?"

"Okay, but bread's like junk food, right? The ducks only eat it because we feed it to them, and it tastes good, but it's not actually good for them. The bread is empty calories. Does that mean you think I'm not good for you?"

"You are human," he says.

"But you don't care about that."

"No." He laughs and looks up with a faint smile. "In that case, maybe you should be the duck. I don't mind if you consider me empty calories."

"Would I ask empty calories to move in with me?"

"Ducks have really small brains, you know."

"What's that supposed to mean?" I ask through stifled laughter.

When he shrugs, I swipe his shoulder. Then he laughs again, wraps his arms around my waist, and pulls me down onto the bed with him. *He's so warm.* My breath quickens. My hands move to his face, and I kiss him.

"Nah, Jayde; you are *too* good for me," he breathes against my lips. "Saving this...stupid slice of stale white bread from the trash. Putting up with my shit, giving me a place to be—a *reason* to be. But what do you get out of it, huh? I mean, besides a headache?"

"A headache?"

I untangle myself from his arms and sit up straddling his hips. His eyes are careful, like he's expecting a serious answer. *Sorry. You're expecting too much.*

"You keep me company," I say.

The ghost of a smile crosses his face. "Anyone could keep you company. Or what? You think I'm the only person on the whole planet who might want to be with you?"

"No," I agree with a fleeting glance at his hands on my hips. "I'm not so conceited to think that, but would anyone else be crazy enough to say they'd die for me after knowing me two weeks?"

"You got me there."

I touch his cheek, resisting the urge to kiss him again. His eyes close as he leans into my hand, and his expression shifts, tender and mild. *And not kissing him is incredibly difficult.*

"So, why are you?" I ask.

"Mm..." He opens his eyes. "Dunno. Maybe it's because I had nothing to lose. Or, maybe, I'm just a touch-starved loser, prone to falling in love with any girl who's nice to me."

"Is that true?"

He snorts. "Not exactly. Didn't I tell you I hated you after we first met?"

"That's fine." I glance away, retracting my hand to draw my hair over my shoulder. "I mean, when I first met you, I thought you were so awkward and weird; it annoyed the hell out of me."

"Are you saying I don't still annoy you?"

I grin. "Only sometimes. But I doubt I'm much better— when it comes to being annoyingly awkward, I mean."

"You're not as awkward as you think, babe."

Ha...

He wouldn't think that if we met earlier. I was hopeless. *The worst.* If we ran into each other before I learned about immortals, it would have been twice as uncomfortable.

But he never would have asked for my phone number the way Ice did. Even if I was nice to him, I would've just been a random human girl who couldn't watch where she was going. Barely able to form a coherent sentence and nothing special compared to the immortals he sees all the time.

Would he have thought twice about me? Would he have bothered to stop and talk in the first place if he didn't find me vaguely familiar?

If it weren't for Night and Ice and the River Sapphire?

"What are you thinking?" he asks.

"Um…"

Before I work out what to say, I notice his hand stroking my thigh. A warm, soft touch prickling my bare skin. I feel my face flush, and, in my flustered panic, I ask if he meant what he said.

Do you really want to marry me?

His hand stops moving, though his smile doesn't falter even as he looks away. "I…just want to be with you. For as long as you still want me. I don't really care how."

"That's all you were trying to say?"

"Yeah, it was…hypothetical. It just didn't come out right."

Right.

* * * * *

My phone vibrating loudly, buzzing against a solid surface, wakes me up. A phone call from a random number. The voice on the other end is automated. A scam call or telemarketer—it's hard to say, but I hang up.

So annoying…

It's just after 9AM, though, so I drag myself up to sit with my phone still in my hand. *Wait, I have notifications.* I scroll down to reveal a text and a missed call. *From—?*

Ah…

> **Ice Monroe**   2:34AM
>
> How do you manage?

Another random message with a photo attached. This time, it's a picture of the night sky, almost pure black except for the bright moon. Together, they're a bit unsettling. But *how do you manage* is a decent question, I guess.

The answer is: *I don't.* At least not well. Everything feels so far out of my control. Like all I can do is hope the situation will sort itself out on its own.

The missed call was from Ice too. He didn't leave a voicemail, but the call was made only a few minutes before he sent the text.

Extra weird.

I wake James to show him the message.

"This is weird, right?"

I tap the photo, expanding it, so he can take a closer look. He instead stares at me a moment longer, groggy and confused, before looking at my phone's screen.

"Ice is weird," he says through a yawn as he rubs the sleep from his eyes. "What more do you want?"

"Doesn't it bother you?"

"Everything bothers me, babe."

I groan. "This seems different, though. Somehow. I can't really explain, but… I mean, the other texts came during the day, and he never called before. You know?"

He sighs. "I think you're overthinking it."

Am I? It wouldn't be the first time, I suppose…

I look at the photo again. It was clearly taken very late at night for such a round moon to be that high in the sky. He must have taken it right before he sent it. But why send something like this? Why was he awake and outside so late? I mean, I guess it's not *that* unusual for Ice to stay up late, but…

How do you manage…?

"Should I…call him back?"

"What? Ugh." James drops his face back to the pillow. "Please don't. It's too early for this shit."

I can't help but laugh, but I pat his back. "Okay, okay. I'll leave him on read for now."

"Thanks…"

With a final glance at the photo—at the fuzzy moon in the dark sky—I lock my phone and set it on the end table. As I turn back, James rolls over and gazes up at me. His hair is a mess. It's longer now than it was when we first met. And he smiles, but he looks sort of nervous—or shy, maybe. Then his expression softens. He reaches up, and I lean down to kiss him.

"What time is it, anyway?" he asks.

"Almost nine-thirty. Is that too early for you?"

He sort of laughs. "Nah. Let's have breakfast."

sixty

James left after lunch.

He wasn't specific about whatever errands he needed to run, but I have no idea what would keep him out this long. Even while staying at his father's house, a place he felt was safe, he'd usually text to check in after being gone twenty minutes. But he seemed fine and unconcerned when he called earlier.

He asked what kind of candy I like. I asked what he was doing, but he still wouldn't tell me exactly.

Shopping. Whatever.

It's not like I haven't enjoyed spending some time alone in my own house for the first time in what feels like months. I thought I might feel more anxious considering everything, but I haven't. I feel fine. It's nice, actually. I'm getting the most mundane things done, and it all feels so normal.

I ran a load of laundry. Made a smoothie using the last of the frozen fruit. Then I checked the locks and turned on the TV and fell asleep for nearly an hour before I woke up to James' call.

He asked how I was. I said I'm fine, because I am, and we worked out dinner plans. He'll pick up pizza on his way home. *On my way home*, he said. I said I wouldn't mind chocolate—I can't even remember the last time I had some—and that was it.

Then I called Rose.

She still won't answer.

So I'm trying to distract myself from the nagging disappointment by cleaning. The TV plays in the background—some wildlife documentary I'm pretty sure I watched a few months ago. Cleaning is boring and tedious, but I'm getting things done that have needed to be done for a while. Like vacuuming. And dusting everything on my desk and dresser. And cleaning underneath the couch cushions.

Footsteps on the concrete outside catch my attention over the music playing behind the documentary narrator's voice. The steps aren't subtle, but I shut the TV off and peek over the back of the couch. The twinge of anxiety fades when I spot James' car through the blinds, parked in Rose's usual parking space.

I fix the couch cushions and half-run to unlock the deadbolt and open the door for him. He has a pizza box that I quickly take off his hands because he's also carrying a few shopping bags. The box is warm and smells like pepperoni.

As I glance up again, he grins. I'm sure he's relieved to see me in a good mood—and in one piece—so I return the smile and step back into the living room.

"What have you been up to?" he asks.

"Cleaning, mostly." I balance the pizza box on the arm of the couch before turning to face him again. "But I could ask you the same question."

Another grin, cheekier this time.

I cherish it even though he refuses to answer and, instead,

closes the distance between us to kiss me. I tolerate the affection, but his unusually good mood has me curious.

When he steps back, he shuffles through the smallest shopping bag—an opaque, black plastic bag—and removes a thin, round box from inside. He hands it to me. The box contains a variety of fancy truffles beneath a film of tinted cellophane.

This is nice and all, but...

I look up from the chocolates. "Is this all you got?"

"No." He laughs, eyes sparkling, but his tone doesn't match completely. "I was out buying new clothes. Most of what I own is from back in high school, and I needed a few more t-shirts or whatever."

"Oh?"

Without taking my eyes off James, I pick at the thin plastic covering the chocolates. His expression, while upbeat, reveals very little. But he spent almost four hours in town. Was he seriously just shopping around for clothes the whole time?

The other two shopping bags are basic reusable cloth totes and do look to be stuffed with clothing. I can make out a pair of jeans and at least a couple t-shirts.

My attention lands on the small, black bag again. I pop a truffle in my mouth. *Oh.* Maybe it's just that I haven't eaten chocolate in a while, but this might be the best I've ever had. I glance at the packaging, but I don't recognize the brand.

"And that's it?" I ask, looking up again.

He shrugs. "Basically."

Why do I not buy that? What reason is there to lie?

Resisting the urge to ask more questions I doubt he'd answer,

I follow James as he heads further into the house. The rest of the way across the living room. Up the stairs. To my open bedroom door. Before I manage to get my grabby hands on the black bag, he turns and kisses me again. With my target out of reach, I play it off by laughing and holding the box of chocolates in both hands.

He looks over the unfolded pile of freshly laundered clothing on the bed. "So, you cleaned the whole time I was gone?"

I haven't put it away yet—it was next on my list before he got back. But I would've held off on washing anything if I knew he was out buying *clothes*.

I sigh. "Well, I took a nap too."

James stashes the small, black bag in his backpack, which he leaves on top of my duffel at the foot of the bed. I *know* there's something else of interest in that bag, but I have a feeling I won't learn what it is any time soon.

It's...fine. I won't die waiting.

He sits on the edge of the bed and starts going through the cloth shopping bags. Pulling clothing out and removing tags and setting them aside in a pile separate from the clothes I washed. He shoved *a lot* of clothes into those bags. Might have even doubled his wardrobe in a single trip. I'm honestly impressed.

I eat another chocolate. Then I shove most of the clean laundry out of the way and sit beside him.

"Did you do anything else?" I ask. "Besides buying clothes and chocolate and dinner, I mean?"

His smile softens. He takes a truffle for himself. I stare him down, but he brushes the question off a second time by admitting that he can't tell me right now—it's a *secret*.

A secret? Time for plan B: weaponized femininity.

"But I'm so curious," I whine. "I really wanna know."

Without waiting for a response, I set the chocolates aside to free my hands. Then I tug on the hem of his shirt sleeve and serve up my best impression of pleading puppy dog eyes.

"Come on, James… Pretty please?"

His breath hitches, and his ears turn red, but he still won't tell me. Even with our eyes wide and our faces inches apart, he resists temptation and shakes his head before laughing and smiling again.

"It's a surprise, alright?" he says. "You'll just have to wait. But it's not a big deal or anything. I swear."

I pout with the goal of looking as pathetic as possible. But I can't think of anything that might change his mind without being outright mean. And I'd rather not be *mean*.

He pats the top of my head, maintaining eye contact and an unwavering smile. I deepen my fake frown, and his soft, vaguely apologetic smile widens to a more playful grin. *At least he thinks it's funny.* But his eyes swirl like warm honey, and my heart beats a little too fast as heat pools in my cheeks.

Then I break into nervous laughter, and my eyes dart aside.

"Sorry." I smooth the front of his shirt, careful to not let my hands linger in one place for too long. "But I think I'm starting to hate surprises."

"Don't worry. This one's a good surprise."

I offer his backpack a final fleeting glance before we leave the bedroom.

We grab drinks and plates from the kitchen, and he suggests we play QuarryKraft while we eat. I'm not confident I can eat pizza *and* play video games simultaneously, but I had fun playing with him the other day, so I agree to try. I curl up beside him on the couch, eating a slice while the game loads.

Our pixelated avatars start up exactly where we left them—building more elaborate houses and chopping down trees or whatever. My character is still inside the small dirt hut I built, wielding a wooden axe. The game doesn't seem to have any real story or clear objective, so I have no idea what to do beyond exploring and collecting materials, but it's nice to relax and hang out.

The past few days have been *perfect*. There's air conditioning. We have tons of space, and we're free to exist wherever we want, whenever we want. It's comfortable. I missed this.

I laugh as I accidentally walk my avatar off a cliff and take a small amount of damage.

For the first time in weeks, everything feels normal.

This feels normal?

You sure?

My thumb freezes over the button I was about to press.

Why would I think about Ice now? Why would the texts cross my mind? *The image of a girl who looks like me but can't be. A gun in her hand, tears in her eyes.*

I snap out of it and continue chopping wood. I want to fortify my dinky shack before it gets dark again, but I can't seem to shake the unease. A tickle in the back of my mind.

What Ice said in the hospital...

One of us has to die.

I don't believe that. I don't, and I haven't. No matter what I've seen. No one can predict the future. Even those with psychic ability can't know for sure, so Ice definitely doesn't. But…

My wrist itches. My character is safe inside their house, so I set the controller down. But my breath falters as my nails scratch the scarred skin.

Why do I feel like this?

Everything's fine. We're safe here.

I look up from my hands in time to watch James glance at me. I try to smooth my expression to keep from looking *too* bothered, but I either reacted too late or didn't do a great job. Because he frowns.

"You okay?" he asks, tipping his head.

"Yeah, I just—"

I try again to take a deep breath, but it catches, and my heart races. *Oh, no. There's no shaking this.* The cool, sinking weight I've felt many times before, in the dreamscape and my waking life. A sinister, oppressive force. A shadowy veil over my senses. *Fear. Danger. Like walking down the street on the Fourth of July. Stepping into the house in Westbrooke. Reaching for the door-knob. Staring at the top of the staircase, holding my breath.*

Something is…

But, *why now?*

James studies me again. His concern is still mild, but a heavy fog clouds my mind. I don't know how to convey how I feel. *I'm not even sure* what *I feel.* I don't know how to explain—

I glance around the room. *Nothing seems off, but…*

"Pause the game," I say.

He taps a button on his controller, and the atmospheric background noise quiets. Another quick look around and over the back of the couch reveals nothing unusual. Frustrated, I turn off the TV to silence the soft menu music too, but I don't hear anything either. Just the AC and distant traffic sounds.

What the hell is this?

Why do I—?

"What's wrong?" James asks.

The hint of tension in his voice only stresses me out further, but I shush him. Straining my ears, I stare through the window beside the front door. The blinds are mostly shuttered, so I only see a crack of the outside world. *The top of the railing. The short grass between the small porch and the empty sidewalk. A bit of James' car. Nothing strange, but—*

A hand touches my shoulder.

I flinch, turning on James with wide eyes. *Why is my heart beating so fast?* He retracts his hand and apologizes, his fingers hovering a few inches from my skin instead of making contact.

He barely touched me.

Why am I so jumpy?

I shake my head and force a smile. "I'm sorry. I just—"

A noise.

My head does not move, but my eyes flick in the direction the sound came from—in the direction of the front door. The faint, musical chime of tinkling glass. *The wind chime.* Did the wind catch it? The wind often picks up in the early evening. Am I freaking out over nothing? Overthinking it again? I hear the wind chime sometimes. It's not that unusual.

But I recognize the sound from my dreamscape.

And this suffocating feeling...

Cool fear. Hot blood. My chest so tight I can't draw breath.

The black handgun.

The wind chime quiets. A brief silence follows, then I hear soft footfalls on the concrete landing just outside. *Not great.* But, no matter who's there, as long as—

I look to James again, and my heart sinks.

Wait—

I remember unlocking the door to let him inside. I took the pizza box. He walked past me. My hand... I...pushed the door shut. I remember my hand on the door. The door closed. And I turned away to follow James.

I forgot.

When he got home, *I forgot to lock the door.*

I don't know if he realizes my mistake, but the color drains from his face. The look on mine must have scared him. *And we both know someone is standing right outside.* But neither of us break eye contact to look.

If I feel this way now—

No. I don't want to think that.

Not now.

Not the one time I forget to lock the door!

But the doorknob clicks as it turns, and the door swings open. It smacks against the doorstop with a crack that reverberates through the quiet house. The sound echoes in my head.

Like a gunshot loud enough to leave my ears ringing.

I can't bring myself to move. To turn toward the door. I don't want to accept it, so my attention remains locked on James' face. *Fear reflected in wide, amber eyes.* The sharp guilt is almost worse than the fear squeezing my lungs.

"Oh." Ice's voice conveys surprise, but it's still too smooth. Too light. "Huh. It opened."

sixty-one

James does not move.

He stiffened the instant Ice spoke, now glued to the couch, wide eyes locked on the GameStation controller in his lap. He doesn't move at all. Not even to look.

But I have to do *something*.

Fighting the crushing weight that pins me down, I rip myself from the couch and bolt for the stairs. Glance over my shoulder. *Ice is still near the front door.* My foot hits the first step. I hear the door close, but no one stops me. No one follows.

I stumble to a stop inside my bedroom.

The door I shoved open cracks against my dresser, but I ignore the sharp sound and glance around, hoping to find...*I don't know.* Anything that might help me. Something to stop Ice. Or to protect James. Or do anything.

My phone? It's in my pocket. But too slow. There's no one to call, anyway. RSP doesn't care, and I can't involve any of James' friends in this level of emergency.

My eyes pass over my dresser. The window. My desk. The closet. So many *things* but nothing useful. I glance down. My bed, covered in clothing. The floor— *James' backpack at the foot of the bed.* My duffel bag pokes out from underneath it.

The handgun! It's still inside.

I move toward it, then pause again, wincing at the commotion downstairs. Sounds like something, *or someone*, hit a wall pretty hard. I almost look back, but there's no point. I can't see from here, *and I don't have time.* Ice hasn't followed me upstairs yet, but James can only keep him busy for so long before he either gets past or someone ends up hurt. So I block out the shouts and jeers coming from the living room and drop to the floor in front of the bags.

James' backpack. The small, black shopping bag.

None of this matters if he gets hurt today.

I knock the backpack aside and drag my duffel out from under the bed. I unzip it and upend the bag, dumping everything out and tossing the empty shell aside.

The gun…the gun…the gun…

Come on!

I sift through the objects scattered on the grey carpet. My heart pounds. Blood rushes in my ears. My eyes, too wide, water as they skim over clothing. My teal bikini top. A plastic water bottle. Cheap flip-flops. A tangle of charging cables. One of those *stupid* designer boots.

Where is it? I don't have time for this!

I fling a t-shirt over my shoulder and return my hands to the pile. More clothes. *Wait— This camisole!* My fingers brush something solid inside, and the relief instantly clears my mind. My hand closes around the textured grip, and I speed back out the door, nearly tripping on the last step on my way downstairs.

"STOP!"

I push my hair out of my face and, with both hands firmly in place, aim the gun in Ice's general direction. He stands several feet away, between me and the couch with his back to me. His right hand is still raised, holding the marbled switchblade. And—

Oh.

He's wearing the long, black overcoat. From the Fourth of July. *From my dream.* My chest seizes. *A cruel sneer on a face that looks like mine. A cracked, green-blue eye, wide and glittering with excitement. A gun drawn from a coat pocket.* But I smother the jolt of fear, force myself to take another breath, and look past Ice.

James stands further away, on the far side of the couch, well out of Ice's reach. He glances at me, acknowledging my return and the gun's presence with a shift in expression, before looking back to Ice with bared teeth.

Both men are visibly ruffled and breathing heavily. A small hole was punched clean through the drywall on the wall between the living room and Rose's bedroom. James' shirt is torn near his waist, but I don't see blood.

Thank god.

James is fine, but Ice and the couch are situated in the middle space between us. Fleeting images from my dreamscape continue playing in the back of my mind like a broken record. *The wind chime's musical tinkling. A gunshot. A body falling to the floor. My dream-self wearing that stupid coat.*

Wouldn't this solve everything? she asked.

I shake my head to clear the worst of the shadows and return my attention to Ice's back.

"Do you have a gun?" I ask, still breathless and too loud.

"Of course not." His voice is mild. He lowers the knife, but I still can't see his face. "I told you; I don't care for guns."

Can I believe him? Should I?

The room falls quiet, save for the blood rushing in my ears. James glances between me and Ice again as anxiety slowly over-takes his anger, but he doesn't move either. No one moves.

What do I do now?

I didn't think this far ahead.

After a long, tense moment, Ice turns to face me.

Wow.

He looks...rough.

His hair is disheveled, but not in the usual intentionally messy way, and his bottom lip is freshly split, oozing red blood. His expression reads as oddly indifferent. Blank, almost. No smirk. No wild frenzy. No inkling of humor. He looks...*tired.*

Then he notices the gun. His eyes clear and narrow slightly as his focus flicks back to my face, but his overall expression doesn't change.

He doesn't care?

My mouth goes dry. I swallow hard and shift my weight to my other leg.

And Ice shakes his head.

He laughs, pockets the knife, and wipes the blood off his lip with the cuff of his coat. *How can he stand wearing that thing? Sure, it's almost 8PM, but it's still hot as hell outside. We're in the middle of a heatwave!*

Ugh. Why, after all this time, does *that* still bother me?

"You won't shoot me," he says with an easy smile, reminding me of the *gun in my hands.* "You couldn't if you wanted to. And I know you don't."

I bare my teeth and square my shoulders.

But he's right.

I don't want anyone to die, and I certainly don't want to hurt anyone—not even Ice. *But what choice do I have?* He already tried to kill James once and nearly succeeded. I can't let something like that happen again. I can't give him another chance to try. This time, if it comes down to it, I have the power to stop him.

Could I do that?

I glance at the black handgun. I can't even hold it still. My whole body vibrates with nervous energy, and my hands are by far the shakiest. I don't stand a chance in this state. I couldn't land a shot if I tried. I don't even know how to use this thing. I've never fired a gun. Until now, I'd never even held a gun like this.

I tear my eyes from the gun and gloss over Ice, who still hasn't moved, to check on James. He watches me with wide eyes. His focus flicks between me, Ice, and the gun. *Me, Ice, the gun.*

What would he do in my position?

What does he want me to do now?

No. Stupid question.

I can't let the pressure get to me. I don't have to fire this gun at all. I can turn this around. *Surely, I can turn this around. Surely. Somehow...*

A deep, shaky breath and another quick head shake fail to

calm me or clear my mind further, but I return my attention to Ice.

In the moment I wasn't watching, his expression shifted to dark amusement. Mouth twisted into a lazy smirk, made no less intimidating by the blood leaking from his lip. He smiles like he finds the situation quite funny, but his eyes are wide and alert and trained on me.

My skin crawls.

I will never understand that man, but I can't back down now. I can't let him walk all over me anymore. I won't let him hurt James again. *I can't.* Not this time. Not if I can stop him.

I don't want to shoot, but... If it comes down to it...

"I'm dead serious, Jayde Palmer." He throws his arms up and out to the sides, exposing his torso—the fitted t-shirt beneath his unbuttoned coat. "If you believe you have it in you, go right ahead. Shoot me."

What?

My eyes lock onto his right hand. It's neatly wrapped in white gauze. I didn't notice before, but the bandages over his palm are stained by dark blood.

What happened?

He laughs again. "What are you waiting for? Do it."

"What?" My voice is hardly a whisper.

"Shoot me," he says, still grinning. The words feel strangely distant and warbled, like there's a thick pane of glass between us. "I dare you."

This...doesn't make sense.

I search his eyes again, desperate for any indication that he's teasing me. *Because this has to be a sick joke.* But there's nothing. Though he smiles, it doesn't read as playful, and his eyes are level and focused, flicking between my face and the gun.

Wait—

Cold, sinking dread crushes my panic. In spite of everything he's put me through, I never expected something like *this*. *Never.* He's screwing with me. He has to be.

He can't be serious.

"Leave," I gasp.

But no one moves.

Ice still has his arms held out, making himself an easy target. James looks like he might faint—*I feel that*—and my hands shake from the effort of keeping the gun in position. But no one moves. For what feels like hours but is probably less than a minute, no one moves.

Until Ice does.

He takes a small, careful step toward me.

And my heart jumps into my throat.

James tenses too. It looks like he wants to move closer, but he hesitates. He makes a soft, disgruntled sound and holds his ground.

That's fine. He's safer there, anyway.

Ice doesn't look back. He doesn't seem to care about whatever James is doing. He watches me like we're alone in the room. Like he just stopped by for a casual visit. Like everything is fine. *Like I'm not aiming a loaded gun at him.*

The muscles in my legs scream for me to run, and my arms are sore, but I maintain a solidly offensive posture. Still, the gun wavers in my tight grip, feeling more and more like a lead weight at the end of my arm.

But I can't back down. I can't. Not after what he did. To me. To James. To Rose. Not after—

He takes another step forward.

"Stop moving! I will shoot you."

My voice cracked, neutralizing the already weak, half-hearted threat, and Ice's smile shifts, almost melancholic. He looks at the gun instead of me.

"Ah… Surely, you realize that taking me out is the obvious solution." Cold, blue eyes flick up again, full of cryptic energy. "Every problem you face now would vanish with me, wouldn't it? You would be free."

Free?

My eyes dart aside.

Is he right? Would shooting him solve anything? Wouldn't it just lead to a whole new mess of problems? There's no way Human-Immortal Affairs would be cool with me killing my sponsor. There's no way.

"The fuck are you going on about?" James growls.

Ice grins, one eyebrow quirked as he glances over his shoulder. "Don't pretend you wouldn't love to watch me bleed out on the floor."

James says nothing, and Ice looks to me.

I ignore him and meet James' eyes instead—this time for *help*, though he frowns rather helplessly. I wish he'd do *something*, but there's not much he can do. He's lucky enough to have come out of their initial scuffle unharmed. His hands are tied now.

Seeing as I'm the one holding the gun, I should be the one in control of the situation. That is *clearly* not the case, since Ice lost his goddamn mind, but I doubt that changes much from James' perspective. The moment I came back with the gun, all he could do is watch and hope for the best. Hope Ice doesn't snap. Hope I make the right choices. Stepping in would only make things worse, and he seems to understand that.

If he stepped in, he'd get hurt. Ice could pull the knife again, and I might accidentally shoot him while trying to break up a fight. *Who knows?*

He shakes his head and mouths, *"It's a trap."*

You always think it's a trap!

Frustrated, I look back to Ice, to reassess his sharp eyes and discordantly easygoing smile. His arms are lower than before, but he seems comfortable despite the incredibly vulnerable position he put himself in. *I hate to admit it, but this feels as much like a trap as it does a joke.*

He takes another step.

Now, hardly four feet away, I can just make out the soft shadow of dark circles beneath his eyes. A subtle gauntness to his cheeks. A bead of sweat at his brow. The slightest hint of tension in his jaw.

I suck in a breath through my teeth, but my mind races.

How the hell is *this* the same man I spent so much time with? We burnt sparklers together on the Fourth of July, and he smiled in that selfie we took. He bought those skyrockets just for me.

And, somehow, that person is the same one who tormented me for the past two months. He laughed as he held a gun to my head. He stabbed my boyfriend and left him to die in my kitchen. He smiled so easily and teased me while James laid unconscious in the hospital.

He seemed fine when we spoke then. Normal. *Totally normal. Like nothing happened.*

But… *Is* this *the man who has been texting me all month?* Stalking my house? Sending those weird pictures? Is this what he's looked like the whole time since I last saw him.

He's dangerous.

My eyes narrow, and I adjust my grip on the handgun, but my hands tremble even more than before.

"Stop moving," I say again, though I can't keep the frantic edge out of my voice. "Don't come any closer."

"Come *on*, Jayde. I'm right here. Right in front of you." He licks the blood off his split lip, and his smile widens. "This is your chance. Take the shot."

He steps forward again, and a trace of wild intensity creeps into his wide eyes. *Why does it look like he's having fun? This isn't a game!*

"Don't you *want* to kill me?"

Another step.

He's too close!

More than anything, I want to step back and put more distance between us, but I can't. I can't move. The most I can do is shake my head.

And he laughs. "You're kidding, right? After everything I've done? Surely, you hate me. Didn't you say you do? Can't you bring yourself to pull the trigger and finish what you started?"

What I—?

A blood-encrusted knife in my pocket. My thumb hit the button. The blade flipped out, and I drew my arm back. But a hand caught my wrist.

The warmth drains from my face.

Gun or no gun, I'm still me.

I'm still that timid, naive human girl Ice Monroe introduced himself to at the grocery store for reasons I've finally accepted I will never understand. *And I know I won't pull this trigger.*

I can't.

How could I?

His expression darkens, sick grin wiped away in an instant. A shadow falls over his eyes as he glances down. His hand touches the gun, and he steadies it, correcting my wavering aim. A final step leaves him just beyond arm's length. The tip of James' black handgun, held in my hands, bumps against his chest, the fabric of his dark t-shirt now the only thing separating the two. And his arms fall to his sides.

Why?

My eyes, watering with sick amazement, lock onto the gun. My hands. The scar on the inside of my wrist. My arms are tired, trembling worse than ever. But the gentle pressure of Ice's chest against the gun's muzzle keeps the weapon steady.

If it went off now—

I look up from my hands.

Behind Ice, James stares at me, white as a sheet, jaw slack in morbid disbelief. He looks as alarmed and sick as I feel, and *I can't...* Slowly, I look back to my hands. My knuckles are pale and sore from gripping the gun so tightly.

And Ice's face—

His expression is level, void of any prior trace of wry humor. His jaw is set. No smirk. No smile at all. None of the annoying, snide cockiness I'm used to, but no sign of nerves either. No fear. He merely seems to be awaiting my next move with an air of mild apathy.

I hate that.

After my dreams, I never expected...

He stopped me before. I tried to stab him, and I failed, and he laughed at me. We both knew I didn't stand a chance against him. But this is different. He's so close. He could easily disarm me. It'd take half a second. *I wish he would, but...*

Instead, he...

How can he stand it?

The gun is touching him!

I want to stop. I want to drop the gun. To toss it aside. But I still can't bring myself to move. The same as James, I'm stuck. Trapped in my own head.

Why do this? Why come here just to do this?

I hate this.

He glances down to study the gun again. After a few, long, *aching* seconds, he frowns. Then he raises his bandaged hand and flicks a small switch on the gun's side.

My breath catches in my throat.

The safety. I hadn't even thought to switch it off.

To make matters worse, he doesn't withdraw his hand like he did before. Instead, he rests it against mine. Gauze scratches the back of my aching hand as he positions his thumb over my finger—the finger that's been hovering over the trigger this whole time.

"Do it," he says. His voice carries no discernible emotion.

My eyes dart between the black gun at his chest, our hands together on the gun, and his unbearably passive face. He frowns slightly before meeting my gaze. The emotion behind his cool eyes, whatever it is, seems more complicated now. He watches me with a careful patience—like he doesn't trust me—but, behind that, he looks...*so, so tired.*

Somehow, it reminds me of James. In July. The rainstorm.

A chill washes over me. Goosebumps prickle my arms. And I can't seem to breathe as it hits me. *He is serious. He's not fucking with me at all. He* wants *me to pull the trigger.*

I...

I never expected...him to be the one—

My vision flashes white. My dream plays over, this time in focus. Everything I missed before, clear as if viewed through a crystal glass. Reliving an awful, unfair premonition.

The sharp BANG as the gun goes off in my hand, pain flaring in my shoulder from the recoil. Ice's smirk falters. His eyes lose focus, and his hand falls away from mine, and he drops to the floor. The gun follows, free from the numb, aching hands that fly up to cover my mouth. I stare at the body for a moment. Ice, lying as motionless as the gun that landed near my feet. And my hands move again, catching in my hair as they make their way to the back of my head.

I... Hey... Wait a second...

I don't want to look at it. At what I've done. At what I let him do to himself. But I can't tear my eyes away. Blood stains the pale carpet, pooling around Ice's lifeless body. His eyes are wide and blank, looking at nothing and seeing nothing, but still as blue as the clear summer sky. The faintest hint of a smile. His lower lip still oozing blood.

No.

This can't be happening.

I step back.

My chest is so tight, I feel like I might pass out. But my eyes flood with tears. A rough, strangled cry escapes my throat, and I drop to my knees. Bare skin squishes against wet carpet—an all too familiar sensation. I hold my head, staring through my tears at the blur of red between me and the corpse I created.

It was me.

I was holding the gun.

I was always the one holding the gun.

The girl in my dream asked a question as she aimed the same gun at me: "*Dare me to pull the trigger?*"

But if I pulled the trigger now—

No.

I... I can't.

I won't.

Ice's thumb presses against my index finger, dragging me back to the present as he edges my finger closer to the trigger. I resist the pressure, but my fingertip brushes metal, and I stop breathing. Still, I can't bring myself to look away from his eyes as he watches our hands on the gun with a quiet intensity.

This isn't what I want.

I don't care what he said. I don't want anyone to die, and *I do not want to kill Ice*. Even after everything he's done. Even if he is an irredeemable monster. Even if he ruined my life. Even if he's right and pulling the trigger *is* the quickest and easiest way to bring this miserable chapter of our lives to a close. *Even if, maybe, he deserves it.*

I don't care.

I can't accept that future—a future where I'd break down and cry over the death of someone like Ice Monroe. But I can't accept a future in which I'd willingly shoot him either.

How could I live with myself if I pulled the trigger? How could I move on from watching someone die right in front of me? *Because of me?* Wouldn't the guilt eat away at me forever? Worse than any other awful thing I've done?

I just want…a normal life…

"Please, stop…"

My voice is barely audible. Just a breath. But he hears me. He hears, and his gaze flicks up, but he doesn't stop. His eyes narrow as they search mine. His head tips ever so slightly to one side. But he does not move his hand.

Since I can't seem to speak, I plead with my eyes. Begging him to stand down. To change his mind. To play it off as a cruel joke. No different from the time he aimed a gun at me. Praying he'll move his hand and make fun of me when I collapse to the floor, sobbing at his feet.

But this isn't a game. Ice isn't joking.

And I'm running out of time.

If I don't do something—

The pressure increases again, my finger wedged between his thumb and the trigger. My eyes dart down, but I catch a flash of bright white teeth at the top edge of my vision. *Like the twisted nightmare Jayde's sick smirk before she—*

And I panic.

sixty-two

"I said *stop*—!"

I wrench my hands apart, knocking back the hand Ice placed over mine. The gun hits the floor and skitters across the carpet, out of sight and well out of reach. *I did it.* But relief turns my legs to jelly. My knees buckle, and I fall, landing awkwardly on my hands and knees.

James cries out from halfway across the room. His voice is frantic, but I can't make out a word over my ragged breathing as I dry heave on the floor. With one shaking hand held over my mouth, I struggle to catch my breath.

Ice makes a soft noise. "Ah... How annoying..."

What?

I saved your life just now!

I stare through my hair and the hot, bitter tears that spill from my eyes and drip from my nose. I stare at my hand. My nails dig into the short, grey carpet. The damp spots left by tiny droplets in the space between my hand and the dark toes of Ice's boots.

Why?

My finger was on the trigger. I almost couldn't stop myself. If it weren't for that dream, I'm not sure I could have. If I hadn't seen what might have happened next, I…

He seriously intended on following through?

He wanted me to shoot him? To kill him? To end things?

That's not fair. That's seriously fucked.

James calls my name again, but he's too far away. He can't stop Ice from dragging me to my feet, and I can't bring myself to react. I don't even *care* as he pins me, wedging my right arm between his chest and my back. I ignore the twinge of discomfort as he holds me tight around the waist.

My mind reels.

Am I scared? I don't know.

But I don't struggle.

There's no point. Fighting back has never helped before. Why would now be any different? I already gave up what little advantage I had. I made my choice. I dropped the gun.

I don't have the energy to deal with this anymore.

James skids into view, stopping in front of the couch, still several feet away. My vision is blurred—I'm still crying, I guess —so I can't make out his face, but my imagining of whatever expression he might be wearing now…

The thought alone spurs a fresh wave of tears.

Was I wrong? Was dropping the gun a mistake? Could I have moved on from the other possibility? I don't know what happens next. Maybe that path would've turned out better than this one? What if we all die here because of me?

I hide my eyes in the crook of my arm. I'd collapse to the floor again if I could. I'd like a minute to sit and feel sorry for myself, but Ice holds my useless, shuddering body upright. He afterglow

shushes me, speaking quietly. His voice is soft. Gentle. I process none of what he says, but, whatever his intention, the effect is far from calming.

Then, somehow, James' voice cuts through the raging storm. "Let her go. Please. What are you trying to prove by showing up now, anyway? Why are you doing this?"

His voice is low and nervous, and each word hurts. *Because I did this. I forgot to lock the door. I put us in this situation.*

"No," Ice says quietly. "I hate it."

His arm tightens around my waist, and the pressure jolts me back to full awareness. My crying stops abruptly as I gasp. I push against his arm with my free hand, trying to relieve the discomfort as his fingers dig into the scar on my side. But I can't pry his arm away, and he doesn't ease up.

"I hate…everything about this. You. And…"

As I register what his other hand is doing, his voice devolves to a static buzz, like the sound of a bathroom fan while you lie in the tub with your ears underwater. Ice strokes my pinned arm from shoulder to elbow. Shoulder to elbow. Slow. Soft. Rhythmic. If it weren't for the *knife in his hand*, I might not think anything of it. But smooth metal warmed to body temperature brushes my skin again and sends an electric chill down my spine.

Oh, god.

Looking away—a single glimpse of the ivory handle was more than enough—I accidentally meet James' gaze and immediately wish I had not. Eyes wide, brows furrowed. He stands in place, still so far away, his posture tense and defensive. But, as he glances between Ice's hand on my arm and my face, he looks more upset and afraid than angry. Then, looking to Ice again, he raises his hands to chest level.

"Please don't hurt her," he says, voice trembling.

"Hm?"

James shakes his head, flashing a weak, terrified smile. "Ice. Hey. Listen, man—for a second, just listen to me. Please. Jayde dropped the gun. She doesn't wanna fight. Just let her go. Please. *Please, Ice.* Whatever you do, don't hurt her."

Ice's hand, and knife, pause near my elbow. I hold my breath —*one, two, three seconds*—until the steady petting resumes.

"Oh… Right." His voice feels distant and hollow. "I said that, huh? I don't want to kill her. I still don't. I don't. I don't want…to hurt her, but—"

"But?!" James throws his arms out in frustration. "But what? What the fuck do you want?"

Ah— I have to do something.

Once again, and with more purpose, I try to pry Ice's arm from my waist. He doesn't relent, instead tightening his grip further, squeezing my midsection. Drawing breath hurts as short nails dig into my ribs through my tank top. Spots form in my vision. It's pointless—*I know it's pointless*—but I continue struggling.

Somehow, I have to get away.

"I can't stand…seeing you—seeing you together." His voice is slow and cold and empty. "I hate it. You're annoying. You're both so…fucking annoying. I can't stand it. Just thinking about it makes me sick. Pisses me off. This has to stop. It has to. Now. I can't take it anymore."

"What does that even mean?" James asks sharply. "Do you

hear yourself right now? You're not making any fucking sense."

I ignore their back and forth and keep trying to jam my fingers between Ice's coat sleeve and my body, desperate for the slightest relief. *But I can't...seem to find any leverage...*

"Ice— *Please*," I croak.

"Oh? What? Can't breathe?"

His voice comes across as indifferent, but the arm holding me in place relaxes, and I manage to draw a proper lungful of air for the first time in what seriously felt like several minutes. Relief washes over me as the panic of struggling to breathe fades, and I stop trying so hard to escape.

I'm tired.

James shifts his weight, looking slightly more focused but still intensely uncomfortable. "There is something you want, then?"

"Hm? Something I want? Is there something? Ah... Perhaps there was..."

"Anything," James says, taking a hesitant step forward. Tears well in his eyes. "I'll do anything. Whatever you want. I swear to god. Just, please—"

Ice cuts him off with a laugh that chills me. "I don't want shit from you, James Reid. Not anymore. No. We're done. Through. I can't trust you for a second. Oh, no. No. You'd take everything from me if you could."

"What—?"

I shudder as the hem of his long overcoat brushes my thigh, and I finally process our proximity. Body heat soaks into my back through his shirt. Fingertips press into my side, not enough to inflict pain but holding me tight, keeping me far too close. *He still has a knife in his other hand. I don't think the blade's out, but—*

My breath hitches, and it isn't lost on Ice, who sighs as though remembering I exist.

"What?" he asks dryly. "You got something to add? Speak your mind, Jayde Palmer. I won't be upset with you. Nothing you say could surprise me. Not now."

I'm...honestly not sure I believe that, but, um...

James glances at the gun on the floor off to my left. When he looks up again, I feel his despondency in my gut. The gun's too close to me for him to reach it without leaving Ice ample time to react, and it's clear now that Ice won't listen to anything he has to say either.

Can I salvage this?

I can't physically fight back in this position, but I dropped the gun because I *don't* want anyone to get hurt. I don't want anyone to die. I don't want to fight, and I don't want Ice and James to fight anymore either. That much should be obvious, even to him.

There must be something... Some weakness in Ice that I can exploit. Words to turn this around, whether they're true or not. Maybe I can say something, just enough to make him back down.

But what?

Night told me that mentioning his personal life is the easiest way to scare Ice off. But I don't know enough about him or his life. I don't know what happened between him and James or whatever. Bringing it up at all might set him off, and it would definitely upset James too.

God... What else *is* there?

He doesn't want to hurt me.

That's right.

He's said something like that several times now, but I don't understand what he means. He doesn't want to hurt me—he never wanted to—but he just...*keeps doing it anyway?*

This isn't fair! I dropped the gun to *prevent* what I saw in my dreamscape. As much as I don't want to be in this situation, I didn't want to watch him die either. Yet he had every intention of forcing me to pull the trigger.

This is what I get for saving his life?

"What *do* you want?" I ask, unable to keep a tremor out of my voice. "You came here for a reason, right?"

"A reason? Not particularly. I don't think."

There's no way.

"But you don't want to kill me," I say. "You don't even want to hurt me. So that's not why you're here, right?"

"No... That's not..."

James shakes his head, but the confused hesitation in Ice's voice pushes me over the edge. Months of pent-up frustration spill over, bitter malice coursing through my veins like adrenaline, and the words come more easily than I ever thought they would:

"You know what, Ice? I don't think you could."

"Tch— What? I could kill you. It'd be easy."

His voice is level, having regained its usual smooth cadence, but his nails dig into my side again. His heartbeat quickens against my shoulder. I caught him off guard. He's uncomfortable.

Should I...keep going?

I glance down, at my hand on the black coat sleeve.

"It's the same for me." My voice wavers, my heart racing too, but I don't stop. "It doesn't matter how scared I am. Or how upset I am. Even if getting rid of you would make my life a million times easier. Even with *your* finger on the trigger. I just can't do it. I could have, you know? Easily." *All I had to do was...not stop.* "But I don't *want* to kill you. It's... It's the same for you, isn't it?"

"Absolutely not," he stammers. "It is not the same. Not at all. No. I am nothing like you. That's absurd."

I laugh. "If it's so absurd, and you're so convinced someone has to die, why haven't you just done it yet? I'm human. I'm weak. Pathetic and defenseless, right? Easy to kill—especially for someone like you."

The color drains from James' face. Ice tenses against my back, and the hand that was stroking my arm freezes near my shoulder.

Maybe I should be afraid, but I'm not.

Maybe I should stop. *But I don't want to.*

I'm sick of Ice. Sick of running and hiding and feeling paranoid and scared and *so small* all the time. Sick of worrying about dreamscape visions and keeping dangerous secrets from everyone I love. And I relish the fleeting sense of power, knowing I can make him squirm for even a second.

"So, do it, then. If it'd be so easy."

James shakes his head again, more frantically.

And, for a second, Ice stops breathing. The flat side of the switchblade presses against my arm as fingernails dig into my skin. A twinge of pain. Nothing I haven't dealt with before.

"Do you want to die?"

"You could've killed me weeks ago!"

Hot tears roll down my cheeks. James *begs* me to stop, but I can't keep the words swirling inside from pouring out, and my voice rises to drown out his soft, desperate pleas.

"So, why let me live, huh? Wouldn't killing me make *your* life easier too?" My voice breaks again. "I just... I don't get it. What do you care if I'm with James? I'm not *yours*, Ice. I never was. You don't *own* me just because you signed a stupid piece of paper. You never even wanted me!"

"I— Ah..."

I squeeze my eyes shut to escape the look on James' face, but I...*can't stop.*

"If seeing me happy with him hurts you *so* much and being my sponsor is nothing but a burden and killing me would be *so fucking easy*, why am I still alive? Why didn't you let me die when you had the chance? Why didn't *you* shoot me?"

A gun held to my head with the safety off. A pit in my stomach. An aching scab on my wrist, a symbol of my worst mistake carved into my skin. The faintest hope that he might just...do it. Just to get it over with. Just so I don't have to deal with it anymore.

But, no.

Why let me go? The first time? Second time? Third time? Why keep my boots? Why go out of your way to comfort me as I bled out on your bedroom floor? Why drive me to the hospital and stay there the entire day? Why leave a new, expensive outfit to replace the one you ruined? Why do anything nice for me at all? If you seriously feel like I betrayed you, how can you act like that? After what you did to me? And then turn around and pull this shit out of nowhere? It's not fair.

I hate him. And, honestly, I'd like to know why it seems like he *wants* me to.

As I stop ranting to catch my breath, Ice's hand closes around the knife and leaves my arm. The skin burns where his nails dug in, but that mild discomfort is the least of my concerns.

I knew I was playing a dangerous game before I opened my mouth. But I lost control of myself. *I have no idea what all I even said.*

"Why?" Ice asks blankly.

I open my eyes, and the first thing I see is James' face. *Pale. Petrified.* And I can only handle it for a second before I have to look away.

He tried to stop me. It's not his fault I unloaded the worst of my feelings on both of them at the worst moment imaginable.

I'm such an idiot.

I stare at the floor, past Ice's arm tight around my waist, with watering eyes. My bare toes. The grey carpet. But, after saying all that, I can't even bring myself to be mad. Maybe I did this to myself. Maybe he's right. Either way, I'm done. My heart is empty, and I feel numb. Defeated. *The same way I felt after he cut a heart into my wrist and left me crying on the floor.*

And all I can say is, "Why?" right back at him.

There's a moment of silence. Then Ice inhales sharply. He shifts his weight behind me, and I feel warm breath on my ear.

"What if you're right, Jayde?" His voice is soft and cold, and I freeze. "Assume, if you will, that I have been restraining myself. Holding back. All this time. Assume...your death...would make life easier. Perhaps, I wouldn't mind if you were gone. Forever. Perhaps...I lied when I said I don't want to hurt you. You're free to believe that. Believe what you want about me. Whatever you want. It hardly matters if it's true. My question...for you is: Would you rather I not...exercise restraint?"

What?

How am I supposed to answer?

Does it make any difference what I say?

I've never heard him talk like this. Not after the Fourth of July or when he caught James outside his house. Not when he first attacked me. Or before he fired three rounds into the crawl-space door. Not even after I pissed him off during our stupid midnight meeting by calling him out on his shit.

I've never heard this tone in my life. From anyone.

So hollow and dark and *dangerous*.

If I say the wrong thing—

"I can show you what I'm capable of," he growls into my ear, sending a shiver down my spine that chills me to the bone. "I won't enjoy it, but if that's what you want from me—if that's who you think I am—just say the word. This can end. For us all. Now."

"I—"

I didn't mean it! I don't know what to say!

"I'm not weak. I'm not like *you*—or *him*. I won't hesitate. I *can* pull the trigger. I can put you out of your misery."

Ah—

This is not *how I hoped this would go.*

I try again to break free—one final attempt.

His hold on me shifts for an instant, like he wasn't expecting it, but the result is the same as before. *The same as always.* I can't pry his arm from my waist with my left hand, and I can't wrench my aching right arm from behind my back. I elbow him in the gut, but I hit solid muscle. He doesn't flinch. I scream for him to *let go*, but he ignores it. He doesn't budge, nor does he seem to put any extra effort into restraining me.

"What? You don't want me to hold back anymore?" Even raised ever so slightly, his voice is frigid. "You want me to end this here? You want me to kill you? Kill everyone? Right now? I can, Jayde. I will—"

I look up. I look to James.

Wide, watering eyes dart from my face to the gun on the floor. He stares at it like he wants to go for it more than anything. But he doesn't move. He just stares. And, as much as I wish he'd do *something*, it's probably for the best. Ice may be ignoring him as things are, but we'd both end up bleeding on the floor if he got in the way.

Might happen anyway, though.

Damn it...

This is my fault. Again.

I shouldn't have said anything.

It's my fault.

"Please," I beg, abandoning any sense of pride I was clinging to before. "I'm sorry. Whatever we did to deserve this, I—"

"Shut up!"

My eyes lose focus, moving past James as he stares at the gun. Maybe I'm looking at the front door. At the tiny peephole. At the doorknob I so stupidly forgot to lock.

"I can't take it anymore," Ice says. His voice is sharp but brittle and wavering, and it pierces me. "I can't...stand the sound of your voice. The way you look at each other. The thought of you together. The...*pictures*. I hate it. I hate it all. I hate...you. I hate everything. All I want— I just... I want it to stop. I—"

The pictures? From the beach?

"Ice, wait—"

"Get out of my head!"

His arm tightens around my waist again, squeezing my ribs, forcing the air from my lungs. His heart races against my back, his breathing fast and uneven.

Oh, no.

This is bad. I fucked up so bad.

I push against his arm as hard as I can, calling on everything within me, but my strength is nothing compared to his. I can't break free. And James is frozen several feet away. Still looking at the gun, tear tracks glistening on his cheek. I can't even imagine what he's thinking.

But I was wrong. I misread the situation and pushed too far. If I could take it back, I would. In a heartbeat, I would. If I thought Ice would accept that. I'd do anything, but—

"I'm sorry," I gasp. "I didn't—"

"I said *shut up*!"

A sharp, metallic click does just that.

I shut up and fall still, able to perfectly picture the polished, marbled blade that just flipped out of the knife's ivory handle.

James looks over, reacting to the sound. Hands grasping the front of his shirt, he starts pleading. But the words don't reach me. I doubt they reach Ice either.

My vision blurs as time seems to slow.

And, for some reason, I wonder what he looks like right now. *Ice. Knowing what he's about to do.* Is he angry? Upset? Nervous? Will he regret it later? Will *he* break down crying because he killed me after I dared him to?

I doubt it.

But I guess it doesn't matter.

I'll never find out.

A flash of movement at the edge of my vision startles me. Ice draws the knife back—a single, smooth motion. Time seems to slow as my eyes dart aside. The knife, blade angled toward me. Light glinting off the marbled steel.

For what it's worth, I am sorry.

I should have refused your first ultimatum.

sixty-three

The knife hits my side, just above the hand still holding me too tightly. *Once. Twice.* It's like being punched. Like, if I didn't know better, I'd think there wasn't a knife in his hand at all.

Then the arm on my stomach shifts. Nails stop digging into my side, and the pressure around my waist vanishes. My right arm is still folded between my back and Ice's chest, but I'm once again standing of my own volition with little help from the body behind me.

And I glance down.

This can't be happening.

Ice's bandaged hand wrapped around the knife's handle. The hilt pressed to my skin. I feel the pressure of it against my rib. *The blade...* The entire four-inch blade is lodged inside. *Inside of me.* Red blooms around the first wound above his hand, staining the pink fabric around the small hole cut into it.

No.

This has to be another nightmare.

This can't be real.

The knife slides out—a familiar sick, wet sound. Then Ice steps back, and I fall to the floor, crumpling onto my injured side.

I drag my aching right arm around to prop myself up and try to catch my breath.

But it *burns*.

I grope across my body, feeling for the wounds. My side is damp. The carpet is damp. Hot liquid slicks my fingers, and I retract my hand to look. Blood drips down, a trickle of bright red over a heart-shaped scar.

Already...? This much?

The wounds don't really hurt—or, if they do, I don't notice. *Because I can't breathe*. Hot pain tears through the right side of my chest each time I try.

"Look at you," he murmurs from above. "What a mess."

Clutching my chest, I take another agonizing lungful of air and look up. Our eyes meet as he stares down at me. His lip is curled in disgust, but his narrowed eyes seem vacant—like there's *nothing* behind them. Then he looks away and steps over me. He walks past James, who rushes by on his way to my side, and my eyes follow him to the front door. He opens the door and pauses to glance back, but I can't make out his expression before he turns to leave.

James blocks my view as the door slams shut, and suddenly everything is *loud*. James is practically screaming as I gasp, still struggling to breathe.

Having dropped to his knees, he helps me sit up—*sort of*. A hand presses against my injured side but quickly pulls away. The red coating his hand crushes me and sends him into a frenzy.

"Fuck— I gotta…" He clambers to his feet and looks around, wiping his hand on his jeans. "We gotta go to the hospital."

Wait— "James, find the…River— Necklace."

Damn it.

"It's—" I cough. "—upstairs."

I'm bleeding a lot. Too much, too fast. I don't know what the knife hit, but I *need* the River Sapphire. Morphing will stop me from losing blood and buy more than enough time to get me to a hospital *alive*.

But James is hysterical. He says he doesn't have time. He needs to find his keys.

I catch his pant leg and ask again.

He looks down at me for a second but steps away without responding, and I don't have the strength to hold him back. *He's freaking the fuck out.* He probably doesn't even understand why I want the River Sapphire, and I'm not exactly in the best state to explain it to him.

Ugh! I'll get it myself.

With a glance toward the staircase, I shift my weight, preparing to stand. But my arms aren't strong enough to push me up off the floor. My hands tingle, pressed against the carpet, and my legs don't fare much better. I barely have the strength to crawl. The first step is only a few feet away, but I'd never make it all the way up the stairs like this.

I look back. I stare at the blood staining the pale carpet. Red left everywhere I've touched. Bright red blood, slicking my right arm and soaking into my camisole and wicking to the front of my denim shorts and pooling on the floor around my hip.

This is worse *than at Ice's house.*

At this rate, I'll die.

If I don't morph soon, I will black out and die.

James is talking on the phone, pacing the room, but I barely make out a word he says.

"The River Sapphire— James, *please*." Fire rips through my chest as I desperately try to take in enough air to speak loud and clear enough to be heard, but I need him to listen. "On my dresser. In the…box…"

"There's no time!"

No time?

No time?!

James, for the love of—

I press a hand to my side. Blood pulses through my fingers with each beat of my racing heart, but I can't tell if I'm applying pressure to the right spot. There are two wounds—*two profusely bleeding puncture wounds*. Breathing hurts. Just holding my hand up to my side is a pain.

This is the same.

Exactly the same as bleeding out in Ice's bedroom. I am *dying*. The only difference is that I don't have the River Sapphire to save me this time. I should've kept it in my pocket. Kept it on my person. Taken care of it…like Ice told me to.

One final fuck you for not listening to him, I guess.

"Hurry," I gasp.

He pockets his phone and kneels in front of me. He touches my cheek, then my side, and he grimaces, glancing away with obvious uncertainty.

"Okay, ah—" His eyes dart from the blood pooling on the carpet back to my face, and he forces a miserable smile. "Just try to stay awake, babe. For me, please."

Ah… This sucks.

James picks me up off the floor. I meet his gaze, but it hurts more than my chest. He's not even trying to put on a brave face now. As he cradles me in his arms, he looks me over with wide, glassy eyes. His face is still pale, cheeks streaked with tears.

And I hate that, right now, I'm so mad at him.

He watched Ice stab me. He can see the blood—the amount I've lost and the rate at which I'm still losing it. Surely, he thinks I'm a lost cause. *So, why?* Why can't he understand that I need the River Sapphire? Did I not explain my separate forms well enough? Did I not tell him that I would've *died* after Ice cut me if it weren't for the necklace?

I don't *want* to die.

I don't, *but maybe it would make things easier for everyone.* Ice won't be stuck as my sponsor. He won't have to think about me being with James ever again. And James… Well, he can move to Los Angeles with Matthew instead. Or Santa Clarita.

Or whatever.

Each breath brings fresh, sharp pain worse than being stabbed. My body aches. My mind spins. The whole world seems to spin. I can keep one hand pressed to my side, maintaining some pressure on at least one wound—*probably*—but I can barely raise my right hand. It's full of pins and needles. Blood leaks between my fingers with little resistance. My shirt feels heavy. Saturated. I don't want to know how much is being left on the ground.

It's too much. I won't make it to the hospital like this.

"I'm sorry," I gasp. "I didn't…think he'd… I can't—"

James' eyes narrow. "You'll be fine, Jayde."

How can you say that?

How can you look at me and say that?

My vision flickers out. *Dark.* Next thing I know, I'm curled in the fetal position, bleeding in the backseat of James' car with no memory as to how I got there.

Groaning, I roll onto my back and stare at the shadowed ceiling. I don't focus on anything in particular. Maybe I can't focus on anything at all. But I manage to move one arm enough to feel for my side. It's still wet and bleeding because I'm still human, but I apply what pressure I can.

Not that it matters. I doubt I'm touching either wound.

I force air through useless lungs and half-listen to James as he speaks to someone. Not me. His voice is sharp and breathless and urgent. I think he's on the phone again, but I can't make out the exact words. He's probably talking to emergency services. Maybe he called 911. Or 119.

Whatever.

What difference does it make?

What can anyone do for me now?

Humans? Immortals? A whole surgical team at the hospital? In the time it will take to get there. To reach them. Without the River Sapphire... *God...*

Why would Ice put me on the spot like that? Why dare me to shoot? Why want me to shoot? And then to stab me like this...

I can't believe I was so...wrong about him.

I mean... I was wrong, right?

Well... Maybe not. Maybe he just wanted to prove *me* wrong.

He can't be *wrong* about anything. He's Ice Monroe. So cool. So suave. So smart. And I'm just a silly, little human girl. I'm weak and stupid. I can't be *right* about him. He said he'd hate to kill me. He didn't want to kill me. But I think, maybe, he hates the idea of being wrong more than he hated the idea of losing *me*, and I called him out in front of James. So, maybe, that's why…

Ugh. Stop thinking about Ice.

Whatever he was thinking back there, that asshole doesn't deserve to be among my final thoughts. I should be thinking about more important things.

Like James.

He's just trying to help. This isn't his fault even if he totally fucked me over by not grabbing the River Sapphire before he stuck me in the back of his car. *But what if he never gets over what I said? What if it eats at him forever?*

And Rose.

I never got the chance to properly apologize for what I put her through. I hope she doesn't blame herself when she finds out I got myself killed. I hope she's able to live a life free from immortals.

And my family…

I haven't talked with anyone in a while. How will they find out about this? When? Will Dr. Corel call my dad? Will James have to look up Robbie's number in my phone and break the news that I was stabbed to death in my living room?

As I take another shuddering breath, I look toward the front seat. The back of James' head. Wild orange hair. Only one hand on the steering wheel.

How could I forget to lock the door?

Why didn't I keep the River Sapphire in my pocket?

I should've kept my mouth shut. Maybe if I'd said anything else... Maybe if I went straight to begging for forgiveness instead of letting anger take over...

This didn't have to happen.

"James..."

His voice falters. Then his hand abandons the steering wheel to adjust the rear-view mirror. *To see me?*

"Ah— She's awake," he stammers into the phone held at his ear. "Right now, yeah... Earlier..."

Our eyes meet in the mirror, and I smile. "Sorry."

"Oh..." *Dismay.* "No." *Denial.* "Don't say that. Please, don't say it like that."

"I...love you."

That's the sort of thing you're supposed to say when you're about to die, right? Just in case you black out again and don't get another chance? *Just so he won't think I hated him after all. Or blamed him. Or...whatever.*

"You're gonna be fine," he says before jumping back into his phone conversation.

Fine?

Yeah, I wish, but I'm not stupid.

I've been through this before, and I only survived because I morphed—and because the damage was easily reversible. James should've listened when I told him to grab the River Sapphire. That necklace was my best chance.

He curses under his breath.

A moment later, something presses into my left side. Soft material brushes my arm. *Fabric?*

I open my eyes to look. *It's the t-shirt he was wearing.* My fingers close around it, and I drag the shirt across my torso to force it against the spot where I *think* the blood is coming from. But I can't apply much pressure. Flexing my fingers hurts, and my arm feels about as useless as my legs did when I tried to stand earlier. *I barely feel my legs.*

And my chest—

I cough once, hoping to clear my throat. But I spiral into a fit. White-hot pain worse than *anything* I've ever felt follows each hacking cough. I roll back onto my right side. I try to keep one hand holding pressure on the shirt and bring the other to my mouth. The coughing eventually subsides, but my breathing feels more ragged and uneven than before. I wipe my lips. The back of my arm comes away with fresh blood.

I'm…coughing it up now?

Like James did.

Is the blood in my lungs?

Will it drown me?

I stare at the back seat, inches from my nose. At the blood my fingers smeared on the pale fabric, made brighter as light from outside the car briefly shines on it. Each labored, wheezing breath threatens to tear me apart until I'm not convinced it's worth breathing at all. It's too hard. I can't keep it up.

This is bad.

I cough. And everything goes dark again.

The sound of static. Like an old TV.

I think of…a black hole. In the freezing cold. In the vastness of space. Like in the documentary we watched. An impossibly dark orb surrounded by the massive halo of light it's slowly devouring. The corpses of stars and planets and whatever else came too close to escape the pull of gravity.

Will I see something like that? Like in my dreamscape?

Or is there nothing?

Either way, I wish it was warmer in here.

Just…a tiny bit warmer…

Something shakes my shoulder.

When I try to move—to address whatever touched me—my arm flops uselessly and dangles over a ledge. My fingers shift. They brush something solid, though I can't seem to recognize the sensation. I hardly *feel* anything. My hand is numb, cold, tingling. Hot liquid drips from my fingertips. A bead forms. And falls. *Forms… Falls…*

I peel my eyes open.

Grey. A small, yellow light. I'm inside a car. Lying on my back. Heart beating far too fast. It's dark. My chest hurts. I can't breathe, but my body tries. Short, shallow, whistling breaths.

Oh. Right.

I'm dying.

Bleeding… Drowning… Dying…

The car door is open. James stands outside. His silhouette is blurry against a bright backdrop, but I know it's him because he's saying…*something*. He's talking to me, I think, and I recognize his voice.

He helps me out of the car, having to drag me because I can't do much of anything myself. I can't stand. Can't support my own weight. Can barely control my head enough to look around. But he doesn't seem to mind carrying me. He straightens himself up, kicks the car door shut, and tucks a strand of hair behind my ear with a hand covered in blood.

"We're there," he says. He might be smiling, but his voice trembles. "Dr. Corel will help you, okay?"

Dr. Corel...?

I want to say *I'm tired.* I want to say *it's cold.* But the gargling that escapes my throat is unrecognizable as words. Like I'm trying to speak through a mouthful of wet bread. I hardly sound human.

If James was smiling before, he's not now.

I manage to choke out his name before another cough cuts me off. Something lodged in the back of my throat breaks free, and a rush of hot, metallic blood floods my mouth. I try raising a hand to cover it. To stop the liquid from bubbling out. But my arm doesn't move, and I cough most of the blood onto James' chest instead.

Shit. Sorry.

"Hang on, Jayde. Please."

Are you crying again?

I guess I can't blame you...

My eyes close for a second. Only a second. But, when I open them again, I can't seem to focus on *anything*. Not even James' face, which I know is less than a foot away from mine.

But I hear several people talking. Hurried footsteps. *Tap, tap, tap, tap.* Among the voices, I recognize Dr. Corel's. A soft, urgent female voice. Another male voice. And another. Everyone speaks at once. Speaks over each other. Too many voices, warbled and fuzzy and blending together.

Next thing I know, I'm flat on my back.

Blinded by bright lights.

Where's James?

I glance around, but I see nothing. Just harsh lights and dark shadows. Trying to ask a question—*where am I?*—leads to another coughing fit and more blood rising in my throat.

Pain tears through my chest, like I'm being torn apart.

It's too much. I'm so tired. I just...wanna...

Wait. No.

No.

I didn't mean what I said to Ice.

I didn't mean it!

James is still here, right? He has to be. Dr. Corel said he never goes far when I'm hurt. And he's worried about me. I can't fall asleep while he's worried. He asked me not to fall asleep. *I don't want to fall asleep.* We're supposed to move to LA next year.

If I fall asleep now, I'll...*never...*

Oh.

Wait. I hear him. James. He's talking. With Dr. Corel. *Yeah.* They're close by. Somewhere. Behind me? I'm not sure. But I hear them.

Am I moving? I think the ceiling is moving. Or maybe the lights are moving. Aah...

"I told you. You shouldn't have brought her here in this form. She can't morph without the pendant, and Centennial Memorial doesn't stock large volumes of human blood."

Blood? What?

"But… Ah… What?"

I can't…feel my hands. Can't…catch my breath.

"Let's see… We can request units from Riverview Gen— *Someone send that order, now!*—but I'm not confident…by the time it arrives—"

My head…

"What are you saying?"

I have to…stay awake…

"Her injuries are severe, James. It'll take time to locate the source of the bleed—assuming there's only one. With so few matching units available to replace the blood she's already lost, the odds are not in our favor."

Blood. Injuries. Time. Survival. Whatever.

"No, but— No. No way! I can't accept that."

"I'm sorry. I know that's not what you were hoping to hear, but—" Another voice interrupts him, and he sighs. "Yes. Take it from here. I need to call HIA, but, please keep me updated. James, with me."

Do I have to stay awake?

"Hey, no— Wait a second! This is bullshit, Corel. You have to save her. You said you would help us. You have to do *something*!"

I'm tired… I'm so tired…of trying to breathe.

And it's so cold…in here…

Their voices grow fainter. They leave me behind, James still screaming about blood when the bright world goes dark.

sixty-four

afterglow

s.k. kelley

.
. .
. . .
. . . .
. . . . .
. . . . . .
. . . .
. . . .
. . . .
. . . .
. . . .
. . . .
. . . .
. . . . . .
. . . . .
. . . .
. . .
. .
.
. .
. . .
. . . .
. . . . .
. . . . . .
. . . .
. . . .
. . . .
. . . .
. . . .
. . . .
. . . .
. . . . . .
. . . . .
. . . .
. . .
. .
.

afterglow

sixty-five

Pain rips through my chest like a bullet.

My eyes flutter open, but the world is a mess of black and white and red. The colors and lights and shadows swirl and melt together. Chaotic. Sharp. Jarring.

Blood fills my mouth. Hot. Salty. Metallic. *And choking me.*

I cough again and again, but there's no end to it. The blood bubbling from my flooded lungs never seems to slow. My airway never clears. There's just...*more blood. Welling up from somewhere deep inside my chest.*

I'd claw at my throat if I could. But I can't feel my arms. Do I even have arms? Or legs? How would I know? I feel nothing but the fire behind my ribs as my lungs move more fluid than air. I can't even cry out for help, my voice reduced to a pathetic gurgling.

This is it. Seriously. I give up.

But my body keeps fighting. Desperate to draw just enough oxygen to stay alive. *My body can do what it wants, but I am done. If this is all that's left for me, I don't want to live anymore.* I listen to the wet gasping and choking as I drown in my own blood. All I can do is stare at the warbling light as I suffer through breath after miserable breath.

A long time passes.

Too long.

Please… If there is a god… If there's anyone…

Let it be over.

I have had enough.

Slowly, the light fades. The swirling red. The flashing white. Both are sucked into a single point in space, and existence seems to blink out entirely. It's dark and silent. Nothing remains. Not even the pain I felt before.

Breathing doesn't hurt. Blood no longer pools in my mouth. I may have stopped breathing completely. Though, if I have, I can't bring myself to care. The absence of pain is a relief, but the pain was replaced by a heavy, oppressive darkness. And a pervasive cold.

It is…*so cold.* But at least nothing hurts anymore.

Just when I'm certain I must be dead, I draw breath.

My lungs fill with air.

Air.

With another gasp, I open my eyes.

It's pitch dark. But I flex my fingers, and both hands respond. No pins and needles. I'm lying on my side in the fetal position. The cold, hard ground leeches warmth from my skin like a slab of frozen metal, and I ache terribly, but breathing is easy.

And I can move.

I look at my hands, loose fists near my chest. My skin is pale and almost seems to glow, bizarrely bright against the inky black ground. I open my hands again. They tremble slightly, but

I can move my fingers. I can lift my hands off the floor.

This light... The dark...

Oh.

The soft, white fairy lights are gone, and it is *freezing*, but this must be my dreamscape. *That means...* I'm asleep, right? Or else I'm... *Or else I'm what?*

Unconscious? *Dead?*

What happens to a person after they die, anyway? Where do they end up? *Here?*

I sure as hell hope not.

With a groan, I sit up and push my frazzled hair out of my face. Moving is the worst, as every part of my body aches in some way, but I can manage. I *can* move. I'm a functional person again. *For the most part.*

I smooth the stiff, floral fabric over my lap and hesitate as I recognize the material for what it is. *A hospital gown.* I am wearing a hospital gown. My arms are clean. No blood. *Scars all accounted for, though.* I take another deep breath as my attention shifts from my arm to my right side. *It is... especially tender.*

Carefully, I lift the gown to check. The two, small stab wounds are there, one above the other on the side of my rib cage, closed with the same type of dark stitches that were used on James' chest after his surgery.

With a sigh, I drop the fabric and look over my arms again. The raised scars almost look white, the surrounding skin pale—like dead-body-in-a-movie pale.

Am I dead?

There was so much blood. Is it possible I survived without

the River Sapphire? *But, if I'm dead, why am I here?*

I glance up from my hands. My dreamscape is dark and empty and bitterly cold. My breath forms faint white puffs that dissipate into the darkness between slow exhales.

What should I do? What can I do?

At the very least, I'd rather not sit on the ground and freeze my ass off forever, so I drag myself to my feet. My head spins at the change in elevation. My balance is shot, and I am physically weak, but I manage to catch myself and remain standing.

As I rub my cold, clammy arms with my cold, clammy hands in an attempt to generate *some* warmth, I look around again. In every direction. I make a full circle. But it's all the same. Nothing but the void and the impossibly black shapes that shift and swirl in the unfathomable distance like deep sea creatures.

Ugh...

This is my dreamscape as I remember it in early July. Dark and empty and unwelcoming. I hate it, but I know this place well enough by now. *And I definitely don't trust it.*

I pick a direction and walk.

It's as cold as the dead of winter. Shivering sets in quickly, but it's not like I can freeze to death here, so I just hug my arms and push forward. One foot in front of the other. One weak, unsteady step after another. I can't tell if I'm even walking in a straight line, but I don't stop.

I continue carefully scanning my surroundings. *But what am I looking for?* Just...something, I guess. Anything that stands out from the rest.

Then, where I'm certain that there was nothing before, I spot something. *No, not something.* Some*one*. A speck of light in the distance. A person, on their knees with their head low and their back to me. I quicken my pace until I'm half-stumbling, half-limping to get closer. As I near the figure, I realize—

The other person is me.

Long, chestnut brown hair pulled up into a messy bun. Wearing a fitted t-shirt, jean shorts, and worn canvas sneakers. Flushed, warm skin. Compared to me, that girl looks…normal. *Alive.* She looks nothing like the me I woke up as.

"H–hey," I croak.

Her head perks up sharply.

My mind turns to a mess of static. A loud, piercing buzz between my ears that leaves me reeling and dizzy. I squeeze my eyes shut, trying to stave off the sick feeling, and raise my hands to hold my head.

The instant my fingers contact my scalp, it stops.

Everything stops.

The ringing. The discomfort. The vertigo. The weight bared on weakened legs. The cold permeating my bones. The soreness in my joints.

I open my eyes again.

But I'm on my knees, staring into the empty depths of my dreamscape with wide eyes leaking warm tears. My heart beats just a bit too fast. I glance down to my hands, planted on the cold ground on either side of James' black handgun.

What—?

When did I end up on the floor?

And the gun…

I don't...

My hands have color now. They're not pale or clammy. My breath doesn't hang in the air. I'm crying—not sure why—but I'm not cold or sore or trembling. I feel fine. *Physically, anyway.*

I wipe my eyes with the back of my hand before looking up. And my heart stops. *Someone...in my periphery.*

The second Jayde is still here. Still standing behind me.

I catch my breath and pop up from the ground, leaving the gun behind as I spin to face her.

One good look turns my stomach.

I still recognize the girl in the floral hospital gown as myself —but only just. *It's worse than I thought.* I knew she was pale when I was in control of her, but... Her skin is ashen. Parted lips tinged blue. Downcast eyes ringed by deep, purple shadows. Long hair tangled and matted as it falls over her shoulders.

She looks *dead.* She is me, and *I look dead.*

That's right, isn't it?

Ice stabbed me.

Blood on the grey carpet. Blood in the back of James' car. Blood I coughed into my shaking hand.

Maybe that is *what I look like in the real world...right now.*

Suddenly, our eyes meet. I flinch back, and the dead girl watches me with an uncomfortable intensity. Her dull, empty eyes seem focused on everything and nothing at the same time. She wavers with the continued effort of standing, but she doesn't move closer. She doesn't speak.

"Am I..." I hesitate, surprised by the clarity of my voice as it echoes around me. "Am I dead?"

She glances away, chapped lips forming a thin line.

Then, after a moment of tense silence, she lifts one arm. She holds her right hand out in front of her, staring at the space above her empty palm as though waiting for something.

I hold my breath, waiting too, my eyes locked on her hand.

One second.

Two seconds.

The black handgun—the one that *was* right behind me—pops into being in the air an inch above her outstretched hand. She catches it just as it begins to fall. Her arm buckles under the gun's weight, but she manages to keep ahold of it.

After staring at the gun for a long moment, her expression shifts, growing serious, and her eyes flick up to meet mine again. She tosses the gun in my direction with surprising ease. It hits the dark ground with a sharp crack and slides across the floor, coming to rest at my feet.

I step back and look up from the gun.

The other me—*that nightmare wearing my skin*—smiles with a pointed, mocking cruelty. "You think what you did back there was brave?" Her voice is cold and smooth, and she doesn't leave time for me to respond as she laughs and wipes an imaginary tear from her cracked left eye. "Whatever, Jayde. Congratulations."

What?

Still smiling, she raises a hand to wave. *Goodbye.* And I fall, the floor having been ripped from beneath my feet.

My dreamscape…shattered. *Apparently.*

I fall and stop falling just as quickly. But I don't hit the ground. Instead, gravity seems to stop, so I'm left floating. Like

I'm underwater. My long hair, free from the bun it was in before, billows around my head like a cloud.

This is new. *And uncomfortable.*

After a moment, soft flickering lights blink into being one by one in quick succession, like a million pinprick stars in the darkest of night skies. They don't drift around like lazy fireflies the way I'm used to, but I take some comfort in their company.

Congratulations, she said…

Congratulations for *what*?

Sure, my original premonition didn't come true. James should be fine, *probably*, and I didn't shoot Ice. I dropped the gun. It never fired. Both men left my house walking. But I messed up. *When I said those things…* I didn't mean it. *I was upset. I was angry. I wanted to hurt him—if there were feelings to hurt, I wanted to dig them up. But I wasn't expecting…*

I didn't *want* him to stab me.

I didn't want to die. I didn't want to end up *wherever this is*. But I kept those toxic feelings bottled up for a long time. Weeks. Months. A little slipped out here and there since everything went downhill in July, but I hadn't…consciously realized how bad it was. For a second, it felt *good*. Knowing that Ice was finally there to hear me out. Knowing the things I had to say bothered him. *The edge of panic in his voice.*

And, who knows? Maybe some part of what I said got through to him. Maybe something will change. *Maybe, even if…*

My lip catches between my teeth. I hug my arms. As I stare at nothing, my tears hang in the air like tiny, glistening crystal beads in the dark. I still don't understand where the light comes from. *I don't understand anything.*

I close my eyes. I curl into a ball. And I make a wish:

If I am dead, don't leave me here.

I can't stand the thought of being stuck here forever, alone in the dark with...*whatever that girl is.* A twisted manifestation of my subconscious. Or my fear of Ice. Or the awful parts of myself I try to suppress and hide because I can't bring myself to face them. I don't care *what* she is. I'd rather there be nothing at all than *only her* and me, trapped within the machinations of my dreamscape.

I'd rather...nothing.

My heart slows. I focus on the rhythm.

A long time passes in silence.

A *long* time. Hours. Days. Weeks. I don't know. It's hard to tell, since nothing has changed in so long. I'd forget my eyes were closed at all if it weren't for the faint stars hanging in the void when I think about opening them to check.

Past the stars, it's dark. And eerily quiet.

I sense nothing around me. I feel nothing. No sensation even when I touch my own skin. I can't even talk to myself—my voice doesn't carry. I'm just falling. Or floating. Or *whatever it is* I've been doing this whole time. I can't tell anymore.

Then...

Something...new.

A sound.

It's faint. So far away, I can barely make it out. It's a...slow, regular pulse. I've heard it before—at least, I think I have—but it's soft and distorted. For some reason...I can't place it.

For some reason…*I'm very tired.*

I wasn't tired before. Not at all. I was hoping I'd get tired, so I could sleep. So I could rest. But, no matter how much time seemed to pass, I never felt tired. Or sleepy. Or exhausted. But, now…

I really feel it now.

Weird...

Maybe… Maybe this is it. Maybe I wasn't *quite* dead before, but maybe I can get what I wished for. Maybe I can leave this place after all.

I just… *I wish things didn't have to end this way.*

To be Continued in Resignation

s.k. kelley

Content Warning

This list includes potentially sensitive or upsetting topics and themes present, mentioned, or otherwise alluded to in Sidetracked (covering all four parts), so readers can make an informed decision prior to reading. Specific context is not included here, but be aware that this information may still be considered spoilers.

Mental illness (including anxiety, depression, and PTSD)
Suicidal ideation and references to suicide and self-harm
Trauma and abuse (mental, physical, and emotional)
Toxic relationships and toxic behaviors
Injury, blood, and physical violence
Guns and knives (including their use as weapons)
Hospitalization (including references to major surgery)
Prescription drug use (as directed by a physician)
Alcohol use and references to alcoholism
Sexually suggestive content (nothing too spicy)
Swearing and offensive language
Nausea and vomiting

Sidetracked contains **NO** sexual violence

As the author, I acknowledge that characters in Sidetracked display harmful and problematic behaviors. However, Sidetracked is a work of fiction, and is in no way meant to condone, promote, or glorify such problematic and toxic behaviors. My characters are heavily flawed and were not written to be viewed as role models.

www.ingramcontent.com/pod-product-compliance
Lightning Source LLC
Chambersburg PA
CBHW030840030726
47495CB00005B/1312